# THE
# DESERTER

Also by Peadar Ó Guilín:

The Inferior

# THE
# DESERTER

PEADAR Ó GUILÍN

**David Fickling Books**

OXFORD · NEW YORK

A DAVID FICKLING BOOK

David Fickling Books and the colophon are trademarks of David Fickling.

Visit us on the Web! www.randomhouse.com/teens

Educators and librarians, for a variety of teaching tools, visit us at
www.randomhouse.com/teachers

*Library of Congress Cataloging-in-Publication Data*
Ó Guilín, Peadar.
The deserter / by Peadar Ó Guilín. — 1st American ed.
p. cm.
Sequel to: The inferior.
Summary: To save the members of his tribe from being devoured by the beasts that share their primitive world, Stopmouth must make his way to the mysterious, futuristic world above, even though a virus is destroying the Upstairs and driving millions of refugees to seek shelter below.
ISBN 978-0-385-75149-0 (trade) — ISBN 978-0-385-75150-6 (lib. bdg.) —
ISBN 978-0-375-98936-0 (ebook)
[1. Science fiction.]   I. Title.
PZ7.O36De 2012
[Fic]—dc22
2011000735

Printed in the United States of America
March 2012
10 9 8 7 6 5 4 3 2 1

First American Edition

To my mother, inventor of beans and mash

Who art Thou, feasting thus upon Thy dead?
*Bhagavad-Gita*, Chapter XI (translation by Edwin Arnold)

Those who gave counsel to build the tower [. . .] drove forth multitudes of both men and women, to make bricks [. . .] Let us see whether heaven is made of clay, or of brass, or of iron. When God saw this He did not permit them, but smote them with blindness and confusion of speech, and rendered them as thou seest.

*Greek Apocalypse of Baruch, 3:5–8*

# PROLOGUE

They're hunting for Indrani, combing the Roof, projecting her picture everywhere. Squads burst into apartments. They wave weapons, shine torches in women's faces. 'Is this her, do you think? Man, for a reward like that . . .'

But Indrani is hunting too. Everything she has seen in her short life has been recorded at ninety frames per second. Almost three billion images per year, and that's just the visual information! Smells too have been digitized and stored away; every odour encountered since the age of four, immaculately preserved on the tiny chance that she might want it again some day.

She can choose to play back the scent of her father's skin from the first fight she had with a rival toddler in the care group.

'Bad girl!' he'd said, but whenever she accesses that recording (one of her favourites), she can hear the pride he'd been trying to suppress over her victory. He was training her even then, whether he'd meant to or not; moulding her into 'the girl who never loses'. Until she lost *him*, murdered by Religious rebels.

What she especially likes about that scene is the slightly damp feel of her father's skin against hers. He'd been sweating, genuinely worried. Proof that he'd loved her, although he used to keep that kind of thing to himself.

But Indrani can't afford to wallow in childish triumphs. These days she spends far more time poring over the events leading up to the moment when she was shot down over the surface of the world. Somebody – *Say it, Indrani, say it*: the Commission, the rulers of the Roof, her supposed friends and allies – somebody had tried to have her killed. She can't understand that, but even stranger is the fact that they later changed their minds and went to enormous lengths to rescue her instead. 'We'll take you back,' they had promised. 'We'll allow your savage to live. Just come home . . .'

The answers to that riddle lie hidden deep amongst the 42,601,850,100 images that make up her life, or in the terabytes of sounds and smells, or the recordings of everything she has ever felt . . . All she has to do to save herself and those she loves is to dig it out.

Impossible, of course. More chance of a blind woman tracking down a single grain of rice on the surface of the world. Indrani cries sometimes at the thought of it. She never cried before leaving the Roof, but she's not 'the girl who never loses' any more. She has killed intelligent beings and eaten their flesh. She has suffered enough horror to realize how fragile happiness is, how eager the universe is to take it away.

So she keeps searching, always searching. And meanwhile the Commission, her pursuers, draw ever closer.

# 1. THE DESERTER

The Globe hovered no more than two man-heights above the injured Stopmouth. Indrani hung out of the door, blood on her chin, one hand stretching down towards him.

'Promise me you'll come back,' he said.

'Of course I'll come back. I'll find seeds for us to grow so nobody ever has to volunteer again. I'll find weapons to fight the Diggers. And I'll never leave you after.' Her voice broke into a sob. 'Never.'

Stopmouth woke with a groan. *I'm dreaming*. And he was. The usual awful dream.

Sweat drenched his body, and all the wounds he'd suffered the day Indrani left ached as though fresh. He missed her. He missed her *so* much. But in his sleep he never got to relive the great times they'd spent together. He only ever saw her leaving. Night after night.

A fire hissed and popped beside him. All around were the moans and whimpers of his poor little tribe, still trapped in sleep. Stopmouth paused. Were they usually this noisy?

He shook his head and grabbed a handful of pounded moss to mop away the chill of his sweat. As he raised his neck to wipe it clean, he chanced to look out of the window, and froze.

*I'm still dreaming.*

Stopmouth's heart began to pound in his chest. Beyond the circle of firelight lay only darkness. *Wake up, fool! Wake up!* The sky was completely black, with no lights where the camps of the dead should be. None at all. As though the Roof itself had disappeared and taken his Indrani with it.

He stumbled over to where the window should be, heart racing, his lips moving to childhood prayers. But even as he reached it, the grid of tracklights came on all at once for as far as the eye could see.

He waited for something more.

'Oh, go to sleep,' somebody groaned at him. It sounded like Kubar, his voice rough at the best of times. 'We've a big day tomorrow.'

Of course. The dream was always more vivid on nights like this.

A single big risk might win his vulnerable tribe a bit of breathing space, might even guarantee survival for generations to come. He'd need his rest. They all would.

He listened. Perhaps it was his imagination, but the fearful sounds of nightmare seemed to have died down already.

'Liven up, Stopmouth!' An elbow nudged him in the ribs and Rockface's foul breath exploded over his face in a cloud.

'Pay attention, hey?'

'Sorry, Rockface.' Stopmouth blinked. High above him the panels of the Roof glared with intense blue light. Once he'd believed the dead lived there – his ancestors and those of his enemies. 'I was just—'

'I know where you were, boy. The whole tribe knows.' Near them, in the shadows, other hunters pretended to be watching the streets, not listening as the big man scolded their young chief. The sisters Sodasi and Kamala whispered to each other, casting sidelong glances at them. Big, twitchy Vishwakarma struggled to keep still.

'Indrani's been gone a hundred and fifty days, but we're still here, hey? And we need you, especially for the next tenth.'

'Of course, of course.' Stopmouth gripped the Talker in his hand, a piece of magic from the Roof that hid his stutter from the others. He could feel himself doing it, though. It happened most when he was nervous or simply ashamed. Before he could pinpoint the cause, something moved in the shadows and everybody jumped.

Stopmouth hissed, 'Vishwakarma, no!'

Just in time.

'Sorry, Chief.' The man's warped spear pulled back from

the throat of a scout, a boy barely tall enough to reach Stopmouth's shoulder and too young to realize how close he'd come to death.

'They're on their way!' said the boy, panting hard.

'Fourleggers?' asked Stopmouth.

'Yes, yes! A trio of them.' The boy gestured into the alley behind him. 'Just one trio.'

Everybody smiled. These beasts always hunted in multiples of three. Had the ancestors wished the tribe ill, as many as nine might have been out there at once.

'Yama's leading them here now.'

Stopmouth nodded and signalled *Silence* to the others. Everybody knew what he meant. Fourleggers had hearing so good they'd be able to tell that Yama was alone and limping. From now on, anybody talking could spoil the plan and jeopardize the future of the struggling human tribe. There weren't enough of them to survive. Stopmouth had always known it. Sooner or later, one too many of his people would be hunted and eaten, or die in an accident, and their numbers would just collapse in a matter of days. It was always the way, always.

This lot would have been extinct already had it not been for the arrival of Stopmouth, Rockface and Indrani. The little group had saved the bigger and had, in return, been granted a home. If only Indrani had stayed. If only he could see her lovely face just one more time . . .

Rockface nudged him. Drifting again. Not allowed, not today. He had to get control of himself. He bit his lower lip hard enough to bleed, then stepped out carefully to where he could see the plaza, glaring in the unforgiving light of the Roof.

A moment later, he spotted the hobbling figure of Yama, moving as fast as his recovering injury would allow him. The boy was arrogant, but there had never been any doubting his bravery – he'd volunteered for this job. 'What if their ears are good enough to hear if someone's only *faking* a limp? They'll be looking out for trickery, but there's no hiding my scars, is there?'

As he ran, Yama never once glanced towards any of the places where his comrades hid. *Good man*, thought Stopmouth. The boy was learning at last, praise the ancestors.

Mere heartbeats later, the shadows stirred in the alleyway that Yama had just fled. A voice the human ear should never have been able to detect said, 'Hunting needs silence to listen.'

'No,' said another 'voice' translated by the Talker, 'hunting needs speed! It flees alone.'

'This one heard two of them,' insisted the first.

'Two, yes, but one strong enough to escape. Another is abandoned to us and waits only for our claws. We must not refuse it by delay.'

Stopmouth's eyes had adapted well enough now to see three Fourleggers, snouts pressed together in the shadow of a wall. They made no sound at all, but the Talker brought him what might have been their thoughts, or a language all of smells. Who knew? His hated brother, Wallbreaker, might have figured it out, but Stopmouth had escaped him long ago and hoped never to see him again.

From the alley through which Yama had run, a rock crashed to earth, and somebody cried out as though in pain and fear. The Fourleggers immediately separated and surged towards the source of the sound, all claws on the ancient road, spraying dirt and moss with each step. Vishwakarma stood up too soon, but the beasts scattered enough rubble to mask the sound. Stopmouth waited for the last of them to disappear into the alley. Then he shouted, 'Now!'

Humans emerged from hiding in every part of the plaza. Almost half the able-bodied men and women of the tribe were out today – a terrible, terrible risk. But this was to be no ordinary hunt; no mere search for food. They had bigger plans than that.

With the help of the ancestors, the Fourleggers would find that their limping prey had reached a dead end. He had climbed a rope ladder and pulled it up after himself.

'In,' shouted Stopmouth. 'Everybody into the nets! Use your clubs, not the spears! Clubs!'

And that was when everything went wrong.

A great *crack* rang through the air, followed by screams of terror from the people he'd placed on the roofs surrounding the alley. One whole house slowly curved itself over, like an injured man bending down. Then it fell in an explosion of dust and flying splinters.

Stopmouth saw the three beasts coming straight at him out of the cloud, running on all fours. Or trying to. One of them held a forelimb clear of the ground, and blood from a scalp wound dribbled over its eyes. Stopmouth knew it would have to dodge him to get away. He took aim with his club, but the wounded creature chose to smash into him instead, knocking him flying and tumbling with him to the ground.

'The pain!' it howled. But it scrambled to its feet before any of the humans could react, and only slingstones caught up with it after that. None struck home.

'Help me,' somebody said from the caved-in alley. Other groans were audible now as the stone settled down.

'I'm cut,' said Vishwakarma, blood streaming down his face. 'I think . . . I think . . . Oh, by the gods, by the gods, don't eat me, please don't . . .'

'Where are you, Vishwakarma, lad?' Rockface's breath was so bad, Stopmouth could actually smell him walking past. He reached the stricken Vishwakarma, a knife held behind his back. But he wouldn't have to use it. Even from the ground, Stopmouth could see that the wound was little more than a scratch. Others might not be so lucky. At least two had fallen from the roofs where they'd been stationed.

Rockface left Vishwakarma and walked back to the plaza, his back hunched over a little so as not to aggravate some of his old injuries.

'Ha!' he shouted.

'Get everyone together,' Stopmouth told Kubar. 'Find out if anybody's missing.'

Rockface was peering at something on the ground, one hand resting on a pile of rubble, the other pressed against his back, as if he feared his spine were about to force its way out into the air. His face showed only triumph, however.

Stopmouth crouched beside him and saw a small pile of rust-coloured scales smeared with sticky black blood.

'You want a live one, hey, Chief? Just able to talk?'

Stopmouth had a bad feeling about this. The big man was calmer since the injuries that had nearly stopped him hunting. Several times, in despair he'd volunteered the flesh of his body to feed the tribe, but small numbers and the battle for survival against the Skeletons had made food plentiful enough, so no such sacrifice had yet been necessary. Now he was almost back to his old cheerful self. A guarantee of trouble.

Stopmouth reached a calming hand towards the man's shoulder, but it was already too late.

'Come on,' said the grinning Rockface. 'We can still catch it, hey? Come on!'

'Rockface! Wait! We have to—'

But the big hunter had lost his hearing and was loping off after the trail of blood. Had it been anybody else, anybody at all, Stopmouth would have let him go, never expecting to see him again. The adults of the tribe had grown up in the Roof and knew little of survival before they'd met him. He'd drummed it into their heads again and again that a lone hunter was little better than a free meal for the first pack of beasts to pick up his scent.

He turned to the others. 'Vishwakarma! There's nothing wrong with you. Now, get up. Sodasi, Kamala, Kubar – you know what to do. You're the scouts. Get everybody home in one piece. No hunting, no trouble of any kind.'

He didn't wait for an answer. Rockface had already disappeared from the far side of the plaza. Stopmouth took off after him. As he ran, he checked his knife and sling. Apart from these, all he had was a club. There was no time to fetch a spear.

He heard his friend shouting from only a few streets away and picked up the pace. His leg hurt a little, and the shoulder he'd dislocated the day Indrani left would probably trouble him for the rest of his life. Yet it felt good to run by himself again, with no pack of inexperienced and clumsy hunters to slow him up. Buildings whipped past and his feet slapped over stone or sank into moss with a scatter of insects.

But then he ran round a corner to find the three beasts, one injured, two unscathed, standing over a fallen Rockface. Humans weren't the only ones capable of ambush.

He knew his friend was finished. In the old days, before the dozen injuries that plagued him and with his Armourback-shell spear in his hand, Stopmouth might have dared this fight with a slim, slim chance of success.

The best he could do now would be to flee, because the moment Rockface was dead, the two healthy Fourleggers would come after him. They were strong enough and hungry enough to drag a pair of full-grown humans home to feed their people.

'Go!' shouted Rockface, his voice hoarse. 'Go!'

'I can't,' said Stopmouth. He knew he had to run – he was the chief. He was *supposed* to run. Nothing else made sense.

One of the creatures looming above Rockface pulled back its arm, the claws aimed right at the fallen hunter's neck. Stopmouth would never get there in time. He swung the club above his head, thinking it might put the Fourlegger off long enough for him to make one final suicidal charge. The two other beasts had gone back onto all fours in preparation for just such a move. Their jaws were working as though they could already taste his flesh.

'Stop!' said a voice.

Everybody, man and beast alike, froze. Stopmouth realized that the words had been made almost entirely without sound and that only the Talker had allowed him to hear them.

He turned slowly.

'Oh, you're for it now, boy,' said Rockface.

Another trio of beasts waited behind. The creature to the fore looked smaller than any Stopmouth had ever seen before: barely the height of a tall man as it reared up on its hind legs.

It said, 'Fine soup needs human bones.'

Stopmouth raised his pathetic club. The pair of Fourleggers guarding the speaker tensed for violence, but it ignored them and fixed its gaze on the human's weapon.

'A sheathed claw does not kill well.'

'It's just a club,' said Stopmouth. 'We wanted to capture one of you alive. To talk. We've tried talking to some of your hunting parties before, but they either chase us or run away.'

It seemed to regard him carefully, but with beasts, who could tell for sure?

'Magicians that can talk to all things . . .' it said. 'Perhaps the flesh of your snout might give me and my sisters such power?'

It stepped closer to him. Stopmouth could see the slight sheen of its scales. By day they were red, and often the creatures made themselves easier to track by shedding them when they ran or scraped up against a wall.

It was so close now that the hunter knew he could strike its skull. His heart beat fast, and faster still when two clawed hands swept out to clasp his shoulders while Rockface gasped and cried out, 'Hit it! Why don't you hit it?'

The creature pressed its sticky, pungent snout up against his dry one. It said, or maybe whispered, 'The little magician needs to talk well to save its bones from the soup.'

Stopmouth took a deep, ragged breath. The up-close stench of the creature tickled the back of his throat and made him dizzy. He hoped it didn't feel the same way about him.

'We want an alliance,' he said. 'We will stop hunting you if you stop hunting us. However, we will exchange our dead for yours. Even better, we will co-operate with your people in hunts. We are not as strong as you, but we run faster. We build good traps. We will allow your kind to hide among us when they are being chased. We—'

'Very well,' it said. It stepped back. 'The scaleless ones will be our sisters.' As it spoke, its pointy snout waved from side to side. Stopmouth jumped when it touched him again, the claws scratching his shoulder.

'New sisters make a gift of blood. Come.' The Fourlegger wounded in Stopmouth's ambush limped towards them.

'Eat this one to make your sisters strong. Her bones carry power. Her seventh mother lived beyond the Roof in a nest all of metal.' It waved a claw at the fallen Rockface. 'Alliance needs an offering from your family now.'

It waited. In the distance, Stopmouth could see the furthest panels of the Roof begin to darken. Right above his head, a Globe, the flying machines of Indrani's people, hovered, watching everything he did. *Are you in there?* But Indrani would have been helping him if she were, Stopmouth knew that much.

He felt a hand on his shoulder, a human hand. He smelled a new stench now – that of rotting human teeth.

'It's time for me to go, hey? Tell the children . . . Tell them—'

Stopmouth shoved his friend's hand away. 'No!' he said.

'Don't be a fool, boy. You know what has to happen, hey? I've gone beyond my time as it is.'

'Alliance needs blood,' agreed the beast leader. 'Blood. Our sister for yours.'

That's the way it had always been when Stopmouth was growing up. The Tribe exchanged its old and its injured for food to keep the rest going, and it was a great honour – the greatest the Tribe had to offer – for somebody to give themselves up, limping but proud, to the needs of the future. The new tribe of poor hunters had yet to learn such vital habits.

'My back has never been right since the Skeletons,' said Rockface.

Stopmouth looked back at the Fourlegger leader. 'The alliance needs blood,' he agreed. 'But not human blood, and not the blood of Fourleggers.'

'Don't be a fool, boy, don't—'

Stopmouth turned in fury, 'I am Chief here, Rockface. You will not contradict me in front of our allies.' He stared at the bigger man, noting the stoop of his back and the many scars that puckered his tattooed skin. 'And you will stop calling me "boy".'

He turned back to the Fourlegger. There were three of its fellows before him and three behind. 'You may have any of our dead in exchange for yours. But this alliance will not be sealed with our blood, or the blood of your sisters. I will bring you *three* corpses of other creatures. I will bring them here in *three* days. If the flesh pleases you, you will bring three other beasts for us.'

He waited, sweat beading on his body, Rockface silent beside him. *And now*, he thought, *we die. Is Indrani watching this? Will she weep for me?*

The leader dropped onto all fours – they all did. Nothing had been said, or the Talker would have translated it. Together, with no signals that Stopmouth could see, the creatures ran off, each trio in a different direction.

'So much for your alliance, boy.' The hunter shook his

head and left Stopmouth to go limping home with no weapons. He didn't even bother to retrieve the club he'd left lying in the moss where he'd fallen.

The young chief looked up. Only he and the watching Globe remained.

People cheered at the sight of Stopmouth and Rockface's safe return. The two men hadn't exchanged a word since their meeting with the Fourleggers. The older hunter shook off hugs of congratulation and made his way into Headquarters alone.

Kubar approached Stopmouth. If anything, the ex-priest was even older than Rockface, but it showed more in his gravelly voice than in his scars. 'Did you catch one?'

Stopmouth shook his head. 'It was them who caught us. We . . . we spoke to them and . . . they let us go.'

The man grinned, his teeth white and straight enough to belong to a child. 'An alliance then? No? What's wrong?'

'I was too . . . I tried to be too clever. Like something Wallbreaker would have done. The beasts come in threes, you see? And they wanted to take Rockface . . .'

Kubar made Stopmouth sit down and explain himself, always probing for more details. 'So,' he said at last, 'they ran away.'

'We lost them,' said Stopmouth.

'No,' said Kubar. 'They didn't attack you and they didn't

say no to an alliance. We have to keep the pledge you made them and hope they don't use it as a way of trapping us. But I think it's good. I think you've done it.'

'I'm tired,' said Stopmouth, and stumbled away from the old priest. He pushed past other people who were babbling questions at him in their foreign language. He could understand more and more of it, but today, even though he had the Talker with him, nothing seemed to make sense.

Cool air inside chilled the sweat on his skin. He followed the sound of children's laughter, as he knew Rockface would have done. On the second floor of Headquarters, future hunters stalked each other between columns of stone and around piles of rusted metal junk that must have lain here for generations before the new tribe's exile from the Roof. Among the humans an infant Fourlegger played. The children had adopted it against Stopmouth's wishes. It could not learn the sounds of their speech and struggled to make itself understood by the adults. But it was for the sake of this small creature, and the fact that it had proven to be so compatible in its play, that Stopmouth had decided to try for an alliance with its people rather than the more human-looking Skeletons.

He approached Rockface, who had stretched out his body against a wall to watch his pupils. The young chief expected his comrade to growl at him, but Rockface never held a grudge for long.

'What you did was stupid, hey?'

Stopmouth nodded.

Rockface waved his hands towards the children. One of them held off three others with a tree branch while the infant Fourlegger circled on all fours to get behind him.

'We can't survive here without sacrifices, boy, and these people know nothing about such things.'

'Rockface, you're all I've got left. I couldn't let them have you.'

The big man sighed and made a waving sound as if chasing insects out of his face. 'It was my fight, boy. A man should charge, hey? At everything.' He jerked a thumb at Stopmouth. 'You, for example, you need to take another wife.'

Stopmouth sat up. 'What?'

Rockface tried to rise with him, but grimaced and lay slowly down again. Then he sighed. 'Without Indrani, you're as much use as a burst skin. Moping about. Dropping slingstones at all the wrong times. Getting knocked over—'

'She'll be back, Rockface.'

'Oh, she's a fighter. I'll give you that. I can see her up there now, kicking all those beardy freakmen in their faces, hey?' He laughed. 'A great one. But she's home now. She has food in her bowl, and who knows what else? She'll come back or she won't. But you . . . These people need somebody whose eyes aren't always slipping up to the Roof to look for

21

her. They need you as yourself, not some boy peeping from behind his mammy's legs.'

'I stayed with the tribe, didn't I? When Indrani left, *I* stayed.'

Rockface jabbed a thumb at him. 'Get another wife and Indrani'll be back before you know it! Get some children. That's what you need. A boy of your own and, I swear by the ancestors, you'll sacrifice anyone – me, Indrani, anyone, to keep him fed.'

Stopmouth tried to imagine another wife for himself. Or maybe more than one. There were women who embarrassed him by brushing up too close against him in a narrow alley, or who followed him when he went onto the roof of Headquarters to look out over the streets and to be alone. Why would they do such a thing when the girls back home in Man-Ways had all but laughed in his face?

But it didn't matter. Every time he tried to imagine life with one of them, he pictured Indrani's return home. Sometimes he even laughed, imagining her chasing some unfortunate woman away with her frightening kicks.

'It's not just about me,' he said. 'Have you forgotten the Diggers?' Stopmouth could never think of the beasts without a shudder.

'Bah.' The bigger man waved his hands in the direction of the hills. 'Those monsters. We left them on the far side, hey? They couldn't tunnel their way through all that rock.'

But Stopmouth knew better, felt it in his bones. What if the beasts found a way to go around the hills? Or if they crawled over them by night? Less than ten days' journey away, the land groaned under the weight of their victims. Indrani would have to come back. The magic weapons she might bring from the Roof were all that would allow these children to grow up.

# 2. Yellowmaws

Aflash of Rooflight from the metal skin of a Globe drew all eyes. But only for a moment. Other things needed the people's attention more: the heavy shadows of ruined doorways; heaps of rubble where a hungry Slimer might rest for days without moving; the uneven patches of purple or red moss that hid sharp rocks and rusty metal spikes.

The small human tribe had long since eaten through their stock of dried flesh from the time of the Skeleton siege. Although their hunting had improved, the surrounding beasts had learned to be wary of them too, especially when they ran in organized parties. So finding three bodies, each from a different species, only to give them over to the Fourleggers, was a luxury they could ill afford.

Many went hungry, but none complained. These were the survivors now. They'd come through massacre and hopeless battle. They'd been banished from a paradise where the food never had to be hunted and never fought back.

And still they lived. A little hunger was nothing to these people. In spite of all their clumsiness, their helplessness, their strange gods and customs, Stopmouth could not help but love them.

His people found the necessary bodies: a Slimer, pierced through the belly; a Wallhanger, brought down by a lucky slingstone before it could swing away; and some unknown shelled creature that had badly wounded Krishnan with a charge.

'New beasts should be studied first,' said Stopmouth to the sorry group that had brought the last one back. But he didn't have the heart to be too tough on them. Tonight they would have to eat poor Krishnan, sharing his flesh amongst those in need of it. Besides, it was now day three and he had a promise to keep.

'What if it's a trap?' asked Yama. The boy limped along beside his leader, while behind them, others carried the three bodies over their shoulders on poles. Guards moved in the alleys that paralleled this one. They had to be wary of ambush with so much flesh at stake.

'They could have had me and Rockface,' said the chief, 'with no risk to themselves. They let us go.'

'But they might want to finish us off all at once.'

Stopmouth smiled. 'They won't find us the easy prey we were when first they met us.'

Yama grinned back and waved his spear in the air. Still

a child, for all the carnage he'd seen. 'We'd take them,' he said. 'We could take anyone.'

Stopmouth said nothing.

Nine Fourleggers waited to meet them. The little one which had spoken last time was not among them, and none of the others would respond to anything Stopmouth said.

'They're insulting us!' whispered Yama. 'We should fight them now – it's what they want.'

The beasts examined the corpses, licking them, scoring the skin with their claws and saying, 'Hunger needs flesh.'

Finally each trio took up a body and left through the far side of the plaza.

'That's it?' asked Yama. 'Shouldn't we even send some-body to follow them?' The humans had yet to find the exact home streets of the Fourleggers.

'No,' said Stopmouth. Then he called out to all the hunters around him. 'We come back in three days. Hopefully we'll get to eat then. Come on. In the meantime we still need to hunt.'

The Fourlegger chief, if that was what she was, stood alone in the centre of the plaza before a small pile of corpses, laid neatly one on top of the other. Stopmouth was curious to see what they were, his mouth already filling with saliva as he imagined new flavours. The hunt-ing hadn't been good lately and he'd forgone his rightful share in the hope that today there'd be no need to fight.

He wondered if he should lick the offered bodies and score them as the Fourleggers had done three days earlier; or if he should refuse to speak. He stepped closer, tummy rumbling with nerves and hunger.

He recognized the first body: a Skeleton. They'd become rare since their disastrous siege of Headquarters. *Delicious*, he thought. Sweet, milky flesh that tasted so much better raw. His stomach rumbled again. He felt weak.

'Hunger needs flesh,' he said, pushing the body to one side. Oh, how he wanted to slice into it now!

The second was a furry beast, its pelt wiry and probably very useful. Four pairs of limbs poked out on either side, and when he pressed fingers into them, he felt good strong muscle underneath. This would have been difficult prey for the Fourleggers and he smiled at the obvious respect they were showing to their new allies.

'Hunger needs flesh,' he repeated.

It was no easy task to pull the heavy beast off the last body in the pile, especially in his weakened state. But when he did, when he saw the last one, the heat of the Roof seemed to intensify, to beat down on his head hard enough to knock him over. He couldn't believe what he was seeing. An eyeless triangular head; a dull pelt riddled with holes.

He brought one shaking fist to his mouth. 'Where . . . where did you find this one?'

'Your hunger has no need?'

'Where did you find it? Your sisters, I mean? Where did they get it?'

The Fourlegger looked straight at him, and he had no idea, no idea at all, what it might be thinking. The Talker couldn't translate its stance, its twitching snout, into anything he could understand. Finally it gestured towards the hills.

'She came with her sisters. At night. Hunger needs them, as hunger needs all flesh. Have you no need?'

Stopmouth stared down at the Digger corpse, beads of cold sweat running over his face. Indrani – she had to come back. Or they were all dead.

'Hunger needs flesh,' he heard himself say. The humans would have to take all the friends they could get. And it still wouldn't be enough.


'Are you mad, hey?' Rockface looked astonished, but there was a grin on his face too that grew the more he spoke. Blood covered him up to the elbows. His butchery class wasn't going well today. The wiry fur of one of the Fourleggers' gifts hid many tricky joints and sinews. Worse, Rockface's little students had been too hungry to wait. They laughed and dodged behind his back or out of reach of his arms until every one of them had faces smeared with tasty gore.

'You are mad, boy.' He sounded proud, and that alone should have filled Stopmouth with worry.

'She should have come back by now, Rockface. I mean, how long could it take to grab a few things from your house? It's not as if their weapons are very large! I've seen one, remember? The green-light thing I took from Varaha. But the destruction . . . whole buildings . . .'

'Ha! That little necklace toy does nothing now! I think you imagined it all.' Rockface suddenly moved to pull a giggling child off the corpse. 'Away from there, you scamp!' He shook her until she dropped the eyeball she'd tried to steal. 'Those bits are for hunters only, see?' Then he turned back to his chief. 'The weapon was even more useless than the man who fell out of Varaha's Globe. Dead within days, but him we could eat, hey?'

'I think she's trapped up there,' said Stopmouth. 'She has enemies now, Kubar was saying. Lots of enemies. The holy ones didn't like her before and the chiefs don't like her now. At least, I think that's what he meant. Life in the Roof sounds so confusing!'

'They talk a lot of nonsense, boy,' agreed Rockface. 'Gabble gabble. Who can understand a word of it, hey? No, you're right. She's our Indrani and we need to go and bring her back. Provided she wants to come back, hey?'

'Of course she does!' shouted Stopmouth. Everybody stopped to look at him; the children covered their mouths with bloody little fingers.

Rockface patted him on the back. 'You're right, boy. Sure, sure.'

'I'm sorry,' said Stopmouth. 'I don't know why—'

'The only thing is' – Rockface stretched his arm out fully, or tried to; he grimaced – 'I'm not ready for a journey yet.'

'Rockface—'

'All the way to the mountains, hey? To the place where the world reaches right up to touch the Roof? That will be some sight. Some sight. Only the Traveller ever saw it before us, or so the old tales would have us believe.'

'Rockface . . . listen . . .' Stopmouth could tell by the way the big man wouldn't look at him that he already knew what was coming next. 'I need you to stay here. I need—'

Rockface threw his knives hard over the heads of the children so that they smacked into the walls. It was a moment before he could speak again, but finally he managed, 'If you think I'm ready for the pot, why didn't you just let the Fourleggers have me, hey? And save everybody a lot of trouble?' But the heat was already going out of him.

'This lot need you,' said Stopmouth.

The youngest girl of the group, Lali, gave the big man a hug. Some of the boys crowded in to pat him on his scarred and tattooed back.

'I'll bring her home,' said Stopmouth. 'I won't risk anybody else to do it. And when I come back, I expect to find enough of you alive to make the return journey worth my while. Only you could make that happen.'

'I'm not so good at the chief thing,' Rockface mumbled.

'Kubar can do that – they listen to him. You just keep them hunting. Don't let them give up! That Digger the Fourleggers found . . . that Digger . . .' He shivered.

In the dark, the whispers of his people seemed louder. Words drifted down from every rooftop, blessings and curses and tears; a soft blanket of sound, wrapping him in need, begging him to stay. Stopmouth stood at the mouth of the U-shaped complex of buildings known as Headquarters. The fixed eyes of every member of the tribe glittered like a second set of tracklights, watching him as though he were life itself. None of them spoke. Not even Rockface.

The chief didn't want to think about their need and how it made him feel. He turned back to face Kubar, who would lead when he was gone.

'You're deserting us,' said Kubar. 'Do you know what that means?'

'You don't understand,' Stopmouth said. 'When the Diggers come—'

The priest growled at him. 'Diggers! I've never seen these Diggers, except for one mouldy corpse riddled with holes. We have Skeletons. Yes, yes, I've seen them eating one of my cousins. And Slimers to drag children away in the night. Definitely Slimers. Real threats that never leave us and will kill us quicker than any number of imaginary *Diggers*.'

'You don't know what you're talking about, Kubar.'

'I know,' whispered the priest, 'that it's just about your woman. The—' He stopped himself before calling Indrani 'the Witch', but Stopmouth knew he wanted to. The Religious had never liked her, and not even those such as Kubar, who had been exiled from the Roof and sent to live here on the surface of the world, had changed their opinion. 'You'll kill us, Stopmouth. You'll kill all of us. Your old tribe was barely getting by with generations of skills to call on and dozens of hunters as good as you are. We need you more than she does.'

'You'll have Rockface to teach you.'

'Rockface!' Kubar didn't dare say more than that.

'And you'll have the Talker.' Stopmouth felt a chill at the thought of leaving it behind. All his life he'd stuttered and stammered, until the magic device of the Roofpeople had made him almost as eloquent as his brother. He'd discovered that he loved to speak. And now he'd be returning to life as the butt of everyone's jokes. But there'd be no people where he was going, not unless he made it to the Roof. And once there, he'd find as many Talkers as he needed.

'The Diggers are real, Kubar,' he said. 'You've seen the

body yourself. And they're already making forays over the hills. What happens when they get a foothold on this side? I could stay here to watch you all die, or I could do something to help.'

Kubar shook his head. 'You know nothing about the Roof, savage. Nothing! Down here you may eat us, but up there, it is they who will eat you. Fighting, rebellion, crowding. Ha! They will put you in a cage and laugh. Or they would if they had room for a cage. It's changed since I was a boy, oh yes. I tell you, the Roof is no place for a helpless savage.'

'You are calling *me* helpless?'

Kubar sneered – he actually sneered at his chief, the wisps of his moustache almost disappearing into the deep wrinkles of his face. He knelt down quickly and grabbed a pebble no larger than the end of his thumb and held it up between them.

'This, you ignorant savage, this is your whole world.' He tapped one end of the pebble. 'You started your great journey here.'

'Man-Ways.'

The priest shrugged. 'Man-Ways. This is where you started. And this' – he tapped the pebble again, and to Stopmouth it seemed that his finger hadn't moved at all, that he was tapping in exactly the same place as before – 'this is where we are now after your epic journey.'

'No! We travelled at least twenty, thirty days. We—'

'Exactly, savage. Exactly. The world is big. Now, this' – Kubar wrapped his fist around the tiny pebble, enveloping it completely – 'this is the Roof. You people think it's like a bowl over your heads, don't you? Well, you're wrong, you're wrong. The Roof surrounds you as a skull does the brain, only touching your world at the highest mountains. You cannot – you will *never* imagine how huge it is. Even we cannot. It has cities too big to walk across in a human life-time, teeming with people – an army of children underfoot. And there are . . . *oceans* inside it. Whole *oceans*. Can you imagine that? It has areas bigger than this whole world just for playing. Or it used to . . . And tunnels without air where men and women travel faster than any stone you could ever sling. You would understand nothing! Nothing!

'If Indrani lives at all . . . *if* she lives and *if* you get there before some devil beast has you for dinner, you will just be a burden to her. And she would be mad to want to come back here.'

Stopmouth gritted his teeth. 'Even if she . . . if she didn't want to come back . . . she could give me the weapons and the other stuff she promised.'

'Seeds,' said Kubar, and spat. 'That's what she promised. But they'd never allow you that, you see? Never allow you to keep any of it. Why, if you didn't have to fight for your food, what would be the point of it all down here? Who would they look down upon? They have banned them, Stopmouth – banned any plants you could eat, just for the pleasure of watching you bleed. Why would they change that now?'

'It doesn't matter, Kubar. I have to try. We've been over it and over it. We won't last a hundred days if the Diggers make it to this side of the hills.'

Kubar nodded slowly, his shoulders sagging. Then, with all eyes on the pair of them, he pulled the chief into an embrace. He whispered, 'Take me with you. I want to go home. Oh, the gods know it's horrible there, but . . . but the – the hunting, the fear every day. I can't . . . I can't . . .'

Gently Stopmouth pushed the man away.

Then he set off out through the gate, every eye in the tribe watching, pleading for him to turn round. The Roofpeople called his ancestors 'the Deserters', or so Indrani had told him once. Something about leaving her people to die a long, long time ago. He'd been offended by the idea. *Lies*, he'd thought then, for what kind of man would abandon his Tribe like that?

He didn't dare look back. His shoulders ached under the weight of food the tribe had given him – food they would need to survive. And he had their gifts to carry too: images of their gods; a child's first attempt at a sling; and other dangerous tokens of their love. All would have to be thrown away as soon as he was out of sight.

The sheer waste of it, he thought. Off on an impossible mission to rescue a woman from a far safer place than this. How his ancestors must be raging at him.

The narrow streets crumbled around him as he walked. Patches of red- and blue-coloured moss swarmed with clouds of poisonous insects. They buzzed past his ears, tasted his sweat, then left him alone. He kept to the cool shadows of cracked buildings, while above him, a Globe floated lazily against the glare of the Roof, never far away. It seemed that his senses were more alert than they had been for ages. The shifting of stones in a nearby alley helped him avoid a Slimer's ambush, and his eye picked out old evidence of a Skeleton hunting party. Now that he was finally heading towards her, Indrani's memory had lost the power to distract him.

Yes, he'd been selfish to leave his people. And yes, he had done so for the wrong reasons. But everything he'd said to Kubar and Rockface had been true too: the whole tribe's future, the *world's* future, depended on Indrani's safe return. He would bring her back, fight her enemies if he had to, and nothing would keep her from him again.

Stopmouth walked quietly, always alert to what might be round the next corner. He avoided open spaces. Where he'd grown up, the ruins had seemed endless, and only the legends of his tribe had ever hinted that anything might exist beyond them. Stories told how the Traveller had taken the best hunters off exploring long ago. He'd returned alone, the lives and flesh of all his companions wasted. But for all his foolishness, the Traveller hadn't lied when he'd claimed to have found a faraway place where the Roof met the surface of the world. Kubar and Indrani had both confirmed it: a *mountain*, it was called, like the hills that now rose to his right, only much, much larger.

The nearby hills marked the border to Digger territory, but Stopmouth, unlike the poor Traveller, had learned to find refuge there. Creatures that hunted mainly lived in houses. When a new group arrived on the surface of the world, they woke up in buildings, never in the forests or on higher ground. If Stopmouth could get himself onto the slopes, if he moved only at night, then the first part of his journey along the length of the river should be safe enough. It would have to be. Every intelligent creature he came across would want to eat him. And he would be alone too. That was only hitting him now. He wished he could have taken Rockface with him after all. Or what about Kubar, or one of the others who understood the Roof?

It stretched above his head, going on for ever and ever. It passed right the way around the world, if he could believe the priest, swallowing everything Stopmouth knew, as though it were all nothing but a scrap of meat in a hunter's mouth. How – how could he ever hope to find her up there? Kubar was right. They had all been right. It was madness.

On the seventh evening, the hills he travelled began to shrink. A barren landscape of rock and scree replaced them, where the glorious colours of the moss paled towards dull greys and blues. Stopmouth saw plants that were totally new to him: single, tapering stalks that reached up pitifully towards the Roof until their own weight bore them down again. The hunter would find no cover here. Luckily, since he'd left the houses behind, he hadn't seen any signs of intelligent life either. Even better, the horizon showed the land rising again further on. He could see a range of hills, high and pointed. Mist clung to the tallest, hiding its peak.

'There,' he said. 'That's it, it has to be. There.' He laughed with relief.

Then, to his left, a boulder *moved*. It rippled; it growled. The rock lifted itself up off the ground. Scaly legs, tipped with long claws, emerged as if from nowhere; eyes rolled open from what he'd supposed to be clumps of woody moss. The whole creature roared and leaped at him. All Stopmouth could see was the mouth. It was almost large enough to swallow him whole, foetid with the smell of rotting flesh.

He staggered back, yelling in horror, slipping on the little stones that lay everywhere.

The monster's first lunge missed. He could see it better now – its long body, its skin slightly too yellow to be rock, the hairy tufts of its eyes.

Its claws came too fast for his sliding feet to avoid, but he ducked to one side, using the supplies to shield his legs. The creature bellowed in dismay and the roar was answered by several others nearby.

Stopmouth parried another thrust. Sharp claws dug deep into the netting that held his food and snagged themselves on cuts of smoked flesh. The human's spear flashed round and sank deep into his enemy's back. It staggered away from him, crying out. But Stopmouth didn't dare hang around to finish it off or even to untangle his supplies from its claws. He could hear scrabbling feet converging on him from all directions but one. It might have been a trap, but he didn't care. There seemed to be dozens of the beasts around him, roaring now, all at once, their great bucket mouths wide open, looking to be filled. A claw caught him on the elbow; an instant of pain. He staggered, skidded down a hillock on his knees, before righting himself and taking off at speed.

The bellowing of the monsters followed him long after he'd escaped. He knew he wasn't safe. He'd left his food behind and, worse, a trail of blood as clear as day.

# 3. THE RUNNING SAVAGE

Despite the rising tension, Hiresh couldn't take his gaze off Purami. Her face had kept him awake at nights, even before she'd been injected and raised to the Elite. Back then, he used to be able to speak to her without having to bow. In the weeks since, the special nano-machines of the Elite had been at work inside her body, firming and strengthening to the point where her slender hands could bend iron bars.

As she faced Chakrapani, those long fingers trembled and clenched at her side. Chakrapani was shaking too. His upper lip rose into an animal snarl that twisted his perfect features. Both were tensed; both were ready to spring.

To Hiresh and the other spectators, it didn't look like the antagonists were standing in the trainee lecture hall at all – the walls that curved up over everybody's heads were projecting images of Earth's Amazon rainforest, while the floor had taken on the colours of soil and had remoulded itself to give a textured, natural feel under the sole of the foot. Almost every surface of the Roof could do that, and the illusion might have been perfect, thought Hiresh, had it not been for the air in the room, heavy with the stench of fury.

Rumour had it that Chakrapani hadn't adapted to the nano-machines as well as his opponent. He had freaked out a few times already, smashing a priceless mahogany table that had survived transport from Old Earth itself. Who knew how long it would take Dr Narindi to balance him out, and what damage would he cause before then?

'In case you didn't know,' Chakrapani said through clenched teeth, 'your savage—'

'Stopmouth,' said Purami. 'He's a human being, which is more than can be said for—'

'Your savage has already murdered one of us. He sold off Varaha's body to some aliens for their gods-damned *dinner*!'

'That was self-defence,' Purami sneered. She was magnificent, truly magnificent. 'And your brother was a second-rater anyway.'

Hiresh, who'd been watching all this from the relative safety of a crowd of Apprentices, felt somebody wriggle through the audience to stand beside him. He knew without looking that it must be Tarini. 'You're staring at Purami again,' she whispered.

He turned to deny it, and in that moment Chakrapani dived across the room at his tormentor. The two untrained

Elite rained clumsy blows on each other faster than the eye could follow, while their body-servants tried to dodge out of the way. More antiques were thrown about at velocities that turned them to splinters and had all the Apprentices ducking for cover or pushing for the door.

Purami should have ended it with a flying kick – Hiresh heard the crack as she broke Chakrapani's jaw with it. It didn't stop him, though. He was a bull, every bit as much a savage as any creature from the surface of the world below them.

Hiresh sent a frantic call through to security. A specially trained squad of Tranquillizers was already on its way. But they were going to get here too late. Roaring in pain and foaming at the mouth, Chakrapani trapped and broke his opponent's left leg. Her neck would be next, and she knew it now; realized for the first time what a mess she'd made for herself. Her cry went out, both from her mouth and via a broadcast that every Apprentice heard, loud enough to deafen.

'Purami!' shouted Hiresh. He found himself running forward, but Chakrapani's body-servant had got there first and, by some miracle, placed himself between his master and the girl on the ground.

'No,' the boy was saying – Hiresh had never learned his name. 'Enough, Master, enough!'

Chakrapani swatted him aside and the boy flew out of the way.

And then Hiresh found himself behind the monster as Chakrapani raised his foot to stamp on Purami's neck.

Hiresh had never been strong, even by the standards of those terrible days of shortage when everybody went hungry.

Back before the Crisis, parents had the full might of the Roof at their disposal and could choose exactly how their child would look. Handsome, of course. A young god, like Chakrapani, his jaw firm enough to carve stone, his eyes large and sparkling.

But then the so-called Virus had come to poison the Roof. Nobody knew exactly what it was, and the Roof itself stayed silent on the subject. But in a matter of months, the creation of new nano-machines – from which Medicine and other wonders were made – had come to a sudden halt.

Only a year separated Chakrapani from the so-called 'Crisis babies' like Hiresh. They were the first generation to be born without modification. They were puny, they were helpless. But they weren't always without talent, and Hiresh had one special knack of his own: he always knew where the weak spot was.

Still new to his status as an Elite, in his rage Chakrapani wasted what little training he'd had. His stance was all wrong, and as he raised his foot for that final strike, Hiresh slammed his puny frame into the back of the other leg. The Elite fell over, rolled once, and was on his feet again in an instant, facing his new enemy.

'Gods help me,' whispered Hiresh. Foam spilled from between Chakrapani's lips in a constant stream. The pupils of his eyes were huge and an animal moaning noise came from somewhere deep in his chest.

Hiresh felt a warm trickle down his legs.

And then Chakrapani fell past him onto his face and Hiresh saw that his back was peppered with small darts. A squad of armoured men and women lowered their weapons and slapped each other's palms. From behind them came a tall, elegant man, stepping carefully over the mess that had been made of the room, his face expressionless. Dr Narindi.

He shook his head over the sight of Purami, weeping in the arms of her body-servant, and tutted at Chakrapani. Finally he turned away from the fighters. 'You must be' – he closed his eyes to access the virtual reality known as Roofspace – 'Hiresh?'

'Yes, Doctor.' It was funny how he used to think 'Doctor' was the man's first name. Instead, it had turned out to be a sort of profession from a time in the distant past before humanity had learned to let technology look after its health. Although why somebody would claim to be one now was beyond Hiresh.

The man pointed at Chakrapani. 'Before the Crisis we'd have had him put down. Can't afford it now, sadly. Elite are too valuable. I'll have to waste Medicine on the idiot.' He shrugged. 'Get him cleaned up, Hiresh.'

'Me?'

'Who else?' The doctor waved towards the corner where the body of Chakrapani's servant still lay. He was twitching, but Hiresh already knew nobody would waste Medicine on an Apprentice. Times were hard and there were other priorities now.

'Your main job is to keep young Chakrapani out of trouble until he balances, all right? If you can last longer than his previous two body-servants, well, I'll make sure you're on the Upgrade List.'

The doctor spun on his heel, leaving the newly-promoted servant to see to his terrifying master.

'You wet yourself,' said a voice beside him.

'Hi, Tarini.' He was still panting after his ordeal. 'Thank you for noticing.'

She was from the same generation as him: another 'Crisis baby' with uneven teeth and one eye slightly smaller than the other. She poked Chakrapani with her bare toe. Apprentices didn't qualify for boots and most wouldn't have wanted them anyway. 'Don't take the promotion, Hiresh.'

Was she mad? 'This is my big chance for an upgrade.'

'It's a death sentence. Do you think Chakrapani won't find out who it was that brought him down? An Elite knocked over by a Crisis baby? He won't like that humiliation one bit. Gods, you shouldn't even stay in the Academy!'

Hiresh shrugged and knelt down to remove the tranquilizer darts from his master's back.

'You'd only miss me if I left,' he said. The darts were sharp little things, and for a moment he imagined himself with a bandoleer full of them to keep his master in check. Would anybody be looking to get them back?

'I *would* miss you,' said Tarini. She kicked him lightly. 'But I'd prefer it if I could see you again with all your limbs in the right place.'

He met her eyes, his only friend. 'You know I can't leave.' He quickly returned to his task.

'You're not the only one who's suffered, Hiresh, yeah? We wouldn't be here otherwise – we wouldn't even have passed the loyalty tests. Those Rebel scum – they . . .' Her voice was thick with pain. When a thousand wildly different religious groups had finally united in rebellion against their Secular rulers, Tarini's parents had been among the first to be murdered.

The Rebels had been well organized. He knew she still dreamed about it: warrior sects armed with glowing truncheons, with knives and home-made axes, charging skirmish-lines of Wardens. The Religious had been complaining of discrimination for generations before that, and Hiresh knew they had good cause – smaller apartments; forced Secular education of their children and so on . . . But the shortages of the Crisis, and the supposedly unfair rationing that had followed the destruction of the Upstairs, had finally pushed them over the edge. Way over. Their revenge had destroyed whole districts and cost millions of lives before the Elite had finally crushed the Rebels.

A lot of people at the Academy had similar stories to Tarini's, and Hiresh had allowed them all to think the same thing had happened to him. But nobody asked too many questions. They all knew the Religious were just waiting for another chance to rebel; that any day now they'd make another attempt to take control of the Roof for themselves.

'Don't worry,' whispered Hiresh. 'We'll be ready for them next time.'

'But we don't have to be here for that, do we? We could join the regular Wardens instead.'

He shook his head. 'I'm going to be *Elite*. It's always the servants who get onto the Upgrade List, isn't it? So it's the first step. I just have to stay on top of this idiot for a few weeks or so until he straightens out. Then I'm in. I'm Elite.'

He was surprised when she suddenly kicked him in the side, doubling him over. Then, gasping for breath, he felt her spittle on his face. In the illusory background, trees and vines jostled together for space. 'You won't last a week, you selfish turd – not a week. And for what? That stuck-up bitch, Purami?'

That wasn't it, but he hadn't the wind to speak. Again she spat at him, and all he saw from the floor was her bare feet disappearing out of the lecture hall.

It took him a good ten minutes before he could breathe properly again. He didn't waste the time. Well, not much of it. First he closed his eyes and fought for the concentration necessary to log on to the virtual world of Roofspace. He sent his thoughts scurrying after Tarini, but she had blocked his calls and the best he could do was to leave a message she could delete later without playing. Next, still gasping, he laid one of the darts from his master's back down on the floor. Living inside the planet-sized computer had certain advantages. Actually, thought Hiresh, it was bigger than planet-sized – the Roof had enclosed within itself an entire world whose surface swarmed with carnivores. The processing power that filled almost every wall, every object, allowed it to answer all questions that did not interfere with the politics or the privacy of its inhabitants.

And so, with total confidence, Hiresh closed his eyes to make his request. *I want to know what this is made of.* The dart sank into the ground, where tiny machines could analyse the chemicals on its tip. A moment later, he had an answer that the Roof would store for him.

*How long will Chakrapani be unconscious?* he asked next. The information slid into the back of his mind like something he had always known and only just now recalled. Three days. Good, good. It would bring him that much closer to his goal. He could be on the Upgrade List in a few short weeks. And if he had to keep Chakrapani drugged until then . . . well . . . he would find a way. He shoved one of the darts into the pocket of his Apprentice's uniform for now.

He climbed to his feet and ordered the floor to rise up under his unconscious master. It re-formed itself into a trolley and led him out of the room towards the quarters he'd now be sharing with Chakrapani.

Hiresh had always wondered if the Elite Academy had been designed deliberately to induce feelings of acrophobia and nausea in its residents. The first thing a new student noticed was how empty, how quiet the place felt. A series of imposing rooms and lecture halls surrounded a small park at the centre. The whole complex housed fewer than a thousand people at a time – why, the place could almost be a wilderness! Most of the Apprentices asked the Roof to augment their vision a bit so that when they looked around, they saw (or rather, they imagined they saw) more comfortably crowded spaces.

Hiresh never did that.

He left Chakrapani in his quarters and discovered he could claim an entire cubby all for himself, with room to lie down and even stretch out a little. It was more than almost anybody outside the Academy had these days; more than he had owned since childhood. 'Mirror.' He spoke aloud for the sound of another voice. The ceiling obeyed, reflecting him back at himself, a skinny, skinny boy who looked barely half the sixteen years of age he was supposed to be. A flaring broken nose poked out from under little eyes.

He whistled sarcastically. The likes of Purami would never be sighing after him, but it didn't matter. What came next always served to remind him of his life's true purpose, the justice of his cause. He removed the top of his Apprentice's uniform. There was somebody from his old life who needed him more than Purami, oh yes. The sticky leggings came next, absorbed into the wall to be cleaned. He stretched out naked beneath his own reflection.

Scars covered the boy in the mirror, all the more horrible against the dark skin of his Dravidian ancestry. A line of pale and twisted tissue ran straight down the middle of each arm, as though some maniac had hacked away at them with a blunt knife. Which was true. The same maniac had then set to work on Hiresh's legs and feet before turning his torso into a twisted mess of knotted skin. He remembered the pain very well – and the other pain, the one that had come before it.

Only Medicine would ever be able to smooth that flesh again. Purami would be getting some for her broken leg, no doubt. And she'd be walking inside a day. But none would be spared for a mere servant. And Hiresh didn't want any. These scars were his proof. He'd paid full price for them and nobody was going to take them away.

After a while he found himself growing maudlin. That

would never do. Others – billions and billions of others – might have amused themselves with the Roof's many entertainments. Its corridors and plazas, its sprawling parks and artificial beaches, thronged with citizens who lay pressed up against each other, eyes closed and hiding from their misery. Dreamers, they were called. Hiresh had tried Dreaming many times since he'd run away from home. It was easy enough: a simple thought would log him on to Roofspace, a virtual environment where all was known and anything was possible.

One night he'd lived as a king, battling giant snakes and their slimy-skinned human slaves. He'd explored the depths of space and loved women far, far more beautiful than Purami. He'd been a sports star and had hunted as one of the savages of the surface. After a while he'd discovered a better game: the Roof would allow him to relive his own memories, editing out the horrors and righting the wrongs . . . But none of it was real. He'd wake sometimes in a stinking, crowded public square filled with hopeless refugees from the Upstairs, and he knew – he just knew it wasn't enough for him, that no mere illusion could heal him.

He looked in on Chakrapani – still nicely unconscious – and decided to find Tarini and make it up to her. She continued to block his calls, but he knew where she must be. He curled his lip.

The argument between his new master and Purami had

started over the plight of one of the murderous surface-dwellers. As the Crisis brought hard times to the Roof, the real life-and-death struggles of the savages evoked an excitement that no virtual entertainment could match. Many of the cannibals became famous, with fan clubs and graffiti bearing their names spreading across the Roof. Never mind that their ancestors had nearly destroyed the Earth with their greed! After poisoning everything, the scum had run away, abandoning the poorer nations of their home world to die in the wasteland the Deserters had created.

Now, one of their descendants, the stuttering killer known as 'Stopmouth', had become the latest heart-throb. That story would probably come to an end today. His fans would gather to cheer him on, or to mourn his passing.

Hiresh shuddered. He'd watched a few times just to keep Tarini company, but the whole spectacle disgusted him. Nevertheless, it was rare enough for them to fall out, and when they did, it was always Hiresh's job to come crawling back.

He retrieved his clothing and got himself dressed. One last check on Chakrapani revealed that the Elite was still sleeping, although he was twitching a bit. Interesting. Hiresh ordered the bed to grow wider just in case his new master should endanger his precious self by rolling onto the floor. And then he was off.

A few servants roamed the hallways, but no sign

remained of the Apprentices. Their training, virtual and real, had been cancelled in honour of Stopmouth's last stand. They had packed their thin uniformed bodies into the trainee common room, laughing or joking or tense. They came from all over and spoke a dozen different languages, but with the Roof perfectly translating every word, nobody noticed such things. Nor were they paying much attention to the walls that were projecting the ruined streets of Man-Ways.

The Crisis generation felt more comfortable in crowds like this. They loved the comradeship and didn't know enough to miss the privacy. Bets changed hands – how long would the Deserter last in his fight? How many would he kill or injure?

Tarini, as always, had gone into the corner of the common room and was pretending to be interested in the conversation of a pair of other girls – as if she had any friends apart from Hiresh! He grinned, and saw her trying to take no notice of him. Crowds meant nothing to those who'd grown up since the beginning of the Crisis, and he passed easily through this one until he stood right at her shoulder.

'Ladies.' Hiresh bowed.

Tarini's companions smiled at him. Both were nearly as thin as he was, meaning they were probably newly admitted to the Academy. They'd be glad of the extra rations here.

Even Hiresh had put on some weight, although his body remained stubbornly puny. That would change when he got the Elite augmentation. He couldn't wait. He squeezed in beside them.

'Congratulations on your promotion,' said the taller of the two girls, giving him a smile. Tarini scowled.

'Is it true what they say,' continued the tall girl, 'that it's really a double promotion? That they'll raise you up as soon as your own master graduates?'

'Pah!' said Tarini, and suddenly her voice was a perfect mimic of the girl who had spoken. '*Is it true, mighty Hiresh, sir, that there's a bigger betting pool on* your *death than there is on Stopmouth's?*'

'How dare you!' spluttered the new girl.

Hiresh only laughed.

'Oh, Tarini . . . Tarini, it's little wonder you have no friends.' He could see she was about to leap to her feet to do her usual storming-off trick. But the crowd had pressed him right up against her shoulder, and a slight lean on his part was just enough to keep her trapped on her backside between her new companions and the wall.

Hiresh smiled at the new girls and continued speaking in a normal voice as Tarini kept up her struggle. 'So, don't bet against me, ladies. I assure you—' He paused with a grunt. Tarini had managed to free an arm and punch him hard enough in the thigh to deaden his leg. 'You see,' he managed, 'I'll be Elite soon enough, and when I am, I'll have a chance to pick my own servant— Ouch!'

'And who will you pick?' asked the girl. She'd turned out really well for a Crisis baby, and she fluttered her eyelashes at him.

'It would have to be . . . somebody . . . who hits very . . . very hard . . . Harder than necessary . . .'

And then Tarini was speaking inside his head – using the Roof to transmit her thoughts to him. *It's only because I care.*

He replied in the same way, still trying to smile for the other girls. *I know. But stop blocking my calls, will you?*

*Why won't you tell me, Hiresh? Why won't you tell me why you're doing this? It's like . . . it's like no price is too much for you to pay.*

*It isn't.*

*You'd sacrifice anything? Anyone?*

His smile grew painful and he dropped it. 'We should log on,' he said aloud. He waved a hand. All around the room, conversation was dying. Young men and women, a mixture of gods and Crisis babies, were closing their eyes and settling back against each other. 'Your beloved Stopmouth will be needing your support.'

Then he closed his eyes, his knees pressed up against hers, his back supporting that of some trainee he barely knew.

The surface appeared far, far beneath him, like a carpet of hills and river-plains. It all looked so innocent from up here; maybe even beautiful. And then he was plunging towards the ground, air whipping past, hurtling like a rock fallen from the heavens. He felt the others gasp around him. Except Tarini. She was laughing like a maniac.

Slowly Hiresh's eyes came to rest on a particular rocky patch of ground that grew and grew until, in the midst of it, he could make out a single human figure, fleeing for its life. Things were about to become serious.

'The savage looks tired,' said Hiresh. He knew his comments annoyed Tarini, yet he could never help himself. But she said nothing. She must have been totally focused on the plight of her cannibal.

Hiresh could see sweat on the man's skin. If he listened hard, he could hear the breathing too, rapid, hoarse, constant. The hunter skidded on a patch of wildly coloured moss before righting himself, and Hiresh caught a glimpse of even paler scars on every part of his body. *We have that much in common*, he thought. In spite of his exhaustion, the hunter pushed on towards a distant hill. He meant to face his enemies at the top.

'Oh, but he's only a boy!' cried Tarini.

'By all the gods,' said Hiresh – he couldn't keep the disgust out of his voice. 'Can't you see that carnivore still has blood on his *teeth*? Am I the only one who sees that?'

Tarini said nothing. In real life, however, she shifted, as though trying to move away from him. *Good luck with that.*

But he wanted to say he was sorry. Sort of. He knew how much she adored the savage. 'Don't you feel anything for him?' she'd asked him once.

Hiresh had moved the palms of his hands from one part of his own chest to another. 'Maybe . . . Wait! Wait! . . . No . . . I thought there was something, but no. I don't feel a thing for him, I'm sorry.'

That wasn't entirely true, of course. He felt disgust. He felt horror. What the cannibals got up to on the surface reminded Hiresh all too much of everything he'd run away from. Things he didn't like to think about. And yet . . . in spite of the muscles he now possessed, the hunter could only have been about a year older than Hiresh and was just as much of an outsider. Other surface-dwellers had called him *Stopmouth*, mocking his stutter. The traumas of his life made even the experiences of the Upstairs refugees seem light in comparison.

But nothing had affected his ability to run!

Hiresh watched him weave between boulders, saw him leap over shattered walls, and smelled (as Stopmouth must have) the sharp burning scent of crushed moss. The hunter had outpaced his pursuers, but the creatures were patient, and blood leaking from his elbow meant they'd never lose him. 'He may be a hero,' muttered Hiresh, 'but he'll be gone soon, and next week we'll be watching somebody else.'

'Enough, Hiresh! You're always so jealous of him.'

'Jealous?' Where did that come from?

The tiring savage had clipped his foot and come to a halt. Tarini's breath caught.

'Oh, why must you all cry over him?' sputtered Hiresh. The savage had ruined one civilized woman already, turning her into a disgusting meat-eater no better than himself. 'He's little more than a beast!'

But he forgot all these thoughts as the hunter turned to face the creatures who'd been tracking him.

At the back of his mind Hiresh was aware of a sudden and total silence in the real world of the trainee common room. A hundred young men and women held their breaths and tried to silence their racing hearts. The hunter's pale muscles quivered. Across his shoulders, the garish tattoo of a snarling enemy shone with sweat.

Hiresh allowed himself to slip further into the broadcast. Again his ears picked up the ragged breathing of the savage. The air down there was warm and thick and full of insects.

Stopmouth pushed aside the dripping mop of his hair. He bent his head back, and for a moment stared his viewers straight in the eyes. The illusion was perfect – so perfect, in fact, that Hiresh muttered, 'It's nothing personal, savage,' as if the Deserter could hear him. A human being, after all. A human being. Sort of.

Stopmouth jerked back to attention. A moment later, Hiresh heard it too: a rain of small stones, some from behind, some ahead.

The exhausted hunter crouched, his spear held before him, his strange grey eyes scanning for enemies. 'C-c-come on,' he muttered.

And they did. Hiresh felt his empty stomach clench at the sight of them. Two squat aliens trundled out of the morning mist. They ran low to the ground like the lizards on distant Earth, and because Hiresh had chosen a point of view right behind Stopmouth's shoulder, they looked like they were running right at him too.

*Yellowmaws*, people were calling them. Huge bucket mouths hung open, wide enough to encompass a man's head and shoulders. Black tongues lolled and jounced at every step. Their yellow bodies sported random clumps of hair where eyes and other sensory organs lay hidden. Hiresh could see the remnants of the creatures' last meal in the form of undigested lumps across their mid-sections – entire limbs of one of their own that Stopmouth had killed the day before. Hiresh felt his gorge rise, and Tarini gripped his arm. Nothing went to waste on the surface.

The hunter braced himself, waiting for the attack.

There weren't any Religious at the Academy, but Tarini muttered, 'Gods help him.' She wasn't the only one in the room who said the words. In a few moments the cannibal might be no more than another undigested lump in one of these creatures' bellies. Poetic justice, some might say, although it would be disgusting to watch, and Hiresh wanted to drop out of the broadcast. For some reason, however, he couldn't bring himself to do that.

Two yellow monsters raced up the hill. They looked so hungry, so terribly strong. They'd slide Stopmouth in and walk on, unconcerned, as he suffocated inside them.

'Look out, behind you!' cried Hiresh in spite of himself. Billions of fans in every part of the Roof must have been shouting the same thing. To Stopmouth's rear, two more Yellowmaws approached, more quietly than their companions, stepping carefully as they climbed the little rise.

The frontal attackers had almost arrived. They picked up their lumbering pace, calling sounds of encouragement to each other. Stopmouth dug his spear-tip into the soil before him and leaned on the shaft until it bent slightly under his weight. When the two aliens were almost upon him, he flicked it up suddenly, spraying soil, moss and poisonous insects everywhere. Much of it landed in the great bucket mouths of the aliens.

'Oh, ingenious!' cried Hiresh. The creatures screamed in fear, their momentum broken. One of them rolled back down the hill, its tongue and little hands working furiously to remove the insects, its sinuses burning under the assault of the acidic juices in the moss. The second reared up nicely on its hind legs. Stopmouth yelled in triumph as he sliced open its throat. Then he turned to murder the first beast, but he didn't get the chance.

The two Yellowmaws behind him were already storming the hill. He whipped his bloody spear round, but the foremost alien, bellowing in triumph, batted the weapon aside and cuffed its owner backwards. The spear tumbled down the little rise, and Stopmouth scrambled after it.

'You fool,' shouted Hiresh. 'You'll never make it!' Tarini must have been thinking something similar, for she crushed her friend's hand almost hard enough to pull him out of Roofspace entirely.

As if to justify these fears, the Deserter fell just as one of his pursuers leaped for his back. For a moment the only thing the viewers could see was the tufted yellow behind of the closest alien.

'No!' whispered Tarini. Her grip tightened even more. All around the room, voices rose in horror.

The attacking Yellowmaw roared in sudden pain, rearing up and waving its front paws. Something had got hold of it – Stopmouth, of course. *Amazing!* thought Hiresh. He'd only *pretended* to be fetching the spear, *pretended* to fall! The hunter's knife sank into his enemy's belly while his left hand twisted an eyeball out of the tuft that protected it. The two other living aliens danced around the savage and his screaming victim, trying to land a blow.

The blood-spattered horror that was Stopmouth shoved his dying prey towards his enemies. He growled, for all the world like the rabid dogs of Old Earth.

'You need your spear,' said Hiresh. Yet he could see the aliens feared the savage, horrified by the groans of their dying companion. They retreated as he limped towards them, passing frantic signals between them as each tried to persuade the other to attack. Their situation was worsened by the fact that their bodies had not been made to walk backwards, and they looked especially clumsy moving down the steep, scree-covered slope.

Stopmouth's calf muscles began to tense, ready to spring. He took one step forward. Perhaps he'd meant it as a feint. It didn't matter: he'd already made his mistake. The alien he'd gutted still lived, if barely. Its last action was to grab the human hunter's foot. He stumbled, and the Yellowmaw to his left hit him with a sudden charge that knocked him backwards to where the other was waiting. He dropped his knife, teetered at the top of the slope, giving his enemy ample time to open its huge jaws. Stopmouth managed to turn round, but still he toppled over, his head and arms disappearing into the waiting mouth.

Somebody in the common room screamed.

With a sickening lurch that should never have been possible, Hiresh found himself back in the real world. For a moment he and the three girls stared at each other, jaws slack. Everywhere, people were blinking furiously, dazed expressions on their faces.

All was silent. And then, like a wave smashing onto the shore, everybody was babbling at once. 'What happened? Why didn't we see the end? What's going on?'

A few Apprentices closed their eyes, trying to log back on to Roofspace. They found they could spy on Stopmouth's tribe, or that of his brother. They could see any location on the surface they wanted – except the one where their hero had fallen into the mouth of the Yellowmaw.

'I've asked the Roof what's going on,' Tarini told the others. 'I've asked it *explicitly*, and it still won't tell me anything!'

'It's politics, then,' said one of the new girls. 'The Roof wouldn't interfere in our own affairs.'

*Rebels*, everyone was thinking. Religious rebels must have sabotaged the broadcasts, and the Roof would keep their secrets, just like it kept everybody else's. Viewing the surface was one of the things they had promised to end if ever they seized control of the Roof. It was about the only matter on which Hiresh agreed with them.

Above the confusion there came the roar of a single voice.

'Hiresh! Gods kill you, Hiresh!'

Chakrapani stood at the door, naked. His jaw, which should have been broken and slack, seemed in perfect working order, and suddenly Hiresh realized that his Elite master must have already been given Medicine by the Academy. The tiny machines would have done more than just heal the injuries of his encounter with Purami: they would have scrubbed the drugs from his system too, leaving him to wake up far earlier than Hiresh had anticipated. What they hadn't fixed was the mood-swings.

'I'll kill you!' Chakrapani shouted, and then he was flinging people out of his way, making a beeline for his new servant.

Tarini jumped to her feet and pulled Hiresh up with her. 'We've got to get out of here.'

'But if I can just calm him down, I'll be promoted – I'll—'

She cured him of that with a sharp slap across the face. 'Door,' she said to the Roof, and he knew she was transmitting the command at the same time. 'I want an emergency door in this wall right now!'

Meanwhile the middle of the trainee common room had turned into chaos, with people screaming in terror, throwing themselves out of Chakrapani's way.

The Roof obeyed Tarini's command and a section of the wall in front of the two friends disappeared. Immediately, hundreds of new smells from the corridor beyond fought their way into the common room. An equal number of faces turned in surprise at the formation of the emergency exit. Some of the outsiders wore veils or scarves. There was long hair and short; shaved patterns and braids hanging over every imaginable style of clothing in every possible colour.

What would the original colonists have thought if they could see this sight now? Oh, legend had it that a few were still alive, made immortal by their technology, but Hiresh didn't believe in fairy tales of that sort. There'd been less than a few thousand of them to begin with. Severe men and women sent from Earth to be prison wardens for captured Deserters and, later, alien prisoners from the many wars of the Expansion . . . Their descendants now numbered over a trillion. They spoke more languages than had ever existed back home, had invented more gods, more strange customs. They had grown a home for themselves that wrapped right around the planet they were supposed to be guarding; that, until the Crisis, had kept growing upwards and outwards into space. It had been the finest, the largest human civilization that had ever existed. And this crowd represented all that for Hiresh. The sound it made – what Roofdwellers called 'the Roar' – washed over the terrified Apprentices within, and transfixed Hiresh, mesmerized him. He always loved this moment, loved it so much. Standing at an open doorway, like a cliff-diver, all vertigo and desire. 'Am I ready?' he'd ask himself. 'Can I do this?' It always reminded him of the day he'd left home. His glorious escape.

'Oh, come on!' shouted Tarini. 'You idiot, you idiot, you have to wake up. He's just behind us!'

She dived for the first hole in the crowd, where an old Religious woman had paused to fix her veil. He found a gap of his own and slid into it as easily as a fish cuts through water in the reservoir. It helped that everybody was so thin these days, so hungry.

A ripple in the crowd told him that Tarini was heading right, and he followed after her in the hope that she had a plan, for he had none. Left to himself, he would have just waited there, and maybe, having failed to talk Chakrapani down, he'd have pulled out the sleep dart he'd stolen and tried to stab his master with it. A stupid idea, since it had taken six of the things to bring him down last time. Soon, Hiresh was running parallel with Tarini, passing through the sea of people, always knowing where the next space would appear, always finding it. Ahead of him in the corridor, a young man had dropped something and was bending over to pick it up. The crowd tried to flow around him, which left enough room for Hiresh to run forward two steps and vault over his back and into the gap beyond. The man spluttered in outrage, but most people just laughed in spite of their hunger. Hiresh was already gone, using the speed he'd gained to slide, low to the ground, between a pair of arguing friends. *Oh, brilliant!* he thought, forgetting his danger for a moment.

But the Roar was rising in pitch behind him. Chakrapani was coming on in a fury, too crazy to find the gaps, spreading a panic that rippled out ahead of him until Hiresh could sense it at his back. Roofdwellers died in stampedes every day, picked up by the herd and smashed against the walls. They lived in terror of these events the way their primitive ancestors had once feared fire and plague, and everybody, even the Religious, logged on to lessons in how to minimize the risks. Keep still and upright. Flow towards open areas. Shield the old.

However, Chakrapani's madness would not be smothered, and Hiresh knew the only way he and Tarini could survive the inevitable panic was by staying ahead of it. *Keep up!* he transmitted to Tarini. *You have to keep up.*

*You think I don't know, you idiot? I've called Dr Narindi – he's sending another squad.* Yet she was falling behind him, her shorter legs tiring before his. He heard screams now and could imagine his master literally flinging people away from him. Hiresh had a sudden feeling of vertigo. People could be dying because of him. People who'd thought they were just leaving their apartment to cadge some extra food for their families. He had to find a way to stop Chakrapani, even if it meant simply turning round and facing the monster.

Not far away the corridor split in two. One branch headed for the shuttle station, where cars shot through tunnels at enormous speeds, while the other led to the great Prairie Park in the next sector. Its wide spaces had been colonized by tens of thousands of refugees from the Upstairs.

Even so, it would never be as full as the corridor at this time of day. There'd be enough room in the park for the stampede to dissipate safely. Of course, with more space to run, the Elite's tremendous speed would soon bring the chase to a bad end. Hiresh felt his legs turn to jelly at the thought. To come so far, to be within touching distance of Elite status – only to be smashed to a nameless pulp.

'Hiresh!' screamed Chakrapani over the Roar. 'Hiresh!'

Hiresh signalled to Tarini that he was taking the right-hand turn.

*No! You'll never get away from him in the park!*

But she stayed with him. A knot of people had clogged up the side of the corridor in front. Most of them wore the blue robes of the Free From Envy sect – a notorious bunch of hot-heads, well-known for fighting amongst themselves. They were packed in around two people whose shouts could barely be distinguished above the Roar. *Religious scum*, he thought, but he slid towards them without slowing.

Any adult born before the Crisis would see the knot of gawkers forming around the argument and think, *There's no way through there! No way in all the Universe!* But they just didn't know how to wriggle very well. That was their problem. They didn't see how a leg could be pushed right *there* or an elbow jostled or a bottom pinched to make its owner jump aside. It was simply a matter of finding the weak spot. Hiresh didn't need to think about it. The tangle of skinny limbs before him might as well have been a highway.

'Stupid child!' somebody said. He was legally an adult, of course, and couldn't help the fact that his whole generation looked so stunted. On another day he might have taken the time to knock the offender's legs from under him. Instead, he squeezed through the group and ran out of the corridor and under the dizzying artificial sky of Prairie Park.

It was so much brighter here, and huge too – seven square kilometres surrounded by the walls of apartments and the gaping entrances to tunnels and streets that projections from the Roof had transformed to look like the gaps between illusory trees.

Nobody had been allowed to live here when he was a boy. It was all grass back then, seeming to stretch for as far as the eye could see, and he'd cried when his mother had brought him that first time. Children often had problems with open spaces. She had distracted him by walking him over a hill to a little pool where creatures known as ducks waited to be fed as they fretted and chased one another over the calm surface.

Nowadays the grass had mostly disappeared under family groups of refugees from the disaster in the Upstairs – a whole layer of the Roof as large as this one, as crammed with homes and people and automatic farms and open spaces. Half the Roof's inhabitants used to live there. It might be a year, people said, before the damage was repaired enough for them to go home. Until then, the Religious and the Secular refugees kept well apart from each other, and even now, in their reduced state, glared at their enemies in constant suspicion and resentment.

And yet, for all that their plight seemed terrible, Hiresh knew that with the virtual wonders of Roofspace to enjoy, a lot of the people he saw were as happy sitting here as they would be in the most luxurious apartments the Roof had to offer. Many of them twitched as though ill. But their minds were drunk with happiness. They'd be living adventures; sharing feasts of the most exquisite chutneys and spiced vegetables while the greatest entertainers of all humanity's long history performed just for them. It was only when their bodies' need for real food woke them that they had to face up to their misery.

He ran through gaps between the groups, exhausted already, feeling a growing fear that his end was coming; that, at best, he'd get away with being maimed. *Keep away from me*, he transmitted to Tarini, for he could see her moving in parallel with him. *Keep away!* He wasn't sure he'd be able to run for more than another few minutes.

He heard shouts of alarm and knew that Chakrapani had already entered the park. He turned, sliding to his knees in the mud as he did so. At the same time Chakrapani saw him and gave a wordless cry, for all the world like one of the beasts of Old Earth challenging a rival.

He came towards Hiresh at a fast walk, his mad eyes fixed on his victim. People along his route woke from their Dreams and rolled out of his way.

The monster looked almost as tired as Hiresh. Medicine made great demands of its host and required lots of food to keep working. But that wasn't all – Chakrapani was now Elite, with millions of tiny machines infesting his body. They had joined their strength to his as he smashed a path through grown men and women. These machines needed energy too, and they had gorged themselves on the last of Chakrapani's body fat, as well as much of his muscle. He looked no bigger than a Crisis baby himself.

But Hiresh wasn't fooled by this. His training at the Academy had taught him enough to recognize that his master had a good hour of mayhem left in him. More than enough to crush the object of his hatred.

Hiresh watched his doom move closer and closer. Where was the clean-up squad? Where were the Wardens? He felt the eyes of the refugees on him. They leaned forward, their talk all stopped. *Am I the entertainment now?* Every single muscle in his body was shaking and his stupid mouth worked like that of a stranded fish. All sounds had a sudden perfect clarity: the squelching of Chakrapani's foot-steps, the final panicked beating of his own heart.

Out of nowhere, a stone flew and struck Chakrapani on the temple. He staggered. Blood seeped from the wound, but the Medicine that still swam in his system closed it up immediately.

'Hey, Chakrapani!' cried Tarini. 'Your brother got what he had coming. He was a coward, a dirty coward. A meat-lover!'

She had crept up close to taunt him. Far too close.

Before Hiresh could do more than cry out, Chakrapani leaped five metres in a single bound to land right in front of her. He lifted her little body and threw her up, out and away.

Luckily she landed in the soft mud of a dying lake. But Chakrapani hadn't finished with her, and strode after her prone body. Many people had woken up from the Dreams now – what some called 'surfing' – and they all watched in fascination. Hiresh couldn't believe it.

He stumbled past them, desperate to come to Tarini's aid. She was gasping in helpless panic, too winded to move.

'Help me!' cried Hiresh to the people all around him. 'This isn't a virtual, gods crush you all! He's going to kill her! A girl – he's going to kill her!'

And it was then the miracle happened – he'd never heard of such a thing before – but a dozen brave men and women jumped to their feet. Secular or Religious, it didn't matter – they all threw their feeble, clumsy bodies at the

Elite. Chakrapani didn't even bother shaking them off but, in his rage, tried to keep walking through the mud towards Tarini.

By the time Hiresh got there, the monster had toppled over, and that might have been the end of it if Chakrapani hadn't managed to get one hand around Tarini's neck.

Hiresh never paused to think that what he was about to do would destroy everything he had been working towards since he had run away. All his promises, all his fears. The scars, the terrible scars. His whole world had come down to one decision that his body took of its own accord. He pulled the dart out of his pocket, saw the weak spot, as he always did, and stabbed.

The dart passed straight through Chakrapani's eye and into the brain and, although the Medicine in the Elite's system probably worked to save him right up until the end, it made no difference.

Those who had been holding down his master fell away, covering their mouths. They'd been trying to save a girl. None of them had expected to be involved in a murder. They melted away, and when the Wardens came a few moments later, Hiresh was still there in the mud.

# 4. THE RACEHORSE

Stopmouth's whole torso slid into the Yellowmaw's bucket mouth, his arms pushed out ahead of him. It burned! Oh ancestors! The creature's insides scorched every part of him they touched. Like landing in fire. Arms and belly; his face, his back. Thrashing and arching and screaming. Even the air tore at his throat and poked hot needles deep into his chest.

He clawed with useless fingers at the inside of the monster's throat. He couldn't find anything to scratch, anything to hurt, although he could hear its great heart thundering nearby, maddeningly close.

And that was all. Or almost all. Before the end, his mind raced with images of Indrani and Wallbreaker. His mother's lap; the scent of her hair. His father's laughter, overheard at night. But these memories boiled away with the last of his air. And then his whole world flashed bright green. And *that* was all.

\*   \*   \*

But after death his eyes opened again. They saw that the afterlife was nothing but a bone-coloured dome, ten steps wide, with a platform in the middle for him to lie upon. He sat up, rising without effort. He felt . . . he felt . . . *hungry.* More hungry than he'd ever been in his life . . . And his skin! He'd expected a scorched and shrivelled patchwork, but instead, his hands shone like a child's, free from a lifetime of scars, cleaner than he could have imagined.

He stood, trembling, starving.

*Am I a spirit?* he asked himself. Would he hear his people if they prayed to him? And what would he be able to do for them if they did, trapped as he was in this tiny space?

'Hello, Stopmouth.'

He spun round, marvelling at the complete lack of pain he felt from even old injuries. A man stood against one of the walls. The hunter hadn't heard him come in.

The newcomer grinned, bright teeth shining in a face as dark as any in Stopmouth's new tribe. But unlike most of them, his features were as perfect as Indrani's – a straight nose, prominent cheekbones and deep black eyes. He was tall and wore a form of clothing that sat snugly over the body of a great hunter.

'I'm in the Roof,' said Stopmouth in sudden realization. He'd made it! Although he was supposed to be dead. The Yellowmaws had killed him. He hadn't even reached the mountain.

'Who are you?' he asked the stranger. 'Where's Indrani?' The second question slipped out of his mouth before he remembered that the chiefs of this place were her enemies. But the man seemed not to have heard it.

'Oh, really, Stopmouth, is that all? Who am I?' He smiled with one side of his mouth. 'My fellow Rebels swore you would launch yourself at me as soon as I spoke.'

'Fellow Rebels?' So the man was *not* one of her enemies, after all.

'They said you would try to gut me with your savage fingernails!' The man laughed, his teeth whiter than the walls of the room.

'I have never killed another human except to end their pain,' said Stopmouth. His mind was racing again. The man claimed to be a Rebel, the people Indrani was going to try and contact. Did that make him a friend? But the hunter had no idea who he could rely on here, and he felt certain he was being made fun of. A lifetime of stuttering had given him practice in dealing with that. He turned his back on the visitor and lay down on the platform again.

The man cleared his throat. 'I told them you were almost civilized, yes? This was when I suggested we rescue you from the Yellowmaws and patch you up. "Risk is what we need," I said. "A bit of risk." And they should have known they could trust you! Most of us have followed your life since you were born, Stopmouth. You have billions upon billions of fans, yes? And these friends of mine, my fellow . . . Rebels . . . Well, some of them worship you. Not as a human being! But as your own ancestors might have worshipped a fine racehorse. Athletic, even beautiful. How lovely to watch them run, to pet their sleek flanks. But who wants to stand behind one in a moment of confusion? Ha! Who but me? I would gamble the world. That's what they say about me. That's what got me where I am today.' He stepped closer, muscles rippling under the uniform he wore.

Stopmouth sat up again, causing the man to flinch. 'How do I understand you?' the hunter asked. 'I see your mouth move, but with a Talker the sound wouldn't match your lips. Also, you speak about *racehorses*. How do I know what a horse is? I *do* know! I can picture it if I close my eyes. I'd love to see one. To hunt it. It would be amazing.'

The man smiled as if delighted. 'Of course you'd love to see a horse. To eat it! The squeal of it as it died! Oh, you'd love that!' He walked over to Stopmouth – gingerly, for all his earlier talk about 'gambling the world'.

'We brought you here to help you find Indrani. We Rebels, that is. She used to be on the side of the Commission, of course, but—'

'The Commission?'

'The government. Rulers of the Roof – big chiefs, yes? Big chiefs and Secular like her. But since they tried to have her killed . . .'

77

'So you really are a . . . a Rebel?'

The man sketched a bow with his palms pressed together in front of him. 'My name is Dharam.'

Stopmouth didn't return the gesture. 'Where's Indrani? Why won't you tell me that?' He placed one firm hand on his visitor's shoulder.

Dharam yelped. 'Please!' His voice rose to a higher pitch than any man Stopmouth had ever heard. 'Don't hurt me!'

'Indrani,' said Stopmouth. 'I just want—'

The hunter found himself lying on his back with his head ringing. He had no idea of how he'd got there. Dharam had disappeared. He climbed back up onto the bed, unsure of what had frightened his visitor so badly. All he'd done was put a hand on the man's shoulder.

He shrugged and then smiled. Indrani lived. So what if he'd scared off one of the Roofpeople. Indrani was stronger than any two men like Dharam. Sooner or later she'd come for him. They'd made it. Both of them had made it to the Roof alive.

He slept and woke again many times. There was always food waiting for him. Disgusting tiny white pellets – vast quantities that he scooped desperately into his mouth. It was never enough for this strange new hunger.

There was no trench in the room for a toilet so he went against one of the walls. The floor drank his waste as though greedy for it.

The longer he waited, the sorrier he became that he'd frightened his visitor away. The Diggers were coming and his people needed Indrani's Roof magic to save them. How long did they have? he wondered. How long before the invincible enemy crossed the hills and established tunnels for themselves? He saw them in his mind's eye, triangular heads bobbing blindly as they streamed down the slopes. His people running, but slowly, far too slowly.

He jumped to his feet, suddenly afraid. 'I'm sorry!' he cried. 'Dharam, I'm sorry! Come back! Come back!'

Hiresh had killed somebody, really killed him. And not in an accident or with the help of a tidy poison. *Blood* caked his fingers and stuck them together – Elite blood, the most precious of anyone in the Roof.

His first instinct was to run away. He had a talent for that, at least. With every public space heaving with refugees, and the Roof, following rules laid down by those who had grown it, refusing to share personal secrets with the authorities, he could have disappeared within moments, never to be found again.

He pulled Chakrapani's fingers away from Tarini's neck. She was still breathing, but he didn't like the hoarse sound of it one bit. He logged on and asked for advice on helping her, but it seemed that without Medicine there was precious little he could do except wait and hope for the best.

Dr Narindi arrived moments later with the clean-up squad. 'You've wasted my Elite.'

The boy nodded. He had Tarini's head in his lap.

The doctor crouched down beside Chakrapani's body and pulled free the bloody dart. Hiresh shuddered, as though it had come from his own eye. 'Do you have any idea how rare the Elite are these days? Any idea?'

Hiresh did.

'I asked you a question,' said the doctor.

Hiresh dared to raise his head and was surprised to see that the man was actually smiling at him, as though they were old friends sharing a joke.

'The cannibal killed an Elite too. Did you know that, Hiresh? Chakrapani's brother, of all things!'

Hiresh lay back in the mud, holding Tarini and checking her condition in Roofspace all the time. The Roar of the crowd seemed to fade a little in the doctor's presence, and even the smell lost its edge. Or so it seemed. He looked up at the artificial clouds and watched them blur in his vision.

'It would be a waste to destroy someone of your resourcefulness,' said Narindi. 'And there is no need. None at all. Do a special job for me, Hiresh, and you will have what you've always wanted. You will be Elite. I can't afford any more knuckle-heads in the programme after this. Are you content?'

'What about Tarini?'

'There's no Medicine for the likes of her, but I am the only person you will ever meet who knows how to take care of her properly without it. Me. Ask the Roof what a doctor is and you will see.'

Hiresh already knew what a doctor was, but his eyes widened at the possibility that Narindi really was part of that ancient profession, from the days – centuries ago! – before Medicine had been perfected. He wanted to ask the doctor how old he was but his nerve failed him. Instead he said, 'Mind her for me, and I will do anything you ask . . . Doctor.'

'Anything?' asked the smiling man. 'I might require you to tell a few lies.' The smile broadened. 'How would you like to meet a real live cannibal?'


Stopmouth tried everything to escape from the white room, but two precious days passed before his visitor returned, seeming to just walk straight through the wall like a spirit. 'Well, my fine racehorse,' he said.

Stopmouth took a step towards him, but paused when Dharam flinched.

'I wasn't trying to hurt you that other time. I'm sorry. And thank you for saving me from the Yellowmaws. I owe you my life.'

One half of Dharam's mouth rose in that funny smile of

his. 'Think nothing of it,' he said. 'I'm the one who is sorry. You are unused to civilized ways, you see. And probably always will be. It must all be so confusing for you . . .'

'I was only worried about Indrani,' said Stopmouth.

'Oh, I know,' said Dharam. 'I know that, and I am worried about her too, believe me. I was hoping we might work together to help her out before her enemies find her.'

The man kept more of a distance between them than he had previously, and his skin-tight clothing showed muscles bunching in the backs of his legs.

'Indrani was very . . . stressed when she got here. Enemies were looking for her and we needed to shield her. Do you recall the time you stole her from your brother's house?' Stopmouth nodded. He knew now that the Roof spied on his people, but it was still a bit of a shock to hear such a secret deed spoken about knowledgeably by a stranger. 'The first time she woke up after the rescue – do you remember that, Stopmouth?'

'She didn't recognize me,' said the hunter.

Dharam smiled, as though delighted at Stopmouth's ability to remember things.

'That's how she was when we brought her here, you see? She seemed afraid of us and ran off down a public corridor.'

The young hunter surged to his feet.

'Oh, don't worry! Don't worry! You'll find no creatures here who want to hunt her!' Dharam's way of smiling and speaking slowly made it difficult for Stopmouth to judge the sincerity of his words. But Indrani had told him herself that flesh wasn't eaten in this place, and if that were true, the beasts here would have no motive to kill her. He forced himself to sit down, aware that he'd almost frightened off his visitor again.

'Good,' said Dharam. 'That's better. Now, the last time she suffered so, you were able to bring her out of it, yes?'

'I thought she just got better by herself.'

'No, my fine savage, our records tell us that the sight of a loved one is often the best cure for such a malady. But listen now – I need to know one thing that might let us help her, and maybe get you to her more quickly.'

'Yes?'

The side of Dharam's mouth twitched. 'Did Indrani . . . did she ever explain *why* she was shot down over the surface? It's how she got to you in the first place, yes? She must have said why it happened.'

Certainly Stopmouth remembered her fall from the sky. How could he not? But all she'd said about the incident was that her attacker had been 'evil'.

He shook his head.

'Not a thing? You're absolutely sure? She didn't mention . . . she didn't mention . . .'

'She said nothing. But I don't see how this can help us find her anyway.'

83

Dharam froze, and his eyes seemed to lose their focus. 'What's that?' he said. Stopmouth didn't know how to answer, but Dharam wasn't even looking at him. 'Where?' he continued, followed by a pause. And then, 'All right. I'm coming straight away.'

Then he turned and walked out through the exact same place in the wall from which he'd entered, leaving Stopmouth trapped behind it. The hunter ran after his visitor, hitting the wall with full force and bouncing off again onto the floor. All he could think of was his poor feverish woman, and the fear she must be feeling as she ran through some never-ending nightmare.

He grew angry. He didn't understand why Dharam had left him here if he was the only one who could help her. It seemed perverse, mad even. He rose again and leaned against the wall.

'Let me out,' he whispered. 'Please just let me out.' And that was all it took, it seemed. He'd only had to ask. The wall dissolved before him and he passed through to the other side.

# 5. The Fan

topmouth gasped.

Immediately, people were bumping into him. Dozens of people, hundreds of people. More than a mind could hold. Their pungent overwhelming stink filled his nose: sweat and filth and a dozen odours unknown.

The first to notice his sudden appearance among them recoiled – or tried to recoil – in horror against the crowds around them. As though Stopmouth would try to hurt them. As if he'd want to! He was far more terrified than they were, shocked by the noises, the sights, the smells. An endless sea of strangers babbling in dozens of languages which were all comprehensible to him, and all at once.

He didn't have enough hands. He wanted to block his ears from the shouting, the echoes of footsteps, the shuffling and coughing, the whispers. But he needed protection for his eyes too, for even when he closed them, the intricate details and mad colours of this place insinuated themselves into his brain: reds, sharp blues and yellows such as he'd never seen in his life. Colours his tribe hadn't words to describe. And there were symbols too, pictures so realistic, it was as though men had been flattened into the wall and left hanging in delicate poses. There were the talking squiggles he'd seen in the crashed Globe too – *writing*, it was called – and it covered every surface, as if in this mass of people a man could be so lonely as to want to speak to the buildings.

He found himself on his knees, shaking and fighting for breath against the hordes around him.

'Help me,' he begged, not sure whom he was asking. 'Help me . . .'

He had a little space on the floor all to himself as the people skirted him. Through the barrier of his hands one word reached his ears more than any other: 'savage'. It was this that brought him back to his feet in the end. 'It's only noise,' he said to himself. 'Colours won't hunt you.' Even so, it was a battle to open his eyes and keep them open without screaming. And to think he had imagined that the Roof was a paradise! How could anybody live like this?

He tried to calm himself by taking his bearings, like any hunter in strange territory. But he felt nauseous and dizzy.

He was standing in what might have been a very broad street were it not for the fact that it had a ceiling two body-lengths above his head. It emitted a soft light, and squiggly messages scrolled across it constantly, sometimes accompanied by moving images of people urging polite behaviour and condemning waste.

'*In case of emergency, walk slowly. Do not push!*'

The walls too writhed with pictures, but here the images had to fit themselves around doors and small trees with an infinite variety of garishly coloured leaves. Most of these plants had been smashed by the passage of bodies, smeared against the bright pictures behind them.

Stopmouth took a few deep breaths. The stink was the worst part. More than anything, he wanted to get out of this place, but he wouldn't leave without Indrani. Not that he knew where he might find her in all this mass of people. Perhaps he'd been stupid to leave the white room. Dharam had claimed to know where Indrani was and had said that Stopmouth would be needed to help her. Perhaps he'd come back here, and if that was the case, Stopmouth should wait for his return.

But something in the young hunter's gut told him not to trust the man. Not because he'd talked down to Stopmouth – he was used to that even from friends such as Rockface. It was more to do with the way Dharam's eyes flicked this way and that when he spoke of Indrani, as if he wasn't really her friend. And if Indrani truly needed to see Stopmouth, why hadn't he been brought to her straight away? No, he'd make sure he was gone by the time Dharam came back. But where?

Just then he noticed that some of the younger passers-by had gathered into a little knot to stare at him from what they might have imagined to be a safe distance. They whispered among themselves, as excited to see him as other people were afraid. But he changed that just by talking to them. He said, 'Help me,' and they scattered, weaving their bodies into the crowds. All except one. This boy – and he could only be a boy even if he looked no younger than Stopmouth – stood his ground. He had a small line of hair across his upper lip. His long, thin face had a certain stillness about it that seemed . . . unreal.

And then, just as Stopmouth had thought he was getting used to it, the clamour became overwhelming again and he fell back onto his knees, forced to cover his eyes with his arms.

*I have to get away*, he thought. *Before Dharam returns. For Indrani, I have to. Up. Get up . . .*

A voice close by addressed him.

'Let me help you stand, Chief.'

Stopmouth peered through his fingers enough to make out the boy he'd seen moments before. He looked barely old enough to hunt and seemed in serious need of nourishment. Stopmouth thought: *He feels sorry for* me! And this brought his courage back again and pushed him to his feet.

'Are you all right?' asked the boy.

'I need to find Indrani. Do you know where she is?'

'I don't know,' came the reply. But he was already leading Stopmouth away through crowds that opened up around them.

'Where are you taking me then?'

'Somewhere . . . calm. I am Hiresh, by the way.'

'I'm—'

The boy laughed. 'Oh, I already know who you are. I think everybody does, except maybe some of the strong Religious. They won't watch that kind of stuff. Come on.'

Somewhere calm. 'Thank you, thank you,' said Stopmouth. The relief was overwhelming, but soon the hunter felt ashamed at being led like this, and pulled away to walk by himself. He ignored his churning stomach and found it easier to move if he concentrated on the back of his rescuer. It wasn't an easy task. The boy always seemed to know exactly where the gaps in the crowds would open, and he slipped into them with no more thought than Stopmouth would have used in crossing Central Square at home. The hunter's advantage lay in his ability to create spaces around himself just by his very presence. Sometimes young men or women would try to tag along, asking bizarre questions about killing. The stench of their bodies, their feet bare or bound in rags, their gabbling voices all threatened to separate him from his new friend. But the crowds that parted for him pushed these questioners away, so that soon he and Hiresh were almost alone in a half-empty corridor whose only other occupants were men and women tossed along the walls in sleep.

They seemed to walk for a very long time. The shapes and sizes of the passageways changed constantly. Every little area seemed to have its own style of decoration. But he was careful not to glance too closely at anything. It was all too distracting, even nauseating at times. Messages urging 'silence' or 'good behaviour'. Promises of 'status' or other rewards for the reporting of criminals. Visions of happy men and women enjoying the fruits of 'obedience'.

Eventually they reached a corridor that was so narrow, so filled with people lying down against its walls, they were stepping over legs and arms. A few times, the hunter's inexpert feet trod on somebody, but rarely did they even look up at him, their minds far away.

'Why don't they wake?' he whispered.

'They're Dreaming,' said Hiresh.

'Are they . . . Are they all right?'

Hiresh laughed. 'They're loving it! Surfing through adventures. Stuffing their faces. You know.'

Stopmouth didn't.

They came to a stop near a tree with broken branches. The scrolling images of the walls did not work so well here and their colours were muted.

'So,' said the boy, 'this is where I live.'

'OK,' said Stopmouth, and plonked himself onto the

floor of the corridor beside some of the Dreamers. Hiresh started making a gasping noise that it took the hunter a few moments to realize was laughter.

'Watch,' said the boy, trying to control himself. 'Watch.' He waved his hand at a part of the wall where a man in filthy white skins lay Dreaming. It opened before him to reveal a little room just like the one Stopmouth had escaped from. The Dreamer fell inside when his support disappeared. Hiresh simply pushed him out again with no more thought than a woman casting bones into the street. The man never stirred.

'Come in,' Hiresh said. 'I'm sorry for laughing, but when you sat down on the floor . . .'

Stopmouth tried to smile, and followed the boy into the tiny space beyond. It was little more than a featureless bone-coloured box with enough room for two people to lie down in. He was grateful for the plainness of it, though. He had an urge to rest his face against the wall and weep.

'It used to be bigger before the Crisis,' Hiresh said. He rubbed idly at the top part of his left arm. And then he too stopped speaking and drew in a deep breath. Perhaps he'd only just now realized he was alone with a . . . a *racehorse*.

Stopmouth looked at his hand and saw that it was shaking, the skin so much paler than that of anybody else he had seen here. He was in a nightmare so terrible that a tiny metal room had come as a great relief. 'Is it . . . Is it all like this? The Roof, I mean? Corridors and boxes?'

The question seemed to steady Hiresh's nerves and his smile came back. His teeth were crooked and discoloured, but he couldn't stop flashing them all the same, and Stopmouth felt himself relax, his own lips responding helplessly.

'Oh gods, no!' said the boy. 'We're in Joy Sector here, my friend – it's all residential, sure, but pick any direction, right, and in less than an hour you can walk to a park or a sea or a . . . well, there are no forests left, I don't think, but—'

'Why not?'

'Oh, with the Crisis it was harder for people to live there. It's the same reason my apartment keeps shrinking. Ever since we lost the Upstairs we need more space for the refugees. They had to come down and live at this level . . .'

This talk was very confusing and reminded Stopmouth of the conversations he used to have with Indrani about the Roof. There was too much going on. Too much of everything. But it didn't stop there. Now his host raised a finger on each hand and pointed at opposing corners of the room. 'Chairs,' he said.

Stopmouth jumped as furniture appeared out of the wall. Hiresh didn't laugh this time. Instead, he showed his visitor how to sit down on one as if it were a step or a ledge, only soft and comfortable. Another wave of the hands brought pictures to every surface until Stopmouth begged Hiresh to take them away again. Magic. Everything was magic here.

'What was that Crisis you were talking about? The one that made your . . . your home smaller. Is it anything to do with the Rebellion?'

Hiresh shifted in his seat. 'Well . . . the Religious – the Rebels – they used the shortages as an excuse. They always claimed we were oppressing them, just because they had to obey the same laws as everybody else. And then they said we were keeping them from their fair share of accommodation and food when they'd have been fine if they'd just been good citizens!' He shrugged and Stopmouth nodded. Here at last was something he understood.

'Shortages always get people fighting, don't they?'

'Yeah,' said Hiresh. 'I suppose. Bits of the Roof have been breaking for years now. Tiny little machines – you know what a machine is?'

'Like a Talker or a Globe.'

'Yeah, like those. Only these ones are too tiny to see, and they run everything and fix everything. Even us, and that's what Medicine is. But these tiny machines – we call them *nanos* – they're not allowed to build more of themselves in case they ever got out of control. Only the goddess . . . I mean, only the Roof.' He grinned. 'There are no goddesses, of course! Only the Roof is allowed to make them, and since the start of the Crisis . . . well, she . . . it . . . can't any more.'

'So everything breaks and doesn't get fixed?' asked Stopmouth. Already he was thinking of the buildings back in the Ways where he'd grown up. Crumbling over generations.

Hiresh looked a little sick for a moment, but he brightened quickly. 'It's only temporary, though! The Crisis, I mean. The High Commissioner himself appeared on the walls a few months ago to say they'd got a Cure for the thing. We've a bad year ahead of us while they roll it out, but after that there'll be food for everybody again and the refugees will all be able to go back to the Upstairs.' His face grew animated with excitement. 'Just think about it! Paradise. Paradise again. Everybody happy. No more bullying by the Religious.'

'I thought it was the other ones, the non-believers, the . . . the *Seculars* who were in charge?'

Hiresh waved that away, his thin face suddenly bitter. 'The Religious persecute their own. And that can't be right, can it? Can it?' He paused, and slowly his expression relaxed. 'But there'll be other stuff too when things get fixed. Games. Concerts. We'll even have Cosmetics!'

'Cosmetics?'

'They're like Medicine. The little machines – except

they can change the way you . . .' He shook his head and looked away from the hunter. 'I'm sorry. It's a stupid thing. I'm not very popular with the girls, that's all.'

Stopmouth smiled. 'I wasn't either. Before Indrani.'

'I know.' The smile returned to light up Hiresh's whole face.

They sat in silence for a few moments, but then Hiresh seemed to snap back to himself.

'So,' he said, 'is Indrani coming here? Now that you have a place to stay, I mean.'

'How would she know to come here?'

'You will tell her, of course.'

'I will? Of course?'

They looked at each other in puzzlement. Then Hiresh gave a nervous laugh. 'You're like a baby, up here! No offence, Chief. No offence! I'm your biggest fan, you know – it's why I helped you back there. I mean, everybody was saying you were dead when the Yellowmaws got you, but I knew it wasn't true. I knew it . . .'

'I'm not offended,' said Stopmouth. 'I don't understand the hunting in this place.'

'Well then,' Hiresh replied, 'let me help you learn the . . . hunting, as you say. Why don't you close your eyes? And keep them closed, no matter what. All right?'

Stopmouth obeyed.

Suddenly Hiresh was standing in front of him wearing

different-coloured skins from before. Bulging muscles had formed all over his body. 'Can you see me? Can you hear me?'

The change panicked the hunter, and he opened his eyes to find his vision filled now with two copies of Hiresh, the new and the old. The old grinned, his mouth closed. The new one, however, floating in the air before him, said: 'I told you to keep your eyes shut. Now you're even more confused!'

'Make the spirit go away!' cried Stopmouth.

The new Hiresh disappeared.

'I don't want that to happen any more!' said the hunter. 'Tell the Roof I don't want it!'

Hiresh sighed. 'Tell it yourself. I mean it. Just think clearly in your mind that you don't want anybody to be able to contact you, that you don't even want to know if they're trying, and I promise you, it will stop.'

Stopmouth took a deep breath and obeyed. A part of him knew he was being stupid, but he couldn't help himself. It was too much like the visitation of a hungry ghost.

'It's all right,' said the boy. 'It wasn't real. Just a picture, like that tattoo you have on your arm. If you asked to talk to me and we weren't in the same room, you could, you know. I'd see an image of you – any image you wanted me to see – and we'd talk all we wanted.'

'I don't want it,' said Stopmouth. And then he froze as

an idea came to him. 'Wait. Can you call anybody you want? Could you call Indrani?'

Hiresh sat forward in his seat and his eyes narrowed. 'Of course. That's what I was trying to teach you for. Why don't *you* call her? Indrani doesn't know me at all.'

But when Stopmouth closed his eyes and thought of her, nothing happened.

'She can't be contacted,' he said. His heart sped up as he said it and he surged to his feet, his eyes wide. 'How do I know that? How can I know that she doesn't want to be contacted? It's like . . . it's like an ancestor slipped the words into my head!'

'Don't worry,' said Hiresh. 'It's just the Roof. The Roof. You were logged on for a second. It's what happens when you try to call somebody, it's—' His jaw dropped open and he stopped talking. His eyes bulged and he stared beyond the hunter. 'Who are you? How – how did you get in?'

Stopmouth whirled round. Behind them, the door stood open.

# 6. JAGADAMBA

The same old Dreamer had fallen backwards into the apartment. A stooped figure occupied the rest of the doorway, its face hidden in orange robes.

'Skinny boy, stop your broadcasting!' said a rough man's voice. 'Stop it now. I can still detect it.' The figure pushed the Dreamer aside and the door slid shut. The room, with three people, had become very cramped indeed.

Stopmouth tried to peer through the robes to the person underneath. Whoever this was, he couldn't belong to the rulers of this place – otherwise, what need had he to hide his identity?

'But why no broadcasts?' asked Hiresh. 'Surely—'

'Let's hear him out,' said Stopmouth.

Hiresh nodded reluctantly, and their visitor, who must have had some way of knowing Hiresh was telling the truth, immediately disrobed.

It wasn't a man who appeared after all, but a feeble old lady, her words emerging as though each had to fight through the constriction of her scrawny neck. To

Stopmouth, she looked older than any of those who'd accompanied his new tribe into exile. Her hair was purest white, jutting up in clumps all over her head. Her teeth looked no better: one of them stayed on the outside when she closed her mouth, all yellow and black.

'You see,' she wheezed, 'they'd have identified me quick enough, yes they would.' She turned to the hunter. 'You think they don't know you're here in this big apartment, savage?'

So intense was her gaze, Stopmouth forgot to take offence. 'Who do you mean by "they"? The ones who kept me in the white room?'

She nodded.

'There was a man,' said Stopmouth. 'I don't know who he was or what side he was on. I'm not even sure what the sides are up here. Religious rebels, Secular rulers – it's all too confusing. But . . .' He shook his head and imagined the thousands of people who'd seen him come out of the white room and how each of these witnesses had the ability to call whomever they wanted with just a thought. 'This Dharam must know where I am,' he said, 'mustn't he?'

'Good then, monster. You're not so stupid. The Roof won't interfere in human affairs, but every Commission lackey that saw you can report back on your movements.' She seemed to become aware that Hiresh was staring at her, a look of horror on his face. 'What's wrong, little hairy lip?

Never seen a Religious before? Ha! I bet you haven't, have you? Not around here, anyway. Well, that's all about to change.' She cleared her throat and spat a blob of phlegm, which was quickly absorbed into the floor. 'We'll be drinking that later!' Her laughter rattled, as though her throat already needed another clearing.

'Just so you'll know me, my name is Jagadamba. Yes, I'm Religious – can't hide that, nor would I want to.' She spat again so that it landed uncomfortably near Stopmouth's bare toes. 'And yes, I can take you to Indrani, because *we* have her. In a place they'll never find her.' She laughed. 'Or so I'm told!'

Jagadamba removed a small package from inside her clothing, which she shook out to reveal another set of robes. They were a dull orange like hers and would cover a whole body. 'You need to wear these, savage. Come on now, no dawdling, you disgusting cannibal. They'll be on their way already.'

Stopmouth grabbed the robes and started trying to get into them. Then he paused. 'But wait. Indrani hated the Religious and they hated her. She was a . . . a Secular.'

'Good savage, good little monster,' said Jagadamba. 'But don't stop putting those clothes on. You, skinny boy. You help him.'

Hiresh remained frozen to the spot as though he'd seen a ghost. The old woman ignored this and hobbled over to

Stopmouth, fussing with folds of cloth. 'In civilization we have mastered the art of talking and dressing at the same time, yes we have. Good, you're not quite right, but those Commission idiots'll never notice the difference.'

'I still don't . . .'

'What, savage? Oh, yes. You are correct. We don't like your Indrani. The Witch, we call her. But we know we weren't the ones who shot her down to the surface during the Rebellion. It was her own side that tried to kill her, and now they're combing the whole Roof looking for her. Why do you think that is?'

'I don't know.'

'And strange how they just let *you* go, isn't it, monster? A cannibal set loose in the middle of the Roof!'

'They *let* me go?'

Jagadamba nodded and grinned at the look of horror that must have appeared on his face. 'Stupid men, always thinking they're the ones who get to do the rescuing. All you are, savage, is a tool to track Indrani down – that's why you're here. Now I'll have to throw the Commission off your scent, gods curse you.'

'I thought . . . I thought . . .'

She wiped her mouth with claw-like hands. 'We'd kill you if we didn't think it would sour the Witch to us. But we need to know her secret.'

Then the old lady seemed to notice Hiresh again.

'What are you going to tell the unbelievers, skinny boy, when the Commission send their dogs?'

'I – I'm just a fan . . . I don't— I mean . . .'

'You've probably recorded my face already.' She reached into her robes. Hiresh flinched, but it was only another set of clothes. 'Yes, you fan-boys always think you want adventure, don't you? Well, you're coming with us. Either you'll answer their questions or they'll lock you up somewhere until you do. Why, they might even send you to the surface you obviously love so much.'

Jagadamba's threat did not seem to frighten Hiresh. He donned the robes she had given him with no difficulty. When the sleeve of his uniform slipped back, Stopmouth thought he spotted some strange scarring on the boy's arm. Maybe they meant something to Jagadamba, for she curled her lip and said, 'You were born one of us. A Religious.'

'Where I grew up is my own business,' he snapped. 'I'm free now – that's all that matters.'

She ignored this. 'There'll be no broadcasting, you hear me, hairy lip?'

'My name is Hiresh.'

'You broadcast my face, Hiresh, and when I'm caught I'll tell them you were working for us all along.'

He nodded, lips pursed.

'Good.' To Stopmouth she said: 'Pretend I'm the murder leader, or hunt leader, or whatever you Deserters call it. Obey me without question. I know how they think as you never will.' The door opened to a wave of her hand and she led them out into the corridor.

'Come.'

The first thing that struck Stopmouth was that this side corridor had suddenly become as full as the main one where he'd first experienced the crowds of the Roof. His stomach lurched as it had then. But these people weren't just walking – they were churning, boiling like a nest of insects. This time, a good half of them were dressed in the same orange robes Jagadamba had made him wear, their faces hidden by veils, their eyes in shadow as they fretted and heaved.

Jagadamba led Hiresh and Stopmouth down a series of corridors, all filled with scurrying robed figures, all identical and anonymous behind their veils. Stopmouth realized that nobody would be able to pick him out of *this* crowd. That didn't stop the old woman from hurrying them onwards, although she herself walked with a pronounced limp.

The images on the ceiling and the walls had disappeared by now, to be replaced with orders to disperse; threats of capture and punishment to anyone blocking public corridors. '*Those who act like savages may have to live with them!*' declared one warning, and Stopmouth, in the stifling, horrific crowd, in the crippling robes, almost wished he could be caught and sent back home.

Then the pressure of the crowd suddenly increased from

behind. 'The Wardens are coming!' somebody shouted. 'The Wardens!'

'Ha!' said Jagadamba. 'The Commission caught on quicker than I'd hoped. They know they've lost track of their savage. We hurry now!'

People were falling over; running as if for their lives. Stopmouth heard screaming, saw men and women hit the ground while others trampled them underfoot. Back the way they'd come, he spied a green glow and heard more screams.

'Wardens! Wardens!'

The crowd ahead became as thick as the one behind, but Jagadamba was always able to say things to get her little group through the press where others couldn't pass. Soon they reached an open space where two corridors crossed. Here, Secular and Religious were jammed in together. Green lights glowed from at least two of the available directions.

Jagadamba tapped three robe-wearers. 'You, tall one. Do not speak any more until they capture you. You, old one: call your tall friend "Stopmouth" and this one "Hiresh". Attempt to escape down the southern corridor and broadcast to the Religious along the way, asking for help. Their spies will pick it up. Try not to get caught for as long as you possibly can.' All three nodded agreement and made off down one of the two corridors that was free of the green glow.

'What will happen to them?' asked Stopmouth.

'Nothing that won't happen to us if we're caught,' said Jagadamba. 'Remember them. Remember what you owe us when we bring you back to your woman.'

The crowd parted to let the three decoys through, and they were soon out of sight down one branch of the corridor. Stopmouth looked after them, wishing he'd taken the time to thank them or ask their real names.

But Jagadamba was already pulling him down the other 'safe' corridor, spitting orders at people to get out of the way. They obeyed her every time, yet progress was terribly slow and the screaming began to catch up with them. Whenever Stopmouth turned his head, he saw the green glow getting closer. Eventually it resolved itself into points of fierce light, rising and falling, pushing panic before them.

'The Wardens!' people were shouting, Religious and Secular alike. However, the former turned back on Jagadamba's instructions and created a buffer between Stopmouth and the approaching enemy. Even so, if their intention had been to slow the advancing hunters, they didn't do so for long. Stopmouth could now see men and women in the tight-fitting clothing Indrani had been wearing when she'd fallen out of the sky. Black visors covered their faces and they wielded little sticks with glowing green tips. They poked their weapons into faces, backs, chests – anywhere they could. Victims screamed and collapsed.

The movements of the Wardens seemed jerky and unbalanced to Stopmouth's expert eye – until he realized they were walking over a carpet of bodies. Brave Religious could sometimes hold them back, or even knock them over. But the advance barely slowed.

Just behind the first line of hunters, Stopmouth could see another consisting of men and women without visors who seemed to be checking the faces of all the fallen Religious. There'd be no chance of playing dead here.

Then the corridor in front of the fugitives widened unexpectedly and the pressure eased. Bright light streamed in from an open space ahead of them where the walls of the corridor seemed to disappear. Stopmouth felt giddy at the thought of open space. 'Come on!' he shouted. But when he started pushing forward, he found that Jagadamba had already fallen several steps behind him. 'Oh.' He had forgotten what it was like to deal with old people. Hiresh seemed fine, but the woman was limping and breathing hard after no more than a few dozen heartbeats. The air rasped in her throat so loudly that the young hunter feared it would be enough by itself to bring the Wardens down on them.

The enemy were drawing nearer. Their excited cries could be heard above the screams of the fleeing crowds. Stopmouth knew he could escape by himself, but without Jagadamba he'd be no closer to Indrani. In fact, her allies might be too afraid to contact him again. There was only one thing for it.

'Follow closely, Hiresh,' he said.

Without asking permission, he picked Jagadamba up and threw her over his shoulder.

'You're as light as a child!' he exclaimed, and started running towards the light, stopping only once to hitch up his robes with one hand while Hiresh stumbled along behind on skinny legs.

The hunter's passenger yelled in outrage.

'Put me down! Savage! Alien-eater! Down!'

And then they were outside. There was no other word for it, although the brightly coloured ceiling – blue with white shapes drifting across it – was no higher than ten houses from the ground. He felt Hiresh bump into the back of him and heard Jagadamba cry, 'Stop staring, fool! Forward! We go forward here!' Ahead of him there seemed to be almost as many people as he had left behind in what Hiresh had called the residential areas. Families lay splayed out on bare earth that stretched far into the distance in front of him. A great dizzying open space. The only break was a small series of what had to be hills. Safety!

'No, go left! Left, you fool! Cannibal! Left!'

He ignored his passenger and ran for the higher ground, skipping between and around astonished spectators, with Hiresh whooping like a joyful hunter at his side. Stopmouth grinned and lengthened his stride, the old woman no heavier than a cloak of moss on his shoulder, the muscles of his legs feeling stronger than they had been even before a wall had collapsed on one of them.

People covered the lower slopes. They shouted questions that the group, already out of breath, ignored. Jagadamba kept shouting too. Or trying to. 'The least . . . you could do . . . you animal . . . is follow the path.'

Sure enough, as the ground rose, a brown track began to emerge. The slope had grown steeper and rockier. People disappeared, having nowhere to sit. Stopmouth paused, astonished. In front of him, in a small crack in the bare rock, some plants were growing – the first he'd seen here that no human had stepped on or crushed. Slender green stems supported blooms of the most astonishing colours. But what stopped him was the scent. Rather than irritating his eyes and nostrils, they smelled deliciously sweet. Intoxicating, even. He had a terrible urge to shove his face into them even though he thought they might be poisonous.

He jumped as he felt Hiresh's touch on his arm. The boy was sweating and clearly in desperate need of a rest. But his smile was as strong as ever. 'Paradise. I told you . . . It will be again . . . the whole Roof.'

'Oh, for the love of the gods!' said Jagadamba. 'Put me down! Put me down at once!'

Stopmouth found he was very glad to do so. All the running was beginning to catch up with him and he suddenly felt hungry, as if he could eat an entire Hairbeast by himself. He lowered Jagadamba to the ground and fell down beside her.

The hunter felt something tapping against his upper thigh. It turned out to be Jagadamba giving him what she probably thought was a good kicking. When she'd finally exhausted herself and shared the latest build-up in her throat, she turned to look back the way they'd come. 'Yes . . . the enemy are still tailing the other three . . . Good. Now get up, you sloths. We need to go and find the Witch. And we don't want to be trapped on top of a hill when the Commission realizes its mistake.'

# 7. EXPECTING FLESH

Hiresh felt sick as he trudged behind Stopmouth and Jagadamba. He'd felt uneasy up on the hills, and at first he'd put it down to the absence of people in that high place. But then they had reached the top, with the whole of the park spread out below them: artificial lakes swarming with the swimming, laughing children of refugees; beautiful bridges arching over the river; athletics fields, barely discernible under the bodies of ten thousand Dreamers who had never run so much as a few metres in their lives.

But the savage hadn't been interested in that. Instead, his mouth hung open in childish joy as he ran the palms of his hands along the bio-metal of the ceiling. Hiresh had to jump to touch it, even at the highest part of the hill. It felt far colder than it should have. His fingers came away damp with condensation that ought to have been drunk up by the metal and recycled.

Things had been breaking down his whole life: the

110

mighty powers of the Roof Goddess were degrading, fading away. Even though a Cure for all these problems was on its way, it still made him uncomfortable whenever he had his face rubbed in them.

'And the fluffy things!' Stopmouth was saying. 'Are they alive?'

'Stupid cannibal!' said Jagadamba. She grinned over at Hiresh. 'They're just holograms of clouds.'

'Clouds . . .' The savage smiled. He had great teeth, as strong and straight as those of any god from before the Crisis. But Hiresh couldn't find it in himself to resent him. Seeing Stopmouth hunt and kill on the surface was one thing; having him here beside you, so gentle and supportive, so . . . so *innocent* – was quite another. How could that be possible?

Hiresh had been called a traitor many times before, when he was growing up. But he'd never felt like that in his own heart until now. It was as if he'd become a sneak, and this puzzled him, because all his actions were born out of the best motives. He served the Commission as he'd always dreamed. More importantly, he was ensuring that Tarini would be safe.

But why couldn't somebody else have been chosen to betray the savage? *That's not me – I'm not like that!* And yet he was the one with the new lump on his arm – a primitive transmitter just under the skin. Human built, because the

Roof would never co-operate in the creation of a tracking device. It had been programmed long ago not to interfere in the affairs of its inhabitants.

*But I'm doing well*, thought Hiresh. And he was. He hadn't even asked to be taken along when the Wardens had pretended to be chasing the little group through the corridors. *I'll pay you back, Tarini, don't you worry.*

They stopped for a rest before starting their descent. At that point Jagadamba took a phial from her robes. 'Know what this is, hairy lip?' she'd asked him. 'It's a Cosmetic.' She grinned at the look of disbelief that appeared on his face. 'Priceless, no? It could make even you beautiful. Maybe even me!' She cackled. 'You want it?'

Hiresh felt his mouth go dry. Luckily, before he could make a fool of himself by reaching for it, she had snatched it away again. 'Come here, savage! Get down from those clouds. I need you to drink something. Come here.'

'Is it blood?'

'Gods curse you, you make me sick! Of course it's not blood! Just drink it and pray to your gods, your . . . ancestors. Pray to look like one of us. Drink!'

Hiresh turned away to keep his jealousy from showing. A Cosmetic! Oh gods!

But he couldn't block out the old lady's gloating. 'His flesh-eating mother wouldn't recognize him.'

Hiresh doubted that. Stopmouth would always move

like a carnivore, a killer. He would give off the smell, different from the hordes around them, of somebody who feasted on the lives of intelligent beings and exulted in the juices running down his chin. Sometimes Hiresh would see the hunter looking at him and his whole body would shiver. But even in those moments he still felt bad about what he had agreed to do.

'It doesn't matter,' he said to himself. His only task was to stay with them until they found Indrani. The transmitter in his arm would do the rest.

The exit from the parkland – a wide, square gap in the walls disguised as the break in a mighty cliff – led them directly into the Boulevard of Birds. Hiresh himself had never seen this wonder before, with its wide sloping canyon and high ceiling. Thousands and thousands of empty niches spoke of the colourful flocks that had nested there in better times and would again just as soon as the Cure started working its magic and the Crisis ended. He craned his neck and was suddenly dizzy. Only the grip of the savage kept him from falling down. Or up maybe, up into the air.

Jagadamba poked him in the side. 'What sect were your parents?' she asked.

'It's unimportant.' Hiresh could feel his heart racing. What he'd had to go through before his escape! And Mother! 'I am my own man now.'

'Man!' she hooted. He could see her exposed tooth pressing against the veil as she spoke.

He looked away from her and his eyes met those of the savage for a moment. The hunter patted him on the arm. Already the Cosmetic was turning his pupils a darker colour. Where had the old hag got hold of something like that? Could she get one for him?

'Tell me, *man*,' continued Jagadamba, 'why you abandoned your duty to your parents so easily.'

Easily? No, it hadn't been easy. He shivered. He'd rather think of anything but his family. But the old lady had stirred things up now, yes she had. And he could see his mother's stick-like limbs. 'Please don't go,' was the second-last thing she'd ever said to him. The last had been uttered as he stepped into the crowded corridor amongst the righteous and the nosy. He hadn't meant to turn round, but he did, and although her lips were moving, the Roar had drowned her out. Perhaps she'd been broadcasting to him at the same time; he didn't know. He'd blocked all messages from his parents a long time before.

Stopmouth interrupted his reverie. 'Why is everywhere so crowded here?' Hiresh had already explained that the Crisis stopped the Roof growing more space, but the whole idea of a world that could do such a thing had failed to sink in. Hiresh tried to think of another way of putting it. Unfortunately Jagadamba stepped into the breach with an explanation of her own.

'It's the fault of those selfish Seculars with their unnatural lifespans. How dare they attempt to corrupt the natural order! And now they pay!'

'No,' said Hiresh. 'It's the Religious, with their large families and their—'

'Even carnivores,' she hissed, 'know the importance of children!'

'Then maybe, honoured elder, you should live with the carnivores and see if they recognize *your* importance.'

She surprised him with a genuine-sounding laugh that sent her into a fit of coughing. She pushed away Stopmouth's supporting hand, then laughed again.

'Honoured elder! He's a cool one, savage, and don't you forget it. And probably mad too.'

'Why mad?' asked Stopmouth.

'Oh, when I was young, most people of Religious families left their parents for the delights of the Secular world. They had the cruel entertainments to enjoy and all the other sins of passion and ignorance to wallow in . . . And more than that, they could live these empty lives of theirs as long as they wanted. But their sins have caught up with them and—'

Hiresh felt his face growing hot. 'Indrani wouldn't listen to these ignorant superstitions, Stopmouth, and neither should you. The Crisis is less than a thousand days from its end!'

'Their machines,' continued Jagadamba, as if the truth hadn't been uttered, 'are losing power. Nowadays it is *their* young people who come to us for salvation. That is why it is so strange to see somebody turning the other way. Poor big man, I wonder what his secret is.'

Hiresh could feel his blood boiling, and he might have lost his cool entirely if he hadn't felt the lightest of touches on his arm from the savage. He felt strangely grateful and then stupid, because what could a flesh-eating Deserter such as this know about the importance of civilized restraint? *I must never forget that he's my target, that* I *am the one hunting him.* He logged on to Roofspace for a second to tone down the quality of the translation. *Let me hear him with his famous stutter!* It might make what was to come, what he had to do, easier.

'But I d-d-don't understand,' said the killer. 'What caused this C-Crisis you all keep talking about?'

'It's just war,' said Hiresh, and now at last he and Jagadamba had something in common.

'Our sacred duty,' she added. 'To rid the universe of demons.'

'To defend ourselves and Old Earth against *aliens*,' Hiresh corrected. 'What your people call beasts.'

'I thought you didn't eat f-flesh,' said Stopmouth.

'Of course not,' spluttered Jagadamba.

'But we do hunt them,' said Hiresh. 'Or rather our

machines, our *warships*, hunt them out across the vast emptiness that lies between worlds. Sometimes one of our machines breaks through and gets the whole lot of them.'

Stopmouth's eyes widened behind his veil and he said, utterly appalled, 'A whole w-world dies and every t-tribe upon it?'

'It's them or us,' said Jagadamba. 'And remember, they *are* carnivores! You've fought enough of them to know that now, right, savage?'

'But you don't even eat them,' said Stopmouth.

Jagadamba shook her head. 'Are you deaf? They are trying to kill us too!' The old woman started coughing again and they had to stop while she got some phlegm up. Her spit landed between the splayed legs of a Dreamer whose own drool spattered the front of a filthy shirt.

'They did get through our defences,' said Hiresh. 'At least that's what people say. Just once. It happened the year before I was born. A small weapon that didn't seem to do much real damage. But it must have been some kind of poison or disease, because ever since then . . . Well, it's like a rot. I told you about the nanos, right? The tiny machines that do all the work?'

'*People* should work, not machines,' said Jagadamba.

Hiresh wouldn't let her put him off. 'They make our Medicine; they build; they grow all our food. And ever since the attack, they've been dying off. First in one area and then another. That's how we lost the Upstairs. Plus a new floor the Roof had been growing for us, because we were already getting too full.'

The Commission had ordered everyone to abandon the upper levels. Crowding and shortages and rebellion had followed. Hiresh remembered it vividly. By that stage, he'd already run away from home to try and join the Elite.

'But we're nearly safe again,' he said. 'I heard the Commission have already started implementing the Cure. The first improvements are imminent, they said.' He turned to Jagadamba. 'We'll see how long your new Religious stay converted then! We'll all have as much Medicine as we want! We'll live for ever!'

'Not if there's a change of government first,' she hissed.

'That's treason.'

'Yes, big man. Treason. That's what we're doing now by bringing this savage to his witch, in case you didn't realize. Welcome to the Rebellion. Once we bring the Commission down, we'll be free from persecution again! Free to live as we please!'

*Believe what you want, old woman*, thought Hiresh. He'd have the last laugh. He glanced at Stopmouth. When the savage nodded back at him, he felt a moment's nausea, self-disgust. *It's him or Tarini. No contest. No contest.*

\* \* \*

Stopmouth knew he did not belong. He was able to adjust to the crowds, to the noise and even the smells for a few hundred paces at a time. But then something would change – the shape of a wall, the dress of the inhabitants, something small – and his knees would weaken enough to make him stumble. Even stranger was the way his skin seemed to be turning darker with every passing moment.

What would Indrani think of that when she saw it? Would she recognize him? Maybe she'd want him more if he looked like a civilized man. He was afraid to find out, but desperate to see her too and take her out of this awful place of too much noise, too many people, and food that would never fill you up.

And then they would come to one of those parks and he'd look up to the ceiling. He couldn't help it: every time, he cried out with delight at what Jagadamba had called clouds. Even more beautiful was the pale blue background. It matched exactly the shade of his mother's eyes. The sight of it drained tension from his whole body. It looked so lovely, so *right*. He felt the pricking of tears and didn't know why.

'The skies of Old Earth,' said Hiresh, one time.

'Yes,' said Stopmouth, although he didn't really understand. 'Thank you, thank you.' He did look down long enough to take in the state of his companions. Jagadamba's aged limbs could only manage a hobble, and yet she never seemed to tire, her pace slow but relentless. Hiresh, however, was panting now, his veil clinging to his dripping face.

'Are you all right?' Stopmouth asked, worried his new companion might collapse. He liked the boy more and more. In many ways he looked like a little child, but he was brave – Stopmouth had seen enough to know that much. Nobody else had been willing to hold out a hand to him, to take him home. And here was the boy now, his thin frame trembling with exhaustion, never uttering a single word of complaint.

'Oh, I'm . . . fine, thank . . . thank you, Chief,' came the reply. Stopmouth knew better and saw that there was only one thing to do about it.

'I'm worn out,' he said to Jagadamba.

'You are?' Her voice was suspicious. They were walking between the husks of dried-out trees where children perched dangerously on branches above their heads.

'Let's eat something,' he said. 'Have we any food?'

Jagadamba nodded and eased herself down into the mud beside a shattered stump. Hiresh made a show of looking around first, but Stopmouth could see the shake in his limbs through the heavy robes. He had run up those hills earlier, when Jagadamba had been carried. The boy was the last to remove his sodden veil.

The old woman pulled out a cloth-wrapped package.

'Ha! Look at your face, savage!'

'But it's rice!' The globby, tasteless little grains of nothing that he'd eaten in the white room. Sometimes there were lumps of other stuff they called protein. Equally tasteless, it seemed to him.

'Were you expecting *flesh*? We have millions of hectares of farmland, savage, that only our machines ever see. We don't kill others for our food.'

Stopmouth shook his head. *Flesh.* The word made his mouth water and created images of feasting and good times that were so vivid, he thought they must be some sending of the Roof. He was beginning to think that no matter how much he ate up here he'd never be full again. All the same, he accepted the cold rice as gracefully as he could.

'How much further?' he asked.

'You don't need to know, savage. Just do as you're told.'

'Indrani is my wife. Among the Tribe, that is a sacred bond. It—'

'What do you know about sacred?' she gurgled. 'Your lives are nothing but a never-ending cycle of passion and ignorance.'

A few grains of rice had spilled into the mud. Stopmouth carefully picked them up and popped them into his mouth. Then he stood up.

'Where are you going?'

'To find my wife. If you won't help me, somebody else here will.'

'You're mad. Oh, sit down, you fool. I don't know where she is either, all right? Only that my friends, my allies have her. We meet my contact just after dark and we'll find out the rest. It's a few hours. No more. And . . . and I'm sorry. Marriage is indeed a sacred bond. Even yours.'

'Were you ever married, Jagadamba?' he asked.

She sighed and lifted her veil to display the single tooth that stayed outside whenever she closed her mouth. 'Has this face ever been loved?' She didn't wait for a reply. 'I'm not like your little traitor friend.' She nodded at Hiresh. 'I was born to an age of wonders that the young here can only imagine. There were fewer Dreamers then among the Seculars, oh yes! I could have put my hand out, savage' – she held a claw up to show him, palm cupped, shaking with weakness – 'I could have put it out to any wall in the entire Roof and said, "I'm too weak to do the right thing. Give me a *Cosmetic*, make me beautiful." But I knew I'd earned all the suffering and the name-calling in a previous life and I didn't crack. Never! I was strong then!'

Other people looked over as she raised her voice. She turned her head to stare them down before she came back to Stopmouth. She sighed again and tapped the filthy ground beside her. For just a moment she looked desperately sad. Then the veil dropped once more. 'Sit down, young savage. Sit down. We all need our rest.'

He sat between the two of them. Hiresh was still

rubbing his arm, but otherwise said nothing. He looked everywhere except at Jagadamba.

Stopmouth waved a hand in front of his face. Hiresh jumped.

'Were you Dreaming?' asked the hunter. He pointed into the crowd. 'Like some of them are?'

Hiresh shook his head.

'Well, what could make them do it? What do they see?'

The boy shrugged. 'It depends on their taste. Stories, history, women . . . My uncle – I haven't seen him in a while, but he used to get the Roof to replay his old child-hood memories again and again.'

'Most of them,' said Jagadamba, 'are probably savouring the murderous pursuits of your fellow cannibals on the surface. Nothing thrills like real death.'

Stopmouth felt a shiver go through his body. 'They – they are the ones who watch my tribe?' For some reason he'd imagined it was only the people sitting in Globes who could see the surface. He should have known better, of course. No more than two or three would ever fit inside one of those aircraft, and large numbers here had recognized him when he'd stepped out of the white room.

Jagadamba stopped. For the first time she seemed hesitant when she spoke. 'You have family, of course, don't you? I never enquired. But yes, you must have. Even such as you.'

'I . . . I abandoned them to come here. They're not very good hunters. I mean, they try, they really try . . .'

'Why don't you watch them?' said Hiresh. 'Just ask the Roof. Imagine what you want to see and it will show you.'

And Stopmouth did want to see it. He'd been worried sick about them all. Rockface, the children. There were some in his old tribe he worried about too, but he couldn't bear to see the Ways. Never again. His loyalty lay elsewhere now.

He closed his eyes. 'Show me . . .' he muttered, not really sure who he was talking to.

Suddenly he wasn't in the park any more. He stumbled to his knees, but all he saw was a view of the world such as he'd seen once from the top of a ridge line. Only higher this time. He was watching from a Globe; he had to be.

Way below, the browns and greys of the land resolved themselves into shapes as his mind focused on them. He saw streets there, and crumbling houses. Up high, it was easy to spot the shadows of other buildings, now gone, swallowed by moss or forest. Wetlanes glittered in the light of the Roof, and rivers shimmered down hillsides and ran all the way to a huge shiny plain that rippled as he watched. Tiny black specks covered most of the area, but when he wondered what they were, the view dropped down towards ground level.

He recoiled in horror at what he saw: row upon row of

Digger-planted bodies. He saw creatures of fur, of scales and skin, of all kinds. Heads lolling, mouths drooling, each expressing an agony beyond imagining, their stench and their moans rising up through the warm air for five days' walk in every direction.

'Take me away,' he cried. 'I want to see my tribe. Just the tribe.'

When he blinked, the landscape beneath him had changed. He heard the hiss of the river, saw it rushing down an ancient pathway between two ridges of hills, with buildings scattered the length of its banks.

The U-shaped complex known as 'Headquarters' separated itself from the surrounding houses and grew in his sight until he could see the unused cooking fires and the miserable people lying nearby. He could hear adults scolding their hungry children into silence.

Inside – he hadn't known he could look inside – he heard Vishwakarma's eternally excited voice calling, 'Huntleader! Can we go? Come on! The boys – oh, and Sodasi and Kamala, of course. I meant the *hunting party*. We're ready to go. Just waiting for you.'

A smile pulled Stopmouth's cheeks apart. He wondered who Vishwakarma was speaking to, so the Roof took him through another wall into a room so small, Stopmouth hadn't known it existed.

Rockface knelt here. At first this pleased the watcher,

but then he saw the look of agony in his friend's eyes, the body bent double at the waist.

It took Stopmouth a moment to figure out that the big man was actually trying to stand up. And failing. Stopmouth gasped when he saw tears, and though one scarred hand tried to smother Rockface's sobs, the Roof obligingly raised the volume.

'Huntleader? Huntleader?'

With a gigantic effort and one last secret whimper, Rockface straightened his back and wiped the tears and sweat from his face.

'A man needs peace to loosen his bowels, hey?' He was still shaking and thinking nobody could see this private weakness. He leaned against one of the walls, gulping in the air as if it was running out.

'We'll hunt back towards the Slimer,' he said when he'd caught his breath. 'The Fourleggers have spotted another Digger and might have seen a few of their tunnels. I won't risk you lot in that direction, hey?' The exhausted face looked up, and his eyes, by some miracle, seemed to stare directly into Stopmouth's own.

'Roof! Get me away from here! Stop it! Stop it!'

He found himself back in the 'park', lying on his side, shivering, with Jagadamba and Hiresh looking on in concern.

'You get used to it,' said Hiresh.

'How can I be here?' was all the hunter could say.

'Yes, it's starting to get exciting again,' said the boy. 'I think we're building up to another climax like that brilliant battle you had with the Skeletons. You remember that one?'

The hunter shuddered. All he could think of was Rockface's humiliation. How many others must have seen it? More than all the insects that swarmed the air, more than the tracklights that lit the Roof by night. The same numbers might have watched Stopmouth going to the toilet; they'd have seen him and Indrani making love. He was trying to save his people for *this*? For the empty sacks around him to laugh and point at them in their most intimate moments?

He grabbed Hiresh's wrist. 'How long have they got?' he asked.

'What do you mean?'

'Before the Diggers make it over the hills and surround them? How long?'

Hiresh's eyes softened and he nodded. 'I'm sorry. Of course. Let me log on.' A moment later he had the answer. 'I'm sorry, Chief,' he said. 'Six days, maybe seven. There's no way to stop it. No way at all.'

'Indrani will stop it.' Stopmouth stood up, feeling light-headed, his vision blurring. 'We have to find her. We have to find her right now.'

He didn't pay much attention to where they went after that. Jagadamba wasn't allowed to know where Indrani was in case she got caught, but she had a contact, somebody who would only meet her face to face. They were going there now. That was all that mattered. A day away at the most. *Oh ancestors!*

After the park, they passed into a new district of narrow and windy little corridors that opened unexpectedly into triangular plazas. The ambient light had been falling with the approach of night. Now, when Stopmouth looked at the walls, the amount of writing he was used to seeing on them diminished, to be replaced by pictures of sleeping or yawning people. Sometimes images of the non-intelligent beasts known as animals would lie in repose alongside humans, with neither threatening the other. This had to be the night-time here. They would meet the contact soon.

'We were getting crowded even before the Crisis,' muttered Hiresh. 'When it ends, it will take us ages to grow floors or to breed enough new nanos to build starships. They—'

'Hush!' said Jagadamba.

But she was too late.

A man and a woman who'd been sitting against the darkened walls of the corridor rose gracefully to their feet, and a green glow sprang into life, harsh in the gloom.

'What have we got here, Sergeant Tarak?' asked the woman, her skin as dark as that of Hiresh and most of those in the new tribe. Stopmouth had a brief glimpse of fierce eyes and sharp cheekbones before she pulled a visor down over her face. Both of the newcomers wore shiny boots, unlike the barefooted people around them.

The man spoke up, his voice too thin for his large frame. 'A trio of superstitious louts, Sergeant Manisha. Look at those stupid robes . . .' He was lighter of skin than his partner, his body, like so many Stopmouth had seen on the Roof, short, but perfectly muscled. He looked the group up and down. 'Why do they have to hide their whole bodies?'

Jagadamba cleared her throat. 'I will be happy to answer your questions on the—'

'You raise an interesting point, Sergeant Tarak. Anyone would think it was an attempt to make the lives of humble Wardens like ourselves more difficult. I've had a severe dislike for their kind ever since they led us on that merry chase over in Mountain Sector.'

'Sergeants,' said Jagadamba, 'I'd be happy to remove my robes if you wish to search—'

'I feel the same way about them, Sergeant Manisha,' said the man; his thin voice seethed with a hatred so pure it must have burned the inside of his throat.

At that moment Stopmouth knew there'd be a fight. Two humans against three others. It happened even in Man-Ways sometimes, but anybody who pushed it too far would have found himself traded off to Hairbeast or Clawfolk. The tribe had too many enemies to be able to afford the luxury of strife.

Other people must have been expecting trouble too. They pulled back from the five of them, waking friends who were sleeping too close and moving them away. But nobody left the area completely. All were watching intently, maybe even thrilled at the thought of conflict – not one happening far away on the surface, but right here before their real eyes!

'Shall we search them?' asked Sergeant Manisha.

'Oh, yes. But what's the rush?' The glow on Tarak's truncheon died and he looked briefly at his companion.

Stopmouth tensed his shoulders even as Jagadamba tried to engage the Wardens in conversation and was ignored. The hunter didn't want to fight other humans. He wasn't really sure how to avoid going for a kill. It just didn't make sense. The only time he'd ever seriously tried to end another man's life – the freakishly strong Varaha – his enemy had proved too quick for him, and luck alone had saved him. But even if he won, it was dark now – time to meet Jagadamba's contact. The tribe couldn't afford any more delays.

'They ought to be questioned and no mistake,' said Manisha. Her truncheon still glowed and Stopmouth knew it would only take one touch from it to knock him out of the fight. She placed a hand carefully on her companion's arm. 'But not here, OK? Somewhere quiet. We can't jam so many broadcasts.'

'All right,' said Tarak. He turned his truncheon back on.

'I know where we can go.' He waved the weapon in Jagadamba's face. 'This way. Move.'

Stopmouth and his two companions had no choice but to follow, wedged in between the Wardens while the crowd dispersed, disappointed.

'Where are we going?' asked Stopmouth.

'What do you care, citizen?' said Manisha, muffled by her visor. 'Whichever god you waste your time on will still be there waiting for you.'

Only now did Stopmouth realize it was the same uniform that Indrani had worn when she landed that first time in Centre Square. It sent a chill through him, and he wondered if all those who wore it could fight as well as she did. They hadn't done so when striking down the Religious in the corridors, but they hadn't needed to. A touch of the baton was enough. And it would be enough now if they wanted to catch Stopmouth and his companions. *They don't know who we are*, the hunter realized. *So why are they taking us away? If they wanted to search us, they could have done so — the truncheons would have ensured obedience.* He couldn't understand it. And yet, when Jagadamba brushed against him, he felt the old woman trembling. *She's afraid.* He hadn't known anything could scare her.

Hiresh, by contrast, seemed utterly calm.

'Why don't you just search us here?' asked Stopmouth.

The two guards paused, forcing their prisoners to stop

too. 'This one's refusing to co-operate, Sergeant Manisha,' said Tarak. He was shaking almost as much as Jagadamba, but his tone of voice reminded Stopmouth of Rockface at the start of a hunt. 'Never mind. Here we are.'

He waved his hand at a wall. It opened to reveal a cramped little room where a man, a woman and two starved children sat. Another wave, and the chairs sank into the floor, spilling the people into a frightened heap.

Tarak stepped in quickly and touched each of the occupants with his truncheon so that they relaxed into complete silence. He slipped the weapon into a holster on his belt. Then, with an astonishing display of strength, he picked up a parent in either hand and dumped them outside. The two children followed.

Stopmouth felt his stomach clench in fear. Were all these people as freakishly strong as Varaha had been? His little group had no hope of escaping these two, let alone of finding Indrani, if that were the case.

'Imagine that!' said Manisha, muffled disgust coming through her visor. 'Breeding during a Crisis! Religious pigs. They don't deserve a big apartment like this. I've told them that before.' She jerked a thumb at her three prisoners. 'Get in!'

Stopmouth felt Tarak give him a shove strong enough to have come from Crunchfist. He landed against the wall, while Jagadamba and Hiresh hit the floor on either side of him. He bent to help the old woman up. She had time to whisper, 'Don't resist!' before Tarak ripped her away.

'You!' Manisha pointed a finger at Hiresh. 'Stop trying to broadcast. In code, no less. Perhaps we have a real Rebel with us.'

'But—' Hiresh hadn't time to say any more before Tarak kicked him in the stomach. 'Are you going to help me with these, Sergeant Manisha?'

The dark woman shook her head and took up a position at the door, her eyes hidden by the visor.

'Thanks,' said Tarak, removing his own helmet. His face was sweating, a tight little smile spread across it. 'Perhaps I should question them about my sister,' he said. 'The one they killed in their Rebellion. You remember the Rebellion, don't you, citizens?' The baton was still in his belt. Stopmouth saw the muscles tense.

'We're at peace again now,' said Jagadamba. 'And you won.'

'Oh, but you haven't given up, have you?' said Tarak. Then he shouted, 'You haven't given up! My sister wasn't enough for you! Was she, you old bitch? *Was she?*'

Suddenly he jerked Jagadamba up off the ground and flung her to the far side of the room as if she weighed no more than an empty hide. She struck the wall and fell to the floor. From where he stood, Stopmouth could hear the air explode from his guide's lungs. Not even Crunchfist had ever shown such pointless cruelty against somebody who was practically a volunteer. Stopmouth couldn't believe it, couldn't bear it. Tarak stood over the old woman with his back to him. The hunter stepped forward, but found the glowing green tip of Sergeant Manisha's truncheon no more than a handspan from his nose.

'This one certainly hasn't given up, Sergeant Tarak. He seems to think an unaugmented Religious like him could take you.'

Tarak spun round, his smile only wider, his face even sweatier. 'Step back, please, Sergeant Manisha. I'm not the soft touch my sister was.'

But Manisha's truncheon stayed between them a moment longer. 'It would be unfortunate if anyone were to die here, Sergeant Tarak.'

'An accident, Sergeant Manisha. Happens to Religious scum all the time.'

'Even so . . . Remember the last one?'

Tarak nodded tightly, clearly disappointed. Manisha lowered her truncheon, saying: 'Of course, it wouldn't surprise me if one as clumsy as this were to fall and break his legs.'

Tarak threw her a grateful look even as a feeling of terror lodged itself in the pit of Stopmouth's stomach. They were going to smash his legs? The memory of agony, of bone poking through his skin, drove him back. He couldn't let them do this to him. In his mind it had become worse than death. And what use would he be to his people then?

'You're . . . you're much stronger than me,' he said to Sergeant Tarak. He knew the fear was coming through in his voice and he felt shamed by it. 'Let me . . . let me fight you fair. Let me take off these robes.'

'What?' said Tarak, clearly confused.

Manisha only laughed from her position by the door.

'Oh, what harm can it do, Sergeant Tarak? He can't be augmented unless the Commission are hiring Religious all of a sudden. He's big enough, but what chance could he have? I want to see the look on his face when his leg bends back the wrong way.'

'Hurry up, then,' said Tarak to the hunter.

Stopmouth wasted no time in shucking the robes. The fake colour of his own skin underneath surprised him. He was almost as dark as Indrani now. Nobody here would look twice at him.

'Well, well!' exclaimed Manisha from her place by the door. 'This one's a warrior! Real muscles there. Must have spent years building that up the hard way, stupid fool. Why didn't you join us, son? Bloody fanatics!'

Stopmouth ignored the banter, for Tarak was already closing in on him in the small space, made more cramped by Manisha's presence at the door and his companions' bodies in either corner.

135

Tarak aimed a punch at Stopmouth's midriff. It almost connected. For some reason the young hunter thought it had been intended as a feint, with a sucker punch to come from another direction. At the last instant he realized the attack was for real and turned his body sideways. Another seeming feint followed. This time it glanced off his shoulder, deadening the whole arm.

'Oh, fair hit, Tarak! He's faster than he looks, that one!'

It was only then that Stopmouth understood that neither punch had been a trick – the man, for all his great strength, was no Varaha. He was *slow*. The hunter almost giggled with relief. These people didn't have to battle for their lives from the moment they drew their first breath. Nobody wanted their flesh, and whenever they did fight, they were used to superior weapons and overwhelming odds. What a pity Stopmouth had allowed a blow to land before he'd discovered this obvious truth.

'Are you laughing at me, scum?' said Tarak. He launched into another attack, and this time his intended victim slipped easily under the punch and kicked his legs from beneath him. The bag of muscles dropped to the floor with an 'Oof!' Stopmouth could have finished him then, and if Tarak had been a beast, there'd have been no hesitation. Instead, he found himself stepping back as if this were no more than a training bout back home. Tarak growled, like something inhuman. His face twisted with rage and humiliation. He was up again in a heartbeat.

'It won't be just your legs for that,' he hissed.

'Go easy, now, Sergeant Tarak!' said Manisha. She made no effort to intervene, however.

Stopmouth edged away from his attacker. He didn't have much space to move in, which was a pity, because the only way to keep his legs intact was to stay out of grappling distance. This was so different from fighting beasts! But here too, his life depended on the outcome.

Tarak advanced a step and the hunter backed off. The Warden seemed to notice this and smiled. He waved his hand in a manner Stopmouth had seen before. Tarak leaped forward and his adversary stumbled back to get out of the way. But a chair had suddenly appeared behind Stopmouth and he tripped over it, falling onto his back, with his head landing on the floor beside Jagadamba. He had less than a heartbeat to realize the old woman was still breathing before Tarak was on top of him, his pungent sweat clogging the air, his weight trapping the younger man's arms and legs.

'Now we'll see! Now we'll see it! You're not so funny now!'

'Tarak!' shouted Manisha. 'I'm getting an emergency transmission! Get off him!'

Sergeant Tarak didn't look as if he had any intention of leaving just yet. *He's going to break all my bones*, Stopmouth thought. He still didn't know how to fight this man, another human. *Got to think of him as a beast. He's not Tribe, not Tribe.*

Even as Tarak was twisting one of his arms, Stopmouth jerked his head forward and smashed it into his enemy's nose with all the force he could muster. There was an audible crunch and a sudden flow of blood. The effect on the bigger man was one of shock and disbelief, as if he'd never been hurt before in his life. But Stopmouth didn't wait. He freed a hand and yanked his opponent's ear so hard it partially ripped away from the head. He rolled and twisted and knocked the screaming beast to one side, hopped to his feet and stamped down quickly on Tarak's ribs. He was about to finish the creature off when, out of the corner of his eye, he spotted a green glow. He'd forgotten the other one! He ducked, and the truncheon swept in over his head. Manisha hopped back and waved her hands. A line of chairs appeared in the room between them.

'Enough!' said Manisha. The truncheon was shaking in her grip and her voice was trembling too. 'That's enough!' She pointed at Tarak. The big Warden was weeping and gasping for breath. He was bleeding everywhere. Stopmouth suddenly felt sick in his stomach at what he'd almost done, what he'd wanted to do.

'We're even now,' said Sergeant Manisha. 'All right? You got your revenge and you know we can't report you. Sergeant Tarak's actions are thought to be a bit . . . exaggerated. You can take your friends. I'm . . . I'm letting you go. We have other orders.' She looked like she was about to bolt and probably had no idea that Stopmouth's rage was at an end.

'Move away from the door,' said the hunter. 'And tell those chairs to go away.'

'OK. OK.'

Stopmouth helped Hiresh to his feet. 'Are you all right.'

'Yes,' said Hiresh, the faintest tremble in his voice.

Stopmouth picked up the old woman as gently as possible. 'You shouldn't . . . have resisted,' whispered Jagadamba. A dribble of saliva swung at the end of her hairy chin.

'Can you walk?'

'Of course not . . . fool.'

Stopmouth edged towards the door, trying to ignore Tarak's weeping.

'I'm recording your face, citizen,' warned Sergeant Manisha, although her voice was higher than it had been before. 'We'll meet again.'

Stopmouth hoped not. He'd had enough of hurting his fellow humans. He carried Jagadamba into the corridor and started running, with Hiresh following behind.

# 8. A KIND OF HERO

Hiresh ran after the savage, not knowing quite what else to do. He couldn't figure out why things had gone so terribly wrong. He'd been broadcasting frantically to the two sergeants: *I'm one of you!* although he wasn't really. He was just one of their 'filthy little spies', as his monstrous father would have said.

*By all the gods, Sergeants,* he'd begged, *you've got to stop!*

In blocking his broadcasts, the Wardens had almost ruined the mission, his one and only chance. He didn't even want to think about the other possibility – that they might have broken his legs too after they'd finished with Stopmouth. What was to prevent them, after all? It was the savage who'd saved him just as Tarini had saved him before.

Stopmouth turned down a side corridor, hopping over sleeping limbs as though they were branches in a forest. The hunter's own people admired him greatly for his running, but it was only when Hiresh had to keep up with him that he really understood. The savage didn't know where he was going; he was carrying an old woman too. Still, he left Hiresh further and further behind.

The boy was about to call out to ask the hunter to wait. But then he had another thought: what if he hung back instead? Allowed himself to be abandoned? Would Tarini really be left to die? Surely not. He'd tend her himself if he had to – the Roof would tell him everything he needed to know . . . He'd never be an Elite then, never avenge his scars. But none of that was Stopmouth's fault.

Part of him heaved a sigh of relief at the idea, even as the killer sped further and further away. It wasn't the danger that Hiresh feared – although he did. Some other weight he couldn't yet name hung over him. Something that made him feel sick and rotten inside. *Tarini wouldn't want me to do this.* He tripped, and found himself face down amongst the tangled limbs of Dreamers. His breath rasped in his ears.

*I needed the rest anyway*, he thought. And then: *I've just thrown away my one chance to save Tarini.*

He had to get up. Or call out to the savage. Something.

Or he could stay. The choice had been made for him by the non-existent goddess.

At that moment a hand grasped his and pulled him easily to his feet. Stopmouth.

'I honour your s-sacrifice,' said the chief, 'but you are needed. I c-c-can't do this without you. I'm sorry. I'll try and slow down, but we must keep m-m-moving.'

Hiresh nodded, afraid to speak. *He thinks I was staying back to hold up the Wardens!* As if Hiresh were some kind of . . . he didn't know what.

He followed on and on, through more corridors than he could count, crossing parks that heaved with people and others where the inhabitants slumbered under fake stars in the pattern of Old Earth's skies. It was only when they came to an area where most of the people wore Religious garb that the savage felt it was safe to stop.

Hiresh watched the gentleness with which he laid Jagadamba down on the ground. She still breathed, but she'd lost consciousness and Hiresh wasn't sure she'd recover. Not without Medicine.

'Are you— Are you planning on eating her?' he whispered to the savage. He didn't want anybody to hear him.

Stopmouth shook his head. 'Jagadamba has neither died nor volunteered. How could I do such a thing?'

'But you would if she did die, would you?'

'I d-don't know. It would be very wrong n-not to, but . . .' He waved his arms to indicate all the people around him, some pressing very close. 'I think the local tribe would be angry if I did. My new f-friends on the surface were just like this lot when they arrived.'

'Of course they were,' said Hiresh. A group of fanatics had got themselves exiled down below. A great lesson for the other Rebels, as their comrades either got eaten or sacrificed or, worst of all, turned cannibal themselves. A great lesson indeed, although Hiresh hadn't been able to bring himself to watch it.

A bubble formed at the side of Jagadamba's mouth. She looked like a wizened baby.

'I think we are about to lose her,' said Hiresh.

'N-no,' said the hunter. 'We can't. We have no other l-link to Indrani. We've lost half a day already! Where is this miraculous M-M-Medicine my woman told me existed up here?'

The boy shook his head. 'Unless somebody has been stockpiling it—'

'What about Jagadamba's allies? She said "we". As if there was m-more than one of her. If we c-could just find them. Do you know somebody, Hiresh? Any of these R-Rebels?'

Hiresh stared back at the savage, a sinking feeling in the pit of his stomach. This was not how it was supposed to be. He was to follow, that was all. Somewhere on the vast Roof, Jagadamba was to lead him to the very nest of the enemy where Indrani was being kept. That was his job. No more. Surely, with the hag's death, it could end at last.

'Or anybody else w-w-with the m-magic cure. I need this w-woman to talk again. It's not like the surface. I know n-nothing here. Only you can help me. P-p-please, Hiresh.' He put a firm hand on the boy's shoulder. 'My f-friend . . .'

Hiresh shivered. But not from fear – that wasn't it at all. It was hard enough to betray this poor savage. Especially after the creature had saved him from Sergeant Tarak. But the stutter he'd allowed himself to hear made everything worse. He'd thought it would prove how superior he was, but the only effect was to remind him of what he and the hunter had in common – a lifetime of bullies and disrespect. *Turn off the stammer*, he ordered the Roof. *Just turn it off.*

To a man as powerful as Dr Narindi, Medicine was so valuable that he only ever gave it to the Elite. Was finding Indrani that vital? It must be, but it would be equally important to Jagadamba, and if she got the slightest whiff of Hiresh's involvement with the Commission . . . He swallowed hard as he realized there was only one way out of this.

'I don't know any Rebels, Stopmouth. But . . . but I may know somebody who does. I'd rather face Chakrapani again. I—'

'Who is Chakrapani?'

'Never mind. Never mind.' He'd already given too much of himself away. He looked at the savage's muscles and realized that he himself would never be more than a stick if his fears got the better of him. And what about Tarini? What would happen to her?

'I will show you,' he said at last, his voice admirably steady, no catch in it at all. 'We will take a shuttle.'

'We can't lose any more time, Hiresh.'

'No.'

Great distances on the Roof were crossed by a network of tunnels. The air had been pulled out of them so there was nothing to slow down a shuttle except for the fragility and comfort of their human cargo. Hiresh logged on to check the location of the nearest station, and in no time at all he was leading the anxious savage across the Plaza of the Abandoned, where great statues of starving men and women looked upwards in despair.

Just beneath the plaza's high, high ceiling hung a genuine primitive spaceship of the type Stopmouth's disgusting ancestors had used to flee Earth with the last of its resources. They'd abandoned the poor to what they thought was certain death, never realizing that one day their past would literally catch up with them.

From this angle, and without the Roof's help, it was impossible to see the great blackened hole on top of the craft where brave soldiers had cut their way inside. They'd pulled hibernating Deserters out and sent them to live on the surface of this world as punishment.

The captured craft, and many others like it in parks all over the Roof, reminded the civilized of something they must never become: Deserters. It made Hiresh feel a little better about betraying the savage.

He led Stopmouth down an avenue strewn with filthy people. Hiresh couldn't see much difference between them and the statues – not good for morale. Some of the Commission wanted them covered up, but it was only these shared images of despair that still united Religious and Secular factions. To pull them down would be madness.

Hiresh was already feeling fear of what was to come, but Stopmouth kept distracting him from it with questions – almost as if he knew what the boy was going through.

'How do you manage to move so fast in these crowds?'

Hiresh couldn't conceal a show of pleasure. 'It's just gap-skipping,' he said. 'I just . . . I just know where the crowd is going to break and—'

But Stopmouth stopped paying attention to him and looked up at the Deserter spacecraft. Hiresh followed his gaze and blinked in surprise. Was the ship supposed to sway like that? Stopmouth said something then, and a horrible chill settled over Hiresh's body as he realized he hadn't understood a word – not a word of it.

As though by agreement, the Roar of the crowd dwindled to nothing. People's mouths hung open in puzzlement. Everywhere, Dreamers were stirring themselves awake, looking around like wild creatures.

And that was when it happened.

The ground lurched and began to shake so hard and quickly that Hiresh found himself on the floor, with Jagadamba and Stopmouth beside him. All he could hear was the screaming of the crowd and a terrible grinding noise. The vibrations rattled his teeth together. People were flung one way and then the other. The light dimmed to almost complete blackness, with only the pale green illumination of the emergency system to take its place. It wasn't so dark, however, that he couldn't see the massive form of one of the statues begin to tumble from its plinth. He tried to stand and back away. He called out Stopmouth's name and heard an answering cry. But the ground flung him back onto his face, and when he raised his head, he saw the dark colossus pitch over into a mass of screaming people only a few metres away. It struck them so violently that warm gore splashed his forehead.

'Oh Mother Roof!' he cried, for surely it was the end of the world. And still the tremors continued. He was so afraid, he even screamed at one point. 'What's going on?' he begged the Roof. 'What's going on?' No response came.

Seconds later, the shaking ended. The lights came on as if nothing had happened. But people didn't stop screaming for some time after, especially around the bloody mess near the fallen statue.

Hiresh staggered to his feet. 'We've got to help them!' he said to Stopmouth.

The savage nodded, his newly darkened features slack with confusion and fear. 'I understand you again,' he said. And then he looked at Jagadamba. 'What if she doesn't last? Who will help her? Who will save my tribe?'

He was right. And even now, hundreds of others were climbing to their feet to help their fellow citizens.

'We'd better go then.'

Confusion reigned at the station. Nobody knew what had happened – the Roof wouldn't or couldn't say and the Commission was still investigating. But everybody looked afraid.

Stopmouth too was becoming more and more agitated by Jagadamba's worsening condition.

'Is anybody here gifted at healing?' he called out.

Hiresh had to shush him. 'You'll only attract attention,' he said. 'Besides, it's pointless. There are no healers.'

'No,' said the savage. 'Nobody does anything here. Nobody can do *anything*.'

'In another year,' said the boy, still queasy after the quake, 'this kind of thing won't be able to happen. We'll have nanos again and it can start going back to the way it was before I was born. Perfect; it will be perfect.'

Stopmouth just shook his head of newly blackened hair. He must have been thinking about his people on the surface, imagining the enemies that were closing in on them with every heartbeat.

Gradually the crowd cleared as shuttles arrived for them. Finally a blue car swept down the tunnel and came to a halt at the platform. It called to Hiresh and he led Stopmouth towards it, his stomach in a knot. He so wanted to turn back. Instead, he found himself asking the car to make a couch for Jagadamba to lie upon while he and the savage sat on another.

He was so nervous over what was to happen, he found himself gripping Stopmouth's arm for support. A cannibal! A killer! And soon to be the victim of a filthy act of betrayal.

The car shot into the vacuum tunnel. *Only an hour*, he thought, gripping his seat. Scratching it. *One more hour.*

When they came to a halt, he led Stopmouth with his burden along a particularly twisty series of alleys. He didn't need to consult the Roof as to which direction he should take.

'Why are we walking so slowly?' asked Stopmouth. 'Jagadamba could die.'

Hiresh didn't answer. All around them, there were only Religious. Most of them were from the Golamatr sect – Roof worshippers, who looked on the living computer as an incarnation of the great Mother. Many of them were as naked as savages, despising clothes and painting their bodies with images of the bones and organs that lay just inside. The more hard-core used tattoos. The Roof could see everything, after all, so why try to hide it?

There were no Dreamers here. None were allowed. Groups of young men ran down the corridors in disciplined ranks, while others tended clumsily to healthy plants under the guidance of the Roof. Eyes followed the three travellers all the way to a door on the last wall of a dead end.

Hiresh took a deep breath. He removed the veil and opened his robes up at the front. He would be strong now. A pity he couldn't keep the shake out of his hands.

The door slid open.

The woman waiting on the far side had whiter hair than he remembered. Her frame was thinner too, bones showing through and pressing against the tattoos designed to mirror them.

'Who is it?' called a hoarse voice from within.

The woman didn't answer. Instead, she pulled her son into an embrace, squeezing hard. He felt her tears against his cheek and a churning in his stomach. His eyes stung. *Not this! Please, gods! Don't let me cry!* But he hadn't addressed the gods in years and there was no reason why they should start listening to him now. He pushed his way inside, hiding his face in the robes again. Not trusting himself to speak, he waved Stopmouth inside past his startled-looking mother.

'Who are you?' said the hoarse voice again, unable to see him through the unfamiliar clothing. 'Why are you in our home?'

Hiresh was breathing too quickly to reply. He wasn't even sure what the answer should be.

'I apologize,' he heard the savage say. 'This woman needs your help. Hiresh said you might—'

'Hiresh!' His name sounded like an explosion in his father's throat. Like some curse from the Atharva-Veda.

'Is that him, hiding his face? As if Mother Roof couldn't see through to his traitor's heart!'

The words helped Hiresh to get control over himself again, anger driving out the tears. He pulled back his robes, ready now to face his father. Instead, he saw the man's heavily tattooed back with muscles underneath such as his son would never have.

Papa had already told the apartment to absorb the furniture and was helping Stopmouth to lay Jagadamba flat on the floor.

Hiresh's mother still stood at the open doorway, trying to take everything in. The sight of her made it difficult for Hiresh to keep his composure, but the shock had passed and now he managed it. He told the door to shut, but unsurprisingly, it no longer obeyed his thoughts. He signalled that his mother should do so.

'Of – of course,' she said.

'Jagadamba hasn't got long left,' Stopmouth was saying.

Papa harrumphed in agreement, his fingers touching lightly against various parts of the woman's chest.

'Mother Roof says she has multiple fractures. Several broken ribs and probably internal bleeding. She has a day at the most.'

'We need to revive her,' said Stopmouth. 'It – it is vital.'

Papa shook his head. 'She's gone without Medicine.'

'Your son said . . . said you might . . .'

And now Papa looked round. Hiresh had expected a glare. But Papa showed nothing for his son to read except startling new creases on his broad, strong face. A missing tooth. And muscle, always muscle, only emphasized by the tattoos that covered every visible part of his body.

Hiresh allowed the disgust into his voice: 'You look well-fed.' It was all he had to say to break the mask that confronted him.

'How dare you, you little Deserter! You traitor!'

Mother said, 'You know I do it willingly, Hiresh! You know our people need him to be strong!'

Hiresh ignored her, hating the sight of her thinness. All masks were stripped away from his voice and he let the bitterness of years wash through every word. 'You're eating her up, Papa. You're no better than the savages below.'

Papa launched himself across the room. Hiresh didn't flinch.

Mother cried out to his father to stop, even as the two fell to the floor together. Hiresh saw a fist raised against him, a great club of gristle and bone and scarred knuckle. He didn't care, he didn't care. He'd said what he'd never been able to say when he lived here. Papa was starving his mother to death. He was starving her to death, and *she* was letting him. And all for the love of a machine they worshipped as a goddess.

The blow never landed.

Part of Hiresh's robe had fallen away to reveal the scarring along his arm where once the tattoos had been. Papa froze. Perhaps he was imagining the pain or the desperation that would drive somebody to such an act. Or perhaps he was simply horrified that a good Religious boy would perform such a blasphemy on himself.

Stopmouth pulled Papa away and set him down next to Jagadamba while the man's jaw worked.

'The lady is dying,' said Stopmouth. 'She needs this "Medicine".'

If Papa ever allowed himself normal human feelings, he wouldn't have been able to answer his guest. Yet the mask came down again remarkably quickly, apart from a little sneer at the corner of his upper lip.

'People are dying all over the Roof,' he said. 'What little Medicine remains is needed for warriors of the coming struggle. Look at her . . . she is close to her final escape. She has given all she can give.'

'No,' said Stopmouth. 'She has more to give. Much more.'

'Father,' said Hiresh. 'She knows where Indrani is.'

'Indrani who?' He didn't look at his son.

'You know, the old High Commissioner's daughter. The Witch, you called her. The one they're turning the Roof upside-down to find. That old woman – *she* knows where to look.'

'And how did you get mixed up in this?' But there was interest in his eyes now. A chance to annoy the Commission would please his bitter heart. 'Shouldn't you be helping the other side?'

'I should be, yes.'

'Perhaps you're changing, at last,' said Papa.

'I assure you I'm not. Please stop wasting time. We need the Medicine.'

'Relax, Deserter. The Medicine is coming. I already made the call.'

Everybody sat in separate corners of the tiny room. Hiresh had a chance to notice the changes since he'd run away two years before. The apartment was smaller, of course. When he'd first started crawling, there was room for a dividing wall that allowed his parents a bit of privacy. He had vague memories of lying in a soft cocoon while the Roof played bright shapes across the ceiling to keep him amused. In his first year or two, or so Mother had told him, the shortages weren't too bad and Father hadn't beaten either of them.

The decoration was more sombre too these days. The glorious scenes of the Roof's bounty no longer played in the background. The pictures in the walls were all of sterner aspects of the great Mother – the palms of her many hands cupping spearheads and spaceships, flinging them into the four quarters of the galaxy to punish aliens and other demons.

Mother served tea to everybody, then came to sit beside him. He allowed her to take his hand, amazed that they were now the same height. *I must have grown*, he thought. Or perhaps she was the one who'd shrunk. Such a thing could happen to the old – look at Jagadamba! But Mother wasn't that ancient – couldn't be.

This was Papa's fault. He was eating all her food so he could pretend to be a warrior.

Jagadamba's breathing had almost stopped by the time the Medicine arrived. Hiresh had never seen any before. It looked no different from a pale cream in a simple green jar. Before Hiresh's birth, anybody could have had as much of this as they wanted just by thinking about it. The Roof could have exuded it from the wall of an apartment, or sent it into the air as a gas.

Papa wouldn't let anybody touch it. 'Not with your bare skin!' he said. 'None of us are perfect and the nanos might expend themselves in trying to heal us instead.'

'Why can't they heal all of us?' asked Stopmouth.

'They're programmed to die,' said Hiresh. 'It stops them maybe mutating in unexpected ways. Imagine how dangerous bad ones could be if they just kept multiplying! They could eat the whole world!' He harrumphed. 'Maybe they already are. That's probably what the Virus is . . .'

Papa's gloves spread the cream on the old lady's skin, as

close to her injuries as he could go. The bruising was horrific and bones moved rather too easily under his strong fingers.

But the miracle took no more than a few hours to accomplish. Before it was time to sleep again, the old woman opened her eyes. They wandered confusedly around the room, not seeming to focus on any one person.

The savage must have been dying to ask about his traitorous wife. Instead, he said, 'Are you all right, Jagadamba? You're with friends, don't worry.'

'Roof worshippers,' she croaked. 'Practically heathens.'

She closed her eyes again. This time, her breathing came easily and quietly. In fact, it was the quietest breathing Hiresh had ever heard her do.

In the morning Hiresh saw a new cubicle in the corner where none had been before. Sometimes, in the old days, Papa would make the apartment grow a wall halfway across the room so he could beat Hiresh without Mother's interference.

'You *will* believe,' Papa said one time, 'if I have to smash every bone in your body.'

'I'll bring you down,' Hiresh snarled back. 'I will, I will!'

'What, you? A blade of grass that couldn't bring down a daisy in the park?'

True, but even so, Father always needed a gang of his

friends to hold his son whenever the time came to give him a new tattoo. The shame it brought on the brute was the greatest satisfaction Hiresh had ever known until his escape.

Just as Mother was handing him a cup of weak tea, the cubicle withdrew into the floor, revealing his father and Jagadamba. The old woman looked strong and straight. The treatment had taken several years off her age, though white still dominated her hair. Hiresh couldn't help wishing they'd given it to his mother instead.

Jagadamba exchanged a significant look with Papa. They were up to something. Rebellion probably. Well, they wouldn't get away with it.

'We'll meet again,' she said.

'Yes.' A nod.

'Get our things together, savage,' she said. 'We're off to find your woman. Let's hope that this time you don't have to kill anybody.'

'I didn't kill anyone,' he said.

She looked puzzled and turned to Hiresh. 'Your father says you were in a fight with Wardens and that you got away.'

'He hurt them pretty badly,' said Hiresh, worried about where this was going.

'But they could have had a hundred friends after us in seconds,' she said.

For a moment Hiresh didn't have a good answer for this,

but then he remembered how the truth was often the most effective lie.

'They didn't know who we were. They brought us into an apartment to rough us up away from any broadcasts. They were in the wrong and they knew it.'

Jagadamba nodded with a smile. 'How typical of them, arrogant Secular scum. And no doubt you were a great help to the savage in the fighting?'

'Savage?' asked Papa, puzzled. Clearly, whatever he'd been discussing with the old lady hadn't included Stopmouth's identity.

'It's just what we call our warrior friend here,' she said, pointing at the hunter. 'He fights as well as the creatures below.'

Stopmouth kept the truth to himself.

Hiresh's father didn't even say goodbye, which suited the boy fine. But Mother clung to him, as if she knew he'd never want to come back again. He hugged her, biting his lip to keep tears from his own eyes. He was shocked by how much he missed her and couldn't believe he was now about to leave her all over again.

# 9. THE HUNGER IN THE DARK

No sooner were they back in the corridor than Jagadamba turned to Hiresh and said: 'I don't care if you are a fan of this savage, we don't need you any more, big man. Why don't you stay with your parents? Important things will happen in this area *very* soon. Great events. You must leave your life of sloth behind you and follow your duty. Your father can show you how.' Her voice rang clear and strong. Hiresh had a sudden flash of what she must have been like as a younger woman – ugly but dangerous, fearless.

'I want to go with you.'

'What for?' She turned to Stopmouth. 'He will only slow us down. Another two days and we'll be there.'

'Two days?' said Stopmouth. 'It's too long. My people—'

Jagadamba ignored him. 'I only let the fool come before because I thought he had nowhere else to go except to the authorities. But look! Proper parents. People who can give his life purpose . . .'

Hiresh would have to insist if he were to complete his mission. Not that he really wanted to now that he understood Stopmouth a little better, but he didn't know what would happen to Tarini. He had to find a way out; a way that would make it look like he'd done his best.

'I want Hiresh to come with us,' said the hunter.

The boy felt his face go warm.

*Why?* he wondered. *What good am I? Why?*

'There isn't enough room for a big man like that where we're going,' said Jagadamba. Yet, when Hiresh turned to follow her, Stopmouth clapped him on the back and the old woman offered no further protest.

The pace was quicker now. The Medicine Papa had obtained from his network of fellow Roof worshippers had removed the hobble from the old woman's gait, and Stopmouth was anxious to hurry everyone along.

'Two days,' she had said. Two more days. Then Hiresh's new life could begin, while Stopmouth . . . Stopmouth would be all right. He'd never be able to prevent the destruction of his tribe anyway. He'd be safer in the Roof.

The same might not be said for the traitor, Indrani.


*Indrani*, thought Stopmouth, *had always wanted to return to the Roof.* And yet most of the reunions he dreamed of with her were lovely. He'd sweep her into his arms. He'd feel her soft skin against his. He'd see the impish glint that had been in her eyes back when she'd taught him to walk on crutches while throwing stones at him for fun.

How he'd missed her. He couldn't help wishing that his guide would just tell him where to go instead of dragging him along at this agonizing pace. But he'd never have made it on his own – not in a world as strange as this one where people ate soggy pellets and swarmed everywhere in impossible numbers.

Jagadamba took them on a shuttle car. 'I've arranged a new meeting for us,' she said. 'And no, savage, there's no way to make it any faster.'

The journey wasted several precious hours interrupted by incomprehensible religious arguments between the other two. Jagadamba hawked, but couldn't find anything in her newly repaired throat to spit at Hiresh. She threatened him with multiple, horrific rebirths. He laughed and promised, 'You have to die to be reborn, right? But I'll be living for ever! Everybody will when the Crisis is over. Everybody except you!'

'Oh, your Commission won't be in charge much longer!' she snarled. 'The savage's woman's got something in her head they're deadly afraid of. They're sweeping whole sectors looking for her, you know. It has them terrified! And she's with us now.'

And on and on in the same vein until Stopmouth was driven back into his daydreaming. As always, he pictured his woman and tried to imagine a life for them together on the surface. This got him thinking about the tribe again, and before he could stop himself, he was asking the Roof to send him back there for a look, a chance to dwell among them as the ancestors must do.

He found them celebrating a successful hunt. Various limbs roasted on spits while the women danced around them and children kept watching the meat turn, licking their lips. For a moment he didn't see Rockface, and panicked. The big man should have been here, rejoicing with the others, boasting of his part in the hunt or telling his fellows where they'd gone wrong. 'You should have charged, hey? All this hanging back, and what good did it do you in the end?' But where was he now? Where?

The Roof took him immediately to the hidden room Rockface had claimed for his own. He sat with his back pressed against the mossy stone and his feet stretched out and braced against the opposite wall. Maybe if he pressed hard enough, his back would straighten itself?

Sodasi sat just round the corner from the room, as if by coincidence. She sat quietly and must have been able to hear Rockface's secret grunts of pain as he ground his back ever harder against the stone. But she said nothing, and Stopmouth suspected that as soon as the food was cooked, she'd be running off to fetch two portions rather than one. Enough, he'd seen enough.

And yet what else could he do? Return to the shuttle and the meaningless arguments between Hiresh and Jagadamba?

Stopmouth found his spirit drifting higher. The Diggers, he thought. He'd find out how far they'd got. He could do that much. Maybe he could also spy out the abodes of other beasts. Once he'd returned to the surface, such information would be invaluable to the tribe.

He drifted out over the hills and saw, on the other side, the horrific fields of the Diggers. A few hundred days before, when his little party had escaped up these rocky slopes, the beasts had still been far away from here. Yet now, Stopmouth could see row upon row of planted, moaning bodies, each kept alive while being eaten from below by the tiny yellow grubs that would grow up to be Diggers in their own right.

He drifted over the fields for a while, never coming close enough to hear the groans of pain or smell the stench of rot he still remembered. However, he felt his heart skip a beat when he spotted the luminous white skins of creatures that could only be Skeletons. So close? Were they really that close? He moved on, afraid he'd see Fourleggers next, or Slimers, or even humans.

The tortured planted beings sank lower in the earth the further he moved from the hills. Soon he reached a place where all but the heads had been consumed. But that didn't last for long. Fat, dirty grubs as large as his arm fought over them, driving off the losers until the victor opened its mouth wide enough to swallow the victim's screaming face whole.

Afterwards, or so the Roof told him when he couldn't help asking, the now huge grub would burrow into the earth and sleep until it woke again as an adult Digger. And there were a lot of these! So many!

Stopmouth looked around and saw nothing but poisoned, devastated land in all directions. The newborn Diggers would find nothing to eat here and would have no way to feed their young, other than with their own bodies. The pain would soon push them over the hills.

'I want to wake up!' he told the Roof. 'Please wake me up!'

He found his companions still arguing with one another – although, strangely, they'd left the venom behind.

'But we are not Indians!' Hiresh was saying. 'Thousands of real years and light years separate us from them, and all the while we've been changing. They would hate us. We're as far from them as Stopmouth is from' – he closed his eyes for an instant – 'from the ancient Romans! Our languages are different, our customs are different, and as for our religions—'

'What do you know about religion, fool?'

'I know our ancestors wouldn't recognize anything about ours: they'd think we—'

'Ah, savage,' said Jagadamba, sounding almost relieved to put an end to Hiresh's tirade, 'I see you've come back to us. It didn't take you long to turn into a useless Dreamer, did it?'

Stopmouth felt groggy, his muscles all stiff. It took him a moment to remember why he'd wanted to leave the Dreamworld so quickly.

Jagadamba continued, 'Your little Secular friend is too clever for his own good. He's going to damn himself with his own smart mouth.'

Hiresh snorted. 'There's nothing you can say to me, crone, that I haven't already heard from *him*!'

'He means his pious father, of course. He—'

'Pious! You call *him* pious!'

'All right!' said Stopmouth. His tongue tasted of sleep and his head throbbed. 'We've got to hurry. I've got to get Indrani and go home to the surface as soon as possible. My people are in big trouble.'

The old lady wagged her finger at him. 'Silly savage, look at the light outside the shuttle – look!'

Stopmouth obeyed. Beyond the glass, all was dim except for a single strip of illumination.

'There are hundreds of lamps out there, each a hundred steps apart. We couldn't possibly be going any faster! We'd be flattened if we tried to leave. But it doesn't matter . . . We're nearly there now, nearly there.'

Sure enough, the single strip of light divided itself into smaller and smaller blurs as the shuttle slowed.

They emerged into another strongly Religious area. The people here wore masks with cold glittering eyes. Some painted their skin blue, some gold or other colours. They spoke a language much like that of Stopmouth's new tribe, or so Hiresh told him.

A blue man with thin arms beckoned them into a room without moving pictures. 'My contact,' whispered Jagadamba.

Inexplicably, he pricked Stopmouth with a needle, stole a drop of blood – something only a friend should get – and ran off for a few minutes. When he returned, he smiled and nodded at Jagadamba.

'So you're the real thing, monster. I told them that.'

But Stopmouth barely noticed. The walls here had been painted (by hand, apparently) with images of other blue-skinned men fighting battles with metal weapons and clever contraptions called *bows* that fired tiny spears over great distances. He studied them, too fascinated to object as he was stripped and daubed with shiny gold paint. A group of masked women performed the same procedures on a squawking Jagadamba.

'A woman should be covered! It's indecent!' But she cried even more loudly at something else her contact must have said to her. 'You are joking! They want us to go *there*?'

Hiresh too looked miserable until they hid his face with a mask. Men muttered and pointed at his thin body – and Stopmouth couldn't blame them.

'You never told me you were a hunter too,' whispered Stopmouth, 'to have such . . . such scars.'

Hiresh said nothing, but he covered up the strange lump on his upper left arm with one hand and refused to let them paint there. A recent wound that might still be delicate, perhaps.

After that, they were shoved into the corridor. A party of masked and golden young men came upon them without warning and bore them along in their midst through a series of twists and turns. They all stopped at a junction to shout insults at some distant Wardens, before running on, laughing.

At one point two strapping young men took hold of Jagadamba and lifted her along between them, whooping and twirling her around as she shouted curses at them.

Stopmouth smiled behind his mask. It was like being on a hunt again, surrounded by comrades and running into danger. But there was something reckless about this group, a carelessness that no true hunting party would dare risk.

'What is your name?' Stopmouth asked one of the men.

'Arjuna,' he replied.

'So am I!' said another. 'And you are Arjuna too, brother, when you wear His mask!'

They came to another junction with a bigger crowd of Wardens waiting at it.

'I don't like this!' wheezed Jagadamba. The young men had let her down again and Stopmouth was beginning to worry about her ability to keep up.

'Go home!' called one of the Wardens, his voice amplified by his helmet.

The youths started uttering ululations. Then they charged, crashing into the black uniforms of the guards, who hammered back with augmented muscles and green truncheons. The youths didn't stand a chance. Stopmouth wanted to go with them, to show them how it was done, but it all seemed like a mad waste to him. Besides, he couldn't leave his companions to cope by themselves. However, another young man was calling at them to move down a side passage.

'I am Arjuna,' he said. 'Like you. Take two left turns and the second right.' Then he started ululating before sprinting towards the hopeless confrontation the other Arjunas had begun. Most of the youths were unconscious already. A few hung back, exchanging threats with their enemies.

'Come, savage,' said Jagadamba.

She led them down a path so narrow that anybody sleeping here would have had to lie on their side. Above them, walls stretched up and up, seemingly with no end. Stopmouth felt dizzy until Jagadamba's bony hand gripped him above the elbow.

'Look, savage. See the colour of the walls?'

'Black,' he said, feeling the dizziness return.

'You must look higher then. See how pale they become further up?'

'*Ice!*' said Hiresh, horrified.

She shot him a look of disdain. 'Yes, big man.' And to Stopmouth, who'd never seen ice before, 'Do you know what that is now? What's up there? The air has been allowed to thin a little, you see, and the temperature has dropped—'

'But we can't go there!' said Hiresh. 'Even if you have the right supplies, what about the alarms? What about' – and here he gulped – 'what about the Emptiness?'

'Your kind are naturally empty,' she said. 'You pride yourselves on it. You will not be welcomed up there.'

'Hiresh comes with us,' said Stopmouth. 'Hiresh is Tribe.'

'Pah. You can keep your tribe. Now, listen carefully. Upstairs, the Roof will not listen to us. Nor will it speak or give us any information . . .'

'The Emptiness,' said Hiresh again, as if he couldn't believe it. 'The Virus has killed all the machines.'

'Stop interrupting!' warned Jagadamba. 'There isn't much time. Those brave boys are selling their freedom for a moment's distraction. Don't waste it! If you don't listen to me now, savage, you won't understand me when we don't have the Roof to translate for us.'

Stopmouth nodded. Hiresh remained frozen to the spot.

'The lift cars are no longer working, so we will be forced to take the stairs. It is not very far, but it may take us a day or more to reach the top. We will have food and supplies for the journey, but listen to me now, because I won't be able to repeat myself later: I am an old woman and this body might not be able to take the strain, despite the Medicine I've had. If I die, you must cut off my left hand and take it with you.'

'Of course,' said Stopmouth. 'You do us great honour.'

Her eyes widened. 'Oh, not for food, you disgusting savage! I can't believe you can still talk like that! Just promise me you will take my left hand with you. And promise me you will not eat it. Is that clear?'

The hunter shrugged, unsure of what he had said to offend.

After that, Jagadamba took them down a set of anonymous streets where a warm mist billowed around them – steam, it was called. Nobody sat in this corridor, nobody at all. It was the loneliest place Stopmouth had seen since his arrival. Hiresh didn't like it at all.

The floor was slick beneath their feet and Stopmouth had to steady the other two when they skidded. Once or twice he even ended up on his bottom, and when Hiresh helped him up again, the floor seemed to suck at the loincloth the Arjunas had dressed him in.

Steam washed the paint from their bodies so that they

left little puddles of it behind with every footstep. *So much for secrecy*, thought Stopmouth.

They came to a small, plain door. Unlike many others that the hunter had seen here, nothing disguised it and it bore the words *emergency only* in the speaking pictures of the Roof. More of the moisture that coated the surfaces of the area seeped out from underneath.

'Remember this tasty hand, savage?' asked Jagadamba, holding up her left arm. 'This is what it can do. Remember this.' She pressed it against the door. It turned green and swung open.

'But are we really going?' asked Hiresh. 'We can't be . . . Surely we can't be—'

'*You* don't deserve to be!' said the old lady in triumph, and then, a little more seriously, 'Once we're in here, we've given them the slip. But we won't be home and dry, by any stretch. It's the Emptiness. Remember that.'

'This is madness,' said Hiresh, rubbing furiously at the lump on his arm, smearing the damp gold paint. He turned to Stopmouth and whispered, 'She's really doing it. She's taking us Upstairs.'

'Not you, big man!' she cackled. 'They've not yet built stairs that could hold a weight like yours! But Upstairs, yes. Where the Seculars don't dare to travel. Where Indrani waits with her secret, which you' – she pointed at the hunter – 'will help us to find!'

'I don't know what secret you're talking about,' he said.

'Neither does she,' said Jagadamba, 'but every Warden, every Commissioner, is looking for her, so you can be sure she knows *something*. When we know it too, they will fall. I'm sure of it.'

Beyond the door, a set of steps lay before them, corkscrewing for ever skywards. Jagadamba pried a panel loose from the wall.

*Clever*, thought the hunter. The old woman or her friends had hidden a large stash of food and clothing there.

While she sorted through it, Stopmouth looked up into the stairwell and immediately wished he hadn't. He felt like he was falling into it.

Some buildings at home stood several storeys high, but not this, not like this, rising up for ever, or what seemed like it. And what would be waiting for them at the top? The so-called Upstairs, with just as many endless parks and corridors and streets as on the level where Hiresh lived.

Stopmouth clamped his eyes shut against the dizziness and made sure that when he opened them again he was looking down, at the steps themselves. Trails of slimy liquid ran along the left side nearest the wall, lumpy and sluggish under a dim green light.

'It feels . . . strange here,' he said. 'Like night.'

'It's cold,' said Jagadamba. 'Don't you have cold on the surface? Never mind. Take this . . .' She handed him a bundle of heavy clothing. 'You'll be glad of these robes now—'

'What are those things?'

'Boots, savage, boots.'

He shook his head, not wanting to trust his feet in them, and she shrugged. 'You'll be sorry. I'm going to shut the door. I have to. After that, no more Roof, you hear me, savage? No more. Just remember my tasty hand in case you need to get out again in a hurry! Now, inside.'

Hiresh didn't follow them straight away. Stopmouth could see a troubled look on the boy's face. As if he were torn between his friendship for Stopmouth and the thought of entering this horrific afterlife of slime and . . . and *cold*. The door began to close in his face, and it was as if he remembered something important. He slid inside, his skinny body just clearing the edges of the doorway.

Jagadamba snorted and made a nasty remark of some kind. Stopmouth had been ignoring her insults so long, it took him a moment to realize he hadn't understood a word she'd spoken. All three looked at each other. Stopmouth could see Hiresh was frightened, eyes flicking everywhere. Jagadamba stopped needling her companions. A convulsive shiver passed through her whole body.

Stopmouth was trembling too and he seemed to have no control over it. But even more disconcerting than that was the way bits of spirit puffed out of everybody's mouths in white clouds with every breath. He tried catching it to shove it back inside his body, but it was useless. Hiresh too seemed to find it surprising, although he made little effort to prevent it.

All three stood there, shivering together, miserable together. Stopmouth's two companions looked like people who'd been expelled from their tribe, whose Tallies were to be publicly snapped in two.

And then the hunter realized something. He wasn't dying. He wasn't losing his soul. If anything, the opposite had happened. All the swarms of people with their colours and their stenches were gone. He was free. Free of the Roof.

Jagadamba made more words and signalled that they should follow her. Then, for the steps were just a little too high for her short legs, she climbed them, one at a time, keeping away from the rivulet of slime near the wall. After a moment Stopmouth followed. Hiresh came last of all.

The small group trudged in silence, Jagadamba moving up a step, pausing, up a step, pausing. Stopmouth concentrated on the sound of her breathing, worried about her, but also wanting to distract himself from this strange feeling of daytime cold. Bit by bit, he picked up other sounds too – a drip-dripping of some liquid that echoed through the stairwell; irregular clattering noises, like bones rolling down steps; a humming sound that dominated everything else.

The hum was not completely constant, but came in

waves and pulses. It reminded the hunter of nothing more than the heartbeat of some great creature on the threshold of death.

He already hated the burning touch of cold metal against the soles of his feet, but didn't trust the foot coverings that Jagadamba had handed out.

'I f-feel like I'm b-being watched,' he said to his companions. 'Don't you?'

They stopped to look at him. He'd forgotten that they couldn't possibly understand him. Strange to hear the echo of his own stutter. Onwards again, up through the sickly green light of the stairs. Fourteen steps followed by a landing, followed by another fourteen steps. Every four landings brought them to a filthy door sealed by grime. Writing covered these entrances, but the hunter had lost the ability to read it. He wondered if somebody had once lived behind them, but clearly no one did now.

After only ten flights Jagadamba sat down and signalled the other two to join her. Stopmouth's body missed the easy exercise and began to shiver. He took the disgusting food she offered – he couldn't remember what it was called any more. It wouldn't fill him, though – that he could be sure of. He ate quickly, then stood again for warmth. He paced around the little landing. He could see where slime seeped and dribbled from under a gap running the length of the wall. The metal around the gap curled away from the liquid, afraid of it. Further up, at face height, thousands of tiny brown holes pitted the surface. He heard Jagadamba heave herself up. Moments later, she was at his side, passing the palms of her hands over the little holes, muttering to herself in what could only be worry.

Then she barked an order and pushed Stopmouth towards the stairs. *Time to get moving, then*, he thought.

There seemed to be no end to the steps or the landings. The stairwell spiralled sickeningly, endlessly upwards, and he still felt as if they were being watched. Friendly eyes, he hoped, anxious for the group's arrival, like the guards in the towers back home.

As they climbed, the pitting in the walls became more pronounced. Holes appeared, some as large as his fist, and soon they were seeing places where only threads of blackened metal held the wall together. Sickly smells of rot wafted through the gaps, where enormous chambers echoed to the sounds of dripping slime. Long rounded objects filled these spaces for as far as the light could reach. When the hunter made moves to step through and examine them further, Jagadamba gripped his arm and shouted angry gibberish at him while her snaggle tooth flew up and down. She was still afraid. So he shrugged and let her lead him away. His feeling of being watched was stronger now.

Jagadamba tired quickly, and the breaks became ever more frequent. It seemed to Stopmouth as if she was trying to find a place to halt for the night, but she didn't like the idea of stopping where the walls had been eaten through.

The travellers were forced to walk right up against the rail, for the slime ran over large sections of the staircase, and the floor looked weak wherever it flowed. Many of the landings were coated with the stuff. Eventually, however, they found a dry one. The wall here held a door that looked much cleaner than usual, and there were only two small holes to either side of it as well as a few pinprick-sized pockmarks.

Jagadamba heaved a sigh. She did not refuse Stopmouth's arm as he helped her to sit, and he could feel a fierce trembling running through her entire frame. She badly needed this rest and the sleep that would come with it, although the loss of time frustrated him. How many days did the tribe have now? He tried to count the sleeps he'd had since arriving here, but couldn't be sure if he'd lost three or four of his precious days.

Hiresh huddled close to Jagadamba for warmth. Soon the hunter was alone. He felt cold too, but wasn't ready to sleep. Besides, he was curious about the chambers they had passed during the day and the strange objects they contained. Perhaps he could find something to use as a weapon. Nobody could live in a place like this – there simply wasn't anything to eat. But he still had that horrible feeling of being stalked and he wanted the reassurance of a dangerous object in the palm of his hand.

He padded down a few levels until he came to a hole in the wall large enough to duck through. The only light came from the stairwell, and within moments his feet were covered in cold slime. He shivered and tried to pick up the pace, but without proper visibility he knew he couldn't move too fast.

The smell of rot was strong here and it was colder than on the steps. He could feel, in the quality of the sound, in the currents of the air, just how large the room was. The ceiling must rise all the way to just below the landing where the others were now sleeping. Perhaps another chamber started there, and another above that, for who knew how many levels? The thought disturbed him and brought home yet again the true power of the Roofpeople. That they did nothing with such power other than laze about, entertaining themselves with the suffering of others, was disgusting beyond measure.

'I hate them,' he said, his voice echoing. Not Jagadamba or Hiresh. Not Indrani – of course not Indrani! But the tribe of them. The great emptiness that was their tribe. The Roof itself and all it stood for. He hadn't fully realized it until now.

His feet began to feel itchy. He ignored the sensation as he padded towards one of thousands of long oval metal cases that filled the chamber. The smell of rotting was particularly strong here. On the top was a hard transparent sheet. He couldn't quite make out what was inside, but his hands, feeling around the metal body of the cylinder, found little knobs that could be some kind of clasp, such as a woman might make of bone and thread.

'Let's see what we have here,' he muttered.

That was when he heard the screaming.

Hiresh. He'd left them alone. How could he do that? He was already running up the stairs on feet that had started to sting.

*It's just a dream*, he was thinking. *There's nothing dangerous in this place except the Wardens, and he could handle the likes of them, surely?*

Heartbeats later, he arrived just in time to see the door beside Jagadamba close with a thump. It had been clean, he remembered. Cleaner than any of the other doors. Wallbreaker would have realized what that meant, but not his stupid younger brother, too distracted by new sights and smells to remember survival. *Idiot, idiot.*

Jagadamba lay where he'd left her. She was up on one elbow, jabbering and pointing at the door. He ran straight past her and yanked at a knob that protruded from it, pulling with all his might. It creaked a little, but held. He pounded at the metal, hearing it ring hollow, but having no other effect.

'Hiresh!' he called. 'H-hang on, Hiresh, we'll g-get you. We'll f-find a way in!'

He felt a tugging at his arm. The old woman had climbed to her feet and was pulling his elbow. He couldn't believe it. She wanted them to run off, to abandon Hiresh!

'He is Tribe!' he shouted at her, amazed by his own anger, the speed of his thumping heart. He shook her off and beat at the door again. Then he remembered her famous left hand. She seemed reluctant to give it, but he pushed it against the door anyway and waited for the magic to work. Nothing happened. He allowed her to pull away. How? he wondered. How could he get in? If this were another cavern like the one he'd visited below, there might be a way through the rotted walls one storey up.

'We've got to go up,' he said to Jagadamba, his voice still full of panic. Why had Hiresh been screaming? What awful things were the Wardens doing to him?

Jagadamba sneered. She wrapped knotted fingers around the door handle and twisted. The whole thing opened easily. She stood back to allow him entry. As simple as that.

He pushed past. Time was slipping away with every heartbeat. Pale lighting similar to that of the stairwell worked to throw long shadows from row after row of cylinders. This room totally lacked the smell of rot he'd encountered on most of the landings below. The air *hummed*, and only a little slime gathered here and there in greasy pools. A large object had been dragged through

180

one of these down the central aisle between cylinders.

Stopmouth tried to get control of himself. *Why am I rushing?* he wondered. This wasn't the surface. The dangers were surely milder and he didn't want to run into an ambush. He followed in the direction of the slime trail, avoiding the pool itself, for the skin of his feet still burned and itched after his last encounter with it. A little further into the room, another pool showed him his quarry hadn't altered direction. In skirting it, however, and with one of the pale light sources directly overhead, Stopmouth finally caught a glimpse through the transparent sheet that covered one of the cylinders. He stopped dead, his heart suddenly frozen in his chest.

Inside, curled into a ball, lay a . . . a *beast*. A non-human creature, all eyes and whiskers. Short tusks sprouted on either side of a wide mouth. How could there be beasts in the Roof? Only humans lived here, or so he'd been led to believe. Down on the surface, yes, there were beasts aplenty there. They fought and ate and died, and when a species became extinct, magic made another set of creatures appear in their place. Magic. In all his life, Stopmouth had never needed any other explanation for where his prey came from. And here it lay before him.

The creature looked as if it was sleeping rather than dead. He glanced into other cylinders. Dozens upon dozens of them held beasts just like the first. All the cylinders were identical except for one. Right near the main aisle, a jagged hole gaped in the clear sheet. Somebody had broken this one open and torn the jaw off the sleeper inside. The rest of the flesh had been left to spoil, and to the hunter, that made no sense at all.

With shaking hands he removed a shard of the broken cocoon. As he'd hoped, it was sharp and dangerous, perhaps as sharp as the worked shell of an Armourback. Brittle, though, so he'd have to be careful with it. He longed for a spear-shaft to attach to it.

He proceeded with caution, trying to concentrate on following the faint traces of slime through the cavern. At the far end stood another door, his probable destination, but he'd be stupid to assume that. The cylinders now held a different type of beast, with scaly skin and no obvious eyes. The sleep of one of these creatures had also been disturbed. A single piece of flesh missing. The pattern repeated itself with two more species before Stopmouth had reached the far side of the cavern. With every grisly find, his fears for Hiresh's safety increased.

He twisted the handle of the final door as Jagadamba had taught him, no longer caring if an ambush waited. He jumped through into a room where long ropes hung from the ceiling, hissing and sparking at their torn ends. Slime ran thickly from holes in the wall. He found himself on a high circular platform looking down into a round room made up of elaborate cages full of shadow. Rivulets of slime ran down walls three times the height of a man, and in several places they disappeared through blackened holes in the floor.

Somebody shouted out below, the voice muffled by humming and sparking.

'Hiresh!' called Stopmouth, then cursed his own stupidity for alerting the kidnappers to his presence. He sprinted around the platform until he found a set of dripping metal stairs. Halfway down, and with Hiresh's panicked voice still calling out, the steps groaned, and suddenly Stopmouth was crashing with them to the floor of the round cage room. He rolled when he hit the ground, coming up in a pile of loose hard objects.

*Bones!* he realized. Hundreds of bones, possibly all belonging to the same species of beast. He had no time to investigate, though, for Hiresh's voice had been silenced.

He shot to his feet. The humming sound was louder down here, the noise a constant throbbing, almost painful. He'd fallen down between two cages. Each could have held a hundred men standing straight, but instead beds filled them, such as the one he'd woken up on when he'd been held prisoner in the white room. The middle of the round space was a mess of heavy metal objects tangled in wires, some of which hissed and sparked. Big pools of shadow lay everywhere. Any one of them might have held an opponent, especially when he had no idea what manner of enemy faced him.

He picked among the bones, looking for a makeshift weapon to replace the one he'd dropped during the fall. Most of them had been gnawed, smashed open right to the marrow, but he found one that had been missed: a long shaft with a heavy lump at the end.

'Hiresh?' he called. No point in hiding now – he'd already made too much noise during his fall. He got no answer. Maybe his only friend in this place had already been killed.

He edged around the room, trying to keep the wall to his back as much as possible. Usually cages got in his way, and once he almost stepped into a hole that some stream of slime had cut into the floor. Nor did he like the look of those sparking wires – they were like living things, spitting and angry. Instinct kept him away from them.

Halfway round the room he spotted a shadowy figure in one of the cages. It loomed so large that for a moment he mistook it for one of the huge lumps of metal that littered the middle of the round space. But then it moved, its skin glittering in the pale light.

Stopmouth stood frozen to the spot. The creature seemed too huge to be real. Three men could not have filled out that bulk. He saw its silhouette turn. A hand-sized, flexible nose curved delicately into the air before snaking in his direction and stopping there like an accusing finger. Then the whole massive body marched out of the cage and strode towards him. Stopmouth could only stare, frozen to the spot. Bones cracked and splintered where the beast walked. How had it got down the stairs that had collapsed under Stopmouth's weight? He couldn't figure it out. As it came closer, he could see more of its features – tiny eyes, little finger-sized ears perched atop its flat head, and beneath the questing nose, a set of heavy jaws, as massive as the rest of its frame. The creature could crush Stopmouth's skull in a single bite.

One great arm swung back behind its head.

*Move!* Stopmouth thought. And finally his body obeyed. He dropped the pathetic bone he'd been carrying, spun round and ran, ignoring the cuts to his feet from the bone splinters that lay everywhere.

Something whistled past his face and shattered against a nearby wall. The creature had strength to match its bulk. He ran halfway round the circular room and then paused, his breathing loud in his ears despite all the other sounds.

It had stopped moving, perhaps hoping he was stupid enough to make a full circuit, all the way into its waiting arms.

Stopmouth crept back in the direction he'd come. He could see no way as yet of defeating such a strong opponent. Study might help. It was one thing his brother had given him, the same brother who'd taken everything else.

He peeked round the great metal objects that dominated the centre of the room and saw the creature standing like a guard before the cage from which it had originally emerged. The hunter cursed, but at least now he could guess where Hiresh was. And the monster knew how to find him too, for its nose still pointed unerringly in his direction.

How could he win? How? With the fire-spitting ropes, perhaps? He didn't know enough about them, and this was not the time to experiment.

He wondered if such a massive beast might also be slow-moving. If so, he could lead it far enough from the cage to determine if his friend still lived. And yet, when it could throw missiles like the one that had just missed him, such a strategy would be pointless. He looked around for more ideas and found nothing.

Stopmouth sighed. He knew he couldn't risk dying here, not with Indrani so close and his tribe only days from destruction. Anyway, Hiresh was already dead. He had to be.

'I'm so sorry, my friend,' he whispered. It felt terribly wrong. Nevertheless, his eyes were already looking for a way out. 'It's for the tribe . . .'

He sneaked backwards again, knowing himself to be disloyal and dirty. He returned to the staircase that had collapsed under his weight. A rivulet of slime ran over the lip of the upper platform and beneath where the steps had been. If they couldn't take Stopmouth's weight, the creature certainly couldn't have been using them either. So there had to be another set of steps in the room, without any weakening slime.

He heard a crunching sound behind him. He flung himself to the side – just in time: a large chunk of metal struck the ruins of the staircase right where his head had been. The hunter picked himself up to see the beast charging, lumbering towards him, its massive feet kicking up splinters, smashing skulls. In one hand it held a long metal pipe.

He darted away, feeling the whistle of the pipe swinging just behind him. The creature was not so slow after all, and it only needed to run into him to cause him an injury. He yelped and stumbled; ran two steps on all fours before his feet took control again and shot him ahead of his enemy.

Stopmouth fled over jagged splinters while the beast pounded after him. It roared, and any second now, the hunter knew, he'd stumble again, never to rise.

A gap appeared amongst the metal objects in the centre of the room. Stopmouth dived for it. His sweaty body slid between two giant, humming boxes. The pipe followed him in, questing and smashing. He managed to turn and grab the end of it. A stupid move – he didn't stand a chance. The beast yanked the weapon backwards so quickly it nearly pulled him out of his burrow altogether. Only hitting his head saved him, for he released the pipe and fell back, dazed.

'Help me, ancestors! Help m—'

The creature attacked again, its blows coming hard enough to knock dents in the walls around Stopmouth. Soon one of its random strikes was bound to catch his skull. He waited for the pipe to appear once more. The moment it withdrew, he leaped from scarred feet to grab the lip of one of the boxes above his head. He howled once when his enemy's weapon clipped him, deadening a trailing leg. Still, he managed to pull himself up while the beast redoubled its efforts below.

He breathed hard, holding in his whimpers of pain and hoping the hum that pervaded the room would mask them further. Slowly, feeling came back into his leg.

*I have to get out of here.*

He wondered if he was strong enough to jump onto the roof of one of the cages. From there, maybe, he might be able to reach up to the edge of the platform . . . But even at his peak, such a jump would have been stupid. So instead, Stopmouth used his height advantage to peer around the room until he saw another set of stairs, intact this time – and near the cage where poor Hiresh was probably lying dead.

He crawled slowly in that direction, trying to keep

quiet. At every push, his hands encountered shards of metal that must have fallen from the ceiling, rotted by slime but still heavy. He shoved a few of them into a pocket of his robes and moved on.

Something had changed. He couldn't figure out what it was. The room still hummed and sparked and dripped. What could it be? The pipe! It was no longer rattling into Stopmouth's former hiding place. Either the beast had tired of its sport and was waiting for him to emerge, or else . . .

The box he was crawling over shuddered. Then it began to rock. It must have weighed more than ten men, but Stopmouth could hear the grunts of the beast pushing it over and back. He got to his hands and knees and spun round. He could see mighty, glittering muscles below him straining against the weight. The top of the box sloped enough now that shards of metal were sliding off the end with every swing. He grabbed some more of them with one hand, while the other kept him from spilling onto the floor. Then he pelted the creature's head with heavy little missiles. They skidded off its bony skull, but it roared, nose pointing upwards, and redoubled its efforts.

A final mighty heave knocked the box backwards to lean against another. The hunter slid towards the second box, and managed to pull himself up onto it before he tumbled to the floor. He didn't wait for his enemy to knock this one down too, but leaped off and rolled when he hit the ground. The stairs were just ahead of him.

He heard the bone-crunching noise of the beast thundering round towards him. He would make it to the steps – just.

He was passing the cage when he heard a voice: 'Shtop-mau! Shtop-mau!' *Hiresh?*

A moment's distraction; a turn of the head was all it took. Then his weary, torn feet missed a step and turned over on top of some old leg bone. He tumbled end over end, and by the time he'd got up again, the creature had put itself between him and the steps.

It walked towards Stopmouth as he scrambled backwards, heart racing. Amidst the panic a coherent thought emerged – *It isn't charging. It's breathing harder than I am.*

The creature was being careful. Now that it had won the day, it wanted to be sure of its kill. Slaver dripped from the great jaws as if they already tasted Stopmouth's marrow.

He called out, 'C-can you m-move, Hiresh?' His voice echoed harshly across the room. The monster took no notice – it might not even be able to hear human speech.

'Can you g-get behind the beast and t-trip it up?'

Of course, Hiresh wouldn't understand him either without the Roof's help, but surely he'd figure it out.

However, the only movement now was the first swing of the pipe, driving the hunter further from the steps and

190

keeping him away from the central metal boxes that had saved his life before.

The swings became more frequent and got closer as the hunter tired. Somewhere behind him, a wall waited. He could hear the murmur of slime running down it. Once there, he'd be trapped. Nobody would ever know about his death in this dark place. There was some comfort in the fact that his flesh would be consumed – better than the fate of most Roofdwellers. But the thought of Indrani never hearing about it made him grit his teeth in anger at himself. He screamed at his tormentor and began picking up old pieces of bone to fling in its direction. Then he remembered the metal shards in his robes. They'd bounce uselessly off the creature's hide. Yet it must have a weakness somewhere, and Stopmouth suddenly realized what that must be.

He ran back a few steps to clear a bit of room for himself, even though it brought him closer to the wall. Then he turned and took aim at the waving nose. Stopmouth had always been a good shot with knife and spear and sling: most of his people were. His first few throws missed, due to the irregularity of the metal. The third scored a line of blood down the beast's face and earned a roar that seemed to shake the entire room. He threw more, missing every one. It didn't matter. The metal pipe swung madly, blindly, in Stopmouth's direction, pushing him towards the wall. In heartbeats he had his back to it. A pace to his left stood a cage, the bars too narrow to crawl through. Five paces to his right, a heavy stream of slime with another cage just beyond it.

The creature was charging at him now, exhausted but clearly enraged too. The pipe swung for his head, but the great body coming on behind it would do the final damage, trapping him and crushing him against the wall.

Stopmouth saw one final chance to turn the creature's own strength against it and save himself. With the last of his energy he dived to the right, rolled through the pool of slime and fell against the cage there. The beast rebounded from the wall where he'd been, but recovered quickly to come for the helpless human again.

It never reached him. The rotted floor – where the slime met metal – gave way beneath its great weight. One leg disappeared up as far as the groin; the other snapped loud enough to echo around the chamber. The pipe dropped and the creature's bloody snout waved and twitched in agony.

Stopmouth watched it from a safe distance, not daring to move. However, his stomach was already rumbling. *Proper food at last*, he thought.

The beast howled its pain while black blood puddled around it, darkening the stream of slime. He wanted to put it out of its misery, but dared not risk it. Instead, he shut his ears to its suffering as best he could and limped back to the cage where he'd first seen the creature's massive bulk.

'Hiresh?' he called. No reply came. He couldn't see his friend anywhere. Stopmouth had an awful feeling that a creature that large might have been able to swallow the boy down in one gulp, much as the Yellowmaws did. But if it ate like that, why did it have such heavy jaws?

There were more bones in the cage than he'd seen elsewhere; piles large enough to hide any number of human bodies. All of them had been cracked open. And they had something else in common too: in spite of their fragmented nature, his expert eyes told him that they'd all belonged to the same species as the creature that had attacked him.

Stopmouth had a horrible vision of the creature waking up in a strange metal place with no food. Except for its own friends and family, of course. What choice would they have had but to fall on each other until only the strongest remained, maddened by loneliness and hunger?

And yet there *was* a choice of other food – it had tried eating the sleepers, one from each species: a little bite before giving up. Why had it stopped?

The hunter shook his head. Another mystery he didn't have time for.

He dug amongst the remains until he found his friend's body. The boy still breathed.

*Thank the ancestors!* thought Stopmouth. One of his friend's arms – the one without the strange lump on it – appeared to have been broken. Not necessarily fatal in a world where people ate 'protein' and nobody had to be traded for meat.

But the sight of the scars that puckered Hiresh's limbs and chest disturbed the hunter. Seeing them all together like this brought back the memory of the tattoos that covered the bodies of his friend's parents. At the time, he hadn't even thought to wonder that the boy had no tattoos of his own. Now he knew: one finger-length at a time, with discipline, patience and tremendous suffering, a knife had cut them away. And Stopmouth knew instinctively who had wielded the weapon.

'I don't know why you'd waste tattoos like that, Hiresh,' he whispered. 'But you're no coward.'

Hiresh opened his eyes. 'Shtop-mau,' he said. 'Shtop-mau . . .' His good hand took one of the hunter's and tried to move it towards the strange lump on his arm. Then he uttered a stream of urgent and desperate gibberish.

'I'll get you out of here,' said Stopmouth, keeping his voice gentle and reassuring. 'First I need to . . . to collect something. I'll only be a few heartbeats.'

His enemy's death cries had ceased. It was time to feed.

# 10. THE VOLUNTEER

Hiresh woke into jolting agony. Stopmouth was carrying him up some stairs, the hunter's breath exploding in clouds around them. He tried to log on. 'Where are we?' he asked. No answer came. The Roof wouldn't speak to him, but he was in too much pain to let that terrify him. Cold, cold air bit at the exposed skin of his face, and every step the hunter took felt like spikes ground into his arm.

Hiresh had something important to say. What was it? What was it? He lost consciousness.

The next time he woke, he saw a doorway. The old woman – her name was Jaga something . . . Jagadamba – was pressing her left hand against it. She must have had some kind of implant like him, for the door swung open at her touch. Beyond, Hiresh caught a glimpse of the Upstairs – it had to be the Upstairs, because it was so cold.

At first he could see no difference between it and the lower floors where everybody lived now. There would be districts divided into sectors, of course – some for recreation, all parkland or water. And residential areas too: great squares and architectural marvels. There was even said to be a re-creation of the Arctic up here somewhere . . .

But all he saw from the hunter's back was a short corridor with only the night lighting switched on. As his eyes adjusted, other things came to his attention: strange shapes on some of the floors; the walls bare of media. Hiresh couldn't stop shivering, even if the continuous movement generated ever more agony for him. The whole place was like the Arctic now.

Jagadamba grunted in satisfaction. She waved her left hand at Stopmouth, making biting gestures and smacking her lips. She cackled at her own joke before leading them into the corridor.

Hiresh could see the shapes more clearly now: bodies, human bodies, huddled as near to the exit as they could get. They must have lain there for years, preserved by the cold, their terror never ending. Why these ones had failed to escape he couldn't say. Almost all were Religious. They lay atop each other, their bodies tangled, all their resentments forgotten. Papa would have raged at the sight, claiming the Commission had deliberately locked them up here to die.

'The Secular refugees got all the spare accommodation! All of it!'

'That's a lie!' Hiresh had countered. 'The Commission wouldn't do that!'

'This is the last straw, the last straw!'

The old woman beckoned Stopmouth onwards. He hesitated and said a few words that included Hiresh's name. The boy felt warm at the thought. Stopmouth had saved his life – he'd taken on an alien that was surely too powerful even for him. He'd risked the only chance he had of being reunited with his wife.

*For me. For his friend.*

The boy felt tears running down his face, but he knew Stopmouth wouldn't mock him for it. Savages lived in an awful world and they cried all the time. No doubt the hunter would weep when his woman was taken away from him for good . . .

'Let me down!' shouted Hiresh, startling the other two. 'You've got to stay away from me! Let me down! Let me down!'

Without the Roof, his companions couldn't understand a word. They hushed him, Jagadamba looking angry. They ignored his protests and moved off along the corridor. After a few hundred metres of frozen corpses, the emergency lighting came to an abrupt end. Beyond them, an even colder draught of air blew in from some large open space, a plaza perhaps, or a shuttle station. Jagadamba produced a power torch from under her robes. It lit only a small area around them, but she led them boldly onwards. It produced heat too, warming his face.

'I have to get away,' murmured Hiresh. The primitive implant in his arm – it was the best that modern humans could make without the help of the non-political Roof – would lead the Wardens straight here. It was simple enough to work, even in the Upstairs. He would betray Stopmouth, ruin the life of somebody who had risked all for a stranger, a Crisis baby. He tried to warn his companions, tried to speak, but soon he found his strength slipping away.

Stopmouth carried him in Jagadamba's wake through the frightening darkness. The light of her torch kept catching on the lumps of meat that had once been citizens. Hiresh imagined the great numbers of them that must be filling the plaza around them and was glad the light didn't extend further. Most people had escaped to the Downstairs, but here, near the exits, the unlucky ones lay gathered in great drifts, like the piles of petals that had filled the parks of his childhood.

He tried to find out what they'd died of, and once again received nothing but terrifying Emptiness in reply. How could the Roof not be active here? He'd been brought up to believe Her a goddess; a notion he laughed off when Papa wasn't there to supervise him. He'd hurt his mother with that laughter often enough. Though without the goddess to answer his every question – to translate for him, to *remember* for him – without Her he was no better than a savage; a blind man groping through a maze of broken glass.

He found himself praying between jolts of pain: 'Forgive me, Great Mother. Do not abandon me. Forgive me, Great Mother . . .'

Jagadamba, who must have felt the Emptiness too, took one turn after another through the dark, never looking lost or afraid. She was humming to herself and even seemed happy in all this devastation.

Somebody had splinted his arm, at least. He only wished they'd used wood for it instead of some dead alien's bone. It eased the pain of movement, but every time he looked at it, he pictured the creature it must have belonged to: massive; frightening; hungry.

At last Jagadamba motioned them to stop for a break. She pulled them into a body-free alcove and handed out little handfuls of damp rice. All three of them shivered with the cold, huddling close to the warm torchlight. Beyond their little circle, the only sound was the trickle of some liquid.

*Slime*, thought Hiresh.

The others looked exhausted. He hoped they'd sleep soon. Then, if he managed to get to his feet without screaming, he could escape, hide amongst the bodies on the floor until he became one of them. The trackers would find him dead here and believe he'd done his duty right up to the end.

'Killed by a savage!' they'd whisper to one another. And they'd *have* to take care of Tarini then. They'd have to. Hiresh's only two friends in the world would be safe at last.

Jagadamba lay down to sleep and he pretended to do the same. Stopmouth, left alone, pulled something out of his robes, bringing it straight to his mouth. He chewed slowly, arching his neck back, his eyes half closed while some dark liquid spattered his chin. Hiresh turned away, unable to watch any more. A savage was a savage, after all. He would not let the fact put him off his decision.

Eventually his friend sighed with pleasure and lay down beside the old woman. The regular breathing of sleep came quickly.

*Now*, thought Hiresh.

It was no easy thing for a weakened body to stand using only one arm while the other was the source of a terrible, distracting pain that grew with each accidental contact. He used his legs to push back against the wall and inch his way up it. With every jolt, he gritted his teeth and refused to cry out.

'What about your revenge?' asked the old Hiresh from somewhere not too deep inside him. 'Your father's getting away with it now, sauntering about with all those muscles. Plotting a new dark age while Mother starves.' They were good questions that he'd have to think through as he walked into the terrifying darkness.

Strength. That's what it was all about. He'd always wanted it, had fought for it, while Papa kept it from him, stealing his food. But he'd been wrong to obsess so much. '*This* is strength,' he said to his old self.

Something caught his foot and sent him plunging to the floor. He twisted in the air to protect his arm, and the wind was driven out of his chest. It was all he could do not to scream. He had landed on a body. Frozen, odourless, lifeless. Rock hard, but at the same time somehow sticky.

He tried not to gag, but as he pushed himself away, his good hand punctured what must once have been somebody's eye and his gorge rose.

'Go back!' said the old Hiresh. 'It's not too late – go back!'

'No, no . . .' He had pretended to be Stopmouth's fan, to be his friend.

He took the first corridor he could find, turned down one side passage, then another and another. He'd lose himself so thoroughly that when the fear inevitably took charge of him, he wouldn't be able to change his mind. Strength – *this* was strength. Not some constant inalienable quality that a man possessed all the years of his life; you had to fight for it, every day and every minute. Hiresh was fighting now, close to losing. But it didn't matter. He'd come far into the blackness, through little corridors and big. By the time his courage finally broke he'd been walking for well over an hour and was thoroughly lost. Even if the others came looking for him, they'd have absolutely no chance of finding him.

Air currents against his face, as well as the reverberating echoes of running liquids, told him he'd come out into another large area, much like the one where he'd left the others. His heart was beating fast, and with every pulse it throbbed pain into his arm. He felt weak and feverish and scared. He wanted more than anything to go back. He turned round to face the way he'd just come. Only blackness awaited him there. All directions were death now.

He'd been strong. Just once in his life. And now it was over.

Hiresh started crying again. He leaned against a wall, facing into the dark of what must have been some public square, or maybe a park. The sobs came fast and hard.

The Commission had promised that the Crisis was coming to an end. Hiresh should have lived to see the return of the times of plenty. He'd have eaten his fill every day; he'd have taken part in sports and other pleasures that were now only memories, while fanatics like Papa faded away. There'd be food and Cosmetics and Medicine. He'd fall in love with Tarini. Why not? They had such fun together. He wished he could apologize for not leaving the Academy as she'd suggested, for being so proud. If only she were here now to hold his hand. The fear was eating him up.

Through all this, the tears kept running. After a while it seemed to Hiresh that they even sparkled and shone. Confused, he brushed his face clean. His eyes were playing tricks on him. In the distance, something seemed to . . . glow.

His jaw dropped open in horror. Had he walked all this way only to come full circle back to Jagadamba's torch? But no. The group had camped in a little niche of some kind. This light, weak as it was, did not appear to be at ground level.

Hiresh walked towards it. The muscles in his legs shook with exhaustion and cold. A small number of bodies – there were fewer here than in the area he'd left – caused him to change course several times. His feet felt dead grass underfoot, and sometimes mis-steps into puddles of slime would cause his skin to itch and burn. He never stopped. An extraordinary sight was awaiting him.

The light rested on top of one of the park's artificial hills. As far as he knew, most of these held hidden machinery whose function he couldn't remember. It didn't matter. The hill looked as though it had been ripped open. Ancient tubes and circuits lay exposed and . . . dripping. That was the only word for it. Beads of slime glittered in the light, much as Hiresh's tears had done earlier. The droplets fell together from one level of machinery to another, gathering in pools and eventually forming little rivulets that ran everywhere.

'I'm impressed,' said a croaky voice behind him.

Hiresh nearly jumped out of his skin. He turned to find himself staring into the broad chest of a Special Operations Warden – an Elite – with a Talker in his hand. Others emerged from the blackness beyond the circle of light.

Men and women like these had engendered so much fear during the Rebellion that Religious had often changed sides just at the rumour that one was coming for them.

And here, despite their rarity in these days of nano-shortages, was a whole squad. What manner of threat would ever need more than one of them to put it down? But Hiresh knew the answer to that too.

The man opened his helmet to reveal a scarred but handsome face such as Hiresh had always dreamed of for himself. It was a young face too, compared with his crackly voice.

'How you found us I'll never know,' croaked the man. 'But you're right. We can't lose them now. Not from here.' He clapped Hiresh on his good shoulder. 'You've done all we could have hoped for and more. Even if a stupid pair of Neanderthal sergeants nearly ruined everything for us.' The scarred man looked around at the dripping, devastated Upstairs. 'Clever of them to hide that bitch up here. She'll be ours by morning, though. And when I get my hands on her savage . . .' He grinned.

Hiresh could only stare back at him.

*   *   *

Stopmouth felt the cold even in his sleep. He dreamed that Indrani was shivering up against him, raving as she had after her poisoning. So fragile she'd been then, where before she'd been so strong. The babbling increased in volume the harder he hugged her. He woke to find Jagadamba beating feebly at his face and shouting in outrage.

He released her and received one more thump for his troubles. She spat a little ball at him, barely a tenth of the volume she might have managed when he'd first met her. Then she busied her stiff frame with gathering up a few small things – packs of food and the like.

That was when he noticed that Hiresh had gone. He cursed, thinking the boy had crawled off somewhere to relieve himself and fallen over. He must have been in great pain – every step would be agony with an arm like that.

'Hiresh? Hiresh?'

He stole Jagadamba's little light-maker and searched the plaza for a hundred steps in every direction, calling his friend's name all the way. Nothing. Except dozens of corridors and passages leading who knew where? The boy might be lying among all the other bodies; he might be crouching in an entranceway. It didn't matter. Stopmouth had no idea how to track someone in this place.

Hiresh had gone, most likely of his own accord. He probably felt he was slowing his friends down and had sacrificed himself for the Tribe. He was 'volunteering', as Stopmouth's people would have said, and nothing in the world was more beautiful or noble. But in this case – surely less than a day from Indrani's hideout! – it seemed so unnecessary, so wrong.

The hunter began looking down one corridor after another, prying apart piles of wasted flesh.

'Hiresh!' Stopmouth called his friend's name several times more, his voice growing increasingly desperate. 'Hiresh!'

The only reply, however, came from Jagadamba. She strode into the small circle of light, her steaming breath like clouds of fire. She grabbed two fistfuls of his clothing and forced him to choose between breaking away from her and looking her in the face.

'Indrani,' she said. She pointed a claw off in the direction they'd been travelling. 'Indrani.'

And his tribe too, of course. How much closer had the Diggers come in the time he'd been sleeping here? How long did they have left now? A day? Two?

Stopmouth sagged and allowed her to take the light from him. He looked back to where he'd been searching. 'Hiresh had many days left in him,' he said. Ritual words used for those who'd given freely of their flesh. They didn't feel right here amidst so much wasted food. He watched Jagadamba moving away from him, allowing the dark to wrap him in its embrace for a few heartbeats more. Then he followed the bobbing light.

In the dark, one corridor looked much like another and Stopmouth still had no idea how his old guide found her way.

They passed very few bodies now. Most people must have escaped the final collapse. Otherwise the Downstairs would not have been so crowded. He wondered what terrible thing had happened here. Sometimes, when he trailed his hands along the walls, he could feel more of the tiny holes that had pocked parts of the stairwell. It was as if something was eating this place one tiny morsel at a time, the way the insects gorged themselves on moss back home. What if this . . . this *Emptiness*, as they called it, came to the Downstairs too? Where would all the people flee to then? He shuddered. He had no way of counting the Roofdwellers, but he knew the surface couldn't support so many.

They came to a small passage, indistinguishable from any other the hunter had seen. But Jagadamba knew it. She turned to her companion, a triumphant smile on her face. She crouched down and touched her famous left hand to a spot on the floor. A green glow formed around it and a panel slid open. Below were the first lights, other than Jagadamba's, that Stopmouth had seen since the stairwell. Two straight sticks of metal stood parallel to each other, joined together by smaller bars. Jagadamba quenched her light and used the bars to climb down into the hole. The hunter followed, his heart beating with excitement.

It was a long trip to the bottom, with Jagadamba's hoarse breathing increasing in tempo all the way down the height of twenty men. The air warmed the lower they climbed, and Stopmouth could feel his armpits growing sticky.

A committee was waiting for them – two old men and a crone. One of the men was practically naked, his bony body painted in swirls, while robes covered the other from head to foot. The woman looked strangest of all: her skin hung in wattles at her neck, and one eye rolled towards the ceiling every now and again, seemingly of its own accord. The other blinked rapidly as though it were trying to send Stopmouth a signal of some kind.

Their faces glowed in the light of a tiny sphere that Stopmouth recognized with relief: a Talker.

The woman with the fluttering eyelid followed his gaze. 'It doesn't work perfectly, for some reason – the translator.' Then she gave a slight smile. 'A bit like myself.'

He'd never heard of a broken Talker before, but nor was he very interested. 'My wife . . .'

'She is well, but . . . exhausted. She is sleeping.' Was

there a hint of pity in her tone? 'I will take you through to the back room in a moment. We are glad to have you here – she might listen to you!'

'Why? What's wrong?'

'She came to us for help when first she escaped from the surface. You understand, my kind – the Religious – we did not like her, but the Commission wanted to catch her and we were happy to spite those sinners in any way we could. Even to the extent of protecting *the Witch* . . .' She patted the hunter's shoulder to take the sting out of her words, to show that she herself did not mean them. 'But we did not bargain for how . . . how fierce they would be in their pursuit, how unrelenting. And as Indrani became increasingly vulnerable—'

'Vulnerable?'

She looked at him strangely, and opened her mouth as if to speak; then closed it once more before finally saying, 'We'll get to that.' She patted him again. 'In the end, the only place the Commission could not find Indrani was here in the heart of the Emptiness. It is quiet Upstairs. It is safe. The gods guard us as machines cannot . . . But your wife insists on leaving now, and you must persuade her to stay. Do you understand, young man? We can no longer protect her Downstairs. Here! Take this Talker. It will help when you see her.'

Stopmouth had no intention of staying in the Roof, let

alone the Upstairs! Nor would he need a Talker to look at Indrani's lovely face, to feel her warm body in his arms. But he had no desire to waste time in arguments, and accepted the little sphere.

'It's . . . it's hot,' he said.

'Yes,' the woman agreed. 'And don't be surprised if it fails to translate for you sometimes. Now, come. But step quietly.' She took the hunter by the hand and led him through a metal door into what appeared to be the only other room.

His heart was hammering in his chest. Pallets lay on the floor. Indrani was sleeping on one of them, and his breath caught to see her.

How had he allowed this woman to leave him? Her features seemed so delicate in the low light, eyelashes as fine as the wings of a mossbeast, hair so black that he thought he might fall into it, longing to lose himself there. Above all, he noticed her skin, having somehow forgotten the smoothness of it as it swept in sweet curves around her body. Stopmouth approached, forgetting the old lady who still stood beside him. He lay down at an angle to his woman, supporting his head on his arms, dying to kiss her, but afraid to spoil the perfection of the moment.

She stirred. Or rather, something stirred beside her. A tiny hand, clutching and unclutching from the depths of what the hunter had assumed was a pile of clothing. A baby?

Indrani had always gathered children to her. When a small group of Religious had been expelled to the surface, she was the one who'd collected up the orphans and tried to keep them safe. In a way, Stopmouth was another of those she'd adopted, falling for him (or so she'd said) when he'd been helpless and vulnerable.

The baby had woken up, but it didn't cry. Instead, it looked over at Stopmouth, and its face— The hunter gasped. He suddenly realized that since coming to the Roof he'd never seen anybody with the light-coloured skin that everybody had in Man-Ways. Except this baby.

The tiny thing yawned and went back to sleep.

The old woman was still behind him. 'Indrani?' she said. 'You have a visitor.'

Indrani blinked awake and cried out. She sat up for a moment, hands over her face. Plenty of time for Stopmouth to remember the occasions when she'd feared the savagery he represented; when she'd rejected him. And did she even recognize him now, with his change of colouring?

She threw herself on him, her skin cool against his, both of them laughing and crying and kissing – she whispering a stream of endearments against his cheek, interspersed with his name. The Talker fell unnoticed to the ground. Behind them, he heard the old woman quietly leave. They kissed some more, passionately now, until the baby awoke with a cry.

Indrani pushed herself away, her face suddenly grave. She shushed the baby, rocking it gently until it calmed. Then she brought it over to him.

'This' – she swallowed – 'is Flamehair.'

Stopmouth's first thought was that this baby (whose hair was almost as dark as Indrani's!) was far too young to have a name. The tribe decided such things, not parents. Then the significance of what it was called hit him hard, so that he gasped. His mother had been Flamehair too. Indrani had picked a name from his family.

He reached out a hand, trembling, to the little girl. 'I have . . . I have a daughter?' The signs had been there before Indrani had left for the Roof – all the signs. How could he not have spotted that his woman was pregnant? Had she been bigger towards the end? He was so ignorant he didn't even know for sure when a women would start to 'show', as the wives called it. It just seemed . . . Well, surely it all took longer than the short time they'd had together. For a baby to grow.

Indrani looked at the floor, not at him. She didn't say a word in answer to his question.

'What's wrong?' he asked. Then it hit him. A cold hand gripped his stomach and squeezed. 'Oh ancestors,' he gasped. 'No . . . Please no. Indrani, tell me it isn't true. Indrani . . . ?'

Once, before he'd rescued her from his brother,

Wallbreaker, she'd almost succeeded in killing herself. She had never fully explained why, but the implication had always been that his brother had forced himself on her.

He tried to pull away, but Indrani held him firm, her face fierce in the Talker's light. 'Yes,' she said. 'Yes, this beautiful little girl has your monstrous brother for a father.'

'I can't . . . I need to—'

'But it's not her fault and it's not mine, you hear me? You hear me, Stopmouth?'

It was too much. It was too sudden. Indrani spoke the truth, of course. She hated Wallbreaker even more than he did. But Stopmouth was like a pot hung too near to the fire, boiling over with hatred and anger and longing and he didn't know what else.

The baby cried again, and eventually Indrani had to let him go in order to shush it. For just a moment he hated it . . . her. And Indrani too. It was wrong – the ancestors knew how wrong it was. He was breathing hard, trembling, his nails digging into his palms. He saw an image of his own mother in his mind's eye. She was looking at this new baby with total love. He could hear her utter the traditional saying: 'The Tribe continues! May she bring us Home!' He blinked away tears, wanting to go back to the surface now more than anything. But he already knew what the ancestors were trying to tell him: this baby was his mother's grandchild. It was Tribe. He would keep it and feed it. He'd see it named and maybe even live to see it jump the fire with a husband.

But he could not love it: Wallbreaker's child and enemy of his heart. He could not.

He felt Indrani's stare against the skin of his back. When next she spoke, it was as if she had read his mind.

'You will come round, poor Stopmouth. And I know you – it won't take all that long. Come . . . Come here.' But Indrani was the one who approached him and put her free arm about his shoulders.

'All this time, dear Stopmouth, all these months, and the only thing I wanted was to have you beside me. I kept dreaming of you – your face when I left you. The gods know it's true, my heart was ripped open. But we're together now, and we will leave together as a family. We have to. I won't find any answers when I can't contact the Roof.'

He closed his eyes, feeling the warmth of her body, until sleep came to carry him away.

# 11. THE MONSTER

A hand shook him out of a vague dream full of mocking laughter. His eyes opened to find Indrani's face close to his. She held the baby scooped up in one arm, worry written across her features.

He started to speak, then shut his mouth at once: Indrani might have been in the Roof for months, but she remembered the hunting signs for *Silence!* and *Danger!*

He held still, allowing his ears to work for him. The snores of old people filled the dark little room. And something else too: a tiny little hiss in the background.

*Up!* signalled Indrani, her free hand jerking. *Up!*

The room smelled of close-packed bodies, with a bitter undercurrent that might have been related to the age of most of the occupants.

*Up!*

He nodded, fully awake now, still searching out the danger that had his woman so worried. Silently she led him to the entrance and pointed at the floor. The hiss was louder here, and so was the bitter tang in the air. A strange smoke was seeping in through a crack near the ground. He bent as if to examine it. Indrani grabbed him by the hair and kept him upright. He bit his lip to avoid crying out, and suppressed the anger the pain had caused him.

She brought her mouth right up to his ear and whispered: 'Don't breathe in that smoke, whatever you do. The enemy are here.' As she spoke, she kept jiggling the baby up and down, afraid no doubt that Wallbreaker's child would give them away.

'They'll have masks on their faces to protect them from the smoke.'

He whispered back, 'We'll take them off, then!' Indrani smiled so brilliantly that he lost his heart to her all over again. But she put one arm on his chest to hold him back from the door. That made sense. If the fumes knocked you out, the men on the other side would be waiting too, assuming their quarry would soon be helpless in the tiny room. The smoke rose to his belly. Already he could feel it tickling his nose and the back of his throat. Its roiling motion reminded him of something – he couldn't quite figure out what.

Stopmouth watched Indrani place the child on one of the high shelves that ringed the room, but the smoke was still rising. He pointed at the door and she nodded, her face determined. They'd fought together before. He could rely on her. Indrani reached through the smoke for the handle and turned it softly. Now he knew what the churning gas reminded him of. The water of the Wetlane that had almost drowned him once upon a time, where pale beasts had fought to pull him under.

'Breathe,' Indrani told him. And so he did as she yanked the door open – a deep, deep breath.

A man and a woman, both dressed in black, fell forward onto the floor. They wore dark masks over their faces, but not for long – Indrani ripped them away and shoved her victims down where they coughed and spat.

The young hunter was already charging past her into the gloom where three other figures waited. They wore uniforms like those of the Wardens, except these ones had bright red lines running up the legs and along the arms. He rammed his fist into the mask of the first. It was made of some soft hide, with clear brittle circles over the eyes that smashed under Stopmouth's knuckles. The man fell back, scrabbling at his face and mewling like a Hairbeast pup before the knife came down. At least Stopmouth wouldn't need the mask any more as the hiss of the sleep-smoke seemed to have halted.

However, the remaining Wardens, a man and another woman, didn't panic, even when Indrani came out of the room to stand beside her man. It had been a long time since the two fugitives had faced such easy odds. And yet Indrani seemed more afraid than ever. It was the child back inside on the shelf, decided Stopmouth; it must be that. She could have handled these two by herself any time.

The male Warden, his voice almost too harsh to be real, said, 'Easy meat for us today.' Both laughed. Foolish and overconfident like Sergeant Tarak had been.

Indrani spat. Then her foot flashed at the woman, aiming for the face. The Warden batted the kick away and drove Indrani backwards with a blur of punches she could barely avoid. These were no muscle-bound slowcoaches like Sergeant Tarak, that was for sure.

But the hunter didn't have much time to be surprised, for his own adversary came after him now, with a shiny knife like the one he'd seen in the blue men's pictures. It criss-crossed the air in front of Stopmouth's face. He could only stumble against the ladder. The knife came again, this time flying past his cheek to slice through a metal rung and embed itself up to the hilt in the wall. The man laughed, and the young hunter realized his attacker had missed on purpose.

In the background, the woman had finally broken through Indrani's guard and rained lazy kicks and punches at whatever part of her enemy's body took her fancy.

'The gas cylinders are empty,' the man said. Then he and his companion both stepped back a pace and removed their masks. The Wardens were young and wore their hair long. Stopmouth's opponent rose above his comrade by a head, his cheeks scarred, possibly by a knife like the one he'd thrown.

Another scar ran right across his throat, a terrible wound that looked as though it should have killed him. He grinned now, his teeth too perfect to be real. Very distinctly he said: 'Activate.'

Stopmouth had heard that word before. Sure enough, in the corner of the room near the empty gas cylinder a fist-sized sphere glowed gently: they had brought a Talker of their own.

'This should be interesting,' said the scarred man. The words sounded cracked and painful in his young throat. He addressed himself to Indrani, keeping a wary eye 'on Stopmouth in case of tricks.

'You've made a mess of my squad, whore. One missing on the surface. Two of my Elite asleep for days, and one crying like a baby over the measly loss of an eye!' He kicked the fallen Warden contemptuously in the ribs. 'Oh, shut up! You can grow a new one when the Crisis is over, but you won't be getting back into the squad, you hear me?' Another kick, hard enough this time to make the man forget about his eye.

'Dharam has decided to let you and your savage live, Indrani. He might even permit you to stay here in the Roof.'

'Dharam?' said Stopmouth, remembering the strange

man who'd visited him in the white room. Everyone ignored him.

In the glow of the Talker, Indrani's face was battered and bleeding. But not seriously, not yet. 'I don't know what information he's after, Krishnan,' she said. She stood straight, like the heroine in an ancestor story, ready to stand over her children no matter what creatures burst through the door. 'And I wouldn't tell you anyway.'

Krishnan spat. 'You'll tell all right.' He looked at Stopmouth now, and the hunter felt chills all over his body. He'd feared the Roof would be full of men like Varaha, but until now he hadn't encountered any. *Elites*, Kubar had called them. No ordinary man could defeat them, and only the arrival of a pack of hungry Fourleggers had saved Stopmouth the last time he'd faced one.

He found himself taking an involuntary step away. His enemy grinned, but there was something other than triumph in the Warden's eyes. *Loathing*, thought Stopmouth. *This Krishnan* hates *me*. The man's scarred face twisted as though the mere sight of a savage made him want to retch.

'The Religious movements are riddled with us,' said Krishnan. 'Only this hole remained secret. But Dharam knows what he's at! He let your' – that look again – 'your *cannibal* run free and pretended to chase him for a bit.' He grinned. 'We always knew where he was, though . . .'

*How?* Stopmouth wondered. *How had they known?* From the first day of his escape from the white room there'd been nobody to tell them where he was except . . . except . . .

'Hiresh?'

He could hardly believe it. His one friend in the Roof. The boy had even volunteered at the end! Or had he?

Krishnan laughed. 'You quite won him over, you know? But he was smart enough to keep doing his job.'

Stopmouth's look of horror must have been obvious, for both Krishnan and his female colleague laughed again.

'Oh, I think, *cannibal*, you'll find the Elites a bit tougher than those Warden amateurs you fought before. They take a few drugs to get bigger muscles and think it makes them one of us! But they cannot twist your head from your neck as *I* will do if your whore doesn't co-operate with me.'

He spoke as if this were a statement of fact, not a boast, and Stopmouth knew enough to believe it. His stomach tightened with fear.

'I don't even know what information you want,' said Indrani.

'Oh, you know.' Krishnan smiled, his scars twisting on his face. 'There's no Roofspace in this hole, but you didn't come straight here – you couldn't have. You'll have had access to your memories before you left the Downstairs, time to find it all out. And when you realized how damaging it was to us, you brought it straight to the Rebels. Isn't that right, whore? They hated you. Why would they take you in if you didn't have something to pay them with?'

Indrani was shaking her head. 'Whatever it was, I didn't find it.'

'I'm not playing with you, Indrani,' said Krishnan. 'I ordered you dead once before. Trust me, if I have to do it myself, I won't slip up. So . . . who else did you tell?'

'Look, I said I—'

He stormed over to her and smacked her across the face. Stopmouth reacted, running at him, but the man sent him back the way he'd come with a twirling kick. Stopmouth found himself bleeding from the nose and clutching the rungs of the ladder for support.

Krishnan was shouting now, his cracked voice seemingly on the verge of collapse, while his comrade stood well clear, looking afraid. 'What did you see, bitch? Who did you tell? What did you see when you took that wrong turn on the *warship*? What?' He was holding her up by a handful of hair and yelling into her face.

'I . . . don't . . . know . . . what you want. I was only on the warship once. I don't remember!'

'Very well, then.' His voice turned cold and he dropped her. 'All right. You don't know. Maybe your savage knows. Your' – that look of horror again – 'your *cannibal*. I'll ask him the questions and keep asking. Feel free to answer on his behalf at any time.' He cracked his knuckles and walked towards Stopmouth.

'What did she see, savage? What did she tell you?'

Stopmouth didn't answer, but pretended to cower away from the scarred man. He didn't need to pretend that much. This was something more terrifying than any beast he'd ever fought: this was another Varaha. People always used to say that no human could ever understand an alien. But he realized that was wrong now. Aliens wanted flesh, that was all. He didn't know what this man wanted; only that he, Stopmouth, couldn't provide it, that his death at hands such as these could serve no purpose except to waste food and bring an end to his tribe.

He waited until he sensed the man reaching for him, then he moved as quickly as he'd ever done in his life. He swung round and punched his adversary in the face, once, twice – hard enough to send him staggering, to crunch teeth. Krishnan howled and spat blood, but, miraculously, he steadied himself enough to start blocking the hunter's attack and, in mere heartbeats, it was Stopmouth who found himself on the floor.

'Loo' at me, shavage,' said Krishnan. His mouth was a ruin of blood and splinters. He grabbed the hunter by the shoulders and lifted him easily from the floor.

'Now,' he whispered. 'Shpeak. Wha' did she tell you?'

He pulled Stopmouth close, as though to embrace him. 'Wha' did she shee?'

He started to squeeze. Stopmouth struggled, but couldn't get free.

'We don't know anything!' screeched Indrani. 'I'd tell you if I did. I swear I would. I swear.'

The embrace only grew tighter.

'I watshh you all your life, shavage. Your people alwaysh dishgusht me.' Stopmouth felt a shudder go through the man's body – almost as though Krishnan were afraid of him, rather than the other way round. It was something to think about, if it weren't for the fact that he was on the verge of being crushed to death. He found he couldn't breathe now. His arms lay trapped at his sides and he fancied he could feel their bones rubbing against his ribs. Krishnan held him as close as any mother would her beloved child. He heard Indrani trying to fight her own opponent in the background and losing.

Somewhere not too distant, the baby had woken on its shelf and was wailing. Indrani begged to be allowed to go to it.

Stopmouth wanted to head-butt the man as he had Sergeant Tarak, but he had no room, his skull pressed against the wall, feeling as if it might burst at any moment, cheek to cheek with his attacker.

'Wha' did she shee, *cannibal*?' The scarred man shuddered again. '*Flesh-eater*?'

Stopmouth's vision turned red and splotchy. He had just enough air for one more sentence, but all that emerged was a growl. Then he did something he could never have imagined possible for any man. He moved his head slightly to the side and sank his teeth right into the throat of a living human being. There was no hesitation, no holding back. He bit down through throat and tendon and windpipe and flesh. He chewed and savaged and drank the screams even before they could be born.

A cry of utter disgust and loathing came from the other side of the room as Krishnan collapsed to the floor. This was followed by a loud *snap*. Indrani had used the horror and the distraction to break her opponent's neck.

Numbly Stopmouth watched her run away from him towards the crying infant next door. He heard her shaky coos of comfort.

He still had blood on his lips. Pieces of flesh in his teeth, and he couldn't close his jaws without feeling them there. It was *wrong* to waste, not to swallow. But he felt more like being sick, like screaming. *What would Wallbreaker think?* he wondered. *I'm even worse than him now.* By his own hands he'd killed another human being – not a brave volunteer, but a strong, healthy hunter. With his teeth he'd done it. What had he become?

Indrani came out of the room with his brother's baby. 'Wipe . . . wipe your mouth,' she said. 'Please? We need to get out of here at once. The woman you came with – all the other old ones will be sleeping for days. We can't take them. They must . . . they must volunteer.'

He nodded, mouth still bloody, and reached for the rungs. She stopped him, though. She led him to one side and sat him down next to the moaning guard that Krishnan had kicked. First she wiped Stopmouth's face, as if *he* was the baby. Then she dressed both of them in uniforms and masks, and this time he knew better than to refuse the boots. The clothing warmed his skin, as though it were a living thing in its own right.

*Krishnan's spirit is trapped in it*, thought Stopmouth with a shudder, but said nothing. He deserved to be haunted.

Indrani secured the defeated guards, tied the infant in a sling on her back and put the Talker in a pouch at her side. Then she tried to lead Stopmouth up what she called a *ladder*.

He shook her off and wandered one last time into the back room.

The strange smoke had drained away by now. None of the sleepers stirred. Jagadamba looked pitifully thin, her hands under her face. What might the Roofpeople do to an old woman like that? They wasted oceans of flesh and killed their fellows at will. They seemed capable of anything.

He threw her over his shoulder in spite of Indrani's objections. He stopped one more time near Krishnan's corpse. He made himself look at it: the stolen life and wasted flesh. He tried to pull the metal knife out of the wall, but it wouldn't come free. Then he followed Indrani up the endless ladder, the mask amplifying the sound of his breath, restricting his view.

Near the top there were other sounds, machinery and voices. Some shouting. They found themselves surrounded by a hundred Wardens of the ordinary type, without the red stripe along the arms and legs of their clothing. All wore masks and carried unlit clubs.

One of them came to the front. His jacket had little patches of coloured cloth stitched to it, almost like tattoos. A chief, then, of some sort, although he seemed nervous of the Elite uniforms Indrani and Stopmouth were wearing.

He took one look at Jagadamba over Stopmouth's shoulders and the blood on his hands.

'You didn't need the backup, then?'

Indrani's voice was harsher than he'd ever heard it. 'What do you think?'

'It's just that Dharam said they were more dangerous than they—'

'Are you questioning the Elite?'

In response, his head shook, almost violently. Indrani was already pushing through the guards, who fell away before her.

'Should we send in a clean-up?' asked the chief. 'Do . . . do you want us to take the baby for you?'

Indrani stopped and turned. 'The boys are still working below. Don't interrupt them. If you hear any screams . . .' She shrugged.

The chief gulped and nodded. Then the fugitives were moving off again, nobody daring to stand in their way.

# 12. THE UNEATEN

In the endless darkness they tripped over uneaten bodies, with only the light cast by the Talker for company. Stopmouth's painful boots gradually loosened as slime rotted them away. His face and body ached with bruises, his stomach rumbled with hunger. And Indrani kept muttering about her need to get back to the Roof, every word perfectly translated by the magic sphere that lit their way. It was all like the old days again. Except for the baby's whimpers and the cold air sneaking through rips in his stolen uniform. None of it sufficed to distract him from what he'd done.

He'd never killed another human being before except to bring mercy. Oh, he'd tried – Varaha came to mind – and had dreamed many times of his own brother's demise.

But now the hunter couldn't close his eyes without seeing the blood spurt from Krishnan's neck. He could still taste it, and sometimes his hands brushed against patches of it crusted on his clothing. It always made him shudder.

After many tenths they came to a door similar to the one through which he'd entered the Upstairs. Indrani pressed some buttons on the adjacent wall, but the only result was a dull voice that made them both jump. '*Authorization required,*' it said, its words translated by the Talker. Stopmouth drew his knife, jerking his head this way and that to peer into the darkness.

'It's just a machine,' said Indrani, and kicked the door. 'A stupid one too or the Virus might have eaten it.'

'I think . . . I think I know what we need to do,' he said. He ignored his wife's surprise and lifted the shivering Jagadamba gently from his shoulder. She was wheezing again as she had when he'd first met her. He suspected the sleeping smoke might have had something to do with that.

He touched her left hand to the cold metal surface. A green glow outlined the gaps between her fingers and the door hummed. It slid open the width of an arm, then jammed on something. It closed and opened several times before coming to rest.

'We have to get out,' said Indrani. She reached her hand through the gap in the door, presumably in search of whatever was blocking it. Scabs and bruises covered her beautiful face. Somehow, they made her look heroic – to overcome so much and still fight on. But she couldn't find any blockage and the door stayed put.

'If we could just get down,' she said, frustration clear in every word. 'I could study my memories in detail, learn what they wanted to steal from me. I finally know where to look. The warship – the—'

'We don't care about that now,' said Stopmouth. 'It's the surface we need to get to! Listen' – he grabbed her arm, more roughly than he intended – 'Hiresh—'

'You mean, the spy?'

Stopmouth shook his head. 'I think he meant to be my friend too. But forget that for now. He asked the Roof how long it would take the Diggers to reach our people down there. Six days, he said. Only six! And that was four days ago now.'

'Are the Diggers really that close?'

'They've crossed the hills,' he said.

'Don't worry,' she whispered. 'I promised I'd find you some weapons.'

'Thank you.' He released his grip. They'd go home together and defeat the Diggers. The baby would just merge into the crowd of other orphans that always surrounded his wife, and she'd be his again without the poisonous shadow of his brother to ruin everything.

'But,' said Indrani, poking one of the nearby bodies with her toe, '*this* is my tribe too, Stopmouth.'

The words made his gut twist. They hadn't embraced properly since she had introduced the baby.

Indrani turned away from him and smacked the door again with sudden rage. 'Oh, by all the gods, we need to get Downstairs!'

Stopmouth had a thought: 'Are there many doors like this around? I mean, wouldn't they know to come here to look for us?'

She stared at him, aghast. 'You're right, Stopmouth. We've been so stupid! We need to get away from here.'

They ran then, seemingly at random, through dark caverns that might once have been parks, Indrani with the baby on her back, Stopmouth with the gurgling Jagadamba. It felt good, leaping over bodies and shards of rotted metal from the ceiling above. The hunter's mind cleared of all memories and all doubts. His whole attention lay focused on staying upright and checking the flickering shadows for ambush.

'Where are we going?' he called to his wife. He saw she was tiring – she wouldn't be as used to this as he was any more, and besides, it couldn't be more than thirty days since she'd given birth! What an amazing woman she was!

'I . . . I don't know . . . I—'

'Stop!' he said. 'Wait!' He wanted so much to hug her, but she was the one to put her arm tentatively around his waist to lean her head against his shoulder.

'Don't . . . don't blame Flamehair,' she whispered, out of breath.

'I'm trying. It's just . . .'

'A shock?'

'Yes,' he said. 'I . . . I hate him. He's not even here,

nowhere near, and I'll never see him again. But if I could get him . . . I'd . . . I'd . . .'

'I know, dear Stopmouth, I know . . . I named her Flame-hair so you could think of her as your mother's grandchild.'

'The Tribe should name her, not the parents.'

'That was your old tribe, Stopmouth. You have new ways now. Any new way you want. Come.' Indrani pulled away from him. 'The exits are at regular intervals. We'll travel to one a few days away if we have to.'

'Won't our enemies expect that too? And they're probably not guarding the high doors anyway. If I were the hunter, I'd just watch exits near the ground. I'd get my prey after they'd exhausted themselves from the journey down.'

Indrani's eyes widened. 'I didn't think of that. We're probably very lucky that door jammed. We'd better sit down and think about it. Come on. The grass here may be dead, but it'll still be softer than one of the corridor floors.'

Stopmouth would have preferred to keep moving – not for fear that anybody would catch them: hunters might stumble around for ever in this enormous place and never find them as long as they stayed away from the exits. It was the cold he feared, this new enemy that sucked the soul-smoke from his body. Poor Jagadamba. He'd wrapped her in the blanket she'd been sleeping in, but still she shivered.

'I wish we could make a fire,' he muttered.

'I bet we could,' she said. 'We're in a park, aren't we?

There'll be dead trees lying about the place. I doubt any of these poor people tried to eat them or even knew enough to burn them to stay warm.'

It proved easier said than done. They found wood quickly enough – old dried-out trees, and plenty of splinters to use as tinder. Getting it to light, however, exhausted Stopmouth and frustrated Indrani, for the baby was crying constantly from the cold. He spun his stick again and again but the smoke was a very long time in coming.

Even after all that, Indrani's gratitude evaporated when he produced a lump of meat he'd collected in the park.

'Where'd you get that?' she demanded.

Stopmouth was saddened that she'd reverted to civilized ways so quickly after her return to the Roof. Worse, though, was a new fear of his own: the thought of eating human flesh brought back memories of the bite he'd taken out of Krishnan's neck. 'Cannibal' the man had called him, as if it was a horrible thing to be. Maybe it was. He had to fight to keep his gorge from rising as he skewered the meat, and it was only when the fire got at it, crisping and bubbling the skin, tickling his nose with that wonderful aroma, that the threat of illness receded in a wash of saliva. His stomach wrenched and spasmed at the thought of food. This was what he'd needed all along to restore his spirits! He'd never felt so hungry in all his life.

He knew it was getting to Indrani too. She'd already lost

the battle between principle and survival once before. Hunger had been victorious. Still, it took many heartbeats of watching him eat before she finally gave in.

'Those poor people have no more use for it,' she said at last. 'And Flamehair needs my strength now.' They supplemented their meal with water from little boxes attached to the uniforms they wore. If there had been any other useful equipment, they'd left it behind on the floor of the hideout.

At last, stretched out in the warmth and sleepy, with Indrani feeding the baby and Jagadamba's shivers gone, Stopmouth said: 'The Religious woman with the twitchy eyes – she told me they couldn't keep you safe Downstairs.'

Indrani nodded. 'A lot of people died trying all the same. I'm sorry for that, but at least down there I had a chance of exploring my memories.'

'You never liked the Religious. I remember that. You called them Rebels.'

'Well, so they were!' Indrani sighed. 'I still dislike what they stand for and . . . and I always suspected they'd killed my father. It's what I'd been told. So it was hard – hard for me to go to them. But . . . I had that same woman arrested once, you know? Ayadara, her name was. Imagine it! A fourteen-year-old in her important uniform, surrounded by her daddy's guards, turning up at your door . . . Yet she didn't send me away when I came back to the Roof needing help, pregnant and alone.

'The Rebels kept me and Flamehair hidden from those who were supposed to be my friends. The ones who had me shot down. Since then . . . since *you*, Stopmouth – since living on the surface I've come to realize that the Religious may be misguided, but my own side, the Commission, is purely evil. What they've done – what *we've* done – to you and your people and all the beasts we exiled there . . . awful things. We . . . we had our nanos alter their body chemistry – did you know that? – so that they could all eat each other. *We* did that. And then we strapped them to couches and sent them below to suffer and die.

'It can never be made right. But it must be ended. It must be. That is the way to protect the tribe, love. Stop the problem at the source.'

Not for the first time, Stopmouth felt moved by her passion. She wasn't one to think of only the next meal. Her plans were never small, never petty. She wanted to change the world, to save it, whether from the frightening Diggers or the Religious. Now she intended to bring down the Commission. The dramatic flame-shadows on her face only seemed to highlight this aspect of her character and reminded him strongly of the time she'd become his woman. 'I'll be gentle,' he'd said, foolishly thinking himself her master. How she'd laughed at that!

'Why are you smiling?' she asked him now.

'Nothing, love, nothing. You were telling me that you

couldn't find the secret even though you had contact with the Roof. I don't understand how that can be.'

'Ah, yes.' She lifted the baby up to her shoulder to burp it. He felt the joy go out of him again. If the baby had been his . . . If it had been anybody else's. Anybody at all.

'A lot of us,' said Indrani, 'probably all of us, use the Roof as our memory.'

'It seems to know everything,' he said.

'Yes, it seems to.'

She smiled again and then spent a few moments encouraging her 'little pet' to expel more wind. The baby obliged a bit too enthusiastically, sending a mouthful of milk back towards its mother.

'Ugh!' She laughed. 'The problem is, Stopmouth, that we grow to depend on the Roof too much and feel we can store as much as we like there. So we do. Imagine, love, if you could see the day you met me again. If you could live every moment of it absolutely perfectly: smell what you smelled; pause to linger at the good bits and fly through the boring parts or the painful parts or any of it at all. Imagine that you could do that with every day of your life. You could go back to when you were a thousand days old and hear what your father said about you or look at him again, examine him in every detail.'

'It would be . . . wonderful,' he said. By mentioning his

father, she'd picked out the biggest hole in his life and shown just how well she knew him. Oh, to see him one more time! To hear the words of advice he must have spoken before the horrible day when he'd decided to volunteer for the glory of his family. 'That is possible here?' he asked. Already he was looking forward to getting back to the Downstairs to try this out. It would be just like spying on the tribe below. He'd close his eyes and think of what he wanted to see until the Roof showed him . . .

Indrani must have seen the look on his face, for she shook her head and reached out for his shoulder. 'Not for you, Stopmouth. Sorry, I didn't mean to get your hopes up. I was just trying to explain what it's like here. If we choose – and most of us do – we can record every day of our lives just like that. We still have our normal memory, but it's so weak in comparison that we rarely use it and it gets even weaker from lack of practice.'

The secret might be something she had glimpsed just once, she explained. A single heartbeat of time hidden among the smells and sights and sounds and tastes of an entire lifetime. That hadn't stopped her trying to find it, of course. Indrani would be fierce, fierce in the hunt! But her hopes of turning up anything had been slim until Krishnan had mentioned 'the warship'.

'But what does this "warship" do?' he asked.

'It kills aliens, Stopmouth. What you call "beasts".'

'Ah! Hiresh spoke about these things. A type of murder machine. You kill them but you don't eat them.'

'Don't be disgusting!' she said, but she smiled sadly as she did so, looking into the fire. Once, before she too had become a savage, she would have meant those words completely. 'The people here believe it is human destiny to control everything. Many advanced beasts – aliens, I should say – dispute this fact. So we need to teach them a lesson from time to time.'

'By killing them?'

'Yes,' she said. 'By killing all of them.'

'And leaving their flesh to rot?'

'We don't eat them. As I said, that's—'

'Disgusting?'

'Yes.'

He added more wood to the fire, wondering if somewhere nearby an Elite was watching them. Even one of them, if he were a bit more careful than Krishnan had been, would have no problem finishing them both off. But nobody wanted them dead. It was Indrani's memories they were after.

'And the warships?'

'Oh, yes ... Well, before the Crisis – I don't really remember that time: I was a baby then, little bigger than Flamehair.'

'In the arms of your mother—'

'Oh, no! My mother died hundreds of years before I was born, so my father and his friends—'

'What? Your mother was dead? Before you were . . . hundreds . . . ?'

Indrani waved it away as unimportant. Things were different in the Roof and that was that. The warship was another matter. Before the Crisis, it seemed, the Roof had built one of the giant killing machines every few hundred days. After that, they flew themselves and fought 'aliens' in the great blackness beyond the Roof. When the Virus appeared, however, it seemed to 'eat' the nanos that built things, and production ground to a halt. All spare capacity was needed just to keep the Roof itself functioning. However, one warship had been near completion when the Crisis struck, and the Commission, fearing alien attack at any moment, had decided that humans would finish the work by hand.

Even with the Roof to guide them, it took years to do what the nanos might have accomplished in days. Apparently Indrani had visited this craft once and once only. That meant she would only have a single day's worth of memories to search now. It would be easy – a matter of sitting down and closing her eyes for a few heartbeats. But she could only do that in the Downstairs. Getting that far would be the hard part.

She sighed. 'Do you really think they'll be watching every exit now?'

'It makes sense. Otherwise they'll have to try and track us in this dark place.'

'If the secret is important enough to them, they'll have the resources to do both. And if we can't use the doors, I don't even know how we're going to get out of here!'

'I might have an idea,' said Stopmouth.

She looked up. 'Really?'

'We need a rope,' he said. 'Where can we get one?'

At that moment Jagadamba's harsh breathing stopped. It had been such a continuous presence since their escape that even the baby woke up and started crying for its lack. Indrani pulled Flamehair away while Stopmouth made sure that the old woman hadn't simply woken up at last. But no. An ear to her chest confirmed that her crotchety heart had finally given up the struggle and her spirit had flown off to join her ancestors.

The hunter shook his head. 'People aren't meant to live so long,' he said. 'But, Jagadamba, you were there when I needed you. We will honour your flesh.'

'We will do no such thing,' said Indrani. 'You know she wouldn't have wanted it, and there are plenty of others around here.'

'Would they have wanted it?' he asked.

'You didn't know them!'

'All the more reason—'

'I said no, Stopmouth! Enough. We have to eat, I accept

that. But you're in my home now, not on the surface. And anyway, look! There is our rope! A lot of the dead Religious around here are wearing *silk* robes that we can tie together. Oh, don't look like that! Yes, it's light, but it'll be stronger than anything you have on the surface! Now, what are we going to do with it?'

'I'll show you!' was all he'd say, knowing it would drive her mad and enjoying the fact. But they had a lot to do, and Indrani was occupied with the baby. So he set to work by himself.

First he took several portions of flesh from a nearby volunteer and put it to smoke over the fire – they might not be able to cook later, and even though they'd only just eaten, his stomach was already demanding more.

*Poor Jagadamba*, he thought. He'd never met anybody so nasty in all his life, and yet he knew he was going to miss her. He thought about cutting off her left hand as she had demanded. But he knew that all the stairwells would be blocked. A pity.

He gathered the type of robe that Indrani called silk. It took him a few goes before he could tell it apart from the other kind. On the surface, he'd grown up with only scraped and cured beast hides for clothing. These silk skins were amazing, though; supple and light, yet so strong.

'Will you just tell me now?' asked Indrani when he'd finally gathered enough of the clothing together.

'I prefer to show you,' he said.

He scattered the fire and hid Jagadamba's body in a niche where he hoped the Elite wouldn't find it and recognize her. Then, by the light of the Talker, he led Indrani to an area where the floor grew rough underfoot with corrosion, and slime could be heard dripping in several places.

'You see,' he said, 'when I was coming from the Downstairs, I saw that there were other floors underneath us – every two levels or so there were doorways, and we came up sixty flights in total.'

'Yes, the *storage* levels, but so what? I heard those areas are in an even bigger mess than here.'

'Well, look at this!' Stopmouth had found what he was looking for – a great, slowly plopping river of slime eating into the floor at the far end of a long corridor. It had probably been flowing here for thousands of days, for it had worn a hole big enough to drop a Globe through. A warm breeze blew in from beneath.

'You're not serious,' said Indrani.

'There's a dead tree against that wall, see? We can tie a free-up knot around it to reclaim the rope after we climb down.'

'And we can do this for every floor? You're sure?'

'The slime is everywhere,' he said.

She smiled, proud of him, and his chest swelled. 'Good,' she said. 'I'm going first.' She raised a finger when he started forward. 'I am, Stopmouth. I'm lighter than you, remember? You get to lower me down. And to mind Flamehair.'

Stopmouth had no chance to protest. A loud *ping* rang against the metal roof of the corridor. Then he heard another, and something zipped past his ear with a sound like the buzzing of a surface insect.

'By the gods!' hissed Indrani. 'Deactivate! Deactivate!'

Their light went out. More pinging sounds whipped and buzzed around them. The darkness was now total. Then Indrani was grabbing his hand and pulling him away, both of them stumbling, the baby crying. He heard a voice shouting from the far end of the corridor, but didn't understand a thing it had said. The noises stopped, but Indrani's tugging hand never lessened its grip. She must have felt an air current from their left, for she suddenly dragged him in that direction, taking more and more turns in an effort to lose those hunting them. How stupid they'd been to keep the Talker alight like that! And who knew what other clues they'd been foolish enough to leave behind them!

Stopmouth heard shouting. Their pursuers couldn't have seen them, but they always seemed to know which were the correct turns to take no matter how much Indrani wove left and right. Any moment now, one of the fugitives would trip on a body – or, worse, fall into a hole, and that would be the end of them.

Forcibly, he stopped Indrani and placed a hand over her mouth to quell her protests. 'Activate,' he said, knowing it would allow him to communicate properly with her.

'It's not the light they're tracking,' he said. 'And with the racket they're making it's not the baby crying either. We've got to fight them. We'll never get away by running.'

The noise got steadily closer in the cramped, echoey corridors they'd been fleeing down. But they still had a few dozen heartbeats before their enemy caught up with them. Stopmouth found a little cross-corridor with a niche halfway down. He persuaded Indrani to leave the baby there. Alone. The little thing started to cry at once and he had to practically drag the poor mother back to the cross-corridor, where the two of them held the ends of the rope and extinguished the light of the Talker.

Right behind the hunter, a little stream of slime rolled down the wall. He realized he was kneeling in it, probably destroying his clothing. Already he could feel the skin of his leg starting to itch.

They heard running feet. Not too many, thank the ancestors, but they'd be strong.

'The baby!' somebody shouted. 'And their uniforms are close. Run, boys! Run! We'll hunt them down like beasts, but keep aiming low! Don't kill the woman!'

The men careered down the corridor in the darkness, the clatter of their boots suddenly thunderous. Stopmouth felt a fierce wrench on the rope and knew the Wardens had fallen in a heap.

He leaped up with the Talker in his hand. He'd had one of the machines on the surface and had learned a few tricks. Like, for example, how to blind an opponent. Keeping his eyes tightly shut, he cried: 'Bright! Brighter than the Roof!' It flared, as it was supposed to, but only for the briefest of moments. Men cursed, but Stopmouth, his stomach tightening, suddenly realized he couldn't understand them any more.

Then he heard Indrani shout; heard an impact as she kicked hard at somebody on the ground. Stopmouth let forth a chilling cry of his own and joined in.

Somebody grabbed at his foot. He knew by the grip that this was no Elite. Still, the man toppled him onto a pair of others. He punched out for all he was worth. His target wore a mask over the eyes. It splintered easily under Stopmouth's fists and he used little shards of it to slash at necks and faces. He kept seeing Krishnan in his mind's eye, kept imagining the blood spouting and hearing screams from all over.

More cries echoed through the darkness. Then he heard footsteps running away. He allowed himself another yell of triumph, then all was quiet again, but for the sounds of his breathing and the baby's whimpers from the niche.

'Indrani?' he called. 'We've done it! We've chased them off. Indrani?'

Only the silence answered him.

'By the ancestors,' he moaned. The men hadn't come for him, of course. They hadn't wanted him at all.

Two of them still lay unconscious on the ground. Stopmouth didn't want to leave them to rot away in the slime, but Indrani mattered more to him than any number of Wardens, so he ran to the end of the corridor until he collided with a wall. He tried to listen for the kidnappers, but all he heard was a wailing cry from back the way he'd come. The baby! He cursed and cursed. His brother's child . . . Indrani's too, and she'd never forgive him if he lost her, no matter what else happened until the end of time.

While tripping over the unconscious men on his way back to Flamehair, he saw that one of them had a faint green light on his face. Stopmouth touched it and found it was the man's mask, similar to the one he'd broken on his other opponent. He pulled it off, ignoring the Warden's groan and the baby's continuous wails, and put it over his own eyes.

Green dots appeared in front of him, the kind he saw sometimes after a blow to the head. He held his hand up and couldn't see it, but his tattered uniform shone before him very clearly indeed, like a spirit. The men on the ground glowed too. Further green shadows, albeit faint ones, drifted somewhere towards the top of his vision. Instinctively he knew they represented his fleeing enemies. He'd heard them, hadn't he? In the last heartbeats before attacking they'd said something about seeing the 'uniforms'

. . . He moved the unconscious men away from the slime before collecting the wailing child.

Stopmouth tried bouncing her as they walked. 'You'll give us away!' he scolded.

She was too young for any food except mother's milk. If he didn't find Indrani, Flamehair would die. He didn't know how he felt about that. Selfish. Despicable. 'You are Tribe,' he said to the little one, to reassure her. Or maybe to reassure himself that he wasn't a monster. 'You are Tribe.'

He came back to the wall he'd run into earlier. The green dots had gone left here, and so did he. What would he do when he caught up with the Wardens? They had some kind of weapon: a powerful sling, perhaps, that threw stones so fast they buzzed as they passed your head. Their aim had been pretty bad, but they hadn't been trying to kill. Not Indrani, anyway. They wouldn't be so gentle when he showed up without her.

He wandered into a huge cavern. A terrible smell filled the air here, like meat that had been overcooked again and again. But that wasn't what stopped him dead.

At the very top, all along the ceiling, were thousands and thousands of tiny lights. They were like the tracklights that surface-dwellers could see on the Roof. Except that these did not march across the sky in orderly lines; rather, they lay scattered at random, as though the ancestors of these people were particularly clumsy in where they lit their campfires. It was a stunning sight. He felt dizzy, his knees weak. Even the baby stopped crying. When he could finally bring himself to look down again and search for the green dots on his mask, he found they were all around him. A light came on, another Talker.

Four Wardens stood in a semicircle before him, their clothing torn and their skin scratched. They'd been in a fight. One of them shifted from leg to leg as though barely able to stand. Two others, a man and a woman, pointed metal tubes at him. *The magic slings*, he thought.

'I warned him,' said the leader. He had little coloured patches of cloth on his uniform that none of the others had. Lines marked his face, and a layer of tiny grey bristles reached all the way down to his Adam's apple. 'I warned Krishnan you'd be a danger even to the likes of him.'

'You were the chief we saw,' said Stopmouth, 'waiting at the top of the ladder?'

A nod, as between peers. 'You may call me Hanuman. I have been a fan since I saw your very first hunt. For that reason I am truly, sincerely honoured to know you. But equally, I would be remiss in my duty if I let you live beyond this point. I'm sorry.'

'What about Indrani?' he asked.

'We've tied her up, but we won't hurt her.' The man grinned. 'She had no such compunction about hurting us, of course.'

The Talker in Hanuman's hand flickered. He glanced at it, puzzled, but the Wardens with the metal tubes raised them and aimed them squarely at Stopmouth's chest.

'And the baby?' asked the hunter. 'Are you going to kill her too?'

Hanuman looked outraged at the question. 'Certainly not! Put it down and step away. Slowly.'

Stopmouth bent to comply. His heart was hammering. The men had him surrounded and he suspected that even if he turned and ran, he'd be lucky not to get one of those magic slingstones in the back. At least they'd promised not to hurt Indrani. But what if they handed her over to the Elite? What then? How could he die here with his woman still in trouble?

The child trembled in his arms, as if responding to his fear. He felt a strange reluctance to put her down.

'There's slime everywhere,' he said. 'Let me find her a dry spot.'

Less than a day ago Krishnan had beaten him half to death, but he felt none of those injuries now. His muscles all but hummed with strength. His flesh did not belong to these people. They were not Tribe and they would not take him without a fight!

Just as he placed Flamehair on the floor, Hanuman's Talker flared once and went out.

The hunter dived forward, hearing a deafening *bang*

that set his ears ringing. Another followed, and another. Then he was among them, just one more green dot. The only difference was that for him, any body he encountered could be safely attacked.

He punched a Warden in what might have been the throat. His opponent fell away with a wheeze, but somebody else caught him by the shoulder, shouting out in triumph. The hunter twisted away from the hand just as one of the strange slings went *bang!* A man screamed and fell.

*Two down!* he thought. But they weren't out of the fight.

A fallen man grabbed Stopmouth's leg, throwing the full weight of his body against it and bending the hunter's ankle until the pain made him cry out. They both hit the floor. Stopmouth kicked back with his other leg and connected with his opponent's face even as two enemies – probably Hanuman and the sling-woman – approached. The newcomers were so close together, their two green dots had merged into one.

The Warden's grip lessened. The hunter pulled his foot free and tried to get up, but the ankle gave way, tumbling him to where the wounded man could grapple with him again, rolling him over into a pool of slime.

The footsteps were now right behind him. When they figured out which dot was Stopmouth, they would shoot. He scooped up a handful of stinging liquid and shoved his fist right into the other man's mouth, as hard and as deep as he could. There was no scream; only horrific, horrified choking. He rolled his victim off him, then pushed the man at the newcomers as hard as he could.

He saw two brief flashes of light, heard two bangs. The body jerked and lay still. The hunter squeezed in beside it, hoping they wouldn't be able to tell his uniform from that of his enemy. He struggled to keep his breathing quiet, almost bursting with the effort.

Hanuman said something; called out what might have been a few names – but with the Talker out of action Stopmouth didn't understand a word of it. There was no reply. Stopmouth felt the body beside him being kicked. Then he heard breathing as the sling-woman bent down to feel the face of the man she'd shot. Even in the dark, it was the easiest thing in the world for the hunter to take the shooting club out of a startled grasp and smack her over the head with it.

'Hanuman?' he called. 'Hanuman?' He listened carefully. He'd hoped to provoke an attack, but the man had already said he knew how dangerous Stopmouth was. The hunter's mask showed the glowing figure of his last enemy moving off a dozen steps before coming to a halt. Did he know the hunter was wounded? Or that he had a super-sling now? Did he perhaps have one himself and was just waiting for Stopmouth to stand up?

*Maybe just as well I can't*, he thought. He pushed one of

the heavy bodies ahead of him as a shield and crawled through stinging slime towards the spot where his last opponent lay in wait. But all he found when he got there was an empty uniform, glowing in the dark. The man had fled. Stopmouth knew he wouldn't be long in coming back with more Wardens. Maybe lots more.

Only one more green dot remained on his mask now. Indrani? Or just her uniform? He heard her terrified voice calling out as he approached. 'Shtop-mouth?'

Only then did he realize how exhausted he was, how unnaturally hungry.

'You'll have to speak Human, love – the Talkers are all dead for some reason.' His own voice seemed far away to him. He picked at the ropes that bound her with clumsy fingers, distracted by his throbbing ankle. Slime had soaked into his clothing and found every scratch on his body. He wanted to wail like Flamehair was doing – a terribly lonely sound. At least they'd be able to find her again in the darkness!

Then he felt Indrani's hands against his cheek. 'To sleeping,' she told him in clumsy Human. It must have been a long time since she'd spoken the language, but her magic worked on him at once.

# 13. THE SHUTTLE

Hiresh opened his eyes. The blurry face in front of him sharpened slowly into features he knew well. 'Tarini?' The sound emerged as more of a gurgle than anything else. He had to spit up onto the floor beside the bed before he could try it again. 'Tarini?'

She beamed at him. Her little eyes sparkled and she grabbed his left hand in both of hers. 'About time you woke up!' she said. 'They've had us in here a whole day.'

'That long?' This was not the Academy, he could be sure of that much. Dense forests decorated the walls, with birds flitting between trees, and insects of every kind buzzing and crawling and burrowing. The whole room glowed with the green of living things, and so it was some moments before he noticed the sheath of the same colour that encased his right arm. A flick to the Roof told him it was a Nurse – nowhere near as valuable as Medicine in that it only healed local wounds. But even then, it was surely too rare to waste on a mere Apprentice. This one looked like it had nearly completed its job. All the swelling had gone down.

Even stranger was the clothing they had given him. It was a uniform. He looked like a Warden.

'Where have you been?' asked Tarini.

Instinct made him check his store of memories in the Roof, but there was nothing to be found there, of course. He'd been out of touch. He'd been . . . and for a moment he found himself back in the cage as jaws the size of his head fixed themselves about his arm. He shook off that nightmare only to dredge up another: an arrogant Elite officer with a damaged voice. The man was congratulating him on the betrayal of his friend. Hiresh sat up, feeling suddenly nauseous. *What have I done? Oh goddess, what have I done?*

'Hiresh, why are you crying?'

'I'm sorry, I'll stop now.'

'That's good, because . . . because I think you're a Warden now and we have an audience.'

He wiped his eyes. 'We do?'

Tarini pointed up to the corner of the room where the foliage of the projected forest had tangled itself into a particularly dense knot. A tiny black box hung there, and Hiresh had to log on to find out what it was. 'A camera?' The Roof refused to spy, so some humans must have spent a very long time producing this clumsy machine for themselves. Or else it was an antique left over from the age of the Deserters.

'I've been trying to rip it down, but I couldn't reach it.'

'For a full day? Why didn't you just make the room grow a ladder?'

She hit him hard on his injured arm, and even with the Nurse there to protect it, he howled in pain.

'Sorry!' cried Tarini. 'I forgot, I'm sorry! I just . . .'

'Why?' he gasped.

'I hate it when you call me stupid. I lashed out.'

'But I didn't call you anything!'

'This room won't obey me. It won't even make a cubicle for a toilet when I ask.' She shrugged. 'And anyway, you enjoy pain.'

Hiresh steadied himself, his arm still throbbing. 'What's that supposed to mean?'

Tarini sat down beside him and reached for his right hand. She shook her head slightly when he hesitated, and he knew that this time she would be as gentle as she was able.

'There,' she said. Through the green sheath a trace of the old scarring could still be seen, although it had mostly healed now. 'You have those cuts everywhere, don't you?'

He tried to pull his hand away, but she wouldn't let him. 'I used to wonder how you could stand it; how you'd even lived through it. But then I remembered a girl from back in Canyon Sector before the Rebellion who used to slice herself all the time. Once or twice a night at least. Why do it if she didn't like it?'

She had Hiresh's sore arm in her grip and must have felt

the tremble that ran through his whole body. It would be agony to pull away. Otherwise he would have been out of the door already.

'I didn't enjoy it,' he whispered. 'All right?'

It had taken months of cutting himself while everyone slept to get rid of the tattoos. Of course it should have hurt, and yet somehow it hadn't. But nor was it exactly a pleasure, just a feeling of . . . relief. That was it. Relief. He couldn't explain that to her; would never be able to explain it to anybody and wasn't even sure he understood it himself. During the day there was the tiny apartment. And around that, for kilometres in every direction, nothing but Children of the Goddess. Just warriors bulking up on the rations that belonged to their wives and children. The starving boys and girls who should have understood more than anybody simply hated Hiresh for his traitorous words. He couldn't bear it, couldn't stand the sight of his mother fading, fading before his eyes, and nobody to talk to and nothing to look forward to but that hour of the night when he dreamed of his escape and cut the holy art out of his skin one millimetre at a time.

Yes, it was a relief, but not one he would ever make sense of.

Hiresh felt the tears coming back. 'Let's just get out of here,' he said.

'There are Wardens guarding the door.'

'Wardens?' He had kept his part of the deal as far as the authorities knew. By now, the hunter and his woman would be in captivity and there should be no more call for Wardens on the door or ancient cameras or anything else. And why had they dressed *him* in a uniform?

He found he was feeling stronger now. He swung his legs over the side of the bed.

'They won't let us go,' said Tarini. 'I've already tried to get to the Academy to collect a few things, but they kept me here.' She smiled. 'I would have come back, you know. I wanted to see you. But I don't like anybody closing me in. Sooner or later there'll be another one of those quakes, and when the Wardens trip over their own big feet, I'll run out of the door between them.'

He nodded, remembering the quake in the Plaza of the Abandoned, and the blood on his face after one of the statues had crushed some people.

'We've had two in this sector since you left,' she said. 'That's a lot, isn't it? It used to be about one a year.'

Hiresh didn't want to think about that. 'You're right, Tarini. I don't like that camera thing spying on us. I'm sick of it.'

He stood up, feeling good now, feeling normal. He waved the door open. The Roof would always let people out of any room it controlled, but not necessarily *in*. There could be privacy, but prisons had to be manufactured by hand.

The Roar flooded in, along with the usual smells of a vibrant humanity. How he'd missed it! Normality. Home. Sure enough, two female Wardens waited just outside the door with their visors up. Both had perfect features, but without Medicine they'd been ageing for years now, and parts of their faces and bodies had begun to sag. The effect was subtle, but it looked to Hiresh almost as though they were melting.

'You're supposed to stay in there, Sergeant,' said the taller of the two, her voice gruff and certain.

*Sergeant?* Was it really true that he was a Warden now? Why else had they dressed him in the uniform?

People were stopping to look. A few must have noticed the Nurse on his arm, for they were pointing and whispering, nudging each other.

'An important visitor is coming to see you as soon as you're up and ready.'

'He's up now,' said Tarini.

'I am,' said Hiresh. 'But if somebody's coming to see me, I'll just go back into the room and wait, shall I?'

That wasn't the message he transmitted to Tarini.

Even as the guards started nodding, the two youngsters ducked between them and disappeared into the crowd. It was easy, far too easy, and Hiresh was amazed that those two idiots had been able to stop Tarini getting out. Unless she hadn't really been trying, of course.

And now they ran, as they had done so many times before, ducking and sliding. Spinning around old ladies, finding some gaps and making others. Whooping and transmitting insults to one another. All the horrors of the last few days got tangled up in the crowd and left behind. Hiresh wouldn't think about his betrayal or his mother or a hundred and one other things. He was escaping.

He struggled through a thicket of angry men even as Tarini pulled ahead of him on the right, but she had a religious procession to cope with – the twirling, unpredictable movements of the dancers would slow her enough to give him the lead . . . Not that they had set a destination of any kind, or a finishing line.

He laughed, knowing his friend well. She liked it this way. She'd announce victory just as soon as she was ahead and starting to tire.

But that wouldn't be for a while yet. They'd been cooped up, and energy flowed in him like he'd never felt before.

For a few minutes a gang of small boys started trailing after him, trying to keep up. Some clumsy parents hunted them down. He grinned, between deep, deep breaths.

A transmission from Tarini: *Wardens up ahead.*

*Turn right for the next shuttle station*, he sent. *If we can get into a car, the Roof won't tell them where we're going.*

*Don't you want to meet your important visitor?*

*I already* had *my important visitor.*

Hiresh saw her stumble before gathering herself again. He loved to embarrass her. But the truth was, he felt sure that any new visitor would just want to talk to him about Stopmouth, maybe to congratulate him some more. Or to gloat a little.

At the end of the corridor he could see a few Wardens coming his way. A little tickling sensation in his mind told him they were trying to contact him, but he shut that off right away. Instead, he and Tarini ran down the ramp to the shuttle station, and although it was as crowded as anywhere else, he simply had to shout, 'I'm a Warden and I'm taking the next car!'

The uniform, as well as the Nurse and his sense of urgency, was all the proof anybody seemed to need. He and Tarini jumped into the car and sent it tearing down the vacuum tunnels towards the far side of the Roof.

They lay on the floor, panting and laughing, too tired to order up seats for themselves. A deep throb of pain pulsed into Hiresh's arm with each beat of his heart. But he felt . . . wonderful. Happy.

'It's better . . .' managed Tarini, 'when somebody chases . . .'

He nodded and allowed his eyes to rest on the tunnel lights that had already turned into a single bright blur with the speed of the car. They lay like that together and he became aware that their shoulders were touching. The normally flighty Tarini seemed content with that, and so, Hiresh realized, was he. Not that it meant anything.

A few more minutes passed and a strange sensation began in his tummy. He sat up, staring at the light outside. 'We're slowing down,' he said, and cursed. Somehow the Wardens had found a way to track their car. But that wasn't it, because all at once the lights outside extinguished themselves, and Tarini shouted something – something that he couldn't understand but knew must mean 'quake'. The shuttle didn't shake with anything like the violence he remembered from the Plaza of the Abandoned, but they were in total darkness now. That made it all the more terrifying.

Tarini's hand found his. He heard her fast, frightened breathing near his ear. She even let a little sob escape – something she was sure to deny later.

They waited. The last quake had lasted only a few minutes, so it wouldn't be long.

*I'll count up to a hundred and it will be over.*

Hiresh was wrong about that. And wrong the next few times too. It was now warm in the shuttle, far too warm. The air circulation had stopped working and soon, he knew, it would become hard to breathe. A little after that, impossible.

Tarini whispered something he couldn't understand, but

it sounded like 'afraid' in his language. He pulled her closer, terrified himself. She whispered something else, and the next thing he felt was her breath on his face, and then her lips against his – not forceful or desperate, not Tarini-like in any way at all. They were soft and full. Her hand stroked his face. And he kissed her back.

His heart still thudded in his chest, but whether through elation at the kiss or fear of their approaching deaths he didn't know. His fingers traced the line of her shoulder, and then, with more daring, slid downwards to lie on her hip. In the blackness it felt as if he were seeing her through his hands. He'd never noticed before how firm her legs were, never seen how sweetly arched was the base of her spine.

'Tarini,' he said.

He felt her lips smile against his, and then the lights came on and, as if nothing had happened, the car started to move again.

Both of them jumped, and Tarini looked around like a trapped animal.

'Embarrassed?' he asked.

'Of course I'm not embarrassed!'

'Of course not,' he said, smiling.

'Anyway, Hiresh, that was the first time you ever got a kiss.'

'No – no it wasn't!'

'Don't worry. It was my first time too.' She shrugged. 'With a boy anyway.'

Hiresh jumped to his feet. 'Tarini!'

She burst out laughing, though about what he couldn't tell. 'By the gods, Hiresh, you'd swear you were a Religious! And what difference does it make? I prefer you.'

He calmed himself, or tried to. 'Thank you. I prefer you too.'

Her grin gave him an awful urge to kiss her again. She stopped him with a finger to the chest. 'You'll have to go back,' she said gruffly. 'To meet your visitor.'

He swallowed and nodded, but when he reached for her hand, she beamed. 'I'm not Purami, you know.'

'I'm not Chakrapani.'

'Gods curse them both!' she said.

'Gods curse them and take them!'

# 14. DAY FIVE

Stopmouth's skin burned and itched. His head rang and his ankle throbbed even through fitful fragments of dream-sleep and the type of ominous messages sent by ancestors that were meant to save your life, but were always forgotten by morning. The burning increased as his body rested until finally it drove him into wakefulness.

He opened his eyes and closed them at once, crying out in fear.

A giant burning Globe hung in the air above him. It shone brighter than the scalding Roof had ever done, fusing itself to his eyeballs so that even when he covered them with his arm, the sphere still danced and mocked in his vision.

'Shtop-mouth! Shtop-mouth!' he heard from right beside him. Indrani was there with Wallbreaker's child. Now that all the Talkers were broken, and the Roof too – at least in the Upstairs – it was hard to understand her. 'Is good, Shtop-mouth. Not to . . . Not to running.'

Dots danced behind his eyelids for hundreds of panicked heartbeats. He had never seen anything so terrifying, he thought. But Indrani stayed with him and spoke calmly in her poor Human. When next he dared open his eyes, he shielded them.

'We name this . . . *sun*, Shtop-mouth. *Sun*. Window in Roof let us to see it. Is good, yes?'

The ceiling around the burning Globe had turned blue. No sign remained of the previous evening's random tracklights. It felt terribly strange to have just one single burning light instead of a luminous, sheltering Roof, but not wrong. It didn't feel wrong to him.

All around him lay a scene of utter devastation, beautifully lit by the glaring . . . *sun*. Bodies, hundreds of bodies, cooking in the heat for thousands of paces in every direction. Many lay half dissolved in puddles of slime, and it seemed to Stopmouth as if they'd been slowly sinking into the floor. It explained the cloying smell he'd noticed the previous night. Behind him were the corpses of the two men he'd killed or caused to be killed. The sight stirred his stomach into a rage of hunger. But the bodies reminded him of something else too, something horrific.

'Oh ancestors,' he whispered. He clutched at Indrani's arm. 'Did we spend a whole night here?'

'Why, Shtop-mou?'

He wanted to be sick. Instead, he tried surging to

266

his knees, but his ankle wouldn't take his whole weight. 'Ancestors, ancestors. Indrani!'

Her face was full of confusion and concern.

'It's the fifth day, Indrani.' Or he thought it was. He couldn't keep track in the Upstairs, and just because the sun made him feel that it was morning didn't make it so. But if it was the fifth day, then his people only had one more left before the Diggers reached them.

'We have to go, we have to get going! Help me – help me up!'

She peeled Stopmouth's fingers away from her arm and set the baby down beside him. Flamehair didn't like it one bit and started crying. The child's soft, delicate skin had turned red where her own little nails had scratched it.

'Where are you going?' he asked Indrani. 'What about the tribe?' Stupid thoughts raced through his head: why had they fallen asleep last night when they needed to be getting back? How had he allowed that to happen? But they'd been exhausted and lost in the dark without the Talker's light to guide them.

Indrani returned with a stick for Stopmouth to use as a crutch. Of course, she was being sensible while he panicked. Then she was binding his ankle with rags from the body of one of the Wardens he'd killed.

'No,' he said, although every heartbeat's delay frustrated him. 'We can't use their clothing. Do you understand?'

She didn't, and was clearly reluctant to take hides from the burned husks of men and women that lay all around. He made her wear the mask to show her the green dots. Curiously it no longer seemed to work. As if the sun had killed it. He flung the device away. So much for the Roofpeople's magic!

In the end, she had to overcome her disgust at the rotted bodies. His ankle prevented him from helping her, but he tried to revive both their spirits by calling out annoying encouragement every time she started gagging. 'Save a bit for me,' he shouted, and was only half joking. His stomach screamed with hunger.

For a distraction, he took the Talker from his belt. It had got covered in slime, and he had to wipe it clean with a piece of old uniform. When Indrani finally returned, sweat was rolling down her face. She dumped an armful of stinking clothing before him.

'Too hot for to wear now,' she said. Stopmouth could only agree.

His hand began to sting. There seemed to be more slime on the Talker. He wiped it off again, and watched in amazement as tiny droplets of it formed on the surface, almost as though the little object were sweating too. Cursing, he threw it away. Then he thought of something else: the broken mask. When he crawled over to the spot where he'd flung it – even though it hadn't landed in a pool of slime –

it was filmed with the stuff. He showed it to Indrani and she shook her head in amazement. This, then, was the alien Virus that seemed to be eating her world.

And still there were more delays. With the Talker dead, they would need torches for the sunless corridors beyond the park. So Indrani had to go back out in search of wood to make a fire.

Once her back was turned Stopmouth crawled to where the dead Wardens waited, praying the meat hadn't spoiled yet in the heat. He took a knife from the woman's belt. His stomach was cramping with a hunger so bad that, in spite of what had happened with Krishnan, he went straight for her liver and gobbled the whole thing down raw. He chased it down with a full container of water from the volunteer's belt. What was wrong with him? He felt so strange. And he was still hungry! He ate as much as he could before Indrani came back, and stored a good bit more in a pouch.

Finally they were able to turn their backs on the sun and set off for the dark corridors beyond, each bundled up in stolen clothing. Even better, they had the rope the Wardens had used to bind Indrani, which was far stronger and lighter than even the one Stopmouth had made of silk.

While they walked, they played a game dating right back to the last time he'd crippled himself. That was when they'd first met. He'd managed to get his legs crushed, and but for Indrani's nursing and her ingenuity in making his legs heal straight, he'd have been dead a long time ago.

While he lay in his sick bed, he taught her words of Human, getting her to repeat them again and again. He'd never met anybody who couldn't speak before, and her pronunciation was so bad that in her presence his own stutter would almost disappear. It was magic, purest magic. She had healed him in every way, and they'd laughed so much that even though she was supposed to be his brother's wife, they caused a scandal throughout Man-Ways.

Now, with the baby sleeping, it was as if the shadow of his brother had disappeared again from their lives. Stopmouth tested Indrani on her vocabulary: *hand, ankle . . . baby, smell . . . nappy, awful.*

This time, however, the word game was different. Indrani tested him too. Because they were now in *her* world, not his, and all around them lay objects for which Human had no expression. Flickering torchlight revealed pictures of men and women relaxing on *couches*, staring into *books*. 'Is good,' Indrani muttered, fascinated. 'Is good good.'

'Very good,' he corrected her.

Other frescoes showing great beasts straining against ropes got her even more excited: 'Look, Shtop-mouth! Look, is more very good! *Wheels!* You see? For *you* good!'

All he saw was circles, and no matter how many times she rolled her hand, he could only shrug and smile. So she abandoned him against a wall and started lobbing little bits

270

of wood at him, until his pathetic attempts to hop out of the way had them both laughing helplessly. Even the baby woke to smile and coo.

But Stopmouth was always aware of the passing time and never fully relaxed until the torchlight revealed a room full of stone pillars with streams of slime cutting holes into the floor. If they were lucky, they could follow it all – or most of – the way to the Downstairs.

'We'll tie the rope around one of these columns,' he said. 'And I'll lower you down.'

'How . . . ?' she asked. 'How you to come?' She pointed into the hole.

'I can do it,' he said, hoping it was true. 'I'm just not sure I could climb back up if I found the rope wasn't long enough.'

'Is good,' she said.

Like all his people, Stopmouth was an expert handler of ropes. Most, however, were made of hide or bark, and no matter how often the women chewed to soften them, none could ever approach the suppleness of the one he'd taken from the Wardens.

'Please, ancestors,' he prayed, 'just let it be as strong as I think it is!' His injury shamed him. He should have been the one going down there, not his wife.

Before anything else, he dropped the torch into the hole. It found the floor easily enough, no more than four times the height of a man down. A few shadowy objects that Indrani referred to as *crates* – no threat, she said – lay just inside the circle of flickering light beside a small pool of slime. Other than that, they saw nothing.

He anchored the rope around one of the pillars. Then he made a large loop for his woman to sit in while he and the baby stayed above in the blackness. Wallbreaker had been terrified of the dark, but his child took it well enough. Stopmouth could hear her cooing beside him and see the little kicks of her feet from underneath Jagadamba's blanket. *She was such a pretty child*, he thought. It shouldn't have made him sad, but it did.

'Is good!' he heard Indrani call as she reached the floor.

'*It's* good!' he shouted back at her, and heard her snort. But he felt nervous for her. She had instructions to take the torch and look for a way out or for another break in the floor – with any luck the same streams of slime would just keep on going down. In any case, the important thing was not to land themselves in a dead end.

He heard Indrani cry out: 'Oh!' He crawled desperately to the hole and craned over the edge, looking for the glow of the torch. It appeared almost immediately, Indrani's face grinning up at him.

'Is good, Shtop-mouth,' she called. '*It's* good – it's much *very* good! Come. Flamehair come!' She was practically hopping with excitement.

First Stopmouth lowered the warm little bundle into her mother's arms. He followed down, still a bit awkward with his ankle, but much less so than he should have been. *Mustn't have been as serious as it felt!* When he got to the bottom and tugged to loosen the knot, Indrani kissed him, making him feel as happy as she looked.

'You're covered in slime!' he said. She'd made efforts to wipe herself off – though it must have stung pretty badly.

'Let's clean you up first,' he said. 'Come on, we'll use one of the spare robes. We'll—'

This brought a frustrated response.

'No good,' she said. 'No good, you see.'

It felt even colder here than it had up above. The torch flickered dangerously in a current of air from way over on the right where Stopmouth fancied he saw another glow. Indrani dragged him towards it over a floor with no corpses and few pools of slime other than the one immediately beneath the hole. Sure enough, a blue light – many blue lights that seemed to blur and merge and blur again – shone from up ahead. All the while the cold grew stronger.

And here, at last, he saw why Indrani hadn't wanted to clean the slime off. A curtain of the stuff hung between them and the source of the blue glow. It dripped in great blobs, thick as jelly. Indrani was able to part it with her hands, and the hole she made lasted for several heartbeats as it slowly healed. A huge shaft waited on the other side, enormous, sheer walls leaping into blackness, thousands of paces wide. It cut straight through the levels of the Roof, all those stairs he had climbed in the company of Hiresh and Jagadamba. Blue lights shone from it here and there, most of them lower down.

Stopmouth shook his head. 'This is our only way out? A hunter would have to be able to fly to travel through a tunnel like this!'

His wife laughed at that, still delighted with herself.

'Globe,' she said. And he understood.

All his life on the surface, Globes had spied on him and his people. Until the arrival of Indrani nobody had realized that humans rode inside these strange objects, studying the descendants of the hated Deserters, amusing themselves with the savages' adventures.

When Stopmouth enlarged the slime gap and looked carefully across the great pit, he could see that each of the dozen or so blue lights on the far wall shone upon metal eggs that seemed to be embedded in it.

'Here too,' said Indrani, pointing first above her head, then to the left and the right.

'On this wall too, you mean?' he asked. 'We have Globes all around us?' She nodded. 'Well' – Stopmouth ran a finger through the curtain of sludge – 'won't all the ones on this side be damaged by the slime? Like the Talker, I mean. Remember how that stopped working?'

Her shoulders sagged. Of course, she should have thought of that before bringing them down here with their only rope. Or maybe Stopmouth shouldn't have been so eager to loosen the knot! Even if they could lower themselves through the ooze and somehow get into a Globe, it might well stop working and send them all plunging to their deaths. Her desperation to get back to the Downstairs had got the better of her.

'I sorry,' she said, shaking her head in disbelief at what she'd done.

'Don't worry,' he said. 'There'll be another way out.' *Please, ancestors, let that be true!*

After Stopmouth had wiped her dry she made a fresh torch and went exploring while he waited with the baby. Whenever the hole in the slime closed up, he'd open it again with a bit of corroded metal. He wondered what people Downstairs were doing to stop this stuff breaking all their magic toys. Nothing, probably. They'd be lying in the parks, staring into some Dream made for them by the Roof. The same Roof that fed them and clothed them, housed them and fought for them. If it couldn't defend itself against this alien Virus, then how could *they*?

And yet these same useless people now claimed to have a solution to the Crisis. He couldn't believe that, but he had his own tribe to worry about.

The baby started crying. 'Stop that now,' he said. He'd

picked up babies before and knew it might help with this one too. He didn't want to. 'Hush,' he said, looking down at her. 'Hush!' The blue light was strong enough to see her face. His brother's features were written all over it, and he knew that when she grew up, she'd have his dimples, and everybody would fall over themselves to do her bidding, no matter what the consequences.

Stopmouth felt a moment of hatred. But Indrani was in there too, especially in the dark, proud eyes. When they looked up, seeming to focus on him, he felt for a moment that it was his wife's spirit that had conquered in the end and that this child would be courageous and loving; everything his brother only pretended to be.

'Stop crying, little one,' he said, trying to keep his voice gentle. 'You'll be safe with me.'

Through the wall of slime he saw one of the blue lights begin to flicker. He counted fifteen heartbeats before it went out.

'Shtop-mouth? Shtop-mouth?'

'Over here!' he shouted, realizing that the torch must have gone out too. Indrani should still have been able to see the blue light behind him, but some of the *crates* resting in piles blocked her view. Sure enough, she appeared with the useless burned-out stub of a stick in her hand.

'We go now,' she said. 'It's good.'

Stopmouth considered telling her about the blue light

that had died, then shook his head. They'd seen enough to be frightened of. Better to keep their minds on saving the tribe.

Indrani helped him to his feet and gave him his crutch. He hobbled after his wife into the darkness. They passed among towers of wooden crates. Of course, they looked inside a few of them. Often they found sweet little crumbs that indicated the presence of Roofdweller rations at some time in the past. All were empty now, many lying on their sides like cracked bones at the end of a feast.

Without the torch, Indrani kept bashing into things, startling the baby into tears. But soon their eyes detected a flickering light that guided them to a new chamber. A few of the lights here still worked. Slime slid down the walls, and in a few places it even seemed to move sideways from the broken lights towards the ones that were still working. As if it were alive and capable of hunting.

Inside lay row after row of the beast sleeping capsules Stopmouth had seen before.

The occupants had dozens of little hooked limbs. Some horrible event, perhaps the coming of the slime, had woken them. It must have, because holes had been smashed in the clear casing of several capsules from the inside, and a few of the creatures had managed to get an arm out into the air. One had battered its strange square face bloody and still failed to escape. Stopmouth felt sorry for the beast. Some of its blood lay congealed on the outside of the capsule. He rubbed it with a wet finger, but Indrani wouldn't let him bring it to his mouth.

'No! Not good!'

'Flesh is flesh, Indrani. Do you see any other food around here?'

She chewed her lip, as she often did when concentrating. 'Not good,' she said again. 'Like . . . like to eat mossbeast, yes? Make to feel not good.'

'You're saying it's poisonous? Because of the slime, maybe?'

She shrugged, and he knew she just didn't have the words to explain it. He thought back to the last time he'd seen a room like this. He remembered how many of the capsules had been broken open, and how one morsel of flesh from each type of beast had been cut away. As if . . . as if something else had tried to eat them and failed. That poor hungry beast – surely the one he'd fought – had been forced to eat its own kind instead because all other creatures were poison to it – until finally it had discovered Hiresh.

Stopmouth shook his head. He came from a world where every intelligent being fed on every other. The thought that flesh could harm him seemed utterly unbelievable. And yet hadn't Indrani said the beasts had to be changed before they were sent down to the surface, so that they and Stopmouth's tribe could eat each other? For a people that hated cannibalism so much, the Roofdwellers certainly went to enormous lengths just to make it possible. He felt his lip curl in disgust.

They edged around the room where there were fewer pools. Many of the green lights here had stopped working, and faint trails of ooze glistened on the wall beneath them. A few others flickered, and when Stopmouth studied them, he made out tiny perspiration-like beads on their surfaces. The slime was coming from *within*. As though some foul insect had laid eggs inside that were only now beginning to hatch.

A door at the end gave onto another chamber, identical to the first in every way, except for the fact that blue light glared from its exit and a cool breeze froze their cheeks and ruffled their hair. Indrani ran towards it, her husband following along at a quick hobble.

She skidded to a stop. 'Slow,' she warned.

He shaded his eyes with his free hand. The floor extended no more than two body-lengths in front of him. After that there was jagged metal and a hole large enough to dwarf those in the previous rooms. Stopmouth could make out the curve of a Globe through a doorway on the far side of the chasm, bathed in blue light.

It should have been impossible to cross, but somebody must have been there recently, because a slice of metal, half an arm wide and as long as five men, bridged the gap.

'Is much very good luck!' exclaimed Indrani. 'Come!' And with that, she strolled across to the far side while the 'bridge' wobbled and rattled beneath her.

Stopmouth wanted to follow, but didn't think the path was wide enough to hold both himself and his awkward crutch. Besides, one little slip would send him plunging down to . . . He moved to the edge and looked over. He gasped. The whole world seemed to spin around him. Beneath this level, no solid ground waited to catch him. Only a shaft, lit by flickering green lights that grew tinier and fainter the further they dropped away until they all merged into one.

'I can't see the bottom,' he said.

'Come,' said Indrani. She mimed crawling on her hands and knees. 'Like this, come. You must to be quick.'

He nodded, his breathing too fast. 'Of course,' he said. He flung the crutch over to her. As he got down onto his hands and knees, the yawning gap only got closer. He wanted to shut his eyes, but they wouldn't obey. They seemed fascinated by the drop, wondering how long it would take a man to fall and how many green lights he'd have to count before he found the bottom. And maybe there was none. What if he just kept going? Still alive, still screaming until he smashed against the rocks below?

'Shtop-mouth? Come!'

'I am coming.' The metal shook under the weight of a

hand. Then he had two hands on it, drops of sweat from his forehead trickling onto it in front of him. Now his whole body hung above the pit, every muscle trembling, as though he'd run half a day with a squad of Armourbacks chasing him for food.

Stopmouth had been in high places before – the tops of buildings, even guard towers. Once, back before he'd ever met Indrani, he'd contemplated throwing himself off one to prevent his enemies taking his flesh. That fall would have been short, the end quick.

'Shtop-mouth?'

'C-come on,' he said. He'd faced down Yellowmaws and Armourbacks; Diggers, Fourleggers and Skeletons. He'd led a whole tribe into battle. And all for the woman who waited now on the other side of this bridge. He saw she was planning on coming back over to get him. He wouldn't allow that.

'I'm coming,' he told her. He kept his eyes away from the drop and looked instead at the beautiful face he had followed through so much terror before. The face that had saved him from a life in the shadow of a deceiving, self-serving older brother. He smiled at her and she smiled back, full of love.

He crawled towards her, growing in confidence with each step. 'Halfway,' he called. Her smile grew wider.

Suddenly Indrani blinked. Her eyes left his face to look

past his shoulder, and one hand rose to cover her mouth.

Stopmouth felt the 'bridge' shake and move to the right. He fell flat onto his stomach, his head hanging over the edge, staring into the unending depths.

Indrani cried out. Then the 'bridge' was still again and Stopmouth heard a man's voice behind him, speaking only a little louder than the sound of his own panting and the thundering of his heartbeat.

Indrani spoke now, in her own language. The hunter wanted to climb to his knees to see who lay behind them. *Wardens*, he thought. No doubt they were bargaining with his wife again. The hunter's life in exchange for co-operation. Stopmouth hated being a burden, hated to think that they might lose everything over him. And yet the memory of that lurch when the 'bridge' moved . . . He could still feel it in his stomach. He wanted to be sick. He brought his face back onto the freezing surface of the metal. Indrani was still talking to the stranger, but she seemed less worried now.

'Shtop-mouth?'

He looked up, vision blurred, ready to retch, and filled with shame for his weakness.

'He say is good. Not to hunt you if you not to hunt him after. Is good? Shtop-mouth?'

He swallowed, his throat so dry it seemed to have got stuck to itself.

'Wh-who is it?' he whispered.

'Warden. Hanuman.'

He dared a glance over his shoulder and recognized the leader of the guards who'd first ambushed him and Indrani with the strange metal slings. The man looked very different now. He'd replaced his uniform with clothes borrowed from the dead. This Warden was no idiot. He'd underestimated the hunter to begin with, but once he'd learned that Stopmouth and Indrani could use the masks, he'd made sure they wouldn't be able to catch him that way. Then, rather than running deeper into the maze of the Upstairs and losing himself there, he'd turned round and followed his quarry in the traditional way, probably spying on their torches and listening out for the sound of the baby crying.

He must have realized that his only way back to the Downstairs lay with them, yet he'd been too afraid to approach openly until the hunter had made himself vulnerable. Now Hanuman had something to bargain with.

He swallowed when Stopmouth met his gaze. If the Warden toppled his enemy into the abyss he'd have no way across himself.

'All right,' said Stopmouth. 'He c-can come, if that's what he wants.' Somehow he shoved his own terror to the back of his mind. Then, keeping his eyes on Indrani, he resumed his crawl. The 'bridge' felt steadier now than it had before. He realized that Hanuman must be holding onto the other end for him. It gave him the strength to continue. In no time, it seemed, he was lying on his back at his wife's feet, thanking every ancestor he could think of for his safe arrival. He didn't move until Indrani handed him his crutch and told him to stand up. Hanuman was coming; she didn't want him to appear weak.

*And yet I am*, he thought. His throat felt raw. He'd have killed for a full water-skin.

But at last three adults and one baby were on the far side of the chasm.

'We should p-push the bridge down now that he is across,' Stopmouth said.

The Warden objected through Indrani.

'He not want' – she pointed down – 'noise. His friends see he hunt with us, much very bad for him! No noise below!'

Stopmouth shrugged; his wife was already eager to reach the last doorway.

His stomach gave another lurch when he followed her through. In front of them lay an amazing sight: they were standing on a platform inside the giant shaft they'd previously only seen through a curtain of slime. It was fifty man-lengths across and perfectly circular. Looking straight up or down was almost impossible for the hunter. But he hated to show weakness before the Warden, so he embraced his wife and used her support to look out at it. The top of the shaft disappeared into blackness, with only a small number of flickering or fading blue lights to push back the gloom. Except at the very top, where a few of the random tracklights he'd seen in the park lay scattered. He wondered if these too might later be replaced by the rising of a *sun*.

And yet none of this was important. A Globe nestled against the wall right beside them, its metal shell glowing blue. Dozens of others lay along the length of the shaft. A few of them flickered, and Stopmouth felt sure that if he could get up close, he'd see beads of slime oozing out of them. But not this one, thank the ancestors. Indrani disentangled herself from her husband to rub her hand against its surface.

'Is good,' she kept muttering in Human. 'Is very much good.'

Far below, one of the craft moved off from the wall, its colour already dulling as it floated down and away. *Somebody must be flying it*, thought Stopmouth. The fugitives were no longer alone.

Indrani opened the Globe. She reached inside and emerged moments later with rations and a few small bits of equipment. These she kept to herself, one eye suspiciously on Hanuman, who didn't look as if he could have lifted them, let alone run away. Then she divided out the little water boxes, which the men consumed as fast as they got them. Stopmouth's stomach was already growling at him again.

Finally Indrani produced the Globe's Talker and brought it to life.

'At last,' she said, all traces of an accent gone.

'Yes,' said Hanuman to her. 'How lucky, though, that you and I spoke the same language!' He gulped down another box of water. 'The bridge might have been a problem otherwise.'

The three sat in silence after that, feasting on the horrible rations. 'This place is worse than anybody thought,' said the Warden. 'I wouldn't have believed it if I hadn't seen it with my own eyes.' He shivered. 'The Roof will need years to bring it all back to normal again.'

'After you get the Cure?' asked Stopmouth.

'Yes. Well . . . I'm sure we already have it, but it will need testing. It had better be quick, though. That stuff in there, that slime – it's *alive*, I'm sure of it. And it *knows* what it's doing.'

Stopmouth agreed. When he looked back through the two doorways, he thought he spotted movement. But no. The only things he could see in the flickering green light were capsules that seemed to be sinking into the floor. Like the houses in Digger territory back home.

'We have to go,' he said.

'What about me?' asked the Warden. 'Indrani swore you'd help me get back to the Downstairs.'

Stopmouth grunted. 'And then you turn us over to your friends in the Elite?'

'I don't have friends in the Elite.' Hanuman laughed. 'Nobody does. They're practically all dead now anyway. But that's not the point. Just get me back alive and I'll say I found my own way out.'

Stopmouth didn't like it. Once he had trusted every promise made to him as though it were a legend of the tribe. No longer. Especially not with these Roofdwellers who fed off his people's suffering and called it 'fun'.

'I'm going to have to tie you up when we get there,' said Stopmouth. 'For a day, maybe. To give us a head start.'

'About time,' said Hanuman.

Stopmouth didn't know what he meant by that until he turned round and saw two filthy Wardens emerging from the room with the 'bridge'. They carried the dangerous metal slings and had cuts all over their faces. Perhaps these were the ones he and Indrani had ambushed with the rope. Or perhaps they'd found Hanuman later on. It didn't matter. One pointed his weapon at Indrani and one at Stopmouth. Before the hunter could react, Hanuman had rolled to his feet and joined them.

'I wasn't completely lying,' said Hanuman. 'We *did* want you to find a way out for all of us. And you have. Don't get up, savage! I told you we weren't going to under-estimate you again. Now, throw your crutch over the edge of the shaft. Throw it!'

Stopmouth did as he was ordered, seething with anger.

If only he'd crossed the bridge quicker and hadn't been such a coward!

'We were thinking of capturing you too, savage,' continued Hanuman. 'If only to use as leverage to make your wife talk to the Elite. But . . .' He gestured to where Indrani stood with the baby.

'It's not my child,' she said. Despite her mild tone, Stopmouth knew she was furious too. She had believed Hanuman.

'I've seen you feeding it,' said the Warden.

Indrani shook her head emphatically and put the baby down.

'Listen to me,' said Stopmouth. Both the metal slings were pointed at his head now. He knew they could fire faster than any weapon back home, and probably with more force. However, the men might well be bluffing. Every other piece of Roof machinery they'd brought to the Upstairs so far had stopped working, and the same must be true for these. And the men weren't in good condition either. None of them had eaten, being too squeamish to take advantage of the banquet all around them. Their hands shook under the heavy metal of their weapons. No, crippled as he was, he'd call their bluff.

He raised his two hands in the air. 'As you can see, I can't even stand on my own, and my wife—'

Indrani chose that moment to throw the Talker with all

her weight behind it. It knocked one of the sling-men backwards in a spray of blood. The other man fired his weapon in panic, pinging off the floor, buzzing past Stopmouth's ear.

The hunter rolled to one side in time to see Indrani kick Hanuman in the stomach. The sling went off again.

'Don't shoot her!' shouted the winded Hanuman. 'Get the sav—'

Indrani kicked him again, while the Warden who'd been hit with the Talker moaned and clawed at his face. The last man didn't care about orders – he intended to live. He pointed the metal sling at the charging woman, but before he could use it, Stopmouth, crawling in from behind, pulled his legs out from beneath him. His head thunked against the floor.

'But I thought their slings wouldn't work any more!' he said.

His wife ignored him. She marched over to the winded Hanuman and grabbed him by the scruff of the neck. Stopmouth grinned. To think the man had been so keen not to underestimate the hunter!

'You threatened a *baby*?' shouted Indrani. '*My baby?*'

Hanuman didn't have time to answer. Indrani transferred her grip to his ears, then dragged him back through the door and over to the pit.

'No, Indrani!' said Stopmouth. 'Don't do that!'

'Don't do what?' she said, her voice bordering on a sob.

She kicked Hanuman twice, but not as hard as she could have. She pointed across the chasm. 'Get over there,' she said to her victim.

'And have you knock the bridge down after? No thanks . . . I'd rather you just threw me over directly.'

'I *promise* I won't knock away the bridge.' Her voice was filled with fury and Stopmouth wasn't sure that even he believed her, especially after Hanuman had broken a pledge of his own. 'I want you to be far enough away that when we take off, it'll be too late for you to follow us. Otherwise, yes, I accept your kind offer to let me throw you into the pit.'

Hanuman swallowed. Indrani let him go and he crawled across the bridge, much as Stopmouth had done that first time. She kicked the man's comrades until they followed after him. One of them was still bleeding and moaning in pain. *Broken nose*, thought the hunter. *Shock too*. They all looked beaten, but Hanuman still had steel in him, the type born of humiliation that would not let him rest.

'You see?' Indrani growled at them. 'We won't knock the bridge away.'

'But how . . . how can you trust us to stay here?' asked the Warden chief.

'Oh, you'll stay, Warden. We have your *guns* now.'

'You don't even know how to use them.'

She laughed, not pleasantly. 'I've seen your men operating them. Point and pull the little lever, yes?'

His eyes widened, and Stopmouth saw that she'd scored a direct hit.

Indrani gathered up the weapons and the baby. 'We have to leave now,' she said. She nodded in the direction of the Globe. Stopmouth limped towards it, surprised at how quickly his ankle seemed to be healing.

The hunter had been inside one of the flying craft once before. They'd been built so that they could never land on the surface of the world – the closer they got, the harder the surface pushed them away. But that one had crashed after a fight with another of its kind. It was little more than a shell that had fallen over the hunter and trapped him alone inside. He'd made matters worse by pressing some of the little buttons in the cabin; firing weapons, disgorging rotten food.

He hadn't seen any seating on that occasion and he couldn't find any now. He paused, embarrassed.

He felt Indrani coming in behind him. She pressed one of the magic buttons and a ledge unfolded right where he needed it. A niche formed above it too, roughly man-shaped. He jumped when straps slithered out from the walls across his chest and lap.

'I need you to hold Flamehair,' said Indrani.

'I . . . OK, I will.' He reached for his brother's baby, but Indrani didn't hand her over.

She narrowed her eyes, and he realized he'd failed to

keep his reluctance hidden. She was still panting from the exertion of the fight, her muscles tensed. *I'm for it now.* But in the end Indrani just shook her head.

'Look at her, Stopmouth. She's a miracle. Look at her. She should have been *his*. Instead, she can be yours. If you want her. If you think you deserve her.'

'I'll . . . I'll try. I promise, Indrani.'

'No, you don't need to try, my love . . .' She surprised him with a sudden, slow kiss. 'You won't be able to help yourself – it's your special weakness, Stopmouth. You love everyone when you get to know them.'

'That's not true. I hate *him*, I—'

She shook her head sadly. '*I'm* the one who hates him. You only think you do. Now, here. Take her. *Keep* her.'

He nodded. His wife strapped herself in and he clutched the child to himself, feeling the warmth of her against his chest.

'Ready?' she asked.

She didn't wait for his reply. She spoke a word and the whole Globe lurched upwards and back. *We've left the platform*, he thought.

'View,' said Indrani.

The walls of the Globe disappeared. The floor too. Stopmouth's gorge rose and he struggled not to be sick. Beneath his feet lay only an eternal fall away into nothing. He dragged his eyes up. He was hovering in front of the doorway. He could see through to the bridge: Hanuman was already halfway across. Indrani grinned, her eyes pure malice.

'They threatened Flamehair,' was all she said.

A green line arched towards the lintel above the doorway and collapsed the whole ceiling. Stopmouth imagined he could hear screams from the other side.

'You killed them,' he said.

'Wrong. I've trapped them. What else could I do? I promised not to touch the bridge.'

# 15. Seeds

The Globe's view swung round as they sank down into the shaft. Here and there along the great walls, Stopmouth could see areas of rot and eaten metal. Sometimes trails of slime dripped down from a Globe, its luminosity dead, to another that was still to be infected. However, more and more as they sank, they saw strong, healthy walls, and soon they were even flying amongst other Globes. Here at last, Indrani's anger gave way to nervousness.

A voice echoed around them – Stopmouth felt sure it had come from another of the craft.

'*Who are you? What's your authorization to be here? No machinery is allowed from the Upstairs – levels thirty and higher are in technology quarantine!*'

Indrani snarled a reply. 'Your rules don't apply to the Elite, idiot. This is Commission business, and if you tell anybody you saw us, you'll find yourself starring in your own little adventure on the surface. I hope you like the taste of *meat*.'

The voice didn't come back, and Stopmouth saw a nearby Globe darting away from them.

Indrani wiped the sweat from her brow and they sank further.

A floor lay beneath them, covered in small flashing lights. Holes opened in it here and there, and Stopmouth spotted other craft arriving or exiting through them. A yellow light shone beyond. It looked familiar to him, reminded him of . . .

'The Roof!' he said. Or at least the part that he had looked up at during a lifetime on the surface.

'Yes.' Indrani smiled in spite of her nervousness. 'I can talk to it now – can you?'

'What about your secret? Do you have it back yet?'

'Not yet, Stopmouth. I need . . . I just need to get us somewhere quiet so I can concentrate. We're a bit exposed here. All these landing platforms will be occupied by *technicians*.'

And because the Roof was with them again, Stopmouth knew immediately what that meant.

No Religious lived here. The local tribes *worked*, all their efforts given in service to the Wardens in exchange for extra rations. His hands felt damp against Flamehair's skin as they neared the floor.

'Open up,' said Indrani, the same arrogant tone she'd used when challenged by that other Globe. 'Commission business.'

'*We need authorization,*' said a voice. '*And your craft . . .
By the gods! You brought one down from the Upstairs! Are you
mad?*'

'All the more reason not to leave us hanging here,' said
Indrani. The sweat sheened her entire face now. Her body
was sopping with it. 'Let us through or start practising your
spear-fighting skills. I swear—'

'*Permission denied. Please hold – we'll have somebody reel
you in.*'

The whole inside of the Globe began to shake.

'Away!' shouted Indrani.

The vibrations suddenly grew much stronger. The
Globe was trying to move, but some invisible force held it
back.

'Forward emergency thrust! Now back thrust! Back!'

The baby was wailing, and Stopmouth's teeth rattled
together like a pouch full of slingstones. He heard a
screeching sound within the cabin – the *siren*, Indrani called
it – and a groan came from the metal at his back as though
it was about to wrench itself apart.

But it didn't happen. Instead, the force suddenly
released them, and they shot right up into the air while
other Globes swerved in all directions to avoid them. Then
the floor seemed to charge towards them again.

'Fire!' roared Indrani.

A green light burst forth and the metal base of the shaft

exploded around them. Molten pieces trailing flames seemed to fly towards Stopmouth's face, only to rattle thunderously against the invisible metal skin of the craft. Everything shook, and the ever more urgent siren drowned Flamehair's wail of despair. Above them, Stopmouth could see that other Globes were gathering now, hunters around the injured prey.

But a jagged hole had appeared beneath them, haloed in Rooflight. Beyond that, albeit a long way down, lay Stopmouth's home.

The Globe surged towards the gap. *It's not big enough!* thought Stopmouth. But they only gathered speed. The hunter had time to clasp his brother's child to his chest, and then they were through – or almost. A huge *clang* sounded next to his ear. The whole craft shuddered and the external view disappeared, leaving only the terror on Indrani's face across from him, and dozens of winking red lights.

Stopmouth's stomach told him they were spinning and tumbling at great speed. Indrani shouted commands – or maybe they were prayers – until the view flickered back into being. Stopmouth wished it hadn't. They had burst through the Roof into the outside world and it twisted beneath them: hills and buildings all melting together in a horrible blur that quickly grew closer. *Globes aren't supposed to be able to land!* he thought. But at least they'd die on the surface. Their flesh wouldn't be wasted.

A hill rushed towards them, all rock and multi-coloured moss. But before they reached it, a great hand seemed to catch them, and bounced them back up into the sky and high over the giant sparkling Wetlane that Roofdwellers called the *sea*.

Their spinning came to a halt.

They stared at each other, unable to speak. From where he sat Stopmouth could see his wife's shoulders trembling. He wanted to remove the straps to seek comfort in her arms, but didn't know how. In any case, he doubted either of them would be able to stand.

Outside, in the distance, a mountain-sized column of metal joined the Roof to some point deep within the surface of the world. Other columns sparkled with Rooflight very far away.

'How's – how's Flamehair?' Indrani asked.

'She . . . she stopped crying when I was sick on her. I'm sorry.'

Indrani smiled, and then threw her head back and laughed.

'My filthy savage,' she said.

'Why haven't they come after us?' Stopmouth asked.

'I think they tried. I detected an explosion a while back. Our passage might have made the hole even more awkward than it was . . .'

'But we saw others going in and out – can't they make new holes?'

'Hatches,' she said. 'We call them hatches.' She shrugged. 'A break in the Roof is classed as an emergency. Maybe nobody will be going back that way until after repairs have been carried out. But don't worry. There's another shaft just like it on the other side of the planet. They'll be coming for us from there.'

They sat for a while in silence, not even taking the time to clean up the baby. The Roof was a blue glare, while below, in all directions, lay only the sea. The lack of any identifiable details allowed the hunter to forget how high up they were and he began to relax. After a moment, however, he sat up quickly enough to startle Flamehair.

'We're outside,' he said.

Indrani cocked her head.

'I mean, we're not in the Roof any more. We're under it. We have a chance now to get back to the tribe.'

'Oh, Stopmouth.' She shook her head. 'The Commission needs me, remember? And it needs me so badly that it risked a whole squad of its precious Elite. What is your tribe against that? They wouldn't hesitate, not for a second, to kill every one of you.'

He knew it was true, had known it all along.

Indrani touched his arm. 'They won't leave me alone until they have the secret. Maybe I'll even give it to them when I've found out what it is, and they'll let us go. Maybe they're desperate enough to save the whole tribe in exchange. And think what they could give us! Weapons to fight the Diggers, and even better: *seeds*, Stopmouth. Seeds. We could grow our own food. Enough to feed the tribe so that we'd never need to hunt again. They've banned Earth plants from the surface up to now. But *I* could make a deal. All we need now' – she pointed up – 'is to get back inside. Somewhere quiet. And then we win.' Her eyes were bright as she painted a glorious future for everybody. It faded though, and quickly.

'But until then . . .' She swallowed. 'Until then, all we have are two of those funny weapons – *guns*, I think they're called. Sure, we can fire them. But how do we power them up again after? We have no idea, do we?'

'Indrani, the Globe is a weapon. You could fire the green light at the Digger burrows.'

She shook her head sadly. 'You're right, but the Commission won't give us a chance, love. I'm sorry.'

Something flashed far away in the Rooflight; several somethings that resolved themselves into a hunting party of Globes arcing towards them through the air. Stopmouth's heart began thumping again, even as Indrani manoeuvred them from side to side.

It seemed a lifetime ago that he'd first seen Globes fighting amongst themselves, spitting fire or light. At the time, he hadn't known that these were the opening shots of the great Religious Rebellion. Not surprising, really: back then, he'd believed the Roof was the home of the honoured ancestors once they'd volunteered their flesh. If he'd thought about Globes at all, it was to wonder what the meat of these strange flyers might taste like if a man could bring one down and crack open its shell . . . And then one day another firefight had split one apart and sent Indrani to the tribe. To him, really. To him.

So, yes, Globes could destroy each other, but surely not with the holder of the *secret* inside.

Indrani sent them into a dive. A bright light, brighter than the Roof at midday, crisped the air above their heads. A dozen more beams soon followed so that it seemed to Stopmouth that his wife was weaving them through a dense, shining forest, the trunks flashing past, deadly and frightening. Several times his stomach rebelled, until it lay empty as a burst sack and the whole inside of the craft stank.

'But they need you alive!' he said.

She ignored him, brow furrowed, and the truth slowly dawned on the hunter that those who were chasing them now didn't know who their prey was, only that one of their precious craft had been stolen.

The enemy had no trouble keeping up with them: where Indrani ducked and dived, they could come on straight, without fear of retribution. If only he had his sling – something to fire back at them; if only— As if by magic, as if they were once more inside the Roof, his mind provided him with exactly the information he needed: he remembered the time he'd been trapped in the broken Globe, reading the little symbols it contained. There'd been a button with *emergency escape hatch* on it, and pressing this had saved his life. But he'd also seen another button that had puzzled him at the time . . . He reached his hand around now until he found it. Sure enough, it was on his side of the wall, right where a hand would need it to be: rear armament.

He pressed the button and a voice filled the cabin: '*Armed. Locating target.*'

Indrani must have heard the voice too, of course, and for a brief heartbeat she stopped dodging and held them steady.

'There!' Stopmouth pointed. 'Shoot there!'

Their nearest enemy burst open in a shower of flame and debris, but that's all Stopmouth had time to see, because Indrani had started dodging again. The enemy beams were now less accurate than before, for they too were afraid to stay in a straight line for long. Stopmouth kept shouting his own targets to the Globe, but it didn't seem capable of hitting them if they dodged. So the hunter aimed for the places he thought his enemy would move next, and once or twice he came close to catching them.

They were now passing through an area of high pointy hills. Stopmouth saw the top of one of them explode when a beam hit it, and a heartbeat later, a rapid hail of stones clunked off the shell of their Globe.

'I know a place we can go,' said Indrani. 'We're close now, very close . . .'

She didn't elaborate, didn't get time: for just then, four other Globes appeared over the horizon, rushing towards them. They didn't open fire at once, perhaps because they couldn't tell which of the oncoming craft was the stolen one.

'Let's see if this works again,' said Indrani. 'Hold on!' She set her craft into a dive, heading at top speed for a pair of peaks close together. She passed between them and steered for a plain beyond, dotted with a number of ruins. On the surface, a small tribe of beasts seated around camp-fires were looking up at them. But not for long: beams from Indrani's pursuers tore up gouts of soil, flinging the beast encampment into the air.

'We're crashing!' said Stopmouth. 'We're crashing!'

But as before, instead of hurtling into the ground, some invisible force bounced them away and straight up into the air, so that they found themselves right in the midst of enemies so confused they didn't know when to stop firing. At least one of them blew up, while another spun away.

Indrani flew them back up towards the Roof and skimmed along just beneath it. Stopmouth's chest swelled with pride. None of the enemy pilots seemed half as skilled as his wife! He shook them up some more by sending a few beams into their midst. His heart still beat faster than a drum, sweat still blinded him, but, strangely, it was no longer fear that did it.

'I think I could get to like this,' he muttered. Maybe Indrani could teach him to fly! Even the tiny Wetlanes and buildings below had lost any terror they'd had for him. Instead, all he could feel was the glory of the speed. It was more exhilarating than anything he'd ever felt in his life, and for the first time since he'd seen it, he realized why somebody would want to live in a place such as the Roof.

'They're not firing at us any more!' he said.

And indeed Indrani had cut down on her zigzagging. 'You're right,' she replied. 'I should have realized they must be under orders not to damage the Roof – it's nearly impossible to repair these days. They'll probably be happy now just to report where we're going.'

'And where's that?' Was she going to take him home? Stopmouth wondered.

'We're here!'

A round hole appeared in the Roof in front of them and the Globe slotted into it. At once, the straps about their bodies withdrew back into the walls. Both of them sagged, suddenly drained.

'Do you think you can stand?' asked Indrani. 'They'll be reporting where we are and we can't afford to hang about.'

'You'll need to take the baby,' he said.

'Flamehair,' she said.

'Yes, Flamehair . . . Of course. My ankle's nearly strong enough to walk on. I've never healed so fast in my life.'

'Interesting,' said Indrani. 'And are you hungry? I mean, does your appetite seem . . . abnormal to you sometimes?'

He nodded. 'It's because there's no real food to eat here, Indrani. Just rations and' – he made a face – 'rice.'

She smiled at his disgusted face and shook her head. 'Stopmouth, we've been eating smoked flesh for days now. Somebody gave you Medicine. They must have! The last thing you remembered before getting to the Roof was an injury of some kind, right?'

'Yellowmaws,' he said with a shudder. 'I should have died.'

She nodded. 'But they needed you alive so they could follow the Rebels taking you to me. That's good news. Very good. It means that as long as you get plenty of food and water, you'll keep healing quickly. At least for a few days, anyway. Had you been older, like Jagadamba, the Medicine would have used itself up right away in trying to make you younger. But don't rely on it – the nanos are made to die two weeks at the most after you get them. It must be close to that now.' Then she shook her head. 'We'll talk about it another time. We should hurry.'

The hatch opened and they toppled out into a long room of six circular niches, each large enough to hold a

Globe. All the others were empty. The floor of the room was transparent, but this no longer made Stopmouth dizzy – he knew he couldn't fall. Still, every muscle hurt and shook, and he could barely crawl out of the hatch and stand up. He was starving too: hungry enough to eat Roof rations and be thankful for them. The effects of the Medicine Indrani said they'd given him. He shrugged, then reached for his little pack of smoked flesh and stuffed a handful of it into his mouth.

'We're not allowed to park in these places any more,' said Indrani, indicating the room. 'During the Rebellion, the Religious came to bays like this one and captured all the Globes. That's how they started the whole thing.' She shrugged. 'Lucky for us the place is empty. Come on.'

They hurried out of the room into panicked crowds. A siren was sounding somewhere. 'The guards are coming,' said Stopmouth.

It seemed that Indrani had managed to steer them into a Religious area. The people here wore simple robes. The men sometimes had bare upper bodies covered in swirls of paint. The fugitives in their rags and their filth stood out. But they needn't have worried. The crowd split to allow the passage of a gang of young men, their faces angry and determined. Each of them carried a heavy stick or a lump of metal. To Stopmouth's expert eye, they held their weapons awkwardly and ran too closely bunched together to be able to swing them properly. Even so, this was a hunting party, off to feed its tribe.

'Looks like the Rebellion has started up again,' said Indrani. 'Come on. We're here now. We're home and dry.'

Ahead of them, the corridor opened out into one of the ruined, refugee-filled parks. As in many others, the wreckage of a conquered enemy spaceship dangled by cables from the ceiling. A strange light illuminated it from above, and the hunter gasped. 'Look, Indrani! Look, it's another *sun*!'

She laughed and hugged him close. 'There's only one *sun* here, Stopmouth – the same as we saw in the Upstairs. We're in the famous, but unloved, Sunshine Park. They cut a shaft all the way through the upper levels and as far as the sky. Do you see?'

Unloved. He wasn't surprised. The burning ball of light could be frightening as well as hot.

'We'll sit down,' said Indrani. 'Here will be as good as anywhere to log on. Besides, this lot are as miserable as we are and stink almost as badly.'

It was true. Hopeless refugees squatted everywhere in family groups, some asleep, some staring into nowhere as the Roof provided them with the illusion of better lives.

'But what if the Wardens come?'

'They'll think we were stealing the Globe as part of a new Rebellion, maybe. They'll certainly assume it was the

Religious who did it. By the time they work out where it came from and realize it was us . . . Well' – she grinned – 'hopefully they'll assume we weren't stupid enough to hang around so close to it.'

Stopmouth laughed too. They found a place to sit, one little family group amongst thousands of others. Indrani settled back, the baby calm against her chest. His own mind was all awhirl. He wanted to spy on the tribe, to see how close the Diggers were. Yet he didn't like the idea of leaving Indrani so unguarded.

She'd be accessing her memories now. It would be easy, he knew that much, like everything in the Roof. She would close her eyes and think, *I want to relive the day I saw the warship.*

But would she even recognize the secret when she saw it? All he could do was pray to the ancestors that she found what she was looking for and that she could trade it for a way to save the tribe. *Seeds and weapons*, he thought. And all would be well.

# 16. MEMORIES

Only a few hundred heartbeats passed before Indrani's eyes snapped open and she drew in a great gasp of air like a woman who'd been on the point of drowning.

'Indrani?'

She looked at Stopmouth as if he were a stranger, and then at her baby with the same expression.

'What did you see?'

She just shook her head.

'Tell me, Indrani. I'm not saying I'll understand. But tell me. Use one of your magic Roof Dreams if you have to.'

'A magic Roof Dream?'

'Yes, or just . . . just words. Whatever you want.'

'I'm lucky,' she said then. 'Whatever else happens, I've been lucky, and if I believed in the gods I'd thank them. But I'm going to have to protect what's mine. You understand me, husband? Do you?'

'Of . . . of course.'

She took a deep, shaky breath. 'I'll show you then. You'd better . . . You'd better sit.'

He loosened the coils of Wardens' rope around his body and squeezed down beside her in the crowd. He closed his eyes, and jumped as a younger Indrani appeared in his mind. *I need your permission to bring you along*, it said. *Do you agree to my guidance?*

'I do.'

*Don't speak aloud.*

'Sorry!' *I mean, sorry.*

In his mind he saw a metal door, or rather, he knew that Indrani had seen it. These were her memories he was looking through, and the colours she saw were not exactly the same as his.

Indrani's eyes never flicked into the corners looking for ambushes, or up to the ceiling where some strange beast might be hanging. A Roofdweller's eyes were carefree.

*It's how I was then*, she said in his mind. *What had I to fear? Daughter of the previous High Commissioner? Nothing wanted to eat me, dear Stopmouth. Or so I thought. I wasn't supposed to be here on the warship. I was showing off. Showing I could go anywhere I wanted.*

To the left lay another hatch, ajar. Her eyes flickered over it. Then, disconcertingly, that glance replayed itself, but more slowly, until the hatch lay square in the middle of the picture. Stopmouth could see through to the other side, where a row of *bunks* waited for somebody to come and occupy them.

*That's the first clue,* said Indrani. *It should have been enough to tell me what was going on. Beds, Stopmouth. On an automated warship. I thought they were for the workers, and I suppose the workers did get to use them, staying long hours, sworn to secrecy . . . Having seen the beds is probably what made the Commission try to kill me and who knows how many others?*

*I don't understand,* said Stopmouth.

An image of Indrani nodded in his head. *I didn't either. You see, no human in their right mind would want to travel anywhere on a spacecraft – not if you can't make fresh nanos to sustain you. You'd die of old age or boredom or vitamin deficiency long before you got anywhere. Our ancestors made ships so big that they were like towns – a whole society with all that society's entertainments moving together to a new life around some colony world . . . Not some poky little warship. Never that.*

*But my ancestors did it too, didn't they? And in smaller . . . smaller Globes?*

*Yes,* she said. *The Deserters used a different method. They tried to sleep away generations of time in order to get where they were going. And that . . . that is the other thing I found.*

The image moved away from the hatch, and Stopmouth had the impression that Indrani too was moving.

*Before I was shot down over the surface, the Wardens were already using simpler technology to get through the Crisis. Like those* guns *Hanuman's men fired at us in the Upstairs. Non-intelligent machines that the Roof gave us instructions to build. The Virus didn't attack those. But even the manufacture of such simple tools has been an enormous effort for a society unused to work and gripped by the thought that the Crisis must soon come to an end. Now . . . watch this.*

She had moved into a new room full of *chairs*. A table lay before her, and on it what Indrani called 'another simple tool' – a thin roll of hide known as *paper*. Pictures of boxes covered most of it. A few little oblongs reminded him of something.

'Capsules!' he exclaimed out loud. *Sorry. But it's where they keep the sleeping beasts!*

*Exactly.* Her voice in his mind was a whisper. *Somebody is planning on sleeping a long time. Do you see, love? They're planning to leave the Roof. To Desert. And that means . . . can only mean one thing . . .*

He felt a chill settle on his bones, and bile rose into his throat. Outside the dream, his whole body had started to shake as he tried to digest what he had just learned.

*There is no cure for the Virus,* he said, shocked. A few chosen ones would escape on the warship. Everybody else in the Roof – *everybody* – would die. His mind whirled with the thought of it. Sunshine Park alone held more people than he'd ever seen in his entire life before leaving the surface. Pretty girls and toddlers and laughing old men. All of them, all of them gone. Rotting and wasted flesh, the worst obscenity his tribe could imagine, on a scale none of them would ever comprehend. If the people heard about this, they'd turn on the masters, surely. Even the Wardens would. No wonder the Commission needed to keep this secret!

*But why, Indrani?* he said at last. *Why did they want you back here? Why not just have you killed? Varaha could have done it on the surface. They deliberately kept you alive.*

For an answer she brought the paper into focus again and enlarged one tiny part of it, where random numbers and letters jostled together all higgledy-piggledy. *There are just enough uncontaminated nano packs and energy reserves for a few hundred people to launch themselves into space and sleep through the rest of the Crisis*, she said. *Viruses burn themselves out when there's nothing left to feed on.*

*Like people*, he said.

*Yes. Like people.* The numbers and letters stood out sharply now in their shared vision. *I must be the only one left alive with a record of this paper*, said Indrani. *Otherwise, why hunt me? And yet a few others at the very least must have seen it too. I just wish I knew what had happened to them. A Rebel attack? Or purged maybe. Killed like I was supposed to be? Until the Commission realized they'd been too zealous*

313

*and didn't have anybody else who had access to the codes.*

*'And these . . . these numbers are magical?*

She smiled – not a nice smile, not at all. More of a snarl. *Dear Stopmouth. Yes. To the ones who plan to escape, leaving the rest of us to die . . . Yes, these numbers are magic of a sort. They're what we call a 'launch code'. The ship won't fly without it. You understand? The scum are terrified they're going to be stuck here with the rest of us when the end comes.*

# 17. THE GREAT MAN

A pair of augmented Wardens had separated Hiresh from Tarini and each held him firmly right above the elbow. The two men thought they had him trapped, but both were too old to know how to navigate a crowd, and he could see a dozen ways to trip them up and scamper off if he had wanted to. But he'd come a long way with them on a shuttle and it was really his own curiosity that kept him prisoner.

They brought him under a huge dome, so high that its top part might well form a hill in the Upstairs. Fish seemed to be swimming there – projected by the Roof, of course, a whole ocean seen from below – and as Hiresh watched, a massive whale emerged from one side of the dome and floated quietly away.

Nobody else cared. Dreamers could do better just by closing their eyes; worshippers were busy at their cere-monies, their prayers and chants competing with the Roar and the laughter of children. Soon the whale disappeared into a part of the dome where the projectors no longer worked.

'Who are we going to meet?' Hiresh asked his guards. They said nothing, only gripped him tighter until his sore arm had him begging them to ease off.

*These two mean business!* he sent to Tarini. *Where have they got you?*

*Take a look!* She sent him an image of a platform with a great drop on one side and a mountain of packaged food on the other.

*Wow! My mouth is watering . . .*

After the dome, they entered a corridor guarded by a group of at least twenty Wardens. Grim men and women armed with a whole variety of weapons, including a rare and precious laser, surely an antique.

Rumours of rebellion were rife, and images of whole sectors full of fighting were being transmitted from mind to mind all over the Roof. But nobody would be getting past here, and Hiresh wondered what – or even who – was so precious that so many Wardens could be spared to guard it.

They parted to let him and his minders pass. Beyond stood a huge shaft, hundreds of metres across and rising up and up as far as the eye could see. Tunnels converged on the shaft at several levels and from every direction. They all ended in a yawning drop, but that wasn't what captured

Hiresh's attention. Directly across from him lay a giant sphere: the warship! The famous warship that people, ordinary humans, had been building by *hand* ever since the supply of new nanos had dried up.

He tried to show Tarini what he was looking at, but somebody was jamming him now. What a shame! He would have to play it back for her later instead. Thousands of primitive tubes and wires connected the warship to the walls of the shaft, and an army of Globes swarmed between and around them. Great engines hung underneath, and in places people could be seen clinging to the surface and working at goddess knew what.

One of the Globes descended to hang right between the end of the tunnel in which Hiresh now stood and the warship. A door formed in the side.

'You're to get in,' said one of his guards.

'Into the Globe?' He'd never had the opportunity to see one, not in real life, and more than ever he resented the loss of contact with Tarini.

'Hurry up,' said the Warden again, using augmented muscles to give him a far from gentle shove. The Globe's door had turned itself into a handy set of steps for him, but no sooner had he placed his full weight on it than it closed again, dumping him into a seat.

'Strap yourself in,' said a familiar voice.

'By the goddess!' said Hiresh. His stomach told him

they were already beginning to rise, but that wasn't what had taken his breath away.

The High Commissioner's mouth formed into that famous half-smile of his. 'Call me Dharam, Sergeant.'

'Sergeant?' Hiresh had heard that before. But he was just repeating words. Babbling. Why was he here? Out of billions, maybe trillions, who lived in the Roof. Why was *he* here with the High Commissioner? It was impossible, impossible.

'Look at this,' said the man. 'Drink in the sight of it.'

One side of the craft became transparent.

Tiny lights throbbed and flickered in the walls of the shaft, splitting to run around docked Globes, and each of these hung snugly next to the surface, glowing gently blue. In other places, sheets of burnished metal turned whole sections into giant mirrors that reflected their craft as they rose ever higher.

'It's beautiful,' whispered Hiresh. 'The Roof is so beautiful and I forget that sometimes.'

'It's a shame the founders made such a hash of the design then, is it not?'

Hiresh turned away from the wall. The High Commissioner's easy blasphemy had shocked him, although he didn't believe in that kind of stuff any more. At least he wasn't supposed to. 'I don't understand,' he said.

'Keep watching.'

Further up, and many of the Globes were dead. The tiny lights blinked only erratically, and tendrils of slime passed between one machine and the next, not dripping, but . . . but lurching, crawling, easing along in a way that made him sick to his stomach. Dharam flew higher until they reached a point where darkness reigned and only a beam of light from their own craft allowed them to see the glistening film that coated everything.

'It's not like the muck you blow from your Crisis baby nose,' said Dharam, his voice quiet. 'This substance is intelligent enough to know what it wants. More nanos to subvert, to turn into more of itself. That's all it desires. More of itself. Same as the rest of us. And it won't die until it runs out of food.'

'But . . .' said Hiresh. 'But that would mean . . .'

'The whole Roof,' agreed Dharam. 'Well, not the structure of it. The slime – *goo*, we're calling it – it only dissolves metal that gets in its way when searching for food. Just as well, or the whole of the Upstairs might have collapsed on us already and we'd be dead. We'd also be dead if it were interested in us at all. It's not, but you'd do well not to take a bath in it. Its caustic nature would dissolve you eventually.'

Hiresh felt light-headed. *Why me?* he wondered again. Why did he have to hear all this? 'Did the aliens make it intelligent on purpose?'

One side of Dharam's mouth quirked upwards. Was he

319

imagining a hint of respect there? From the most important man in the world?

'You know for certain it was aliens, do you, Sergeant?' said the High Commissioner. 'Don't you think a dozen simple nukes would have been a more logical means of destroying the Roof?' He waited for the boy's uncertain nod before continuing, and when he did, he leaned forward in his seat. 'Sergeant of the Wardens, Hiresh . . . Somebody, some person or persons, made this virus. *Humans* made it. And they had a reason.'

'Humans? That can't be—'

'You see, the Roof treats us all like children. It obeys its own laws and not ours. Thus, when your father so callously began starving your mother—'

Hiresh jumped. 'How did you—?'

'Spies, of course. The Roof would not report such a crime to us, and that in a way is its downfall. And ours too. It keeps the secrets and the privacy of even the monsters who live amongst us, and so, Sergeant Hiresh, you and others like you had to grow up in suffering . . . That's why the temptation is always there to . . . to *meddle* with the workings of the Roof.

'No aliens did this, I am afraid. It's just a story we put out after Indrani's father was murdered. He was investigating a plot. A plot to create nanos that would subvert all others to the commands of a shady group, giving them full control of the Roof. Even I as Commissioner can only dream of such power. But the fools didn't know what they were doing and lost control of their creation.'

'Rebels . . .' whispered Hiresh.

'Of course.' Why was the man grinning so much? 'Who else would dream of it? So clever, so daring a plan. But when the previous High Commissioner found them out, they murdered him, and poor Indrani hasn't been the same since.'

Hiresh nodded. How strange that Dharam should admire the plan so much, almost as though he were proud of the enemy's cunning. But not nearly so strange as the fact that the Commissioner would confide in a mere boy. 'What about the Cure?' he asked. 'You kept saying you had a Cure.'

Dharam nodded. 'Oh, we certainly have. Or we almost do. That's what the whole warship is about, you know? It's not really a ship at all – it can't even fly.'

'It can't? But it has engines!'

Dharam shook his head. 'We needed to make a laboratory. One consisting only of the most primitive machines. Ones we could build ourselves by copying records from the Roof's archives. The goo cannot subvert that kind of stuff . . . And so, when we first spotted the Crisis, we began working on a way to end it. And now, finally . . . finally . . . we are at a point where we can save humanity from total destruction.

'But there is one crucial piece of information we are missing. A technician got herself killed during the Rebellion, and her work, carelessly left lying about, was destroyed.' Dharam leaned across and grabbed Hiresh by the front of his uniform. His eyes stared into those of the boy. 'We don't have time. Do you understand me? Have you seen the quakes? We don't have time to repeat the idiot's research, and only one other person has seen it and might have a record of it in her memories. Only one person can save us all – every man, woman and child on the Roof.'

'In . . . Indrani?'

Dharam released him at once. It was all so clear now why Hiresh had been chosen for this. 'She got away?' he asked. 'And Stopmouth too?'

'A dangerous creature,' said Dharam. 'And I should know, for he attacked me when I interrogated him.'

That did not sound like the Stopmouth Hiresh knew. There must have been some kind of misunderstanding. 'But why did you question him personally?'

'For the same reason I have taken a Globe, filled with delicious nanos, on a little jaunt around these goo-covered walls.'

Hiresh blinked. He had not realized they were in such danger. But they had a long way to fall if the machine they were riding in became infected.

'And,' continued Dharam, 'it's also the reason Indrani's

. . . very valuable father went after that conspiracy all by himself. Some of us have lived a long time, my friend. Hundreds of years in some cases. Or more. At my age, you have to roll that dice every chance you get so your heart can be bothered to keep pumping. Now' – he leaned forward again – 'here's my offer for the boy who befriended a wild cannibal and lived to tell the tale. Here it is.' He gestured, and the inner surface of the Globe filled with images, a hundred of them. Everywhere Hiresh looked he saw violence, rebellion, burning and death.

'It has started again. Rebels. Murderers. And we have no Elite left to face them.'

Hiresh was shocked. 'None?'

Dharam shrugged. 'Well, a few dozen perhaps. They've been getting themselves killed, or falling ill.'

'Ill?' Hiresh realized he kept repeating everything the High Commissioner was saying, but couldn't seem to help himself.

'And as if that wasn't enough, the Roof itself is failing underneath us. We are going to die. Your mother. That new girlfriend of yours. The other students at the Academy, the Religious, the pacifists, the Seculars. Everybody. The savages on the surface might live on a little longer, but without the fresh aliens we add to their food-chain, without *light* from the Roof, even they will succumb in a few months.'

'Oh goddess,' said Hiresh. 'Oh goddess.'

'The old goddess is dying,' Dharam agreed. 'There is only one chance left for any of us.'

'We have to get Indrani to come in.'

Dharam waved the screen away. 'Exactly. We have to make her come in, and more importantly, we have to get her to co-operate. She had a bit of a thing for me once, but I knew she was far too young, and now she . . . distrusts me. Blames all kinds of bizarre things on me, and this will lead her to lie to you about what she knows. But' – and now he leaned forward to grab Hiresh's arm – 'she must, *must* be brought back here.

'Now, Dr Narindi tells me we have one dosage left. We can make one more Elite. And I'm prepared for that person to be you.'

It was funny, how long and how hard Hiresh had struggled at the Academy to become Elite. He'd wanted it back then to protect his mother; to oppose his father and all who were like him, the bullies, the fanatics. But now he had a higher purpose. 'What do I have to do?'

'Whatever it takes. We will take care of' – a second's pause to log on and check his memory – 'Tarini for you. No harm will come to her, or anybody. If you can only bring Indrani in.'

'What . . . what if she won't co-operate?'

Dharam grinned. It was as if he had no other facial expressions, as if time had worn them to nothing. 'Unless the late Commander Krishnan gave the game away before he met his horrible end, there's a chance the savage still trusts you. That should help. It's partly why we chose you, after all. But there's more. Apparently Indrani has a small child with her. She will want that child to live. That alone ought to bring her in – and voluntarily too. If not, Sergeant Hiresh, you had better figure something out.'

Yet again the Commission were going to use him to catch Indrani, to betray Stopmouth. But as the Globe began its descent and slime glittered and winked at him all down the wall, Hiresh knew that this time it was different.

*It's for your own good, Stopmouth. We're all dead otherwise.*

# 18. NOTHING LEFT TO SEE

After sharing her memories, Indrani fumed quietly to herself, upsetting the baby.

'I'll take her,' said Stopmouth, relieved the horrible vision had ended, but feeling terribly shaken too. The baby's parentage seemed less important in the dreadful light of the secret. She was just another poor child in distress. And she did look a bit like his mother.

He whispered nonsense to the child as he'd seen countless women do in the tribe. 'We can go back to the surface,' he said. 'You and me and Indrani. She'll be mine again. No more Roof to take her away and spoil everything . . .'

But all around them sat other people. Dreamers and Seculars, Religious adults and boisterous children. Corpses, all of them corpses. The thought of it made him dizzy and sick.

Once he'd believed his tribe were the only humans in existence. He did not know what a stranger was, and his language had no word for it. He would have given his life, and gladly, to keep his people from extinction.

He would still die for the Tribe, but the meaning of that word had changed. Now it meant Indrani, and maybe . . . maybe even this little girl. He'd have to see about that last part.

A piercing sound cut through all the clamour, and every wall in the plaza turned red.

'Your attention, citizens!' boomed a voice loud enough to jolt even the deepest Dreamer and shock the fussiest child into silence. 'A vital announcement from the Commission follows!'

A man appeared on the walls now, his handsome face the size of a house. 'Dharam!' exclaimed the hunter. This was his visitor when he'd been trapped in the white room just after his arrival in the Roof.

'You know him?' asked Indrani. But she didn't have time to say anything else before the High Commissioner began speaking.

'Citizens! Our victory over the Crisis approaches its final stages.' Pictures appeared of gleaming, empty corridors; parks full of healthy trees. 'More areas have been reclaimed from the Virus.' Some people in the crowd cheered at the sight. 'But these free sectors will not be ready again for human habitation for six more weeks . . .'

Everybody groaned, for they knew what was coming.

They'd be crushed together even closer than they were now. Rumour had it that in some sectors people were being forced to sleep standing up. A shiver of fear ran through the crowd. It only got worse when the announcement added that the newly 'cleared' area had contained food-purification centres. Stopmouth could actually feel the anger building around him. An explosion was coming: one of the great, horrific riots that would leave thousands trampled. Stopmouth's little tribe would be right in the middle of it . . .

'But there will be no shrinkage,' cried Dharam. 'No loss of space or rations.' He waited a few heartbeats to let puzzlement replace anger. 'Why should upstanding citizens like yourselves have to suffer when the very ones who have sabotaged us – those who introduced the Virus that now plagues us – still get to share in the fruits of our civilization?'

Somebody, some human group, had actually planted the Virus? Stopmouth looked at Indrani. She looked shocked – everybody did. How could humans do such a thing?

Images of empty parks on the wall disappeared, to be replaced by pictures of an angry chanting crowd of Religious. Their clothing differed greatly from that of the people around him. 'A dangerous and ruthless minority sect,' called Dharam. 'They hate technology and sought to bring about the end of our civilization.' The picture expanded to focus on a single hate-filled face. A young woman, ugly and thin, spittle flying from her mouth as she shouted some slogan.

Around Stopmouth, even the Religious bellowed the young woman's hatred back at her until the High Commissioner drowned them all out. 'Well,' he said, 'I have decided to give them the primitive society they crave and save the rest of us from more shrinkage. Let's see how these fanatics take to life on the surface!'

The people cheered. Religious and Seculars together. Stopmouth had thought that some alien was responsible for the Crisis. No wonder the crowd was furious. He felt that itch in the back of his head that meant Indrani wanted to 'call' him.

*This can't be right*, she sent. *Why would somebody plant a virus like that? They'd have to know they'd be killing themselves with it. Unless it was meant to accomplish something else and all the rest of the effects were only an accident. But it doesn't sound like a tactic the Religious would use. Many of them worship the Roof.*

*He lied to me*, Stopmouth replied. *When I first woke up here, he told me you'd gone mad, but he was just using me to find you.*

*He interrogated you personally, Stopmouth? Of course he did. He wouldn't trust it to one of his minions in case you knew anything useful. Dharam can be very convincing. I used to believe every word that came out of his mouth, and then it was me on the wall, spreading his poison for him. 'The face of the Commission', they called me.* Her image shook its head. *The Religious were closer to the truth with 'the Witch', if only I'd known it. I was his puppet. I thought he was a god.*

*So are they really sending these people to the surface?* he asked.

The walls answered that question directly: the same fanatical men and women appeared now, in their thousands, strapped to the floor in cages that, in turn, rested in a huge pit. Stopmouth had seen a place just like it before, although its floor had been covered with bones and the sole occupant had been a huge beast, crazed with loneliness and hunger.

A flash of light had the audience cursing and cheering. When the spots cleared from Stopmouth's vision, the fanatics were gone, the cages empty. Screams of joy filled the air. People jumped up and down and hugged each other. A dancing group knocked Stopmouth over, forcing him to twist his body to keep Flamehair safe. She was so tiny! He felt their feet against his back, but then a dozen hands reached down to pull him to his feet, and men hugged him and laughed until he found himself laughing with them, while Indrani scowled from a few paces away.

'We've done it!' shouted a handsome but ageing Secular. Stopmouth didn't know whether he meant the defeat of the

Virus or the demise of those now being blamed for setting it loose.

'What's your wife so sour about?' asked somebody else, a Religious woman who'd tried to give Flamehair a kiss but couldn't bend far enough in the press.

'Tummy ache,' he responded.

She laughed, her hood falling back to reveal twinkly eyes. A nice woman, as good as dead.

'What's wrong?' she asked. 'You got tummy ache too?'

Nobody had the energy to keep the celebration going long. After a few hundred heartbeats everybody sat down again, telling each other that they'd soon be moving into the cleared areas, and not long after that, each and every one of them would have their own apartment again – like the old days when the Upstairs had been barely full and the Roof had a whole new floor under construction.

'Hey,' somebody shouted. 'They've arrived! The Commission already has a Globe watching the traitors!'

A wave of silence spread through the plaza as more and more people – even Religious, who were supposed to be beyond such things – submerged themselves in the sounds and images broadcast to them by the Globes that spied on the surface.

Stopmouth didn't have to look to know what was going on. The 'traitors' would still be asleep, their bodies distributed in the buildings of some empty streets. Hungry beasts would have noticed the arrival and were probably already on their way to exploit this new, inexperienced flesh.

*If your world is ending, we must go home*, he sent to Indrani. *We can steal another Globe, or find that place where you said the land touches the Roof. The – the—*

*The mountain*, she said.

*Yes! The mountain! You can't save the Roofpeople, and I'm sorry, truly I am sorry about that. But our tribe still have a chance. If we can get back to them before nightfall . . .*

She was still staring at the pictures of empty cages on the walls. Finally she said, *Can you see in the dark, Stopmouth?*

*What do you mean?*

*I mean, where will your light come from when the Roof turns black with rot? How will the trees grow that give you firewood? Where will new flesh come from when you've eaten all the beasts on the surface or when they've eaten you? Because when the Roof dies there won't be any more.*

*We'll find some seeds before we go back. You said yourself—*

*You're not listening, Stopmouth. Seeds need light to grow, and there won't be any light down there. Ever.*

'What—?' He shouldn't be speaking aloud, so he shut his mouth and thought, *What can we do?*

*You won't like it*, she sent. *I know you. I don't like it either, but we have no choice.*

In real life, Indrani sighed. The picture of her in his

mind remained totally calm. *The Commission have a means of escape for a few hundred people*, she sent. Her red-rimmed eyes looked straight into his. *And they can't get away without our help . . .*

She didn't mean it. She couldn't. To leave billions to die here. To abandon his people to generations of darkness followed by a slow extinction.

'We can't do this,' he hissed aloud to Indrani.

She reached over and took the baby from him. 'I won't let her die,' she said, and whispered, 'Or you, dearest Stopmouth. There is no world without you.'

'We can't,' he insisted.

*I'm going to call Dharam*, she said. *We'll make a deal.*

*But you're the one who told me about the Deserters, Indrani! This is what they did, exactly what they did. Sneaking away and leaving the innocent to suffer! You're saying we should be no different?*

'Flamehair,' was all she could say, and Stopmouth had no answer to that.

She and the baby fell asleep beside him. He didn't know how she could do that, for he doubted he would ever sleep again. The tribe, the tribe! Even his brother's tribe. How could he abandon them? Some of his ancestors may have been Deserters who left their people in their hour of need instead of fighting to the last to save them. But he was not like that.

'Show me my people,' he whispered to the dying Roof. 'I want . . . I need to see them again.' Even if it was just to witness the extinction he had failed to prevent.

Night had fallen on the surface, but in Headquarters, nobody slept. His first sight of the complex of buildings was a confusion of lights – torches, Stopmouth realized – rushing this way and that. And then the shouting reached his ears: Kubar calling for more fires to be lit; Rockface yelling for spears and hunters. Something was moving out in the streets. It was like a river flowing past and between houses.

'Closer,' Stopmouth commanded, and the Roof obeyed, swooping him down over the alleyways. Of course, it wasn't like a real fall; he felt nothing in the pit of his stomach. He just knew he couldn't be hurt. But he gasped anyway at what he saw there. Beasts, all kinds of beasts: Fourleggers and Slimers, the ones that looked like the Clawfolk back home; hairy ones, and others with segmented bodies, ignoring everything around them, running, running for their lives. No species took the time to hunt any of the others. When a beast fell, feet trampled it and left it to die uneaten.

Rockface shouted: 'Hunters, to me!' He looked fierce in the firelight and the young flocked to him. He was limping, but his face showed only joy. 'There'll be good eating tonight, hey? Hey? This will keep us for a ten of days.'

'Wait,' said Kubar. 'You mustn't go out there.'

'Are you mad?'

The old priest pushed his way past an excited Vishwakarma and grabbed Rockface by the arm. 'We'll capture some, yes, but we can't kill them. We need to know what they're running from. Maybe we should be running too?'

Stopmouth found himself nodding. 'Listen to him, Rockface,' he muttered, knowing he couldn't be heard, knowing there was nothing he could do.

The big hunter shook off the older man. 'To the doors!' he shouted.

'What about the Fourleggers, at least?' said Kubar.

Rockface paused. 'Maybe,' he said. 'All right, all right. No Fourleggers, but kill anything else you can find and drag it inside.'

The stampede had almost ended by the time the humans got outside. Nevertheless they brought down seven or eight beasts of all types, the young men and a few women whooping as they fought creatures without the heart to resist them.

Yama managed to cripple a Slimer. He laughed as it put up no fight, but kept trying to crawl around him. The boy continued poking it here and there until an angry Kubar finished the creature off.

Sodasi had abandoned her sister to take up a place

beside Rockface. When a beast got behind him and raised its claws, she was ready with her sling. She gave no shout of triumph as she broke its momentum with one stone and stopped it dead with another. Stopmouth felt sure she wanted to hide from Rockface the fact that she'd helped him. She'd never tell him how slow he'd become.

'Enough!' shouted Kubar. 'Bring it inside – bring it all inside.'

'Yes,' Rockface agreed. Sweat streamed down his face, although he'd fought for no longer than a few hundred heartbeats. 'Get . . . get it in, boys. In. And bar the doors tight.'

Stopmouth followed them inside, passing through the walls to where a tiny machine spied for him, sending all images to a nearby Globe. He had a bad feeling. The streets were silent again.

'Hey,' said Yama, 'there's one still alive here!' Sure enough, a hairy creature with two legs and six short arms growing from its chest and back lay slumped but breathing in a corner. The boy grinned and strode over to it with his knife drawn. But once again, Kubar was there to deny him.

'This one's mine, boy,' he hissed.

'We'll see about that. Nobody made you Chief. Look at your grey head – you're just about ready for the pot yourself.'

'I have the Talker,' said Kubar. 'I'm going to question it,

and if it answers my questions, I'm going to let it go. We have more than enough flesh.'

'Let him ask his questions,' said Sodasi. 'Right, Rockface? We'll let the priest talk to the creature?'

Rockface shrugged. He hadn't stopped sweating since the fight.

'There,' said Sodasi, her pretty face serious.

The priest approached the hairy creature. 'Did you hear?' he asked. 'Did you understand?'

The six arms waved and a strange perfume filled the air. 'Yes,' said the Talker. 'I wish to go. I wish to go or not to live.'

A child came rushing down from the roof, all excitement. 'A house,' she cried. 'A house just fell into the street!'

Everybody jumped as a crashing noise came from outside. And then another, closer to them. The Sixarm suddenly shoved Kubar aside and rushed for the door. It was still trying to find a way to open it when Yama's spear took it in the back. 'What a kill! Another kill for me!'

And then a crack ran up the walls in front of him. Dust sprayed down from the ceiling.

'I can feel it through my feet,' said Kubar. 'There's something in the ground beneath us . . .'

Stopmouth saw Sodasi whisper in Rockface's ear. The big man nodded even as more dust rained down from the ceiling. 'The walls are falling!' he shouted. 'We need to get to the roof on the other side of the U before—'

Abruptly Stopmouth found himself back on the Roof, snatched away from what was happening on the surface of the world.

'I need to see,' he cried. 'I need to know!'

But the floor beneath him groaned and shook as if the Diggers had come here too, and though the crowd shouted and prayed, he understood none of it. The tremors continued, heartbeat after long heartbeat. Flamehair woke crying while her mother cradled her from the buffeting of surrounding bodies.

Liquid fountained into the air a hundred paces away – sewage, its foul stench billowing over the people with every lurch of the ground. The whole event lasted no more than a dozen heartbeats this time. At the end of it, the little family had to fight to hold onto their space as filth-covered refugees from the sewage spill fanned out, looking for somewhere cleaner to huddle.

Stopmouth tried to see what was happening to his tribe again. But the Roof showed him nothing, nothing at all. As if it couldn't; as if there was nothing left to see.

Again Indrani went back to sleep, leaving him alone with his thoughts. All around him came grunts and curses; farts and snores and fighting; talking, and even the sounds of a couple making love not too far away, unconcerned by the presence of the crowd. Overhead, the random and twinkling *stars* shone through the same hole in the Roof's many layers that had earlier brought him the *sun*.

His people were probably already dead. Or worse, they might survive this night; prey to dark-adapted Diggers and who knew what else while he fled with a gang of cowards who despised him.

Nearby, some doomed child angered the adults around it with its wails. He tried to roll away from the noise, but came up against some stranger's back.

Stopmouth wondered if the rulers of this place – the Commission – were able to sleep at night. They'd been planning their escape for at least as long as he'd been alive. That was the time they'd spent fixing up the warship. They'd kept the secret; they'd diverted resources away from saving the lives of everybody else. A whole generation of sickening selfishness.

His body twitched, hatred threatening to overwhelm him, to make him stand up and scream out what was happening to all those around him, even if it meant the certain doom of his small family. The people had a right to know, didn't they? A right to prepare for death, if nothing else? He couldn't bear it, he *couldn't*.

'I won't Desert,' he whispered. 'I'll get Indrani onto the ship, but *I* won't go. I'll die with my own kind.'

Stopmouth's dream of taking Indrani home could never happen now. He knew that. But at last he had found a way to keep her safe while still doing the duty to his people that had been bred in him since before he could talk.

As he made the decision, his body relaxed. It was as if he'd been holding his breath ever since he'd gone looking for his woman, and now, finally, he could take a fresh gulp of air, and another, and another. His eyes closed out the stars.

# 19. THE FALLEN LEAVES

Morning came too quickly to Sunshine Park. This was one of the reasons people disliked the place, or so Indrani said. The days were all the wrong length.

Stopmouth heard laughter nearby and saw Indrani sitting up in the midst of a cluster of women. Most of them were Religious, he thought, and getting on in years, but a few had unlined faces. They were smiling at Flamehair and seemed to be competing for a chance to pick her up. She didn't cry, but looked wide-eyed at each of them in turn. When she burped a bubble of milk, everybody thought it the funniest thing they'd ever seen.

One elderly lady on the edge of the group looked too frail to hold the baby and contented herself with a wide toothless grin, half hidden behind curled fists. She noticed Stopmouth, and one feather-light hand drifted onto his arm.

'Such pale skin! You're the father?'

For a moment he thought the fake pigment of his body had come off. 'I—'

'Where did you get the nanos to colour her so?' wondered the woman. 'A Cosmetic, was it? Oh, she's so beautiful.'

It was true, he realized. What a shame Flamehair wasn't really his. If he could learn to fool himself, to pretend . . . His eyes met Indrani's and she grinned at him, her despair all pushed aside for now.

Eventually Indrani asked the women if she might have a bit of privacy to rest the child, and the flock scattered, some of them moving surprisingly far away into the crowd. Stopmouth crawled over to his wife and her sweet baby. He put his arms around them both.

'We'll have to leave at once,' she said. 'I've . . . I'm sorry, Stopmouth. I've made contact with Dharam. I told him I won't be sharing any information until we're all safely aboard.'

Stopmouth opened his mouth. He too had made a decision. 'I—' He paused.

'What is it?'

He shook his head. There'd be plenty of time to tell her about staying behind when he'd got her safely to the warship. The later they had the argument, the fewer chances she'd have to weaken him and change his mind.

'Will they send somebody for us?'

'They want to, but I won't tell them where we are. I don't want them marching us in there as prisoners.'

'What difference does it make?'

She refused to answer, but he could guess easily enough. His wife didn't trust Dharam, not one bit. She must have feared the Commission would beat the information from them, much as Krishnan had already tried to do. Then there'd be no need to keep a place on the warship for any of them . . .

After that they ate, sneaking smoked flesh from beneath their cloaks to their mouths in the midst of the starving crowd. Then they set off, picking their way from space to space with sometimes a word of greeting from Flamehair's admirers. 'Oh, she will be back, won't she?' cried one girl. Indrani just smiled, and they moved on until they reached the end of the park and squeezed into the still, dark boulevard beyond it.

They spent the rest of the day queuing at a shuttle station. Stopmouth wondered if all the tribe was dead yet, but no matter how often he closed his eyes and prayed to the Roof spirit, the vision would not come. *If only there was something I could do . . . Oh ancestors, ancestors.*

Their long wait was made worse by local men who lined the platform with sticks, preventing most of the passengers who arrived from disembarking. 'We're too crowded here!' they'd cry, brandishing their weapons. 'Move along! There's more room in River Sector!'

'But we've just come from River Sector! We couldn't even breathe there. We—'

'Move along!'

When an empty car did arrive – a box big enough for six passengers – it brought forth a surge of desperate people until the stick-men shoved them back into line.

Their leader, a burly man who strode the platform with a tight grin, cried, 'Who's got food to pay? This shuttle for a single ration pack! No takers? Are you sure?'

Nobody came forward with a bribe for the stick-men.

Their leader shrugged, picked a few people out of the line – regardless of how close they were to the front – and shoved them towards the car.

Shortly afterwards, a siren came over the speakers on the wall, announcing yet more expulsions to the surface. Footage showed the usual terrified men and women being herded into cages. The stick-men cheered, along with a few of the Seculars. But the Religious stayed quiet, some of them openly angry. 'They won't stop till they've killed the lot of us,' said a tall, thin-featured man. As if to emphasize his point, a shuttle trundled in, its windows too fogged up to see through. When the doors opened, far too many people spilled out onto the platform.

'They're dead!' shouted one of the stick-men.

'Keep your voice down!' said another, but it was too late, and people crowded forward to gaze in horror at the victims. Stopmouth noticed that the fingertips of the corpses were raw and bloody.

'Who wants this car?' shouted the leader of the stick-men. He looked shaken, and already many in the crowd were heading back to the park or the corridors they'd come from.

'Don't be stupid!' he cried. 'There were too many of them in there, that's all that was wrong!'

'We'll take it!' said the tall Religious man. He had a family with him, two pretty daughters and a wife who barely came up to his elbow.

'So will we,' said Indrani, pushing forward.

'We can share it with you,' said the tall man.

'Are you mad?' said his little wife. 'The last lot ran out of air. We can't crowd it.'

A hubbub was rising from the people off to the sides, and some of the stick-men were gazing at the walls.

'She's right,' said the head stick-man, ignoring all distractions. 'Only one family will have it. So what will you pay me?' His gaze went from Indrani to the tall man and back.

Stopmouth knew they needed a car – Indrani had assured him that no amount of walking would ever get them where they were going. But the stick-man was no longer watching them. Stopmouth recognized the look of somebody receiving a communication through the magic of the Roof.

The noise from the edge of the crowd was growing louder. The hunter glanced around, but all he could see was other people craning their necks to stare at the wall. He turned back, having no interest in watching further expulsions.

'Boss!' said one of the stick-men to his leader.

'Hush! I have received an urgent communication from the Wardens.' He fixed his eyes on Indrani and her baby, and then Stopmouth. He smiled.

'Boss! You need to look!'

Stopmouth sent an urgent message to his wife: *When I tell you, take Flamehair and run for the car.*

*But, Stopmouth—*

*Do it! Now!* He shoved her forward, and moved immediately into the gap she had left. 'Run!'

She did, sprinting as only somebody who'd learned to flee for her life on the surface could. The stick-man boss turned to follow her, but Stopmouth's foot took him in the stomach and sent him reeling into a crowd too fascinated with what was on the walls to care.

Stick-men moved in on him from all sides. Puny men, some of them grey and feeble; others fat with extorted food. Yet even children could take down the fiercest beast if there were enough of them.

A blow landed on Stopmouth's shoulder. Another found his kneecap and he howled in pain. He grabbed someone's club and beat a space for himself. He ducked under a blur of movement to his left and hooked the legs out from under some bumbler with a wild beard.

*Come quickly, love!* sent Indrani. *They'll take the car from us!*

He didn't know who she meant or how to escape the predicament he'd got himself into.

'Out of my way,' shouted the head stick-man. He was trying to climb to his feet and, stupidly, some of his inexperienced hunting party paused in their attack to help him. Stopmouth screamed to distract the rest, then leaped forward. His knee almost gave way on landing, but he managed to ignore the pain and launched himself onto the rising back of the head stick-man, who bellowed and fell, but not before the hunter had clambered over him and was running towards the car. Lots of people were fighting at its door. He could hear Indrani's rage.

The head stick-man shouted, 'Leave me! The Wardens want them! Get them!' But his comrades had already started the pursuit.

A struggling knot of men and women had blocked the door of the car, with Indrani just inside trying to push them away.

*Get back*, Stopmouth sent to her, amazed at how easily communication came in the Roof. *They're just behind me. Get back and be ready to close the doors!*

He dived forward, knocking a man and a woman into the car and falling in with them.

'Close it!' he shouted.

And then silence took over, cutting out the noise of the platform. The two strangers lay stunned on the floor, with Indrani pushed into the corner and Flamehair wriggling in a little cot the car must have grown for her.

Outside, everybody seemed to be fighting. Stick-men and Seculars and Religious. The tall man they'd seen earlier was protecting his wife and daughters as best he could in a corner, and Stopmouth felt ashamed.

'Did we cause all that?' he asked.

'Look at the broadcast on the walls,' said Indrani.

'Oh,' he said.

The expulsion hadn't gone as well as planned. In the picture, Wardens were sheltering behind the couches, firing metal slings. Blue Religious warriors had overrun the rest of the scene. They too carried weapons, and whenever they fought their way to a cage, they dragged its prisoner free with much rejoicing. The Wardens they captured were not so lucky.

'We need to leave,' said Indrani. 'I can't give orders to the car until we all agree on a destination.' She looked at the strangers, the man and woman who'd been fighting to get in until just a few moments before.

'Freedom Sector,' said the woman.

'Anywhere,' said the man. 'Somewhere less crowded.'

'All right,' said Indrani. 'We'll drop you both off at Freedom Sector. Then we're taking the car.'

They shot away from the violence and entered the tunnel. None of the adults in the car looked at each other, but everybody had time for the baby.

'How did you do that skin?' said the woman. She was quite young and must have been desperate to reach Freedom Sector – she'd been willing to fight the bigger man to get there. 'It's amazing. Almost like . . . Please don't take this the wrong way, but it's almost like the skin of the savages below, you know?'

Indrani laughed to show she wasn't offended.

'I never had a child,' said the girl. 'I suppose I never will now.' It was the first time Stopmouth had ever heard anybody in the Roof other than Indrani doubt that the Crisis would come to an end. He couldn't bring himself to correct her. Nobody could.

Night-time reigned in Freedom Sector.

'It's too early!' said the man, and the woman nodded. 'It shouldn't be dark here yet.'

People crowded the platform. Most were asleep, their bodies scattered right the way over to the drop where the car floated. A few stared up at the arrival before lying down again. None of them tried to get on board.

'You still want to leave here?' Indrani asked the woman.

'I have to, you know?' She didn't say goodbye. She took

one last look at Flamehair before hopping off into a tiny space left free between somebody's splayed legs.

'What about you?' Indrani asked the man.

'I thought it might be less crowded – with enough room to go for a walk, maybe. I mean, only a few months ago . . .' He shook his head. 'The population can't have increased that quickly in so short a time, can it? *Can* it?'

Indrani said nothing, and the man hesitated a full hundred heartbeats. By now the young woman had hopped a few dozen paces down the platform towards the corridor beyond.

'See she gets where she's going,' Stopmouth told the man.

'All right,' he said with a sigh. The doors closed behind him.

'Where are we off to now?' asked Stopmouth.

'A long way,' said Indrani. 'We should follow Flamehair into sleep while we can.'

But the hunter wasn't ready to close his eyes just yet. 'What about the head stick-man?' he asked. 'He got a call from the Wardens just before he tried to stop us. Why are they still after us if we have a deal with Dharam?'

'It's very simple,' she said. 'We can't trust them. Space on the warship will be limited, and if they can get what they need from me without having to provide room for all three of us . . .' She shrugged. 'We have to be in a position to bargain when we get there, love. We have to be in charge.'

He nodded, not yet ready to tell her that he wouldn't be taking anybody's place on the warship.

They whipped away into the tunnels. Indrani commanded beds for them and darkened the windows. 'How's your ankle?' she asked suddenly.

'My ankle? Oh, you were right. It healed really quickly. The . . . the Medicine must have fixed it. Like you said.'

'Good. Good. Now, come here.' Indrani must have communicated something else to the car then, because their beds moved closer together and joined to become one. He felt her arm slide over his chest and her warm breath against his ear. 'You came after me,' she whispered.

He woke, unsure how long he'd been asleep. His bed was a single again and Indrani was rocking Flamehair on the far side of the car, singing to her. '*A lovely smile on my lovely girl, her lovely ears, her perky nose . . .*' Each feature was touched and tickled as it was named, and Flamehair's little face bore a huge smile.

Indrani looked over at him.

'Can you understand me?' she asked.

'Of course.'

She seemed relieved.

He sat up. 'Is it day or night?'

'I . . . I don't know.' And now he saw the worry that had

been hiding behind the game she was playing with her daughter. 'The Roof won't tell me the time,' she said. Flamehair started wailing until Indrani remembered to rock her again. '*Her dainty knees, her little toes . . .*'

'I don't understand.'

'It's political,' Indrani said. 'The Roof, right at the beginning, was made to work for the Commission. But those were peaceful days when everybody had plenty of anything they wanted. It was created to be . . . to be fair to all; to respect everyone's privacy and to prevent itself being used in any way that would bring harm to another citizen. The longer the Crisis has gone on . . . well, the more obsessive it has become about being fair. This is the first time . . . the first time it ever refused to give the time of day. It's like . . . I thought we were having another quake. I thought the car was about to trap us here like those people we saw who ran out of air.'

Stopmouth reached across to hug her and absently tickled the baby, whose little eyes wandered vaguely over their faces.

'How long before we get there?' he asked. 'Or is that . . . political too?'

'An hour,' she said. 'Do you know how long that is?'

He found he did. It was the time it would take a hunter to walk right up to the walls of Blood-Ways from Central Square at home. It might be the last time he ever saw his wife and he hadn't even told her yet. But how could he be sure she'd be safe after he'd left?

'We should get out before then,' he said. 'If, as you say, they plan to go back on their deal, they'll have a hunting party waiting for us.'

'You're right, love. You're right. We can't trust them.' Indrani closed her eyes a moment, and when she opened them again, she reached into her robes and pulled out the last of their smoked flesh. 'I'm going to stop us a few hours' walk from the shipyards. With any luck they won't be expecting us to start from so far away. Let's eat. I'm sick of carrying this stuff around.'

The car, however, no longer provided them with water, and both struggled to get their meal down without it. It had been hours since their last drink at the shuttle station. But shortly after that, Stopmouth's body felt the drag of the car's deceleration. The strip of light in the tunnel turned back to a series of blurs separated by longer and longer stretches of blackness, until finally they were replaced altogether by green lighting such as he'd seen in the Upstairs.

Indrani blinked, and they both moved right up to the windows of the car to peer through the glass. They saw very little until she ordered the car's own lights to dim.

'Oh gods,' said Indrani.

Stopmouth could only agree. Bodies lay piled up like dead leaves under a fallen tree.

'They . . . they were waiting for a car,' said Indrani, 'and they just . . . they just lay down . . .' She was breathing very fast, clutching Flamehair to her until the baby cried.

Stopmouth saw Wardens lying with the others, weapons beside their hands, faces peaceful. 'Well, they can't harm us, right? We can just walk over them . . .'

'But we don't know what killed them, or even if they are dead.'

'We should at least search them for food or weapons,' he protested. 'Let me go. I'll be able to hear if any creature gets close and I'll jump straight back inside afterwards.'

'You don't understand,' Indrani said. 'Do you remember the strange smoke the Elite tried to put us to sleep with?'

'Oh,' he said. 'Oh!'

'Bad air can drown as surely as water.' She waved the car on.

*All those volunteers*, thought Stopmouth as the corpses disappeared. And all the surface-dwellers too, soon to follow them into death. They rose up in his mind, a mass of empty ghosts, mourning the shocking waste of their lives and their flesh. He saw them screaming at him, weeping, begging.

'You're shaking,' said Indrani. 'Are you all right?'

It was anger – anger at the rulers who'd abandoned their people while lying to them that salvation lay just round the corner. A leader should share the risks of his tribe. To hide while others hunted was something his brother would do.

Worse! At least Wallbreaker's schemes provided food for all.

'Stopmouth?'

He looked up at his wife. 'Do you think you could fly the big Globe?'

'The warship? Probably . . . But they'll already have a pilot. They—'

He took her free hand and stared into her eyes. 'We'll steal it, then,' he said.

'What? Are you mad?' Indrani tried to pull away, but he was stronger and more desperate.

'Your chiefs don't deserve it, Indrani. They're doing what the Deserters did and should suffer the same punishment. We'll throw them out of their Globe and fill it with our people from below, if they still live! If not, we'll find somebody deserving up here. Young ones. Anybody but Dharam.'

'But we wouldn't have a hope. We—'

'We'll save the tribe. Like we promised, Indrani. Like *you* promised. Those other people would prefer us dead in any case. You know that. No matter what they've told you, sooner or later they'll find a way. Even the baby, Indrani. Even Flamehair.'

She sagged.

'Gods help me,' she whispered. 'It's true . . . And yes, of course, if we could find a way to rescue the tribe . . . But these people will have weapons, love. Maybe a few Elite, even. I don't see how we could do it.'

Stopmouth grinned. Suddenly he felt light and strong and wonderful. 'The one thing we know about these people is how much they fear for their lives. And they're scared of savages too.'

Indrani nodded and finally grinned back at him. 'I think I know where we might find one of those. Perhaps if he were to capture a few of the Commission and threaten to eat them . . . ?'

They both laughed and hugged, the baby wriggling in protest between them.

They sobered as the next few stops brought more eerie scenes of piled-up bodies. Finally they reached a station where the lights worked properly. Here, however, there were no people at all. It was like the paradise so desired by the man who'd shared their car the previous day; a place to walk where nobody would ever bump into you.

'Can we get out here?'

Indrani bit her lip and jiggled the baby. It was so strange to see her like that with her own child. As if she'd skipped past Stopmouth in the race for adulthood. He didn't feel like a chief beside her. He was still just a boy.

'I don't know,' she said.

'Remember, you didn't want to stop too close to the warship? They'll only be waiting for us there.'

'All right. You can go out. It's just . . . Where are all the people?'

'I don't know,' he said. 'Let me have a look. I'll wait a few dozen heartbeats next to the car and if I feel I'm getting sleepy, you can let me back in.'

She nodded.

As soon as the door had hissed shut behind him he took a deep breath. The air *did* taste strange. Like metal on his tongue. But he didn't feel drowsy. On the contrary, he now realized how much he hated huge numbers of people; how close he'd been to collapse over the last few horrible days. The sight of an empty corridor in front of him pulled his lips up into a smile. The only thing strange about the platform was a slight tremor he could feel in the soles of his feet. It was as if the Roof had a pulse he'd never noticed before, like a dying person, irregular and faint. He shrugged. Perhaps Indrani could make sense of it. He waved. 'I can breathe fine,' he said. He wanted her to hurry, desperate for a drink.

A moment later she stood beside him, and both turned to watch the car close its doors and speed away.

'We're stuck here now,' she said. 'Come on. We need a north corridor.' Whatever that was.

Stopmouth followed her into a passage as eerily empty as the station had been and longer than any he'd seen before. Windy, sinuous beasts wriggled along the walls, some of them eating their own scaly tails.

'It goes on for ever!' he said. 'I can't see any turn-offs,

can you?' The far end was nothing but a speck, and all the doors along its length were shut. None they passed would open to Indrani's command.

'They were locked,' she said, 'not abandoned. The people are either still inside or planning to come back soon. Maybe this is one of those clean areas they showed on the walls, remember? Where the Virus has been burned out and everybody can move back into it afterwards?' She smiled sadly. 'Except we know that can't be true, don't we, love?'

Even more disturbing was the fact that none of the walls would give them a drink. But surely they didn't have far to go – surely not.

A little way down the corridor they found an open doorway. An apartment, much larger than any Stopmouth had seen in his time in the Roof. Homes were supposed to be getting smaller, but ten people could have lain down here in comfort.

Indrani held out her hand. 'Apartment, give me some water.'

A beaker emerged from the substance of the wall, but it was empty. It clattered to the floor and was not reabsorbed.

'We've found a desert,' said Indrani, her voice hoarse. 'Nothing but a desert.'

They continued along the endless corridor, not finding any trace of recent occupation. The scaly beasts of the wall – *snakes*, they were called – undulated around sealed doors and across the ceiling. Sometimes their great bodies dived under the floor, only for the head to surface on the far side of the corridor.

Stopmouth and Indrani walked for a whole two tenths of a day, and still they could see no end to their journey.

'Are you sure we stopped only half a day's walk from the warship?' Stopmouth asked.

'I can't be sure of anything any more . . .' Indrani said. 'It's what I ordered. A sector away, I said.'

'And all these sectors are the same size?'

'Mostly,' she muttered, and saw the look on his face. 'I know, I know. I should have been more careful, but the Roof isn't co-operating very well, is it? Ideally, each sector holds the same number of apartments.'

'Maybe they're all in this one corridor,' he said. 'Those snake things are just a single long creature, aren't they? And this is Snake Sector.'

She sighed. 'You must be right. What a place to run out of water! Come on, we have to keep going.'

They passed more open apartments on their way. None of them had anything to drink. One room was choked with furniture, and no amount of waving from Indrani could make the floor reabsorb it. Even as they watched, a box emerged from the wall to land on a table. Other shapes jutted from every surface – half a chair, a cup – unable to emerge fully for lack of space.

And the snake continued. Finally the little black dot in front of them resolved itself into a doorway filled with flickering light. 'Can you hear that?' asked Indrani.

Stopmouth shook his head, afraid to speak.

'Listen.'

He did, straining with all his might. A faint draught ruffled their hair. The baby stirred sleepily in her mother's arms. And then he heard it. The dripping of water falling into a pool. Indrani saw the look on his face and grinned.

'Come on!'

She led the way at a jog that woke her daughter. Indrani greeted the baby's wails of complaint with laughter and didn't stop moving. Stopmouth smiled, his eyes now on the exit from Snake. It was further than it looked, and he wondered at the perversion of the people who could design such a place where water would retreat from a hunter even as he ran towards it.

He'd never been so thirsty in his life. It had to be the Medicine, he realized. He'd hurt his knee fighting the stickmen and the nanos needed large quantities of food and water to heal him properly. No problem, no problem at all for a normal Roofdweller living in normal times. But dangerous in a desert. His throat felt like it was burning and his vision made the whole corridor waver before him as though he were looking at it through the haze above a fire.

A hundred paces separated them from the exit. No

lights shone from beyond it, but they could feel the cold air that wafted from out of the blackness and hear the delicious tinkling of liquid. They had to stop as soon as they had passed the end of the corridor, for what little light they had came from the corridor behind them. A large pool blocked their way.

'You can't swim, of course,' said Indrani.

But Stopmouth didn't care about the possibility of being trapped here – or indeed anything else. He got down on his hands and knees and scurried towards the pool. He cupped his palms and had them halfway to his mouth before he realized that something was wrong. His skin *tingled*. His parched tongue didn't want him to stop, but as he hung there over the pool, the tingle turned uncomfortably sharp.

'Oh no!' he croaked. Not in the Downstairs!

Trails of slime ran from holes of rot in the ceiling and were spreading along the walls.

# 20. The Air of Pride Sector

iresh received no training, for the Academy staff had all been sent to quell the Rebellion or to keep the fighting away from the warship. There wouldn't have been time, anyway, to make him a proper Elite.

He found he didn't care. After the injections his whole body had burned with a fever. He'd heard about this in the Academy; about the tiny machines even now digging into the muscles of his body, re-forming them for speed and strength and endurance.

But he just felt sick and cloudy all the time, with none of the pride he'd expected. He'd always been small and skinny and starved. Now his clothing was beginning to tighten around his arms and legs, and all he cared about was what Tarini would think of that.

He hadn't been allowed to speak to her again from the moment he'd heard about the end of the world. Any attempt to communicate met with the blank wall of an ancient jamming device. So whenever he was conscious he recorded as much of his experience as he could to share with her later.

He kept playing back memories of holding her hand after their one long kiss in the shuttle. The kiss itself, because it had happened during a quake, had not been recorded, although he tried again and again, in the midst of his fever, to re-create it.

Sometimes the walls of his room would come alive with pictures of Rebels in exile on the surface. The forces of the law sent down thousands of them every day. Others, the peaceful ones, the co-operators, earned rewards. Smiling, they frolicked in the vast open spaces of the 'cleared areas'.

'*Live free!*' blared the wall. '*All contamination gone and the old days restored!*'

Hiresh turned away, shaking with fever and longing for those 'old days' that he himself had never experienced. But he knew the truth of the smiling faces; knew what lay in store for Tarini and his mother and everybody else he'd ever met if Indrani could not be found and made to part with her secret.

Dr Narindi woke him with a call. *You're needed*, he said. *We've found them. Quickly now!*

Hiresh looked at his apartment wall. Some strange boy stared back from its burnished surface. He looked haggard. Sick, even. Strangely sheened with sweat. But his body had become that of a man, a hero. As though the Roof had manipulated the mirror to play tricks on him or to flatter his vanity.

A uniform emerged from the wall, a single red stripe running down each leg, and it moulded itself to his new form while instructions from the doctor wrote themselves into his memory.

*One last thing*, sent the doctor. *There is a present for you. In the corner.*

Sure enough, a strange object lay gleaming on the floor. The Roof identified it as a *hammer*. A priceless antique made of steel rather than the more flexible bio-metal he was used to.

He picked it up, unsure what the doctor wanted of him.

*Bend it.*

'What?'

*You heard. Make a little arch of it.*

Hiresh had to strain to obey. But not much – not too much at all. In moments he had the head of the hammer butting up against its own tail.

*Good. I wanted you to see. Now go. You have your orders.*

Outside the apartment, a squad of Wardens waited for him. Most carried pistols, a technology so simple it could be relied on to survive the coming downfall. Two others bore little lasers from the early Age of Expansion.

Such weapons were so dangerous that their manufacture

had been banned long ago. Only registered Wardens could fire the few that remained.

A tough-looking middle-aged woman came forward. She limped ever so slightly. 'Captain Hiresh' – even the newest of the Elite automatically became Captain – 'I'm Sergeant Divya. I am to be your second in command.' She kept her face expressionless. All the others stared, confused perhaps by the new officer's extreme youth.

'He doesn't look well,' somebody muttered from the back.

'I'm not,' said Hiresh. 'But I'm what you've got. Come on. They've found Indrani and we need to get there fast.'

It was easier said than done. Many in the crowd were packed too tightly to move out of the way. Sergeant Divya fired over heads with her laser on the lowest possible setting.

'No,' said Hiresh. 'We could cause a stampede!' Tarini would be disgusted. But the Wardens were too old to have learned gap-skipping, and in the end they had to rely on forming a wedge and pushing through, with their truncheons flashing in warning.

Nobody wanted to rely on shuttles any more, so instead, the squad spent twenty full minutes shoving their way towards the old docking bay where the squatters had been expelled and five Globes lay waiting for them.

'How's the fever?' whispered Divya.

'Better,' Hiresh told her. Perhaps it was a lie. He wasn't

really sure how he felt. But a thrill went through him as soon as he strapped himself into a Globe and felt it take off. The pilot made sure he had a perfect view as they soared out over the plains and hills of the surface. Darkness reigned down there, in every sense of the word, but its barbarous inhabitants fought back with the little fires that seemed to drift by beneath his feet. All too quickly they docked again.

'Why are there only four Globes now?' he asked his pilot. 'Has the fifth come in to dock elsewhere?' There was nothing about that in the briefing Dr Narindi had slipped into his memory.

'It – it fell,' said the pilot.

'Fell? Globes don't "fall"! They can't "fall".'

'I know,' the pilot whispered. 'But it . . . fell.'

Some of the Wardens had lost friends now and they looked angry. Hiresh felt that way too, remembering that it was probably the Rebels who had caused all these malfunctions when they had invented the slime.

One of those missing (though not, thank the gods, Sergeant Divya) had been carrying a laser. Still, ten armed Wardens no more than two sectors away from their target should be capable of anything.

They came out into another corridor with half-melted walls and air that stank and tore at the throat. The Wardens coughed, but none seemed to be in any difficulty. The crowds here were thinner than he was used to, and more lethargic too.

'Help us,' said one woman. She may have been pretty once. Now, like a great many of those around her, she had sores around her mouth and just under her nose.

'I'm trying,' he said. 'We're all trying.'

Everybody here was lying down and nobody had to be shoved out of the way. The odd accidental step of a Warden onto somebody's body elicited no complaint other than a low groan. But it made Hiresh wince every time. He didn't even want to ask what had gone wrong here. Every area seemed to be dying in its own unique manner and he had to smother his pity. 'There's only one way to help these people,' he told himself, but it was hard not to look.

Another hundred metres brought them to the beginning of a new sector, or should have. Instead, they found that the corridor had been blocked off with piled-up furniture. The people on the near side of the barricade had given it a wide berth, and only the twisted corpse of a Warden could be seen on the floor. The sight turned his stomach. Was this how the last Rebellion had started? It made him feel shaky, strange.

'We're armed,' called a rough voice from behind the barrier. 'Pride Sector belongs to the Rebellion now.' The speaker then started coughing and another voice could be heard speaking quietly. Apparently the bad air didn't respect the new border.

'Religious scum,' growled Sergeant Divya at Hiresh's side.

Hiresh nodded. His head felt so cloudy. He was facing a thousand men and women who were just like his father – destroying the Roof in their ignorance and hate. Robbing all the food from the mothers to feed their warriors. His heart started beating faster, rattling in his chest, and it was only with a huge effort that he managed to calm it down again and push away the wave of sickness he felt.

He took a deep breath. 'Pride Sector is nothing to us,' he called back. 'Let us pass through to Snake and you can keep your barricades for all I care.'

'Snake is ours too.' *Cough, cough!*

'I don't care. We want to go in, collect some of our friends and leave.'

'Yeah,' called a new voice, female and clear, 'and send them to the surface to be eaten. We know all about what you've been up to. Well, your time is over now. You and all your kind. Turn round and we won't kill you where you stand, even if you are only a little boy.'

The mocking tones of her voice stirred an anger in Hiresh: all his limbs seemed to stiffen with it, and he pressed his hands to the sides of his head. His face was burning.

'Are you all right?' asked Sergeant Divya. 'Should I . . . should I burn down the barrier?'

The unseen woman continued her tirade. 'We have some of the new pistols your kind have been hoarding. We're prepared to waste a few bullets if that's what it takes to send you home to your mammy!'

Hiresh didn't know if it was the mention of his mother that did it or the earlier insults. Or the fact that the Elite injections had simply turned him into another Chakrapani.

He roared like an animal, and all the Wardens jumped away from him. And suddenly Hiresh found himself charging across the open space, leaping over his dead colleague and smashing into the pile of furniture. It barked his shins, and an outstretched table leg bruised one thigh. It didn't matter – nothing mattered, not even the hurried orders from the far side and the clicking sound that indicated the loading of a weapon. The shot never came. Instead, the whole pile of chairs, a bed and tables toppled under his machine strength. Laughter turned to fear and screams. He heard the woman's voice calling: 'Go back! Get the others. We'll hold him here!'

He flung wreckage out of his way and caught her, middle-aged and lanky, reaching for a fallen gun. Her back broke under his fist. Such a satisfying snap! Others came at him, their knives pricking his skin, hurting and stinging, building his rage. Hiresh roared again. He grabbed one man from among the others. A boy really, his own age, with blue-painted, sweat-soaked skin. Hiresh used the body as a shield until it stopped screaming, and then as a weapon. He swept the boy in a circle, driving his enemies back into the usual corridor crowds. He saw their faces. He saw their terror.

'They're gone, sir! They've run off!'

Other Wardens stood around him, as if they had appeared out of nowhere. His enemies lay like empty sacks, no more alive than the pulped rag doll still clenched in his fists. Slowly, slowly, with none of his squad approaching too near, his heartbeat calmed and he managed to unclench his fingers enough to release the dead boy.

He saw concern on the faces of the other Wardens. And fear too. And disgust. Hiresh found it hard to look them in the eye, but it was even harder to catch a glimpse of his own fingertips, which had been strong enough to sink right into his victim's back.

'I need . . . I need water,' he said. His body wanted food too, yet he preferred to punish it for having betrayed him so badly. If only Tarini could see him now. *Oh goddess, oh goddess.* It was the revenge he'd always dreamed of on those nights when he'd been cutting himself. But it would have been better if his father had never let him escape.

Divya dared to place a hand on his shoulder. 'We need to go on. Unless . . .'

'All right,' he said. He owed Stopmouth his life. And these people too, the ones he'd murdered in his mindless rage. It would all be for nothing if he didn't find Indrani.

Hiresh lurched to his feet and moved on through the exclusively Religious crowds of Pride Sector in the Quiet God District.

These were non-combatants. He could tell by their skeletal look – far worse than that of any Secular, even these days. It would have been easy for them to lunge at him as he passed, with a knife maybe. Nobody dared. They'd already done what damage they could by feeding up warriors instead of themselves for a rebellion they could never win in a world that could never last.

Many religions had clubbed together here: he saw Roof Worshippers like his own family; Blue Warriors with dyed skin; and orange-robed Ascetic Faithfuls. Each group kept to its own part of the corridor, but all their eyes bore the same bleak resentment.

The further the Wardens progressed, the greater the stench of unwashed bodies, the more bitter the air. Nobody spoke aloud, but they might not have been heard anyway over the never-ending coughs that sputtered from all quarters; the hacking and spitting that flecked the walls with poorly absorbed saliva. The whole corridor glistened with it, as though the sector were sweating in some special fever of its own.

Further on, as the malfunctioning walls of Pride Sector darkened, he and his squad passed into a corridor staked out by the Veiled Mystics. Here, only the top half of a person's face was visible, peeking between folds of filthy cloth that damped the noise of coughing.

There was something about the eyes that bothered Hiresh and he couldn't put his finger on it. He transmitted his concern to the squad, hoping somebody might be more observant than he was.

*They're young*, somebody sent. *Young eyes.*

*Stop!* ordered Hiresh. He looked around, feeling a sudden chill in the stifling corridor. *These aren't non-combatants*, he sent.

He was too late. All around him, the Veiled Mystics surged to their feet and threw off their robes. Shots rang out. Divya's laser beam turned one wall into slag as Hiresh's squad panicked around him. A trap! He'd led them into a trap!

Men and women ran at him with knives. He tried to throw them back, but in the press of bodies there was nowhere for them to fall. He caught a glimpse of apartment doors opening all along the corridor as more fanatics squeezed into the fray.

He sent a panicked message to Dr Narindi. *Reinforcements!* Though where they might come from, he had no idea. He punched and kicked and head-butted with all the savagery he could muster. His enormous strength crunched through fragile bodies until the live ones were crushing him back against the wall with a barrier of corpses to protect them.

He heard cries of panic from his squad, and pain and fear. 'I give up!' somebody shouted. 'Oh, please!'

The back of Hiresh's uniform was sticking to the damp wall. All he could see was knives and hate-twisted faces. They couldn't reach him any more than he could them, but the crush and the bad air were making it harder and harder for him to breathe.

He saw Divya go down. They had caught her arm and forced it up where she couldn't bring her laser to bear. They must have knifed her then, for she sank quickly. Hiresh was on his own. He was starving for a breath of poisoned air.

The wall, it turned out, was an apartment door. Suddenly it opened behind him and he fell inside onto his back. More warriors waited within, eager for their chance to finish a real Elite, one of the very few remaining in the Roof. He felt overwhelmed by terror, more frightened than he'd been since Stopmouth had saved him from the giant alien.

But he was stronger than they expected, and more athletic too. He rolled his entire body backwards into the room before they could fall upon him. He threw one man straight through the door into the crowd and spun round a girl coming at him with a knife. She dropped her weapon and he picked her up and held her facing the crowd.

'I'll break her neck!' he called. 'I mean it!' He didn't, of course. He couldn't. The Chakrapani rage had already left him.

Hiresh didn't expect them to stop, but strangely they did. A sudden hush had fallen on the crowd, broken only by the continual coughs of this district. He realized that the sounds of gunfire had long since come to an end.

The crowd parted to reveal a young Blue Warrior of excellent physique. A handsome boy of the last blessed generation before the Crisis. Only sores around the mouth and nose marred an otherwise perfect face.

'Your Wardens are all dead,' he said quietly.

'More of us are coming,' Hiresh told him.

'We'll kill them too.'

'And me,' said Hiresh. The youth nodded, and the Elite felt bitter laughter rising in his throat. The crowd muttered, but waited patiently. 'All I wanted was to pass through your sector,' he said. 'Not for my sake . . . There's somebody who can put an end to all the bad air and the shortages. I swear to you. Let me get her out and all this can end.'

The youth shrugged. 'We stopped believing the likes of you long ago.' The crowd muttered approval. 'Your only decision now' – he pointed to the terrified girl in Hiresh's grasp – 'is whether you die with the karma of another butchered innocent on your soul, or whether you choose to go with dignity.'

Hiresh shook his head. He could feel the anger rising, and struggled to put it back in its box. He knew it wouldn't save him against such numbers. 'Why should I choose either? The guilt would be yours and not mine. You can let her go by freeing me.'

'We cannot allow an Elite to escape. Little Manju knows that, don't you, pet?' Hiresh felt the girl nod in his grasp, though her whole body trembled. 'Any of us here, from the youngest up, would make the necessary sacrifice.'

'Even if that sacrifice is somebody else? This girl? You will choose it for her?'

The youth smiled sadly.

# 21. THE
# DROWNING

Stopmouth stepped back from the pool of slime, shaking his head, until he felt Indrani's hand on his shoulder.

'It's only thirty paces across,' she said. 'If it's not too deep, we could wade . . . And we've been through it before, love. It stings, that's all.' Her voice lacked conviction. She must have known the damage would increase the further they walked. Thirty paces would almost certainly kill the baby if she couldn't be kept out of it. And who knew what condition the floor might be in? What hazards lay decomposing at the bottom, ready to catch their feet or trip them up? And water? More than anything, what about water? Stopmouth's whole body was screaming out for it.

'I'm going to tighten Flamehair's sling,' said Indrani.

Stopmouth ignored her.

He pressed his face against the clammy surface of the nearest wall. It vibrated ever so softly against his cheek. Had it done that before? He felt so sleepy now, all his limbs warm and achy at the same time. Stopmouth had never seen an old man when he was growing up. Hunters too weak or weary to lift a spear gave their lives and their flesh – usually willingly – for the sake of the tribe. After he'd fled his home with Indrani and discovered a new people, he'd noticed men and women with strange grey hair and wrinkled faces. He'd tried teaching a few of them to hunt and had been amazed to see their pathetic shambling attempts at running, as if their legs might give way at any moment.

*That's me now,* he realized. *A drink, though. A drink will win back my strength. Just a sip. A swallow. If only I could swallow!*

'Stopmouth? Stopmouth!' He felt a stinging slap across his face. 'I'm sorry, are you all right? You looked a bit . . . I didn't want you to . . .'

'Fine,' he whispered. He was concentrating on staying upright. But it didn't work out like that. Suddenly the lights dimmed and he was thrown off his feet. Indrani fell on top of him, with Flamehair wailing. The ground shook and the Roof closed off all knowledge from them. It went on and on. The hunter's teeth shook in his jaw, and they all slid together across the floor of the corridor.

Towards the station, the door of an apartment burst open, spewing fragments of metal and other materials he couldn't identify. He tried counting the heartbeats that the shaking lasted, but was constantly distracted by the need to keep his family close and safe from flying debris. He felt sure that the forces around them were strong enough to smash puny human bones if the ancestors willed it.

Eventually – although it felt like an eternity – eventually it stopped. The lights came back fully for a few heartbeats, then turned dim.

'Can you understand me still?' whispered Indrani.

Stopmouth nodded.

'We have to hurry. The next one of those . . .'

'Yes.' The Roof surely wouldn't survive another day. Certainly not in this area. Soon Snake Sector would look no different to anywhere in the Upstairs. High up on the walls, light sparkled off the little droplets that were beginning to form there. Many didn't drip straight down, but instead drifted left or right or, in one case, upwards.

Voices were coming from the corridor at the other end of the pool. A middle-aged woman ran through the door there, her appearance dishevelled, her clothes torn. She skidded to a halt when she saw them, her mouth working.

'We won't hurt you,' said Indrani.

'I'm going into the cleared area,' called the woman. 'I'm going to Snake.'

'No,' said Indrani. 'There are no cleared sectors. It's all just propaganda. I'm sorry.'

More people came in behind the woman. Some might have been Religious, but under the filth it was hard to tell.

Four more women; a knot of men; feral children who didn't seem to belong to any adult there.

'You can't stop me,' screeched the woman. 'I'm going – I'm going to the clear sector!' Screams came from the corridors behind her.

'There's nothing here!' shouted Indrani.

The woman and several others surged forward into the slime. They waded through it, the woman at the front. A few paces in, a look of puzzlement crossed her face, but she didn't slow down. Two thirds of the way across, her teeth were clenched, and she emitted a faint whine. She shrieked once, floundering and splashing in the heavy liquid around her. Those behind her did the same thing, their wails rising in a chorus of terror. Stopmouth leaned out towards her over the edge of the pool, but he didn't even reach the tips of her fingers before her knees gave way and she sank. Most of those who'd come into the pool with her followed her under the surface too, but it didn't put off others who were only now entering the room. They came forward in a frightened wave, while Indrani begged them to stop. The hunter helped the tiny minority of half-dead survivors over the edge. They lay panting around his family, too tired to crawl any further, their skin eaten away to the bloody flesh beneath.

'You're wasting your time!' cried Indrani. 'It's a desert over here!' The wails of those who were sinking and dying drowned her out. Dozens of other people tried their luck, pushing floating bodies out of their way, or clambering over them, until the hazards at the bottom of the pool drastically cut down the successful crossings.

In the end, a few dozen Religious milled around on the far side, unable to get up the courage to run across; even less willing to turn back to whatever horrors they'd fled. Indrani had fallen to her knees at the edge of the rising ooze.

Stopmouth stepped up beside her and laid a hand on her shoulder. 'Get up,' he croaked. 'I need you to talk to them.'

'Who?' she muttered.

He pointed across at the people on the far side. For most of his life he'd been poor at speech, his stutter a never-ending source of fun to other boys and some of the adults too. He'd become adept at gestures. Now that thirst had turned the inside of his mouth to old fur, he needed them again.

He showed Indrani the Wardens' rope he still carried around his waist and mimed holding it under strain. Then he pointed back at the men and women on the far side.

'It can't work!' she said, but already she was rising. She pulled him close and kissed him deeply. He felt the sting on his peeling lips and a growing determination that he would not fail her, that he'd get her to the far side.

'You there!' she called. 'Listen to me, if you want to cross! Listen!'

Many were still panicking and wouldn't shut up, but others stilled them, sometimes brutally, with punches.

'We want to get over there and you want to be here,' she stated.

'You're mad!' said a big man on the far side. 'The demon's coming. If you're as Religious as you look you'll want to be staying there, believe me.'

Indrani didn't tell him about the lack of water. Stopmouth felt bad about that, but made no effort to alter what she was saying. She clutched Flamehair tightly to her chest. She had but one loyalty now, one tribe. These others were only beasts: their skins for clothing, their skulls for plates.

'We're going to throw you a rope. My husband is strong enough to hold one end by himself. Your men will take the other. I will climb across. Then some of you can come here. Enough to support my husband when he crosses. When we're all on that side, we'll hold the rope for anyone else who wants to go. Agreed?'

There were a few frightened arguments that Stopmouth didn't listen to, distracted as he was by his own over-whelming thirst. But he bucked up when he heard Indrani saying, 'All we ask in exchange is that you give us water. If any of you have bottles, throw them over here now, or it's all off.'

'Indrani!' he whispered. 'You can't! They'll die in Snake with nothing to drink. You know it!'

She spared him a glance, but all he saw was the cold eyes of the Tribe, choosing volunteers so that the rest might live. It was an idea he'd grown up with and knew to be right. Yet volunteers always understood why they'd been chosen. They too were raised with the same customs and accepted them. No deception took place.

'They are not beasts,' he said.

'They are not my child,' she replied. 'They are not my man.' She touched a hand to his face, and now he saw the turmoil that hid beneath her cold façade. The sight of her doubt made him feel better.

Moments later a ten of bottles flew across the pool. Half landed in slime, but the others fell around Stopmouth, and his qualms dropped away in a madness of thirst. He'd heard it said that a hunter deprived of water shouldn't drink too much. But his body with its Medicine was different. He swallowed three full bottles, while Indrani wiped his face, and then went back for more. She took little herself, for all that she must have needed it.

Indrani stroked the muscle on his shoulders and ran a hand down one arm. 'You're so strong, my love,' she said. 'But you're going to need an anchor for all that weight.' She pointed to a heavy piece of furniture half poking through the door of an apartment. 'You might want to tie yourself to that bed.'

He nodded. The fog had started clearing from his mind,

at last. It was amazing what those nanos could do. He was beginning to understand how these people had become so dependent on them.

They tied some empty bottles to one end of the rope and flung it across to those who waited for it. More people had arrived in the meantime and anxiety was growing. In the distance, great cracking noises echoed down corridors, and once the floor shuddered so much, the hunter thought they were having another quake, the one that would end everything.

He was glad that Indrani would be the first across. He wasn't sure how long the patience of the refugees would hold out.

'Now,' she said to him. 'I'm leaving you Flamehair.'

'No!' His voice was already stronger than it had been. 'No! What if . . . What if—?'

'You'll wear her on your back, like I do. I know what's going through your oh-so-noble savage mind and I won't have it.' She gripped his shoulder. 'You're not staying behind. I need you with me. Both of you. We're Tribe. All three. Or none. And remember the plan! I can't capture the warship without you.'

Five strong men took up the strain at the far end. Family men, he saw. Desperate to get their people to safety. He felt renewed guilt, but swallowed it.

Indrani gripped the magic rope and began to climb

across, upside down. It gave a little under her, seeming to stretch so that her bottom almost touched the rising surface of the slime. He felt the strain of her weight across his shoulders, but the bed he was anchored to carried most of it. The men on the far side had only themselves, and their faces creased under the unaccustomed effort.

Bodies floated beneath Indrani, already eaten away, while on Stopmouth's back, Flamehair wailed for her mother.

'All right, little one,' he said. 'All right.'

An explosion came from the far corridor. People cried out, and new refugees rushed in, calling out in panic. *What are we getting ourselves into?* Stopmouth wondered.

The other men's concentration seemed to slip and the rope dipped so that Indrani's hanging robes trailed in the slime.

'Get me up!' she cried. And they did. They steadied themselves. She pulled herself forward another few paces. Only ten steps from safety remained! Only ten!

A sharp green light that Stopmouth had seen once before lit up the far corridor. The man who'd hunted him on the surface, Varaha, had carried a weapon that could do such a thing.

'He's coming!' somebody cried. 'The demon is coming!'

The men didn't drop the rope. They grimaced, and one of them opened his mouth, perhaps to call out. It didn't matter. Everybody surged forward towards the slime at once and knocked those faithful men over.

'Indrani!' screamed Stopmouth as she plunged upside down into the slime. She might have been fine. She might have risen to her feet and taken the burns suffered in the last few paces to the far side: others had lasted much longer. But a surge of refugees was splashing in around her. They'd trample her under before she could get up. She had no chance, no chance at all.

'Indrani!' he screamed again. Flamehair joined in his lament even as Stopmouth abandoned the rope and sprinted forward. He leaped from the edge, jumping high to cover the most distance, with the baby still wailing on his back. He didn't think how his landing might scare her; he didn't think of anything. He came down with a splash, and his whole head went under for a moment before he surged to his feet.

Other people struggled around him. They stood between him and his Indrani, and thus became enemies; flesh for his spear. He threw the beasts out of his path as the first tingles pricked at his skin. The sensation turned into tiny needles, and then, as he reached the spot where she'd gone down, became knives, each one tearing at his still sensitive flesh. He howled and moaned, slapping creatures aside, reaching down into the burning liquid to pull her up. In the back of his mind, some calm part of him noted a baby crying in great distress.

Stopmouth raised Indrani's body above his head and staggered towards the shore. By now, the knives had become teeth. Like thousands of Armourback young tearing at him, ripping gobbets of flesh from toe to chest.

More of the enemy were getting in his way. More beasts. Many had already died, their floating bodies carpeting the surface. He battered them out of the way, living and dead alike.

Only a few paces remained now. He felt a terrible weakness. He managed to slip Indrani over the edge of the far side, but only just. He had no remaining strength to pull himself out after her. It didn't matter: his ancestors were already calling him. He could let go now, slip away. He felt his knees buckle.

Something crying . . . Some creature on his back . . .

Flamehair! He tried to untie the sling. Such a simple little knot – nothing really, nothing at all. But even that was too much. He was slipping, he was slipping . . .

The girl squirmed in Hiresh's grasp as the crowd closed in on him. She was about to be murdered by her own people, and for what? It wasn't anger he felt now, but a rush of despair. 'Stay down,' he whispered to his prisoner. Then he threw her to one side and rushed forward. The Roof was going to die and all these stupid people with it.

He smashed into them. But after the first rush he

ducked down and burrowed through their legs, his eyes finding the weak spots, for all the world as if he were gap-skipping a crowd. Except he was stronger now. He stayed low to the ground and tore through ten whole metres to where Divya had fallen.

People where smacking at him with their puny arms. A few had clubs or knives, but now the lack of space was working against them instead of him. And at last he found the body of the sergeant and, in the pulped flesh of her hands, the laser that only a Warden could use.

Did they know the danger they were in? Did they know? A green flash blinded him temporarily. Reflected heat scorched his skin. But before the spots had even cleared from his eyes, the horrific smell of roasted flesh was smothering all other odours. He had no time to think about it.

'Rush him!' shouted the blue-skinned boy.

'No!' screamed Hiresh. 'Please!'

He fired again, setting bodies on fire, melting flesh and charring bone so that he found himself advancing over bubbling corpses. 'Please,' he cried again. 'Please, pleeeee-assseeee.' But the Chakrapani rage was already rushing back to the surface, taking over. He kept moving forward and killing, long after there was any need for it, unable to stop himself. It was all just history. As if he were watching a recording of his own memories with no way to change course.

A call came through from Dr Narindi. *I've tried to get reinforcements, but they won't reach you in time. We had a . . . a crisis here. A huge quake. Are you all right? Will you be able to get to Indrani?*

Hiresh showed him an image of what he was seeing: the smoke, the scorched corpses, the continual firing of the laser at panicked and fleeing civilians. He expected the doctor to be appalled by what was happening, to order an end to it. But the only thing the man said was: *Good work! Now, for all the gods, try to hurry. You know what's at stake.*

He did, yes, he did. He'd been chosen for this horror, because they must have known only he could be weak enough to allow it to happen. Or maybe it was the implants. They'd turned him into a monster and it would be weeks before his moods balanced out.

He finally managed to stop when a huge quake threw him off his feet and kept him from getting up again for what must have been ten whole minutes. He couldn't judge time without the Roof's help.

As Hiresh lay there, he imagined Tarini's disgust over what he had become. Other ideas crowded into his thoughts too. Words and pictures and feelings. Were all of them side-effects of the Elite drugs? Or did they come from the Roof Goddess, random firings of a dying brain? And something else was tugging at his mind. Something about Dr Narindi, about High Commissioner Dharam too. Whatever it was, he couldn't figure it out, and part of him didn't want to.

After it ended, he heard people running away, screaming all the while. They were safe. He wouldn't hurt them now. He wanted to just lie there until the goddess sent somebody to punish him. But of course he couldn't do that. *The Roof. Got to save the Roof. Got to find Indrani.*

Hiresh finally picked himself up. He came into a park where the air was so terrible, it had him walking double with the force of his coughs. His eyes streamed and mucus ran down his face. The view waved and blurred in front of his eyes. But he didn't have far to go: Snake lay only a corridor away.

Even here, the odd Rebel popped up to fire at him. Their aim was poor, and so was his when he shot back, his laser seemingly blowing up things at random, melting walls and driving a wave of screaming people before him down the last few hundred metres.

He was breathing more easily now. At the end he passed into a great hall that echoed with people's cries. Many crouched pleading in the corners. Others were so desperate to escape him that they plunged chest-deep into a pool of slime and tried to wade across.

That's when he saw Stopmouth, his disguise all but worn away by the goo, a baby tied to his back, sinking out of view.

*Leave him*, said Narindi, back online again. *Indrani and the baby should be enough.*

Of course, Hiresh couldn't obey that order. He lifted man and wailing child free of the slime and sluiced them off with water taken from those around him. Indrani was all that mattered, it was true – he knew that, he knew it. Billions of lives depended on getting her to the warship as quickly as possible.

Narindi agreed. *He's dangerous*, sent the doctor. *Dangerous!*

*Not to me*, sent Hiresh. *We are Tribe, he and I.* 'My friend,' he whispered, eyes stinging. 'My friend.' He hugged the savage fiercely to his chest, hoping for a sign, a whispered word of forgiveness, but the hunter didn't wake up.

# 22. THE LAST MISSION

The famous statue of Haputal Plaza had no face, but it was far from expressionless. It strode forward relentlessly; a giant, stocky woman, every limb working as she leaned into the future. At night it . . . *she* would slow down, make a show of yawning, before her great chin finally came to lie against her own chest. Children must have pestered their parents to ask the Roof where she was going, or why she never lost hope when all her movement failed to advance her a single step.

Hiresh, ten years past the age of his first Log On, experienced no urge to ask the questions for himself. All his thoughts led him back to the same places and the same foul deeds.

He slumped away from the barracks window and its fine view of the statue and the hordes camping at its feet. His movement caused a pair of nearby Wardens to flinch away from him. He ignored them. He'd been feeling feverish and nauseous since his rescue of

Stopmouth's family. But at least it hadn't been for nothing.

He had carried the two adults and the child back with him through most of the same corridors he had followed on the way to Snake Sector. People fled from him and made the Religious signs against evil that he knew so well. Sometimes he understood the conversations around him and sometimes he didn't. The start of a prayer or a shouted curse would turn to gibberish in mid-sentence as the Roof flickered on and off. The baby cried all the way and there was nothing the Elite, with all his powers, could do for her when he failed to revive her parents. If they even *were* her parents.

Indrani in particular looked dangerously fragile, with so much skin eaten away. *What if she dies*, he had wondered, *before I get her to the Globes?*

Another wave of heat passed through Hiresh's body and he shuddered with it.

'The doctor is here,' said one of the Wardens, a handsome woman with proportions like the statue beyond the window. She needn't have spoken, for no sooner had she stepped back from him than more Wardens came into the barracks, all armed to the teeth, with Narindi safe at their heart. He rushed to Indrani's side. He slipped on a pair of gloves and began smearing what had to be Medicine onto her face and shoulders.

'This is the last of it,' he muttered. 'The very scrapings of the barrel.'

There was something about Narindi's movements that didn't seem quite right to the young Elite. It had crossed his mind during the quake in Freedom Sector, but his thoughts were too cloudy to focus on it right now. Flamehair started crying again, ignored by everyone until Hiresh staggered to his feet and took her in his arms. She must have been starving, poor thing. She smelled too. Really bad. He jiggled her a bit, taking great care not to hurt her with his new strength until, to his great surprise, she fell asleep. *Exhausted*, he thought. *We're all exhausted.*

The doctor now stood in front of him. A few minutes seemed to have passed. Indrani was already gone, and a group of Wardens was taking Stopmouth away on a trolley. Hiresh felt he should stop them, but he couldn't think straight.

'You don't look well,' said the doctor.

'My bones are hot,' said the boy. 'I can feel every one of them.'

The doctor muttered to himself, 'Like the others . . .'

'What others?' Did the man look worried now? Hiresh stood up, the baby still in one arm. Yes, the doctor was definitely worried.

'A few of the other Elite were sick too. But it doesn't matter, Captain. You'll recover.'

'How do you know I'll recover?'

'I . . . I'm a doctor. I . . . you'll recover. You'll be fine.

Had we known it would be so difficult for you, we would have sent somebody more experienced.' He held out his arms to Hiresh. 'The child . . . please. I'll take her.'

Hiresh swayed on his feet. 'You think I'm a fool, don't you?' The words felt right as he spoke them, although he had no proof of anything. Passion brought hot spittle to his lips as his anger rose. 'And the High Commissioner too. He spoke to me himself, practically laughing in my face with every word he said. Who knows what lies he told me in there . . . during my *private audience*.'

'Hiresh,' said the doctor, fear in his eyes. '*Captain* Hiresh. Your work today has saved us – the Roof, that is. The Roof. What difference does anything else make compared to that? Please. Please give me the child. We need Indrani to talk.'

Perhaps he handed over Flamehair, or perhaps he let the doctor take her. The next thing Hiresh saw was the man walking away from him, and something . . . something was not right. His vision started to blur again, but he reached out and grabbed the departing man's shoulder. He squeezed it just a little – just until Narindi groaned.

'Doctor. Something has been bothering me about you. About Dharam. I want to know. Why aren't you Elite?'

'Please . . . you'll break the bone . . .'

Hiresh did not let go. 'You've lived so long. Since the time when there were doctors in the world. Since before there were shortages. You could have had anything you wanted. Cosmetics, Medicine, *anything*. So why aren't you, or Dharam, or any of the Commission' – *squeeze* – 'why' – *squeeze* – 'aren't you' – *squeeze* – 'Elite?'

'Stop it! Stop it!' The baby had woken in Narindi's arms and was crying again. A number of Wardens milled about in confusion. A few had truncheons or even guns pointed at Hiresh, but nobody fired.

Hiresh eased his grip slightly. 'Tell me.'

'None of you last,' said the doctor. 'You get ten years at the most. We don't know why. Nobody knows why. After a decade the Elite just . . . they just drop. And we always claimed the deaths were from combat. I'm sorry, I'm so sorry. But you got what you wanted, didn't you? The ones we accepted at the Academy were . . . were . . .'

'Fanatics,' said Hiresh.

'No!' babbled the doctor. 'Patriotic! Brave! All of you. You – you wanted to rescue your mother, didn't you? You can. You can, now. We have no further orders for you. And . . . and don't forget, we have your girlfriend too. You can have her.' Hiresh said nothing. 'Or any woman you want! That Warden over there, the pretty one – you could—'

The old anger rose in Hiresh again. His stomach churned as he pushed it away. He wanted to hurt this man so, so badly, but he knew if the anger returned he might well kill everybody here, the baby included. And he didn't want to be a killer any more. He didn't want that and couldn't believe he ever had, no matter how much his father had ruined his life.

'Where is Tarini? Show me where she is.'

Narindi transmitted the information. A room full of hostages with plenty of food and water, but with all communications from the outside blocked off. Narindi also supplied directions for getting there, and when the Roof vouched for the accuracy of the information, Hiresh let him wriggle free.

The Elite found himself back at the window, looking out at the marching statue. Distracted by the heat from his bones, he had no idea how much time had passed since the doctor and the Wardens had left.

'You wanted to rescue your mother,' Narindi had said. And that was still true. Hiresh would use this magnificent strength to see her one more time and to persuade her to get out of her husband's clutches. He was aware the task might get him killed either by Rebels or the failing Roof. So there was one other person he would have to see first. He would kiss Tarini again. He would kiss her goodbye.

Boxes and boxes of food climbed up one side of the room, tumbling over each other and forming little avalanches at the edges. And there was water too, glistening in tall containers with tops that could be twisted off. 'Bottles,' Stopmouth whispered. 'They're called *bottles*.'

A cool draught blew against his sweaty, stinging skin and his stomach growled so loudly that he felt his whole frame tremble with it.

A woman screamed nearby while a dozen other voices tried to hush her. He ignored them all. His body had taken over, driving him in a frenzy over to the supplies. He guzzled his way through five days' worth of what these people called 'ration packs', tearing through the inedible skins, drained bottles spinning at his feet. Finally he fell back against the wall in relief, rejoicing in the cool breeze that soothed his raw body.

He found a dozen pairs of eyes watching him. All Seculars, their clothes cleaner than any he'd seen in a long time.

'Is he . . . is he going to eat us?' asked a middle-aged man, one of the very rare overweight people in the Roof.

'No,' said a teenage girl beside him. 'Don't you know anything? That's Stopmouth.'

It was then that he noticed the drop. The room had three walls only; instead of a fourth, he found himself looking out at a vast open space large enough to hold the streets he'd grown up in. His full stomach lurched. He'd been sitting a mere arm's-length from the edge!

A sphere hung in the middle of that space, with various

pipes and tubes and walkways reaching out to it from the walls on all sides. He saw figures crawling over various parts of it, while above, two Globes hovered, each tiny against its bulk. What really frightened him, however, was a brief glimpse of what lay beneath – it had to be the surface of the world. His longed-for home was no more than a fatal drop away from him now.

The hunter threw himself backwards to the sounds of more screams from his new companions. Had he been any less terrified, he might have tried to calm them. He'd forgotten how much he feared these yawning spaces. It had been different in the Globe, when he knew he couldn't fall; here it felt more like that terrible bridge in the Upstairs.

'It's all right,' said a nervous voice beside him – the funny-looking girl who'd known his name. She had put herself between him and the others. He puzzled over how they had recognized him, but a quick glance at his skin showed that the last of his disguise had burned away under the slime. He was just himself again. An out-of-place savage among the civilized.

He smiled at the girl. 'You know me,' he said.

She nodded back at him. 'I saw the Yellowmaws get you, but I knew you weren't dead. Oh, by the gods! When I play this back for my boyfriend . . . I can't – I just can't believe it!'

'Who are you?' he asked.

'Tarini,' she said, her funny little eyes bright with joy.

'No – I mean, thank you, Tarini, I do want to know your name. But why are we all here together like this with all this food? Who brought us here?'

'I think we're hostages,' said one woman. She was every inch the Secular: young and thin and tired. Nobody else wanted to talk, but she seemed to be the type that couldn't bear silence for more than a few moments. 'My husband has been working on some project in the shipyards.' She pointed out past the missing wall. 'He wasn't allowed to talk about it. Two weeks later he came home and said, "I'm not going back, Yogita. No way! I want to spend what time I've got left with my family." And no sooner had he said it than Wardens were at the door, dragging us away just like that! He started shouting something about . . . I don't know, the Deserters or something, and they truncheoned him just like that! Like that!'

Her husband must have known the truth, Stopmouth thought. He asked the others why they were here, and none had any answers except that all of them, apart from Tarini, seemed to have somebody working in the shipyards.

But the talkative woman, Yogita, hadn't finished. 'And my man wasn't the only one,' she said. 'Some of the engineers revolted. They'd heard something – something *terrible* – I don't know what. And they threatened to change the launch codes so the warship couldn't be used, but I couldn't tell you what happened to them after that – I was in here.'

She was looking at Stopmouth as if he had the answers, but what could he say? 'The world is ending and you're all going to die'? or, 'Don't worry, your brave leaders will be escaping and will think kindly of your sacrifice'? How could such words possibly help her? Or him, for that matter.

However, it *was* interesting about those workers changing the . . . he'd forgotten the word already – something 'launch'. But he knew it referred to the magic *paper* Indrani had seen. If Dharam only had the old version, it would explain why he needed her so badly now.

'I have to get out of here,' he said. 'We all do.'

He didn't answer their questions. Instead, he tried the locked door, asking the Roof to open it for him, asking for furniture that might have helped in smashing it – all to no avail. He tried contacting Indrani, calling her to say he was all right, to ask about Flamehair. She didn't respond to his messages and he had no proof she was even alive – except, of course, the fact that they had bothered to keep him safe.

'Are there guards?' he asked the other hostages. 'When do they open the door?'

'When there are more people they want to keep safe,' said Tarini. 'We have everything we need here,' she added. 'I've never seen so much food in my life!'

'They'll come for those rations, don't you worry,' said the hunter. 'But it may be too late by then. My wife . . . I need to find her and her . . . and *our* child. I'm sure they must have been taken to the warship.' It was the only thing that made sense. They'd want Indrani aboard and they'd use Flamehair to make her do their bidding. Or maybe they'd threaten Stopmouth himself.

'I know a way out,' said the girl.

Yogita snorted. 'Oh, not again, you crazy child!'

'I went some of the way already,' Tarini confessed. 'Just some of the way. I was too scared, and besides, they told me to stay here. My boyfriend is working for them.'

Stopmouth bit his lip. 'Will you help me leave, then?'

She nodded, and pointed out towards the impossible drop. 'We need to go that way.'

'Oh no!' was all he could say. 'I can't.'

'But you're a hero,' she said. She pushed a strand of hair out of her face. 'I've done it. Watch me.'

'I don't think I *can* watch.' But he let her take his hand and pull him a few steps closer to the edge. He felt his breathing quicken, and halted a good body-length from the drop. His heart beat faster than a wedding drum and he realized that if by picking this girl up and throwing her over the edge, he himself could be spared this task, then he would have done so. The thought shocked him. *I am Wallbreaker, after all*, he realized. He remembered the sweat on his brother's lip; the nightmares he was said to have, and the way he'd turned into a chief who directed others to hunt, having become too scared to ever do so himself. Wallbreaker.

'Are you sick?' asked Tarini. 'You're sweating.'

'I know.'

'We don't have to go,' she said.

Stopmouth looked at her, shamed by her bravery, and thought, *Oh my ancestors, this one is worthy of the greatest of you. Possess me. Give me the strength to get this girl onto the warship alongside my family.* He didn't worry that this might mean one of the rulers of this cursed place losing out.

'We're going,' he said. 'What do I have to do?'

'You're both mad!' said Yogita again.

Tarini ignored her. 'We climb over the lip,' she said. 'There are pipes and things, bars of metal. We can clamber over them as far as the edge of the room and then move up a level. After that, though, it gets hard.'

He smiled. 'Hard? Don't . . . don't let's talk about that yet. We'll just . . . go. I'll need you to guide me because I might . . . I might have to keep my eyes closed, all right?'

'All right,' she said.

Stopmouth shut his eyes and allowed her to lead him to the edge, trusting her when she said to stop. His heart hammered in his chest and his imagination created a vision of the fall every bit as terrifying as the real one he was trying to block out.

'Sit down here,' said Tarini.

His legs locked in position.

'I said, sit down!' She had a remarkably hard punch for one so small. It didn't hurt, but it woke Stopmouth's pride enough to allow him to obey.

'Sorry,' she said. 'I know what it's like. But you're a hero, right? I know how you guys work. You just have to think of the person, you know? The person you can't let down.'

'Indrani,' he said.

'Yes,' and he could hear the smile in her voice.

He opened his eyes and closed them again immediately as his stomach spotted the void and tried to leap towards it. However, his brief glimpse had shown him plenty of strong, predictable handholds – the pipes Tarini had promised.

Stopmouth backed over the edge while Yogita whispered loudly about how stupid they were, how they'd never make it back and so on.

He shuffled along after the girl, a stout tube taking the weight of their feet.

'We're just coming to the wall now,' she said. 'You're going to have to open your eyes to find the handholds.'

He nodded. A great draught was at their backs, the air cold enough to chill the sweat on his skin. When he forced the lids of his eyes open, all he saw was the edge of the room where he'd been held prisoner and the fascinated faces of the other hostages staring back. *Not so terrible*, he thought. Above and to his left, Tarini hung from a clump of metallic fibres that looked as though they'd just sprouted there. Her eyes were so full of encouragement for him, and no little belief, that he knew he could do this. *As long as I don't look down . . .*

They climbed easily after that. So many curious protrusions, cables and pipes poked out of the walls, he felt he could scale them all day and never tire. But they didn't get far. Little lights ran here and there on the wall, flicking on and off, but Tarini showed no fear of them, so neither did he.

'This is where I had to stop last time,' she said.

The wall above them had grown smooth for half the length of a body. Polished metal that Stopmouth could see his face in, his pale skin. Above the mirrored section lay a mass of loose cables and the lip of what might be another room. 'Look at the shape of it,' said Tarini. 'I think it's the end of a corridor.'

The hunter nodded. There seemed to be entrances to other corridors all over the wall, although only one was within reach. Or almost within reach . . . He could see why the girl had been forced to stop here. To get onto the lip, she would have had to climb as far as she could before leaping in the hope of grabbing onto the edge, or maybe onto one of those cables. Somebody of her height and strength was unlikely to succeed, and if she missed . . . He shuddered and wished he had more control over his imagination.

At that point Stopmouth felt some kind of vibration thrumming in the pipes to which he clung. *A quake!* he thought, horrified. But it never rose beyond a slight tremble that he felt in the palms of his hands.

'Oh, look!' said Tarini. 'Over there!'

'I . . . I don't want to. Could you tell me what's happening?'

'A bridge,' she said. 'It's growing out from a corridor near the one we're trying to get to, and going towards the warship. Maybe we should head back? They'll see us when they start to cross.'

'No,' he said. 'If I don't do this now . . .'

She said something back to him, but he'd already stopped listening. All he could hear was his own blood pulsing through his head. He pushed himself up as far as he could go. His limbs trembled, but whether that was the bridge extending itself or his own terror, he didn't dare consider. He crouched down, ready to spring. His muscles locked in place, but he was in charge, not them. Indrani needed him, and Flamehair too, his mother's grandchild. He screamed, and launched himself upwards. It was so easy to pass the height of the lip, he almost forgot to grab onto it. His sweat-slick hands clung tight.

'I can give you a push,' he heard from below.

Tarini's strength helped him over the edge, although the loose cables scratched at his chest and the remains of his robes. Thank the ancestors, an empty corridor. Another one paralleled it no more than twenty paces away, and that was where the bridge was coming from. He was sure he'd be able to reach it through one of the many side passages he could see ahead of him.

A little further in lay a pool of what had to be slime. He shuddered, imagining what would have happened had it been closer to the edge when he was trying to hold on.

'My turn,' said the girl. 'We need to hurry – the bridge is almost complete. There'll be somebody crossing it.'

Stopmouth had hoped to find a rope, or something to pass over to pull her up, but his clothing had been so corrupted by the slime that he wasn't sure it would hold her weight. Some of the cables hanging there might do, but he would still have to look over the edge in order to pass one down to her. He swallowed his fear and reached down for her, careful to concentrate on her hands rather than the fall. Her voice and her own brave eyes steadied him. 'You won't drop me,' she said. And she jumped. Not a moment too soon. The bridge reached the side of the warship with a deep *clang*.

'We should get over there if we want to cross,' said Tarini as he dragged her over the edge. 'They can pull their bridge back just as easily. And if it's the ship we're heading for—'

'It is. Come on. No, wait—' He paused. 'We should

agree to talk from now on into each other's heads. I'll allow you and—'

'We can't,' she said. 'The Roof is still translating, but messaging isn't working right. There might be a jammer nearby. I couldn't get through to my boyfriend.'

Maybe her friend was already dead, Stopmouth thought, but decided not to mention it. There'd be time enough for bad news later on.

Ahead of them, past a massive pool of slime, the corridor curved off in the direction of the bridge. Yet the side passages appeared to offer a more direct route, full of smashed machinery and other good cover. 'We'll go this way,' he said.

It proved harder than he'd thought. Little doors no higher than his arm lined the walls three high. Most were open, as though they'd recently burst, and spewed forth wires and glittering scraps of hexagonal metal that made the ground between the machines slippery and uncertain. The gaps they passed through grew smaller. They squandered hundreds of heartbeats tripping over one obstacle after the other while Stopmouth imagined the bridge pulling away again, leaving him stranded here for ever and making rescue of Indrani impossible. Deep down, he still hoped that some of the tribe on the surface had managed to barricade themselves into Headquarters. He might yet be able to scare Dharam into saving them.

They kept pushing forward as fast as they could go, until Stopmouth, pulling ahead, fell off the last metal box to land in the light of the corridor beyond.

'Well, Captains,' he heard a voice say, 'I doubt we'll ever have such an easy mission again! He came right to us.'

The hunter looked around. He found himself in a clean, wide corridor no more than twenty paces from the bridge. Three Wardens waited there. Three. He might just about be able to handle that many – they frightened easily, that was the trick. And they stood between him and his Indrani. This could only end one way.

Two of the Wardens – both young women – already looked a little worried. They leaned heavily against the rail of the bridge they had grown, and their faces ran with more sweat than seemed natural. The man at the front, however, only grinned. He stood with hands on hips, his head tilted back like a chief surrounded by friends at a feast.

Beyond them lay the circular shaft. It stretched upwards for ever, all glittering lights and polished sheets of metal that sat next to each other in complex patterns. Stopmouth craned his neck, drawn towards the terrifying vastness of the space even as his stomach rebelled. Globes swam up there, always moving, always working, tiny as insects until they came lower to buzz about the warship. Even then, they grew no larger than his fist.

The foolish Wardens didn't interfere with him as he sat

up. They just stood there, watching, the one at the front still smirking beneath the visor he wore.

Stopmouth glanced back into the clogged passage. Good, he thought, Tarini had been smart enough not to come out from hiding where he'd have had to worry about her too.

When he turned round again, he found, to his astonishment, that the leader of the three Wardens had somehow managed to appear right beside him.

'Surprise,' said the man.

A lazy kick sent the hunter sliding and tumbling across the floor. 'Get over here, Captains!' said the Warden. 'We've been warned about this savage. "Take no chances," they said. He's killed our kind before. And more than once.' A smack. 'Too young, too cocky, the lot of them.' The women still hadn't moved and it made the man angry. 'I said, get over here! What are you waiting for?'

Stopmouth felt something grip him round the neck and raise him off the ground. A hand, a single hand, at the end of an arm so strong it didn't need to bend as it hoisted him into the air. It was only now, in that crushing grip, that Stopmouth glimpsed the red stripes that marked his three enemies out as Elite.

The visor watched as Stopmouth scrabbled at the sleeve of the Elite's uniform, digging fingers into the iron muscle beneath. He saw wrinkles on the man's chin, as though he was as old as Kubar back home. Strands of grey hair poked out from beneath his helmet. Old people were supposed to be weaklings.

The Elite could easily have crushed his victim's wind-pipe, but did not. Nor did he ever bend his arm. Perhaps he'd heard how the hunter had eaten Krishnan's face and was keeping a safe distance.

'Hurry up, Captains. Bring the chains.'

Tarini chose that moment to make her move. She darted out from the side passage, a shard of metal flashing in her grip. One of the sick Wardens on the bridge called out a warning, but quick little Tarini had no more than five paces to make up before slashing at the sergeant's back.

The man cried out and dropped his captive. His first swipe at Tarini was too high. Before he could take another, the hunter dived forward to take him round the ankles so that he crashed to the ground, striking his head hard enough to stun.

Stopmouth saw a familiar shape in the man's weapon belt – a metal sling; a *gun*, as they called it. He pulled it out, intending to strike the Elite warrior before he could regain his senses.

'Stopmouth!' cried Tarini.

The younger Elite had finally steadied themselves enough to run towards Stopmouth. One of them had a funny kind of metal rope, but her feet caught in it, slowing her down.

'Run, Tarini, hide!'

Stopmouth raised the iron weapon, pointed it and pulled the trigger. A deafening bang thundered around the walls of the corridor and the weapon jumped in his hands like a living thing. He had barely time to realize he'd missed everybody before the nearest woman reached Tarini and knocked her to the floor. The other had recovered her feet and was approaching fast. Stopmouth flung the weapon at the face of the nearest. Then he dived into the gap between a few rusty machines in a side passage and wriggled for all he was worth, desperate to get away.

They wanted him alive: the older one could have killed him at any time, and had called for the younger ones to bring chains – that was the metal rope he'd seen. The only use they could possibly have for him was as a hostage to ensure Indrani's good behaviour. Once Dharam had made his escape, he would have the hunter killed. Indrani would know this, but would still be forced to do his bidding.

*I must not be caught.*

He heard conversation from the other end of the little tunnel: 'No, Captains, I'm fine, I'm fine! Just follow him down the tunnel so he can't come back this way. I'll do the rest. "Crippled and in chains," they said! It will be my pleasure.'

A great racket filled the passageway as one of the Elite

struggled through the tunnel, lifting machines out of her path, pushing others aside like the branches of trees.

Stopmouth's own progress was not so swift. He was tired and hungry again. New cuts and bruises collected on his body with every step. They would catch him – there could be no doubt about that. They'd use him and little Flamehair as weapons against his woman. Then all three would be killed while the tribe died out on the surface. Hopeless, all hopeless.

He came out into the corridor sooner than he'd expected.

The drop lay waiting for him only twenty paces away, with the small stream of slime he'd passed through earlier glittering under all the reflected lights of the shaft. His pursuer was making quite a racket in the passageway he'd just left, but other footsteps approached beyond the curve of the corridor in front of him.

Sooner or later he'd have to fight them. A terrible prospect. All his previous successes with the Elite had involved a mixture of luck, outside forces and arrogance on the part of his opponents. None of these could be relied upon now, especially in the case of the sergeant, whose voice he heard coming round the curve of the corridor, shouting encouragement to his younger, weakening comrades.

Stopmouth looked around for some help in fighting his enemies, and laughed even as his heart almost seized in terror. This place was full of weapons he could use, full of them. And all he needed to win was a desperation strong enough to overcome his fear.

Luckily he didn't have much time to mull it over. First thing first: he ran over to the pool of slime and coated his body in it, feeling its awful sting. The next part would be more dreadful, for he'd have to put his head over the edge of the drop. He shivered. *I'll be looking*, he thought. *That's all, just looking . . .*

'I know you're there, savage,' came the voice of the leader. 'I need you to give yourself up so we can fix the Roof, all right?'

Stopmouth was glad of the voice and the distraction it brought. His hand was scrabbling over the edge of the drop, and all he could see before him was an eternity of falling. It was daytime down below now, and yet several places lay in almost complete darkness.

'I'm not here to hurt you,' said the voice. 'But we need your woman's co-operation, see? Without her, the Roof is doomed – the Roof and everybody in it. Even a savage could understand why we need her help. She shouldn't have to be forced to co-operate. If you were to ask her—'

Stopmouth had finally found what he was after, thank the ancestors. A few more adjustments, a few more heartbeats . . .

'They've lied to you, Warden,' he called back. He was

almost ready now. Terrified, terrified, but ready. 'There is no Cure for the Crisis. The only way out is on that ship. Why do you think they built it?'

Stopmouth scrambled to his feet just as the man rounded the corner.

'It's a laboratory, savage. Not that I'd expect a Deserter to think of anything but running away. And the Commission might well lie to the masses, but they wouldn't dare lie to us . . . Captains? Captains? Hurry up!' The sergeant had come into view round the curve in the corridor, his powerful body blocking out most of the light. 'Your woman must talk, savage. She must. This is your last chance. Come willingly or I'll break every bone in your body to keep you still. Do you understand? I'm no monster, but I would do this to save my people.' All the while he spoke, he was drawing closer. He stepped through the pool of slime, leaving streaks of it behind him as he drew nearer to where Stopmouth stood at the edge of the drop.

'I'm going to throw myself off,' said the hunter. 'You'll never use me to make her talk.'

He moved back half a step, heart pounding. He felt his heel touch the edge. *Don't look! Don't look!* His sweat mixed with the coating of slime that tormented all the many cuts in his skin.

'Easy,' said the warden, inching closer. 'Go easy now – you don't want to do that.' His voice projected calm, but a lifetime of hunting and being hunted made Stopmouth aware of the muscles that tensed and bunched under the man's uniform.

'Easy,' the man started to say, and then pounced. The hunter was ready for him. He pushed back hard, adding all of his strength to the momentum of his enemy, so that both fell out and over the drop. They screamed in fear, clinging together like drowning men. The cable Stopmouth had tied to his ankle jerked them to a halt, and they hung for only the briefest of instants before the Elite lost his grip on Stopmouth's slimy skin and fell away and down for ever.

Stopmouth hung there, looking out into nothing, his stomach screaming for him to get away, but also robbing him of the strength he needed to obey it. He could fall now and they'd never be able to use him as a hostage. This was it – one way, at least, to help Indrani. His body would hit the surface and become food for his tribe, or some other creatures. He'd be going home.

The Roof chose that moment to give him a last look at his people. Perhaps it was pity. Or perhaps a Globe simply happened to be passing by on its way to fight the Rebels somewhere. Stopmouth would never know.

One whole arm of the U-shaped complex of buildings where his tribe lived had collapsed entirely. Many other houses in the area had disappeared, or seemed to be sinking into the ground. A hill on the near side of the river groaned under the weight of planted beasts, in eternal agony. In eternal blackness too, for the Roof panels above their drooping heads lay dark and would now be dark for ever.

The only light in the area consisted of bonfires on the surviving roofs of Headquarters. Stopmouth was amazed to see that some of his people still lived, despite the arrival of the Diggers.

A small band of maybe two hundred humans fought desperately to repulse the creatures that dug claws into the very stone of the walls as they swarmed upwards. Stopmouth saw Kamala being dragged screaming from the parapet, her useless sling wrapped around one fist. He saw Yama covered in blood, and Sanjay lying broken in a corner. A weeping Sodasi held down Rockface, who was bleeding from the chest, but who still wanted to fight next to the children he'd trained. He grieved for each one who disappeared from the walls.

And then the Globe, if that's what it was, had swept out of range again, and Stopmouth was back in his body.

He felt pressure on the cable. Somebody was pulling him up. The other Wardens. The sick ones. The hunter had no spare energy to fight them. He'd been hoping, half hoping really, that they would have seen or heard the fall and assumed Stopmouth was dead.

The women raised him easily. Soon the hunter lay on

the ground at their feet, a volunteer waiting only for the knife to fall.

They took him through the corridor the long way. Two young women, one of them extremely pretty. Both ill, muttering under their breaths, swaying at odd moments. But their grips never loosened enough for him to break free, and he knew that either of them could have snapped his arms without so much as a thought.

'We're going to chain you up and hang you off a bridge,' whispered the pretty one. 'Indrani will be able to watch us from there. Then we'll break your bones, one at a time, until she talks.'

A hostage. As he had expected. But if they needed to use him for this, did that mean Flamehair was dead? Killed by the slime? The thought closed his throat and weakened his knees so that they had to drag him along. His whole tribe was dying. Everybody he knew, right down to the last beautiful child. What else was there? What else could there ever be again?

A new Elite waited for them at the bridge with Tarini's unconscious body, but Stopmouth paid him no heed. He felt the grip of the pretty Warden loosen on his arm.

'Hiresh?' she said.

Stopmouth blinked in astonishment. The boy was supposed to be dead, but here he stood.

The female Warden spoke again, her voice hoarse and

weak. 'So you were picked? You graduated? I thought that girl seemed familiar. She's the crazy one who used to moon after you all the time. That weird Crisis baby . . .'

Hiresh staggered to his feet and fumbled something out of his pocket. He pointed it at the other group, and both Stopmouth's captors released their hold on him at once. The hunter recognized the object too, but he had no fear left in his body.

'Put the laser down,' said the pretty one. 'Hiresh?'

He only raised it higher and clicked some button on the top of it. Stopmouth heard the uneven sound of the Wardens' footsteps as they ran away.

The boy lowered his weapon and knelt down beside the girl again. Stopmouth joined him. Part of him wanted to be angry with Hiresh for his betrayal. But none of that seemed important as the whole world died around them.

'It's true, isn't it?' whispered Hiresh. 'They're Deserting. That laboratory story is so . . . so stupid. Why would it need engines? How could I have believed any of that?'

'They won't get away,' said Stopmouth. 'I think somebody changed the . . . the magic words . . . the . . .'

'Launch codes.' Hiresh nodded. There were tears running down his face.

'Indrani's the only one who knows them now, I think.'

'Take Tarini with you. She took a knock, but she'll be all right.'

'Of course, Hiresh, but what about you?'

Hiresh smiled sadly and shook his head. He caught one of Stopmouth's wrists and brought the hunter's hand up to touch his own cheek. His tears stung the hunter's skin. Slime! The boy had slime running out of him like the machines of the Upstairs. Stopmouth jerked his hand away.

'You need . . . to go,' said Hiresh. 'Before there's another quake . . . And . . . and I don't want her to . . . see me. But tell her . . . please, tell her . . .' He shook his head and shrugged.

'I will,' said Stopmouth. 'I'll tell her something.'

Hiresh took one last long look at Tarini. He stood and turned as if to go. Then he paused and threw something back at Stopmouth. It was the green-light weapon. 'Only a Warden can use one of these,' he said. 'I think . . . Indrani might still count. I don't know.'

And then he was limping away.

Stopmouth waited until Hiresh had gone round the curve in the corridor before gently slapping Tarini awake.

She was groggy. 'Did they hit me?'

He smiled.

'Scum,' she said, and groaned as she tried to sit up.

'You want me to carry you?' he asked.

She surprised him with a weak punch to his arm. 'Who carried who when we were climbing up the shaft?' She forced herself upright. 'What's next, Chief?'

'I need your help, Tarini. I need you to come into that thing with me. They have my wife and my . . . my daughter.'

'You don't sound too sure about that.'

Flamehair was his brother's daughter, of course. But Stopmouth was the only father she would ever know or love. It was an amazing realization: he had seen her as yet another thing Wallbreaker had stolen from him, when in reality the opposite was true. Flamehair was his, now and for ever. An unexpected joy.

'I'm sure,' he said, and smiled so broadly that a filthy Tarini could not help but laugh at him.

'Come on then,' she said. 'Let's get them back for you.'

# 23. THE SEED

Stopmouth and Tarini entered the warship through a clunky metal door that looked nothing at all like those in the rest of the Roof. They found themselves in a narrow room where straps and rungs grew on every surface.

'It's so quiet here,' said Tarini.

'And shouldn't there be guards?' asked Stopmouth, his voice echoing slightly. This was the secret, after all. The only way out of a dying world for numbers of desperate people so large, his mind could not imagine them. And it was the only possible escape for the tribe too, he reminded himself.

'I'm not sure they need guards. They already know we're here. Look up there, Chief.'

Stopmouth obeyed, and saw a funny little machine with a red dot flashing on top of it. He didn't know what that meant, but the device hadn't hurt either of them yet and it didn't look like it was about to start. All that mattered was that his family was close. He felt elated at the thought.

They had to climb up to another door, no easy feat after

their recent efforts, and here at last they found some guards: two men and two women in filthy white overalls, each of them wielding a metal gun in nervous fingers. They all looked tired, but well-fed. Two of them, a man and one of the women, had grey hair.

'You're not Wardens, are you?' said the hunter, earning a snort from Tarini. She showed no fear before the guns, and Stopmouth wondered if the girl who'd dared to climb out above the void was even capable of such an emotion.

'Stay right there, savage,' said the grey-haired man, terror in his voice.

'I'm not going to eat you,' said Stopmouth. He toyed with the idea of licking his lips, feeling giddy now that they were finally on board.

The gun of the youngest woman wavered in his direction. 'Don't listen to that primitive,' she said. 'Deserters can't be trusted.' The laugh that had been bubbling up inside Stopmouth burst out at last, and more than one nervous finger closed tighter over a trigger.

'Deserters?' said the hunter. He looked at each of them in turn. 'I take it *you're* not Deserters? You'll be leaving this ship before it abandons everybody on the Roof?'

'What?' asked Tarini, her voice shocked. 'They're doing what?'

The grey man lowered his weapon.

'We mustn't let them on board, Gurdeep!' cried the

younger woman. But the man was weeping. He covered his face, his whole body heaving behind those flabby arms.

'I . . . I can't stay here,' said Gurdeep.

Stopmouth patted the man's shoulder. 'I'm just looking for my family,' he said. 'You'll let us pass, won't you?'

'I'll shoot,' said the woman.

'Your chiefs wouldn't want that,' the hunter replied. 'Come, Tarini.' He pushed his way through their useless guns and down another corridor.

'They're Deserting?' asked Tarini. 'But why? Where is there to go? Why can't they stay for the Cure?'

He stopped a moment to look her in the eyes. 'I don't have time to explain it right now, Tarini. But please, will you trust me?'

'I have a friend . . .' She gestured back the way they'd come. 'Out . . . out there.'

'Hiresh,' said the hunter. 'I know. I'm sorry. I'm so sorry.'

'How did you . . . ? Wait! He's . . . He's dead? Are you saying he's *dead*?'

'Gone,' whispered Stopmouth. 'Please trust me. I wouldn't lie to you if there was a chance. I knew him too. He was Tribe to me.'

She just stared at him, and when he tried to give a reassuring pat to her back, she threw him off.

'OK,' he said. He strode forward into the centre of the

ship as if he knew where he was going. After a brief pause he heard Tarini starting to follow him.

They came to a corridor, almost as large as those in the Roof proper. They opened a series of chunky doors, one at a time, to reveal rooms full of strange (Tarini said 'primitive') equipment. One of them held about a hundred capsules, each about as long as a hunter was tall. They covered every surface, even the ceiling. A pair of white-suited women paused in their incomprehensible labour to stare in fright at the visitors.

'You won't . . . you won't damage the coffins?' asked the older of the two.

'Or us!' said the other woman hastily.

'I wouldn't hurt you,' said Stopmouth. 'Where are my wife and child?' The ship couldn't be any bigger than the streets where he'd grown up. Everybody would know everybody else here, and their business. Tarini walked past him into the room, while the women looked at each other.

'We're not supposed to tell,' said one of them.

'Oh look, Stopmouth,' said Tarini. Her eyes glistened even as her lips twisted in anger. She was tugging a wire attached to one of the capsules. 'I bet I could pull this right out.'

'No,' said the older woman, her voice rising almost to a screech. 'Don't do that! You could kill somebody.'

Tarini pulled harder.

'Last door down the hall on the left!' said the woman. 'We didn't tell you.'

'No, you didn't,' sneered Tarini, much to Stopmouth's puzzlement. He shrugged, and followed the girl out into the corridor.

His heart began to speed up. 'It's all been too easy,' he said to the girl.

'Easy? There were three *Elite* on the bridge.'

*Four*, he thought, but said nothing. As they walked towards the last door, he heard something – the wail of a tiny baby in terrible distress. 'Flamehair!' he said. He ran the final few steps, put his hand on the door and stopped. He turned back towards Tarini and whispered, 'Make sure nobody sneaks up on us.'

'Nobody will.'

Stopmouth flung the door open, glimpsed a table and dived to one side of it, rolling smoothly to land in a crouch. Flamehair lay on the tabletop, wrapped up in fresh cloth, still wailing. The walls and floor were black with scorch marks and smelled vaguely of burned meat.

*I know this place*, he thought. He'd never been here before, but Indrani had. He'd seen it in her memories. It had been cleaner then, with more furniture. There'd been that funny stuff – that *paper* that had caused so much fuss. Otherwise, the room was completely empty except for some half-familiar metal bottles. As he picked up his daughter,

Tarini shouted from the corridor. 'Somebody's coming, Stopmouth! I think—'

The door swung shut and all the metal bottles began hissing at once, quickly filling the room with sleep-smoke. One breath was enough to show him how foolish he'd been. 'But the tribe! We have to . . . We have to . . .' He sank to his knees next to the door, the child beside him.

As he tried to claw a way out, he realized he wasn't the first to do so – scratch marks covered the metal surface of the door. Indrani had marvelled that nobody else had seen the paper. But somebody had. Judging by the soot under his knees, there'd been a lot of them. Maybe this was all that remained of the workers who'd changed the launch codes. Locked in and burned alive. Whether this had been an accident or murder, Stopmouth might never know.

The gas continued to rise. Some of it disappeared through slitted holes high in the walls, but it was too late for him to climb up there or push the baby through. He felt himself topple over.

In Stopmouth's dream, a hole opened in the ground on the surface of the world. Everybody he knew and loved was falling into it. His parents were there, clinging by their fingernails until the rocks they gripped slipped free of the earth and tumbled into the void. Everything shook. The streets of Man-Ways rose up to become a slope, rolling its inhabitants one at a time into the starving gullet of the ground. Kubar and Rockface fell past. Yama and Sodasi followed too, dragging Hiresh and a cursing Jagadamba in after them.

The hunter woke into pain, crying out, horrified that the shaking had followed him into the real world. If anything, it seemed worse here. Straps and ropes held him down in a metal room crowded with long, soft chairs. These were occupied by other people, some with eyes tightly closed, and all afraid. Loose objects flew through the air, bringing yelps of pain and terror when they struck somebody.

A large window took up one side of the room. Indrani sat before it – strapped as tightly as Stopmouth was, except her hands had been left free to wander over a hedge of buttons. Dharam sat to her right, shouting at her.

'It's the last quake! We need to go! You said you'd memorized the launch codes – now use them!'

'I'm trying,' said Indrani. 'There's still a bridge. I can't make it disengage without help from the Roof!'

'We have weapons systems,' he cried. 'Shoot it away! Away!'

Impacts came from outside as well as in. On the big screen, Stopmouth could see slabs of wall breaking away from the sides of the shaft. A few were clean, burnished like mirrors, flashing as they passed; but most were pitted, rotten with slime. Some of them struck the bridge that was holding them back, but bounced off into the void.

'I can't hit it!' said Indrani. 'There could be people nearby.'

'You must, you fool! Think of your baby, your savage! Shoot!'

But although flashes of green light lit up the screen, Indrani didn't seem capable of bringing her weapons to bear so close to the ship.

The warship rattled and shuddered as a few smaller pieces struck it. Stopmouth wondered what damage he'd see if he could view its skin. As a boy, he'd believed metal could not be harmed by anything but time. After he'd seen his first smashed Globe, after pieces of one had rained down on Man-Ways, killing a child, he'd had to change his mind.

The green-light weapons of the warship still weren't getting any closer to the bridge. Dharam was screaming, 'Hit the thing! Hit it!'

'I can't,' Indrani shouted back. 'I—' Then she got that look on her face that meant, *I have an idea.*

The wild firing stopped for a moment as Dharam continued screeching and the cabin shuddered with impacts. Then she aimed one single shot far from the bridge. The only effect was to bend a glittering section of the wall forward. Now she aimed for it again, and everyone gasped as the beam of light bounced off the polished surface straight down to the bridge below. Two more strikes, then the hunter felt himself pressed back into his seat and the vibrations lessened. The walls began sinking in front of his eyes.

'We're on our way,' said Indrani, her voice trembling.

*The wrong direction*, thought Stopmouth. *Away from the tribe. Away.* They were all Deserting together.

Dimly he wondered why it was Indrani who had become the pilot. Certainly, their earlier escape from the Upstairs in a stolen Globe had shown that she was a better flyer than anybody else. But how could Dharam trust her? Except, of course, now that they were all in the warship together, she would have as much to lose as any of the cowards in the Commission.

Stopmouth felt tears in his eyes. He wept for the loss of the tribe; he wept in anger at his own stupidity. Instead of taking the ship, he'd been the one to be caught. Like a fool, a fool. No doubt later, sometime when Indrani had done her job, one of Dharam's friends would bring a knife to finish the tied-up hunter. *No more than I deserve.*

The craft shuddered under more impacts as the view on the great screen shifted to show the top of the shaft. Stopmouth wished it hadn't: a solid curtain of fragments was shooting towards them. Beams of light leaped from the warship to take out the bigger ones, but others penetrated the defence. One impact was so strong that the whole craft tipped over, and everybody in the room screamed until it righted itself again.

'The shaft doors aren't opening,' cried Indrani. 'I'm going to have to shoot them.'

'If they tumble down on us—' Dharam shouted. There was no need for him to finish the sentence. Doors large enough to cover the entire shaft were bound to crush the ship when they fell.

Dharam screamed as Indrani fired off her beams of light. They had no effect that the hunter could see, but she kept them there while sweat snaked over her lovely face, changing course with every impact to the spacecraft's shell.

Then the doors seemed to burst into flame and fly upwards. Huge slabs of metal paused in their flight, hanging like the Globes that had once hovered over the world's surface. They waited above the warship for what felt like a dozen heartbeats. Then they dropped down the shaft again, tumbling like spinning knives. Everybody in the craft cried out at once. Everybody except Indrani. She'd been watching, watching, ignoring the smaller impacts that constantly shook them now.

She threw the warship into the sky. As the great pieces of metal fell, their tumbling pulled them apart for no more than an instant. Indrani found the gap and shot them through into sunlight and a field of scattered stars. In moments, the great curved Roof lay far beneath them.

Stopmouth spent the rest of the day sagging against the straps of his couch as everybody else seemed to float into the air. How was that even possible? The sight of it roiled his stomach, and he wasn't the only one, by the looks on some of the faces around him.

'Can you let me out?' he asked the white-coated people who were now moving about, engaged in incomprehensible tasks. They ignored him, except when he wet himself. Some woman took the time then to sneer 'dirty savage', until Indrani shouted her into terrified silence. 'She's another meat-eater,' muttered somebody else under his breath.

They could be smug now, thought the hunter. They'd escaped. They were free. And it didn't matter that the price of their freedom had been paid by their fellow Roofdwellers and would soon be paid by the savages who lived below. His rage built against them. So this was how it felt to be Deserted. He strained against his bindings but could not move. He tried to force calm on himself, to save his energy for any opening that might come to him later on.

'Not all our technology is primitive,' Dharam was saying. A tenth earlier he'd been screaming his lungs out, but the experience seemed, if anything, to have raised his spirits and he grinned like a madman as he spoke. 'We have the Talkers, of course, and some of the most powerful lasers ever produced. But everything we know tells us that the higher-level stuff is already infected. We have ten days at

431

the most before the last Talker stops working, and we must be prepared for when that happens – yes? We need to know who can speak which language and so on. We need to decide who wakes and tends to the farm every few years, keeps it producing oxygen, gets it ready to feed us . . .'

'I thought you'd have had all this worked out already,' Indrani said.

'Oh, no!' Dharam shook his head. 'Some things the Roof wouldn't help us with, and some we couldn't risk doing for fear that word would leak out. We wouldn't want a stampede for the escape now, would we?'

'No, we wouldn't,' said Indrani, her tone frosty.

'We've got most of the skills we need, and that's what counts. We always knew we'd have a bit of organizing to do when we got this far.'

'And then we all go into the coffins?' she asked.

'Not just yet,' he said. 'We need you to take us to the Seed that the new Roofmind will grow from. It is programmed to obey only me, of course. But you mustn't worry. I will order it to create a habitat for us with its own orbit around the star. We just need to make sure we're close to where our new home will be when we emerge from hibernation, yes?'

Stopmouth slept a few times, although probably not for very long. He thought he must be getting feverish.

Sometimes he felt as if a great hand was pushing him back into his chair. At others, his whole body screamed at him that he was falling. He'd close his eyes when this happened, and try not to think about all the terrible things that crowded his mind.

Mostly, when he slept, he had visions of those he'd abandoned on the surface. It seemed so wrong. They'd lived good lives; they had hunted well and would one day give their flesh in love so that others might make it Home. If any should be saved, it was them and not those who had laughed at the tribes' struggles for centuries while keeping them imprisoned below. But even he knew there was no way back to them now. The injustice of it! And Indrani must be feeling it too. Sometimes she took time from her tasks to look at him. All he saw on her face was exhaustion and shame.

'We're nearly there,' Dharam told her, triumph written on every feature. Stopmouth could see him watching Indrani, his eyes running over her body. 'We'll go into *orbit* near the Seed, and then you can join your baby in sleep. We'll have a brand-new Roof to wake up to. A Roof that does not choose which orders to obey! Oh no! My . . . *our* civilization will finally have the unity it needs to flourish properly.'

She ignored him, her eyes on the screen. Finally she said, 'I see it. The Seed.'

A black cube floated in the sky, made visible only by the thousands of stars that hung behind it.

'Strange,' she said. 'It looks . . . blurred or something.'

'It's just the screen,' said a man others referred to as Dr Narindi. 'There'll be dust in our primitive sensors.'

'Then why aren't the stars blurring too?' she asked. 'We need a closer look. Magnification by one hundred!' The screen obeyed, turning the blurring into a fine mist that, under further magnification, became tiny droplets: a million perfect little spheres.

'Water?' asked one of the white coats.

But Stopmouth felt a chill settle on the room.

'Slime,' he said aloud.

'Impossible!' shouted Dharam. 'The Virus wasn't designed to live in a vacuum! We've been sabotaged. We—'

He stopped suddenly, and the look on his face made it plain he'd said something stupid – though what that might be, Stopmouth couldn't tell. Other people, however, were just staring at him, jaws hanging slack.

A grey-bearded man whispered, 'How . . . How could he possibly know what the slime was *designed* for?'

'He said aliens planted it,' a woman added.

'He changed it to Rebels after, but why would they do that? They worship the Roof!'

'I . . .' said Dharam. 'I was just speculating. Of course *I* didn't make the stuff. I mean . . . What I meant was—'

Indrani punched him hard in the nose, rocking his head

backwards. Tiny globes of blood seeped from his right nostril to hang around his head.

Everyone started crying at once – some, like Dr Narindi, in terror, for with the Seed's infection, their plan to survive the downfall of the Roof had failed. Others yelled in anger, and a dozen of them pushed their way towards Dharam with murder in their eyes.

The hunter felt almost glad the end had come. Except he had never wanted his wife and child to suffer. Flamehair deserved a chance at life. So did poor Hiresh, for that matter, and all the countless thousands who must be choking on bad air or starving on the decaying Roof.

'Somebody let me out,' he said. He wanted to go to Indrani. In the end, she used her free hands to release herself. She magically floated over to him from her seat. So many people were crying, their tears filled the air much like the mist of slime that surrounded the Seed. Dharam had backed himself into a corner and could be heard threatening and begging.

'I have a knife, husband,' said Indrani. She sliced through the straps. Stopmouth's arms were itching to hold her. She did not resist.

'Flamehair?'

'She's already in a coffin. The gas could have . . . but it didn't. They got her out of the room in time and put her into the long sleep. Your friend too. That girl.'

'Why . . . Why were you the one flying this thing?'

'I memorized the launch codes. I'm the only one it will obey now. I think they were going to torture you to make me write the numbers down, but I managed to waste a bit of time until the last quake came along and forced them to trust me.' She looked sadly out to where the 'Seed' floated in a cloud of slime. 'Not that any of that matters now.'

'None of you have to die,' Dharam was shouting. 'I swear it. We still have a way out! Narindi sent a plea for help to Earth. The signal will reach them in another eighty years. All we have to do is sleep until they get to us. We just have to sleep.'

'And why,' said one of those hunting him, a cross-looking woman with bruises all over her face, 'would anybody from Earth come here with your filthy Virus floating about?'

'Oh, where is your courage?' shouted Dharam. 'We can beat this! It's an adventure we're on. The adventure of a life-time! If we just—' They converged on him all at once, as clumsy a group of killers as Stopmouth had ever seen. The angry knot floated in front of the view screen, blocking most of it.

Suddenly shafts of light flashed through the gaps of their thrashing limbs as the sun came over the curve of the Roof. Indrani turned to look. She froze, her left cheek a sudden crescent of white. Then she burst out laughing as the glare spread further and further into the cabin.

'What's wrong?' Stopmouth asked. Other people were now staring too.

She looked back at him, eyes shining in the new white light.

'Do you still wish to save the tribe?' she asked.

'You found a way?'

'Oh, yes,' she said. 'But' – she pointed a finger at the heaving mass of people – 'things are about to get bumpy. Do we have any savages available to scare that lot back to their seats?'

He grinned.

'And,' she whispered, 'you'll need to keep them there. Use the knife if you have to. They won't like what comes next!'

# Epilogue:
# Falling Metal

It was Kubar who had saved the last of them, and he was proud of that. Nobody had congratulated him, but then again, what was the point and what had he saved them for? Their numbers had probably been too low to survive before the great Digger attack. Now extinction had become a certainty.

As the fuel ran out and the fires died, the enemy swarmed over the walls, gripping masonry with diamond-hard claws. *I won't hide in the dark,* he'd thought. Death would come quicker if the demons could see him.

So he'd replaced firelight with the Talker's illumination, and when he saw that the monsters feared it, he made it as bright as it could go, until the grubs on their backs shrivelled and died and the grieving 'mothers' fled before him. To think Stopmouth had gone to the Roof for a weapon, when they'd had one here all along.

But the Talker wouldn't last long without light from the Roof to power it. He knew that much, even if the others did not. So he kept it switched off now, while everybody waited to die.

The big old savage, Rockface, stirred himself in the blackness. Kubar could tell it was him by the careful way he moved these days. 'That's not right, hey?' said the big man.

Kubar knew what he meant. He could feel the vibration in the parapet under his palms. Something was happening. Another Digger attack? Or were they trying to collapse the building again? People crept forward to join the two men.

'Daylight!' shouted Vishwakarma. 'The day is coming back!' Kubar wondered if the young man's injury had driven him mad – but no. An enormous section of the Roof, maybe ten times the size of a park, had begun to glow only a few kilometres from their current position, close to where the Diggers had made their huge underground nest.

'It's the wrong colour,' Kubar muttered, but nobody heard him. At first it was deep red, then orange, until finally it turned to a blinding white.

'It's melting,' he said. Balls of molten metal dripped onto the plains below or splashed hissing into the river. Finally a portion of the Roof burst asunder with a sound that rolled over the surface and shattered many of the buildings the Diggers had weakened. The noise and the light had everybody scrambling back from the parapet, shading their eyes.

But not Kubar. He saw it all. A spacecraft – a real

439

spacecraft! – fell through the enormous hole it had made for itself. It plummeted towards the ground, only to be saved at the last moment by weak jets. Then it moved – quite deliberately, thought the priest – to hover over the Digger nest that had appeared on this side of the hills. A blast of flame, hotter than the sun, plunged into the earth, searing to nothing the field of victims and – surely – cleaning out the tunnels underneath. Then one final wobbly manoeuvre tilted the craft back towards Headquarters.

'It's coming this way!' shouted Vishwakarma. 'It will burn us all!'

'Let's kill it!' said Rockface.

He really hadn't a clue, thought Kubar.

'One last hunt, hey? We'll go out with blood on our spears!'

The spacecraft hovered and roared. It managed to lower itself to within a metre or two of the ground before it crashed. Everyone started shouting and running.

'Let's get it,' said Rockface again.

Kubar didn't bother correcting him. One of the children would do that soon enough. He stayed alone on the parapet, blinking away the blotches the spacecraft had left on his vision.

When he could see properly again, he gasped at the beautiful destruction that spread out for kilometres before him.

In all directions, the hillsides and plains lay covered with shards of metal and plastic. They sparkled brilliantly in the light that poured through the giant gap in the Roof. *Sun*light! Sunlight! Incredible, shocking, thrilling. The *sun*!

'Now,' the priest said to himself, his voice shaking, 'if that ship only has a few seeds aboard, we might actually make something of this place . . .'